Ethereum

Scott Edison Adventure Series: Episode 1

N C Mander

This is a work of fiction. Names, characters, places and incidents either are the product of the author's imagination or are used fictitiously. Any resemblance to actual persons, living or dead, events, or locales is entirely coincidental.

Copyright © 2019 by N C Mander

All rights reserved. No part of this book may be reproduced or used in any manner without written permission of the copyright owner except for the use of quotations in a book review.

First paperback edition May 2019
First e-book edition May 2019

Book design by N C Mander
Image by Robert Bye on Unsplash

ISBN 978-1-0968-5093-9 (paperback)

www.ncmander.com

For Dominic

Beware the fury of a patient man.

John Dryden, Absalom and Achitophel

Vengeance is in my heart, death in my hand,

Blood and revenge are hammering in my head.

William Shakespeare, Titus Andronicus

Prologue

One year ago

The vast trading floor at Billingsgate Market teems with fishmongers peddling their wares, crying out their inventory.

'Langoustine ... Squid ... Finest North Sea cod ...'

Rubber-booted men shuffle through the slush of melting ice that overflows from the polystyrene boxes displaying every type of fish anyone could care to name.

Buyers traipse past boxes of cod, whole salmon, sides of tuna, lobster, still clawing lazily after their freedom, and prawns piled high. Occasionally, punters examine the merchandise on offer, commenting on the freshness of the produce to no one in particular. The clock, hanging from the rafters in the cavernous warehouse, reads just before 6.15 a.m. when two men take delivery of a wooden packing crate. A forklift truck, that had nosed its way through the crowds to their stall, reverses with a deafening beep. Customers scatter to allow it clear passage.

The two men examine the box. One stands no more than five foot four inches tall. He is black, sports a single earring and wears a gold chain round his skinny left wrist. The other is also slim, but white and fair-haired. His chin is mottled with three days' worth of stubble. They are both dressed in white coats like all the other fishmongers. The taller of the two men wields the crowbar but has difficulty getting into the crate, struggling to gain purchase on the slippery concrete floor. The surrounding area gets wetter as the ice-packed crate thaws and water seeps from between the slats.

The trickle is tinged blood red, but nobody pays it much

attention. Blood and guts are a familiar sight at Billingsgate Fish Market.

The other man takes over the attack. Eventually, the side of the crate gives way. Torrents of crushed ice, a sickly shade of pink, pour onto the ground. The tidal wave subsides, and everyone's attention is drawn to the horrific sight of a severed human hand, resting palm up, on the ice. Chewed nails appear to claw at the air. A further shift in the ice reveals a leg, an ear and a nose. A clean-shaven head pokes from the frozen packing. Silence descends on the busy market as dozens of pairs of eyes survey the scene. Eyes widen, jaws drop, aghast.

The two men back away, looks of horror and shock on both their faces. The market erupts into noise and activity. Nearby fishmongers crowd around the broken crate and its macabre contents, jostling for the best view. In the melee, the men make a dash for it, separating at the end of the aisle and disappearing in opposite directions.

An officious, elderly stallholder inexpertly manages access to the scene. He proclaims loudly that he has experience of police matters and tries to usher people away from the crate with little success. 'Experience of police matters? You mean you've served a stint inside,' somebody calls from the back of the crowd. A ripple of sniggers washes through the mob of onlookers. Another pipes up, 'I've called the police. They're on their way.'

*

This was to be the last shipment. I promised myself that once Metin was here, I would close it. Close the shipping line for good. Although they *wanted me to keep it open. And now this!* They *send me Metin's body in thirty pieces. I turned on the television as I waited for my beloved brother to knock on the door. After all the heartache. Losing Houda and Samar. It gave me hope to know that Metin would be here. In England. Even if that bastard Johnson had denied him a visa. I had his new passport ready. A new life. For both of us. And then I turn on the news. Police all over a crime scene at Billingsgate. And I catch a glimpse of my brother's body.*

A message from them.

If only, if only he had been granted asylum. Like Houda and Samar, who gave their lives to the waves because the Right Honourable Timothy Johnson has no compassion. Just a visa, a simple visa, was that too much to ask? He does not know the suffering endured by ordinary, righteous people. He decided he did not like me, and that was why Houda, my darling sister, may she rest in peace, was denied her escape from the living hell back home.

I was going to give it all up. To live a life my beloved Houda would have been proud of. But now my cherished brother too has fallen victim to his callousness. He is a vindictive man.

*

It's later now. The dust is settling. My heart aches for everything I've lost. And they *have been in touch. They have offered an opportunity for me to avenge my family. Avenge the injustice brought against them by these British pigs. It will be done. They will know and remember the Dastans. They do not go meekly to their graves. But you, Timothy Johnson, and your loyal subjects, shall know terror as you reach your day of judgement. Inshallah.*

Chapter One

2136, Saturday, 24ᵗʰ June, Moniedubh Estate, nr. North Ballachulish, Lochaber

'*The biggest scandal to hit the British Security Service in decades culminated today in the formal dismissal of one of the country's most senior civil servants,*' the immaculately made-up news anchor said from the laptop screen. The picture then cut to a clip of crowds of jostling journalists gathered outside Thames House, cameras flashing, Dictaphones waving. The newsreader went on, '*Sir Donald Hughes left MI5's headquarters today with his reputation in tatters but was assured that all charges against him have been dropped. His demise was precipitated by an anonymous whistle-blower within the Security Service. Exact details of the accusation against Sir Donald – knighted eight years ago – have not been released.*'

The commentary continued, not adding much information, as the footage showed Sir Donald in the doorway of the formidable building, dressed in a heavy overcoat against the February wind. He paused momentarily – a choreographed move – at the top of the steps to place a smart tweed fedora on top of his thinning hair. Sir Donald was flanked by his lawyer on one side and the demure figure of his wife on the other. They descended the steps, his solicitor protesting and explaining that his client had no comment at this time. They were bundled into a waiting Mercedes saloon car which pulled away, leaving the media circus behind.

Hughes paused the clip just as the cameras panned back to the doors of Thames House. In the frozen image, he spotted a man, twenty-five years younger than himself, dressed in a navy-blue greatcoat that made him appear even more imposing than his well-over six feet and broad shoulders normally did. He had his chin tucked into his chest, trying to blend into the hubbub of people that milled around the doorway. His hands were thrust deep into his pockets. Hughes clicked through the film, frame by frame, to find the moment the whistle-blower looked directly into the lens. His intelligent blue eyes were set deep in sunken sockets, and Hughes noticed they were rimmed with grey bags. Suddenly, and just for a moment, those tired eyes looked up into the camera.

It was a moment, Hughes delighted in recalling, when that man's world fell apart. All in his absence.

Their eyes met.

Scott Edison.

Sir Donald snapped the laptop closed, feeling energised. He looked around the lavishly furnished study. Its big windows had far-reaching views over Glencoe. The events from the clip had taken place over a year ago. Since then, the expansive family home in the Highlands, technically his wife's, had been his refuge and his prison. He had rattled around in it, occasionally bumping into his wife. His engagement with the outside world had been limited to the few choice contacts still loyal to him. He had been careful not to throw anyone under the bus as his distinguished career at MI5 had unravelled. He was shrewd. He knew there was far more value in maintaining the trust of a handful of pawns in London. He could conduct some master puppetry from north of the border.

His first act had been to manoeuvre that snake Edison out of the Security Service – that had taken a couple of months, but he had achieved it – helped toward his goal by Edison's own self-destruction. It appeared that the young man couldn't cope in the Service without him. However, the latest intelligence coming out of London was that Tanya Willis, the director of counter-terrorism, was making noises about Edison's return. Such an outcome would not suit him at all, and he was intent on manipulating his pieces accordingly.

Sir Donald released a long breath and sat back in his leather upholstered desk chair. It would be ok. Edison could be dealt with. He could always call on dear old Johnnie for assistance if necessary. And soon, he thought with glee, he would escape this mausoleum. There were a few more strings to pull. A few more pieces to slot into place, but escape was nigh.

He pulled open the top drawer of his antique mahogany desk and drew out an old Nokia mobile phone and a piece of paper on which there was printed a list of eleven-digit numbers. A handful at the top of the list had been struck out. Placing the sheet on the green leather of the desk, he ran his finger down to the next visible number and carefully punched it into the phone. He typed the message – *10 minutes* – and clicked send. The screen lit up briefly with the words – *Message sent* – before dimming. He shut the handset down, removed the plastic cover and battery to reveal the slot for the SIM card. He slipped the existing card out and replaced it with another from the drawer. He reassembled the phone and laid it carefully on the desk.

There was a knock at the door, and without invitation, his wife appeared holding a tray bedecked with a teapot, cup, saucer and milk jug. 'Maggie's day off,' she told him in the matter-of-fact tone that seemed to infuse all their exchanges. Donald and Elizabeth Hughes barely spoke, bar to exchange information about the whereabouts of the domestic staff and, very occasionally, the weather, but the latter only as it impacted the exercising of their two lurchers, Dolly and Angus.

Elizabeth set the tray down on the coffee table next to Donald's wing-backed leather armchair near the window. 'Shall I pour?' she offered. The phone on the desk began to buzz.

'No,' Hughes said, glancing at the mobile. 'Thank you. I'll help myself.'

'Ok, dear,' Elizabeth replied, eyeing the phone on the desk as it buzzed impatiently. She backed out of the room, wondering where the phone had come from. Her husband, despite his advancing years – he would be sixty-two on his next birthday – was a technophile to rival any teenager. He had the latest of everything. What relic of his past was that brick of a phone? What did he really do, holed up in the study for most of the day? He had told her, months ago, that he was writing a memoir, but that did not require archaic technology. She shrugged as Dolly trotted up to her and accompanied her into the drawing room where her own tea tray lay and where she planned to spend the next hour perusing the latest edition of *House & Garden* which the postman had delivered that morning. Then she would go to bed.

As the door closed behind his wife, Hughes snatched up the phone and pressed the button to answer the call. Too late. The caller had rung off. 'Damn,' he said beneath his breath. He consulted the list of numbers and typed the next one into a text message with the word – *Now*. Hurriedly, he replaced the SIM with a fresh one from the drawer and waited. The phone rang just seconds after he had clicked the battery cover closed.

'Bantam,' Hughes addressed the person on the other end of the line without any pleasantries being exchanged.

'Yeah,' came the reply.

'Next shipment. Twenty-ninth. Deal with the collateral as per usual.'

'Sure, Guv. Should I worry about what happened last time?'

'Enough time has passed, and that is of no concern of ours,' Hughes lied.

The man on the other end of the line grunted.

Hughes changed the subject. 'Is the physicist in play?' Hughes was referring to Edison. It was not a particularly sophisticated alias and being frank, he'd be surprised if anyone was listening, but it paid to be cautious. He knew better than to overcomplicate things. Bantam, his man on the ground in London, was a valuable contact, thanks to his network in the East End, but his abilities did not extend much beyond surveillance and safe transportation of goods. He was not the brain of Britain – a term Donald's mother had been fond of using.

'All set, nothing new, but I've got tabs on 'im,' Bantam replied and hung up.

Hughes took a pen and struck through the two burned numbers on his list. The SIM cards were slipped carefully into an envelope. He returned the handset, the SIM cards and the list of numbers to the drawer before locking it.

He pondered the resurrection of the Billingsgate import channel. It had been a year since a dead body, hideously mutilated, had brought unwanted attention to what had been a straightforward line of business. He had been bringing high-quality cocaine into the capital under the cover of a fishing channel in the North Sea. He had no idea who the man was or how he had met such a grisly end, a dispute amongst the crew that had got out of hand, he had assumed. Ideally, he would have liked to change the route or at least suspend the operation for another six months, but she had been most insistent that now was the right time. It was alluring, the urgency with which she wanted to raise the money they needed to start their new life together. A few risks were worth taking for the promise of a future with her.

He stood and stretched. 'Eye on the prize, Donald,' he muttered to himself. There was a scuffling at the door. He crossed the room and opened it. Angus, the other lurcher, bounded into the room and Hughes ruffled his ears affectionately. The dog trotted over to the coffee table before hopping onto the sofa and looking back to Hughes expectantly. His master poured himself a cup of tea and sat down next to the enormous dog. His mind whirred as he considered what needed to happen in order to ensure the next phase went smoothly and, almost as importantly, that the son-of-a-bitch Edison suffered adequately. As he gazed out of the window, lost in concentration, he idly fondled the dog's belly. Angus could not have been happier.

Chapter Two

0612, Saturday, 24th June, Penn Street, Hoxton, London

Edison raised a hand, rubbed it across his face and under his stubbly chin. With some effort and a groan, he rolled onto his side and tried to focus on the red digital display of the clock by his bed. He realised it wasn't there just as the body sleeping beside him shifted beneath the unfamiliar duvet. Through the haze of his hangover, Edison attempted to recollect what had happened the previous evening. Come on man, he thought to himself as he struggled to piece together a coherent picture, you're a spy after all.

Former spy, his inner monologue corrected him.

He hauled himself up onto his elbows and surveyed the room. There was grey light creeping in from around the hastily drawn curtains. He guessed it was still early. Probably shortly after six, judging by the quality of the light and the time of year, late June. The room was large and sparsely furnished. All he could see of his companion was a slim outline underneath the duvet, a neatly manicured hand reaching out onto the pillow and some wisps of chestnut hair. Gingerly, he got up, hoping not to disturb his bedfellow. His clothes were scattered about, and he crept around the room, disentangling jeans and a T-shirt from sheer tights and a lacy black bra.

Out in the hallway, Edison worried about waking the mythical flatmate. Kat spoke occasionally of the party animal she lived with. He had skulked out of this apartment a handful of times since spring but not once met Sarah. Kat was a former colleague. Ten years younger than Edison, she was manoeuvring her way quickly through the ranks at the British Security Service, thanks to her sharp intellect and commensurate skill. In the bathroom, he considered a shower but thought better of it. He completed perfunctory ablutions and tiptoed back into the corridor. He picked up his shoes and made his way noiselessly toward the front door.

Edison descended in the lift and left the block of flats, striding purposefully in what he thought he remembered was the direction of the station. His phone buzzed deep in the pocket of his jacket. It gave him a start. Who was texting him at this time of the morning and, as an afterthought, how the hell does the ruddy thing have any battery left? Most days, it didn't last much beyond mid-afternoon, even with his carefully rationed usage. He rummaged in his pocket and pulled out the phone. *You're better off walking to Old Street than trying to take the Overground on a Sunday* – the message read.

Turning, he looked back up to the ninth floor. Kat, wearing only an oversized T-shirt, was watching him from the full-length window overlooking the courtyard. She lifted her hand and wiggled her fingers at him. Edison slowly raised a hand and returned the wave, adding a perfunctory nod for good measure. With a sigh, Edison turned on his heels and set off in the opposite direction from which he had started, bracing himself for the long walk to Old Street tube station and hoping to pass somewhere that could service him with a good, strong cup of tea.

*

Kat cradled a mug of coffee in her hands, wondering whether Edison was likely to reply to her message. The previous evening had been fun. The old gang back together, enjoying a drink and one another's company in The Prince of Wales, just across the bridge from New Scotland Yard. As the night wore on, Mo and Natalie made their excuses and Jock wasn't far behind them, leaving Kat and Edison nursing their drinks and chatting amicably. It had been

Edison who had suggested another drink, the evening was following their usual pattern, and Kat, dutifully adhering to the script, had proposed heading back to Hoxton, closer to her flat.

'He's making a habit of skulking off early in the morning,' said Sarah as she entered the kitchen and interrupted her flatmate's thoughts. In contrast to Kat, who was petite, dark-haired and fine-featured, Sarah was tall and blonde.

'I guess so,' replied Kat. Sarah picked up the coffee pot and poured herself a cup, adding a generous spoonful of sugar and a glug of milk. She flopped onto the sofa, opposite the window where Kat still stood, and pulled a peroxide lock away from her face.

'You having fun?' Sarah asked.

'Yeah,' said Kat. She meant it, although her reply didn't come out as convincingly as she had hoped. Sarah raised an eyebrow. 'He's a good guy. We have a good time.'

'I thought he left the Home Office under suspicious circumstances.'

'Hardly suspicious,' Kat protested. Working for the Home Office was the standard cover story for MI5 employees. 'He'd had a difficult time after the death of his wife, and he and the boss really didn't get on.'

'That guy's gone too though, hasn't he?'

'Ummmhmmm,' Kat confirmed.

Sarah hoisted herself out of the sofa, sensing that the conversation about her flatmate's lover had run its natural course. 'I better shower.' She crossed the room and gave Kat a squeeze. 'Did you say you were working today?'

Kat rolled her eyes. 'Yes, I'd better get going.'

'Jeez, they work you hard as a civil servant. But I already called first dibs on the shower.' Sarah lunged at the coffee pot for a top-up and skipped out of the room.

Kat had turned back to the window, her thoughts returning to Edison. 'He's all right, you know,' she said to no one. 'Bit messed up, but aren't we all?'

*

Edison sourced a strong cup of tea once he was almost on top of Old Street tube station. He handed over what he considered to be a ridiculous sum of money for a teabag and hot water with a dash of milk. Despite this, he was grateful for the paper cup of steaming tea he received in exchange. He parked himself at a table by the big glass windows and absentmindedly bobbed his teabag up and down, waiting for the colour to turn from what he called 'mouse piss'. Tea too weak to crawl out of the pot, his father used to say. Edison preferred his, like his father had, creosote brown.

London was awakening, although it was not yet seven, and he watched as workmen made their way to building sites and confused tourists emerged from the underground's many entrances to discover they were on the wrong side of the enormous roundabout. They would take an age to navigate their way above ground, and the more intrepid would revert to the subterranean concourse only to reappear minutes later, more often than not barely a hundred yards from where Edison had first seen them.

Edison gulped down a few mouthfuls and began to feel more himself. The hangover was receding with the fresh air and tea, but he popped a couple of paracetamol, which he had made a habit of carrying in the last year, just to make sure. Leaning back, the chair groaned under his bulk. He breathed out deeply.

*

Emerging at Waterloo, Edison pulled up the collar on his jacket against the driving rain and hurried along the South Bank. Usually teeming with tourists, he encountered only the hardiest of sightseers, all reconsidering their choices for the day. There was a short queue for the London Eye, huddled under too few umbrellas. He hurried past St Thomas' where he had spent those last few painful months with Eloise, although crucially, not the last moments, and pressed on toward his apartment block.

Closing the door behind him, he was hit by the silence. Even after all this time, he couldn't get used to it. He retrieved his phone from his pocket, shook off his wet coat and left it to fester in a crumpled heap by the door. Without unlacing them, he pulled off his shoes. He left those where he removed them, knowing that he would trip over them later. His phone vibrated in his hand, and he looked down, expecting to see another message from Kat. But it was telling him that finally, it was giving up, its battery empty. An angry red warning flashed on the screen before it went black.

Edison considered plugging it in. Instead, he chose to leave it on the sideboard and embrace the peace that being severed from the digital world offered. There had been a time when that would have been unthinkable to him. He needed to wallow for a while. He flicked on the kettle and assembled the necessary components of another cup of tea whilst he waited for the water to boil. Tea made and stewing, leaving the teabag in the cup, he started to undress. The flat's floor-to-ceiling windows afforded views over Westminster, but its position on the twenty-first floor of the high rise offered privacy without the need for curtains or blinds. In just his boxers, Edison returned to the tea just as the phone rang.

'Damn it,' he said out loud. He regularly forgot that Eloise had insisted on installing an old-fashioned landline in the flat. There was only one person who ever called that number. It could only be Eloise's mother – the formidable Jane de Courcy. Edison took long enough deciding whether to pick up for the answering machine to kick in. '*You're through to Edison and Eloise,*' his dead wife's voice rang out around the open-plan apartment. '*We can't get to the phone right now.*' Eloise went on to promise that if the caller left a message one of them would be sure to get back to them. Edison felt sick. The machine beeped loudly, reminding Edison that his hangover wasn't to be readily forgotten, and he winced.

'Scott,' said the familiar plummy voice of his mother-in-law, 'you really ought to change that message. It is not fair on anyone. We will be in London on Thursday to meet with agents. We need to expedite the sale. Make sure the place is respectable. I will let you know times once I know.' Jane paused, considering what to say next. 'Well,' she stuttered, 'I may see you then.' She hung up. The subtext was clear. She hoped not to see him. It was too awkward. The unpleasantries that had passed between them in the period after Eloise's death were not easily forgotten. Now Jane was evicting Edison from the marital home. It had been bought for Eloise when she moved to London, but she had never officially owned it. This was Jane's master move that would end the game of one-up-manship chess they had been playing ever since Eloise had taken him home to meet her family, seven years ago. The de Courcy's lived in a chateau, surrounded by expensive vines making expensive wines, near Dijon. Edison seethed. Jane de Courcy had been born plain Jane Wright from Manchester with an accent to match. Leaving school at sixteen, she had worked hard on her diction and her secretarial skills before taking a job in the typing pool for a London-based wine merchant. It was there that she had met and married Gauthier de Courcy.

Edison looked around his home. Hardly a home – in the last two years, he hadn't thought of it as anywhere other than a place to occasionally sleep and to store his meagre possessions. When Eloise has been alive, the apartment had effervesced with her unique French style. Modern, elegant and slightly eclectic, just like her. The surfaces gleamed white. The expensive furnishings were islands in the sea of space, around which Eloise would host parties with people who didn't drink beer and didn't spill their red wine onto the leather upholstery. Edison had been a curiosity amongst the curious in those gatherings, but he engaged with the crowd amiably, a skill for which his expensive education (underwritten by scholarship after scholarship) had equipped him.

Since the gathering of London-based mourners in the flat, none of that crowd had crossed the threshold. Only a sweet colleague of Eloise's from the fashion magazine had occasionally texted, checking in on her friend's heartbroken widower. The party, as Jane had insisted on calling it – *'I can't abide the word "wake"',* – had been hosted a month after the actual funeral. The funeral had been in France. Of course. It wasn't a subject for discussion. Check. Your turn, Edison.

Edison's next move had been to get horrendously drunk on Eloise's father's red wine at the reception following the funeral. He had smashed a full bottle of vintage burgundy, and the contents soaked into the plush cream carpet of the drawing room.

'Are you still my in-laws?' Edison had asked through the misty fug of his drunkenness, as his father-in-law had guided him gently out of the room and up the grand sweeping staircase before his wife discovered the scene.

Gauthier was an ally. He had adored his daughter and, by extension, loved anything she loved. He led Edison into a guest room and encouraged him to sit on the edge of the bed. This wasn't the room Jane had allocated him for his short stay. She had put him in the room he had always shared with Eloise – her daughter's childhood bedroom – in which Edison struggled to sleep, overwhelmed by the memories of his dead wife.

Gauthier reappeared with a large glass of water. 'Perhaps,' he said, 'you should take a little time out.' His English was perfect, but he spoke with a strong French accent. Edison nodded, accepting the glass and drawing a long sip. The cold water flushed through his foggy head, and he felt his hand begin to tremble. Water sloshed onto his suit trousers. Gauthier took the glass, placed it on the bedside table and sat down beside his son-in-law. He reached upward and placed a slender arm around Edison's shoulders. He was not a short man, but Edison towered over him, filling every bit of his six-foot and four-inch frame. The act of tenderness opened a dam in the younger man, and Edison exploded into heart-rending sobs.

'Gauthier,' Jane called, she was halfway up the stairs. Hastily, Gauthier withdrew his embrace and patted his son-in-law on the thigh. He hurried onto the landing, closing the door behind him just as his wife reached the top of the stairs.

'Oh, there you are,' said Jane. 'We need more of the red. Have you seen Scott, and have you seen the mess in the drawing room?' She reeled off the questions in French in a single breath.

'Oh yes,' Gauthier replied with studied nonchalance, 'it was one of the dogs.' Jane raised an eyebrow. 'I'll sort out the wine,' he went on, heading for the stairs.

'And Scott?'

'It's been a difficult day, he's just having a lie-down.'

'It's been a difficult day for all of us, people expect to see him,' Jane said to the empty hallway. Her husband had already descended the stairs and was making his way to the kitchen cellar where he could retrieve a case of the estate's more recent vintages.

*

Edison had slept through to the following morning when he had made his half-hearted apologies to his mother-in-law for his absence and left to return to the sparse flat in which he now sat.

He moved over to the windows, lost in thought. He leant his

forehead against the cool of the glass and surveyed London spread out below him. The window offered views over the Thames and many of London's most famous landmarks. An estate agent's dream, thought Edison and turned to survey the room. The flat, grey light revealed a sparsely furnished room. At least it won't take long to pack.

Right, he thought, and pushed himself away from the window on which he was slouching, what now? Shower probably. He turned on the water and went to plug in his phone.

Washed and wrapped in a towel, he revisited the three missed calls on his mobile he'd been ignoring all morning. There were two accompanying text messages and a voicemail. They were all from Charlie, one of his oldest and dearest friends. He played the first message.

'*Eddie*,' Charlie addressed him in his familiar Scottish accent, pausing as if expecting his friend to reply despite speaking to Edison's voicemail, '*Everything ok?*' Another pause. '*Shall we get a drink?*' Edison nodded as the voice message ended and read Charlie's text messages. The first left instructions of Charlie's preferred location for meeting. The second qualified the time. There was no need to confirm that he was referring to today. They both knew that Edison not only had nothing else to do but even if he had prior arrangements, they would be cancelled in favour of a drink with Charlie.

Edison consulted the clock. He had enough time to dress and eat before making his way to the pub. If he walked, he might even think up a story for why he hadn't picked up the phone the previous evening.

*

1035, Saturday 24th June, Thames House, Westminster, London
'Anything from Skagen?' Tanya asked as she swept past Kat on her

way toward her office. That Kat should follow her boss was implicit.

She jerked her head at Mo, 'You had better come with me. You've been on point with the guy in Denmark.' Mo grabbed his tablet and trooped after Kat.

'Are we in a position to put an asset in the bank?' Tanya demanded as the door closed behind her two intelligence officers.

Kat was momentarily caught off balance by the director of counter-terrorism's change of topic.

'Yes,' Kat said, gathering her thoughts, 'I spoke to Tom, the MD there, yesterday. The recruiter rouse has bedded in nicely, and he wants to see my candidate next week. He's pretty jumpy about the regulators cracking down on his trading activities, so it's a perfect opportunity for us to put someone in with carte blanche to dig deep.'

'Perfect. I know exactly who we need.'

'Really, who?'

'Scott Edison.'

Mo drew a sharp breath at the mention of the Security Service legend. He had joined MI5 just after Edison's departure the previous year but had been regaled by the team with stories of his exceptional field skills and ability to hack into any corner of the internet.

'Edison?' Kat argued, 'I'm really not sure he's the right fit.' Forgetting the fact that she had been sleeping with Tanya's proposed agent, Kat didn't like the idea of her predecessor being brought onto the biggest operation she'd ever handled at MI5. She had been promoted in the wake of Edison's exit from the Service. She didn't want her authority undermined.

As if reading her thoughts, Tanya said, 'His involvement will be very much off-grid. His interaction with the team limited. It's an unofficial role.'

'I was thinking Mark could do it.'

'I've made my decision, Kat. Get Colin to run up a legend for Edison. I'm briefing him tomorrow.'

Kat opened her mouth to disagree, but Tanya's expression brooked no argument.

'What do we have from Skagen?' Tanya changed the subject again.

Kat gave Mo an encouraging nod and he spoke, 'Six's asset in Skagen has seen the *Boston Jubilee* a handful of times in the past six weeks.'

'But there's been no activity at Billingsgate?'

'No, Jock's had eyes there since the guys in Vienna suggested that the route was up and running again. I'm wondering if they're bringing the contraband in somewhere else,' Kat said.

'Or they've changed their cargo. That's what Martijn thinks,' Mo interjected.

'Who's Martijn?' queried Tanya.

'Six's asset in the port at Skagen. He's seen a few new faces floating around. One boarded with the crew of the *Boston* last week. He left port but didn't return when the boat did later in the week.'

Tanya narrowed her eyes. 'Human assets being brought into the country. That suggests VIPERSNEST is on the move don't you think?' She paused, a pregnant silence hung in the air before Kat nodded. 'It's time to up the threat level on HAPSBURG. Kat, this is to be everyone's priority.'

Kat nodded again, feeling the mixed thrill and fear that came with any operational escalation.

*

1905, Saturday 24th June, The Windmill, Clapham Common, London

The Windmill on Clapham Common on a Saturday night was

buzzing with drinkers. Edison pushed his large frame through the crowds to find Charlie sat in their usual spot, toward the back of the main bar. He stood up as his friend approached and gave him a broad grin before embracing him in a manly hug, pounding him on the back three times. 'I've set us up,' said Charlie, waving at the two pints of real ale in front of him.

'Thanks,' said Edison, loudly, struggling to be heard over the noise of the busy bar. He jerked his head back toward the door, 'Shall we get some air?'

Charlie paused, unwilling to give up his hard-fought barstools and nook but conceded it was difficult to have a proper conversation over the hubbub of Saturday-night revellers. The pair struggled back the way Edison had just come, holding their beer glasses high above their heads to avoid spillage. The long tables outside the pub were sparsely populated with a few smokers and drinkers. Although it was June, a long spell of wet weather had left the city cold and damp. Charlie and Edison pulled their coats around themselves. The pair took a couple of seats as close to the outdoor heaters as they could.

'Cheers,' Edison said wearily, holding up his glass and grimacing.

'Cheers, mate,' Charlie said with more vigour.

'Layla on duty tonight?' Edison asked after Charlie's wife and their children.

Charlie nodded, taking a long draw on his pint. 'Yes, so I'm all yours, for you to regale me with your stories of last night's conquests.' Charlie's green eyes flashed, and an impish look Edison had become familiar with since childhood filled his features. Edison rolled his eyes. 'Oh, come on mate,' Charlie cajoled him, 'who is she?'

Edison looked at his oldest friend. They had known one

another for nearly a quarter of a century, ever since Edison had arrived from inner city Newcastle at Harrow on his scholarship. Edison had been a fish out of water amidst the ceremony and ritual of the British boarding school system and would have been a prime target for the school's bullies had Charlie, the son and grandson of Old Harrovians, not plucked him out of the lion's den on his first day.

On that first day, swamped by his oversized new school uniform, Edison had found himself backed into a corner in the dorm as a crowd of merciless fourth formers who, having got wind of the new arrival, were taunting him for his northern accent. Charlie was supposed to be playing rugby but had returned to the dormitory to retrieve his socks. He elbowed his way through the crowds. The gaggle quietened when they saw him. Although Charlie was only in the third form, a minnow by the school's strict, unwritten hierarchy, his older brother, Toby, was an influential sixth former. Toby was captain of the squash team and known to offer a beating to anyone who dared even threaten Charlie.

'All right, mate,' Charlie had said. Edison was white and bristling, not knowing who to trust, and didn't reply. 'You forgotten we have rugger this afternoon?' Charlie freestyled. 'He prefers computers,' he explained to the startled crowd, 'but it's not an option this term. Come on, mate.' Charlie placed a hand on Edison's arm and firmly directed him toward the door. The crowds parted as they came through. Charlie grabbed his socks on his way past his trunk.

Once they were out of earshot of the startled mob, Charlie turned to Edison, 'Where are you supposed to be then?'

Edison shrugged and pulled a crumpled timetable from his pocket. Charlie studied it. 'Oh, you are meant to be in PE.' He looked more closely at the piece of paper. 'You're in most of my lessons. Just follow me about, and you shouldn't go far wrong. I'm Charlie Harrington-Smith. What's your name?'

'Scott Edison,' Edison told him.

'Scott Edison,' Charlie played with the name for a while whilst they headed toward the changing rooms.

As they hurried through the enormous school that Edison was sure he would never be able to navigate, he asked his new friend, 'How did you know I'm into computers?'

'Lucky guess that you're the computer whizz that won the special scholarship. Toby, that's my big brother, he's a Monitor, told me about it. There aren't many boys who start a term into the year,' Charlie replied matter-of-factly without looking at him.

'What's a Monitor?' Edison asked.

'Oh, they call them prefects in most schools. You'll get used to all this stuff. The stuff that makes this place weird,' Charlie assured him. Edison wasn't sure he believed him.

When they arrived, the rest of the boys, already bedecked in their rugby kit, looked up expectantly. 'All right lads,' Charlie said. 'This is Eddy. He's all right.' He paused, looking around at the collection of early teenage boys. 'Ok?' he added rhetorically.

Five years later, Charlie and Edison went up to Oxford together. Edison walked away four years on with a double first in mathematics and computation. After university, they'd lived together briefly as they began their careers – Edison in the Security Service and Charlie on a fast-track scheme at the Met which saw him quickly working for Special Branch, the division of the Metropolitan Police that would later become Counter Terrorism Command. Their professional paths had crossed regularly on joint operations and via the Joint Intelligence Committee.

Twenty-five years on from Charlie's heroic rescue at Harrow, he was looking at Edison expectantly. Edison studied their surroundings, feeling disinclined to share too many of the details of his affair with his former colleague. Charlie and Kat still worked together frequently.

'Don't make me guess …' Charlie threatened. Edison sighed, he knew better than to hold out too much longer.

'Ok, I've been seeing Kat, very occasionally,' he stressed. Charlie's face broke out into a grin. 'What's that look for?'

'She's hot!'

'You're married!' Charlie eyed Edison's left hand where his wedding ring had remained for the sixteen months since his wife's death. 'Touché,' said Edison, his right hand going to the ring and twisting it on his finger.

'How long?' asked Charlie, more seriously.

'It's not exactly a regular thing.'

'Fair enough, how many times then?'

Edison raised an eyebrow. 'Handful of times.'

'How big a handful?' Charlie pressed.

'Ok, ok, I've been back to her place every time we've been out drinking for the last three and a half months.'

Charlie quickly ran through their social calendar. With the exception of last night, he was a regular in the drinking crowd – a group of a dozen from across all the services MI5, MI6, Counter Terrorism Command and GCHQ. 'Wow,' he said eventually, having worked out that in the time period to which Edison referred, there had been pub sessions on fourteen separate occasions. 'You have been having a good time.'

Edison snorted but then ventured a smile. 'Yeah,' he conceded, 'I guess we have.' He was admitting it to himself for the first time as much to Charlie.

'Anything more to it?' Charlie asked.

Edison shrugged and drained his beer. 'Another one?'

'Thanks.'

Returning from the bar with two pints in hand, Edison hoped that the conversation about Kat had run its course. It was a complicated and uncomfortable part of his life. He couldn't forgive himself for enjoying the time he spent with her. He felt like he was cheating on his wife. It felt dirty, and Kat, a young, intelligent, not to mention stunningly beautiful woman, deserved better, he knew. To his relief, Charlie turned the conversation to Edison's living arrangements without any prompting. It was another uncomfortable topic but marginally better than romance.

'So, what's happening with the flat? Are you homeless yet?'

'Soon to be. Her majesty left a message today to say they will be in London on Thursday to get it on the market.'

'What are you going to do?'

Edison shrugged.

Charlie considered his next comment carefully. 'Jock told me that Tony has been looking for a roommate.' Reclusive and unpopular, Tony was an analyst at MI5.

Edison opened his mouth to protest Charlie's suggestion but knew he was backed into a corner. He had limited funds and even fewer options. 'Not sure how I feel about shacking up with that particular desk monkey,' he said.

'At least Five would love it. You know they like to keep you close even once you've left the Service. Anyway, Tony's all right. Keeps himself to himself. Bit nerdy. I've heard he spends his life holed up in front of his computer, playing video games. You'd never see him.'

'I'll think about it,' said Edison, making it clear that this was another topic of conversation that needed to be brought to a close.

'And job?'

Edison glared at his friend over the rim of his pint glass. 'Three strikes, Charlie,' he threatened. 'Romance, living arrangements and work. You've covered all my least favourite topics, and we're only two pints in!'

'Eddie – I'm worried about you,' Charlie said in the soothing tone that was familiar from their boarding school days. 'It's been a year and a half since Ellie …' His voice trailed off, his own grief following the loss of his best friend's wife had been all consuming.

'Sixteen months,' Edison snapped then breathed deeply, fighting back the desire to throw up defensive barriers and retreat into silence. If he did, he would down a few more pints alone. Drinking had been his coping mechanism. It had ultimately cost him his job.

He had rushed back to work just a week after Eloise's funeral, worrying about his assets, set adrift, rudderless in London without him. He had been running a handful of agents across three live investigations; a straightforward people-smuggling operation, regular surveillance on a north London mosque suspected of cultivating terrorist sympathisers amongst their young worshippers, and a more complex drugs and people-trafficking ring in West London, the profits from which were being syphoned off to fund weapon purchases in Palestine. His asset on the latter operation had tried to reach him late one night, worried that his cover had been blown. At the time, Edison had been slumped over a bar, having made his way to the bottom of a bottle of whisky alone. Jan was Edison's mole. He was a well-connected pimp in West London, embedded in the import operation that saw women and drugs being brought off lorries from the continent in Dover and distributed through a network of brothels across the South East of England. Jan was found under the Hammersmith flyover the following morning, with his wrists slit and a knife at his side. To the untrained eye, it had all the hallmarks of a suicide, but the investigators saw through the clumsy staging. The knife was Russian. The direction of the cuts was inconsistent with suicide. There were multiple missed calls to Edison's mobile and finally a voicemail. '*They're here,*' Jan had whispered into the phone. '*Help me ... they know ...*' The message had served to corroborate the theory that Jan's cover had been blown, and he'd been disposed of.

The subsequent investigation had resulted in a swift dismissal for Edison. The details of his failings were kept quiet by his sympathetic head of section, Tanya Willis. 'He's a fantastic officer,' she had told the committee convened to investigate the matter. Only a couple of them had known of Edison's connection to the Sir Donald Hughes affair. Eventually, Edison's departure was explained on mental health grounds, and he received a significant stipend from the agency.

'I'm not drinking so much now,' Edison assured his friend, finishing the remainder of his beer in a single gulp. 'Another one?'

Charlie rolled his eyes but didn't decline. 'My round,' Charlie insisted. 'It's getting cold, and it's quieter in there,' he nodded at the building behind him as a dozen women, bedecked in pink sashes, burst out of the door and made their way unsteadily toward the tube station, 'now the hens have flown the coop.'

Whilst Charlie went to the bar, Edison settled himself into a cosy armchair and surveyed the pub. In another snug, was a couple in their sixties, barely speaking to one another, occasionally sipping at their gins and tonics. Further away, at a big slab of a table surrounded by benches, was a crowd of students, nursing their drinks through to opening time at the nearby nightclub. The only other drinker in the vicinity was a short, slight, black man poring over his smartphone. Briefly, he went outside. He reappeared, sat down, only to jump up moments later and slip out the door once more. Edison assumed he was taking a call but noticed the smartphone still sat on the table. Had he forgotten it? Edison swiftly crossed to the table, picked up the phone and followed its owner out the door, hoping he would catch him before he got too far. To his surprise, the man was just outside. Edison was sure he saw him slip a mobile into his pocket as he turned. He seemed startled to see Edison. 'Sorry mate,' Edison said hurriedly, proffering the mobile he was holding, 'thought you might have forgotten this.'

The man stared at Edison's outstretched hand, holding his smartphone, for an instant before composing himself. 'Thanks,' he said eventually, taking it from Edison. 'Would've been well annoyed to forget that.' He paused. 'Thanks again,' he said, slipping the phone into the pocket of his leather jacket – the same pocket Edison was sure he'd put another phone into moments earlier. The man turned on his heels and loped off in the direction of Clapham Common tube station. He moved quickly for such a short man. Edison watched him go, committing to memory what he was wearing, out of habit rather than any genuine suspicion. Some habits die hard. Converse trainers, dark jeans, black leather jacket, single earring, gold chain round left wrist, no other jewellery, dark beanie hat, he repeated to himself three times as the man disappeared into the darkness.

'Are you ok?' Charlie's voice interrupted Edison's focus. He had backed the door open whilst holding the newly acquired pints in both hands and two bags of crisps under one arm.

'Yeah, guy forgot his phone,' said Edison as he relieved his friend of one of the pints. They made their way back to their table. Once they were seated and the bags of crisps were opened, Edison said, 'So work …' offering the topic before his friend had a chance to bring it back up. 'I think I'll look to take on some private stuff.'

Charlie scoffed, 'Really? Errant husbands cheating on their wives? You'll last a month.'

'Beggars can't be choosers,' said Edison, picking out a phrase his mother loved to use.

'Hmmmm,' was all Charlie said, not disguising the scepticism in his voice.

The conversation moved on to more mundane topics, mostly centred around Charlie's family life; the sporting activities the children would be engaging in over the coming weeks, an early summer trip up to the Highlands, Charlie's eldest son's entrance exams for Harrow. Edison allowed the conversation to wash over him as the effects of the beer began to do the same. Together, the friends enjoyed a fourth and a fifth pint before Charlie declared that he had better be getting home if he was to make the following morning's five-a-side match.

They embraced outside the pub and made promises to meet up again soon. Charlie set off unsteadily toward the comfortable semi-detached home on the west side of the common where his wife and three children waited. It was the life for which Edison had been destined. It was the life he and Ellie had been planning. It was the life that had been cruelly taken from him the day the doctor had told them both that it was cancer that was aggressively consuming Ellie's body and that there was nothing they could do but manage the pain.

Edison pushed these thoughts out of his mind, along with the almost overwhelming desire to return to the bar for a whisky. He trudged toward the tube station at the north side of the common. It was quiet for a Saturday night – the early evening's revellers had headed into central London, leaving only a handful of people milling around the tube station. The fried chicken shop would be busier later, and Edison would not usually have paid it a second glance but for a familiar diminutive figure disappearing into it, dressed in dark jeans, a leather jacket and wearing a single earring.

Two hours had passed since Edison's brief exchange with the solitary drinker in the Windmill. Why was he still loitering around the station?

'Pull it together,' Edison muttered to himself. Fifteen years in the Security Service had left him on a default setting of 'suspicious'. Edison admonished himself, burying his hands into his pockets and deciding that he would walk the three miles home rather than getting onto the tube.

He strode off purposefully along Clapham High Street, sidestepping a couple of the sash-wearing hens who were noisily smoking a cigarette outside a nightclub. As he went, Bantam watched him from the fried chicken shop, cursing himself for his earlier misstep that had brought him face to face with his boss's quarry. Nothing to be done, thought Bantam, as his mind turned to how he was going to get back to Poplar this late at night.

Chapter Three

1140, Sunday 25th June, St George's Wharf, Vauxhall, London
Compared with the previous day's overcast weather, Sunday dawned bright, and light flooded Edison's flat. He perched at the kitchen island, absentmindedly dunking a teabag in and out of his mug until it reached a suitable shade of turpentine. Tea brewed, Edison padded across to the window and drank in the view. London's skyline basked in glorious sunshine, and the rays of sun danced across the Thames. To the right, the river curved past Vauxhall, skirting the imposing golden building that housed MI6 and on to Westminster, where Thames House, the home of the domestic Security Service, MI5, hid behind an effusion of summer leaves, and the Houses of Parliament rose in all their majestic grandeur.

That corner of London was always infected with crowds of tourists, but from Edison's lofty vantage point, he thought it looked even busier than normal. Where were his binoculars? He found them amongst a selection of his few belongings in what had been the drinks cabinet. Back at the window, he put the binoculars, a relic from his former career, to his eyes, only to see a foggy grey mist. The lenses were filthy, having been neglected for so long. Edison untucked his shirt, breathed heavily on the glass and rubbed vigorously at the greasy residue with his shirt tail. Now, with a clear, magnified view of the crowds on the corner of Westminster Bridge, Edison recognised the barriers and banners of a charity run.

Edison hung the binoculars round his neck with the strap and let them fall onto his midriff. He looked down at his ample girth with a twinge of embarrassment. He turned to view his profile in the full-length mirror Ellie had installed to reflect as much of the pale northern light into the flat as possible. She loved the light. Edison was taken aback by what he saw. His face was haggard, his hair unkempt and he was sporting three days of stubble on his once defined features. His chin was now jowly with weight gain. Below his broad shoulders and ample chest, the binoculars rested against his protruding belly. The untucked shirt added to the study of dishevelment which he had subconsciously cultivated for the last year and a half. He glanced at his watch, it read eleven forty-five. He turned back to the window and raised the binoculars to his face again. The Service issued good quality lenses, but these had been a gift from Donald Hughes, bestowed on Edison in his early days in the Service. They magnified every detail by ten times. He watched the fit, lithe runners streaming around the corner from the Embankment for their final push to the finish. He glanced back at his reflection. He swallowed the final mouthful of tea. Something was going to have to change.

He headed to the kitchen island, grabbing the pad of paper and pen that lived next to the phone, still flashing its bright red LED light at him – a reminder that Jane's message needed attention. Blank sheet of paper in front of him, he ruminated on his options. Carefully he wrote down three headings.

Flat.

Work.

Life.

He paused. Then crossed out the last one and replaced it with '*Health*'.

The first one was easy to deal with, thought Edison. He pulled out his mobile phone and scrolled through to find Tony's number that he had taken from Charlie the previous evening with the promise to consider it as an option. He took a deep breath and hit dial. It didn't ring for long before the call was answered.

'Hullo,' said Tony. His voice was gravelly, as if he hadn't spoken for a while. He coughed to clear his throat.

'Hi, Tony.' Edison tried to sound casual, 'This is Scott Edison.'

'I know.' Tony's voice was cool. 'Got your number in my phone.' He paused. 'What can I do for you?'

Edison wondered why Tony had his number saved. They had never been close. He pushed the thought aside, focusing on the task in hand. He considered asking his former colleague how he was doing but decided that small talk wasn't necessary, and there was a strong argument for keeping their engagement as transactional as possible. 'I understand you have a room to rent?'

Tony drew in a breath. 'Mother-in-law finally kicking you out then?' Edison couldn't work out whether Tony was being scornful or sympathetic.

Edison relaxed his shoulders, releasing some of the tension that had crept in as he tried to engage with the analyst who had, when they'd been colleagues, made life very difficult for him, failing to supply the appropriate or relevant intelligence about his operations. He laughed off the question, 'Yeah, something like that.'

'Well, the room is available.' Tony went on to list the rent and bills. 'Want to think about it?'

'Not got much time for thinking,' Edison said. 'I'll take it.'

'But are you good for it?' Tony asked, needling Edison on his employment status.

'Yeah,' Edison lied. 'I've got a few final interviews lined up.'

'Really?' Tony's voice dripped with scepticism. 'Do Five know?'

'Listen, Tony,' Edison snapped, 'do you want to rent out the room or not?' Edison knew Tony had money problems. He was servicing debt on a handful of credit cards whilst supporting his estranged girlfriend and their nine-year-old son and fourteen-year-old daughter on a junior civil servant's salary. Not easy.

'When do you want to move in?'

'Tomorrow?'

'Sure. Want to drop by Thames House, and I'll give you a key. You hiring a van?'

Edison surveyed his meagre belongings and thought of the paucity of clothing hanging in the wardrobe next door. 'I'll probably manage without.'

'Ok,' Tony said.

'Ok,' Edison replied, unsure how to end the conversation.

'See you tomorrow, roomie,' Tony tried a joke and hung up. Edison shivered, placing the phone back on the table and picking up the pen. He struck out '*Flat*' on his list.

*

In Bethnal Green, Tony ended the call with a flourish of his bony finger and grinned. He was a pasty-faced man, with a tousle of lank brown hair. His front teeth were too large for him, which gave him an unfortunate resemblance to a rat. Spinning on his high-backed office chair, he turned his attention back to his computer screens. He had three large monitors arranged on his corner desk. In addition, there was a fifty-inch flat-screen television, showing the coverage of that day's race in central London, on mute, hung on the wall nearby. Tony tapped a complicated password into the wireless keyboard, and the screens flickered into life. He had better let the boss know. He opened an incognito browser window and navigated his way to a suitably anonymous spot on the Dark Web. From there, he typed out a message: *Physicist inbound. Tomorrow.* He encrypted the message and sent it.

He turned his attention to another screen on which two

warriors, one mounted on a dragon and the other a phoenix, were duking it out in a battle. The phoenix-rider won, and Tony manipulated his victorious avatar onward to claim his bounty, three ingots of gold and a magic potion that would heal the wounds inflicted by the vanquished opponent. He accepted the congratulations of his fellow players over the game's direct message system. He consulted the map which he kept open on the third screen and resolved to send his warrior off to explore a section of uncharted territory in the south-west of the domain.

*

Edison turned his attention to the next item: work. This would require some fuel. He made himself another cup of tea. What were his options? On leaving the Service, he had been advised on the suitable career paths from here as part of his debrief. Spies rarely made it to retirement age, but for the majority, they would usually be shuffled into a desk role, often in Cheltenham, once their value on active duty started to wane. Special individuals ascend to the senior ranks, are given a big desk and a suitable title. This had been Edison's trajectory at one time. He fitted the bill. Astute and exceptionally good at his job, his private education had set him up well for playing the political game that came with promotion and increasing exposure to Five's neighbours at Whitehall. Plus, he'd had the sponsorship of the Service's top dog for most of his career. Those opportunities had evaporated somewhere between the decision he'd made to expose Hughes' misdemeanours and the loss of his best asset. Those who did make it out of the civil service to seek employment in the private sector were quickly snapped up by a select group of approved private security firms as advisors on how to secure government contract work. Edison's tainted reputation had meant these opportunities had been slow to materialise.

There had been one genuine job offer, managing IT security

for the University of Croydon. Edison had allowed the email exchange with the recruitment officer to fester in his inbox, such was his apathy for the job. Reluctantly, he pulled up the last missive he'd received, in which a paltry sum of money had been tabled. He shot off two lines to enquire about whether the position had been filled before pushing his phone away in disgust.

*

Tom rounded the bend at the bottom of the mall. The crowds, standing a dozen deep on either side of the course, were pounding on the hoardings that prevented them from surging onto the final stretch of the route. He snuck a peek at his runner's watch. The clock was ticking toward the four-hour mark. There was a little over four hundred metres to the finish line, and Tom pushed hard to cross it inside the time he had set himself when he took on the challenge at the behest of Jamie, a junior member of his team at Penwill & Mallinson.

Crossing the line, his legs nearly gave way beneath him, and he hobbled through the finish area. Tom felt a clap on his back as he queued to pick up his bag. 'Nice one, old man,' a voice beside him said. Tom turned to see Jamie's grinning face and he grunted. 'Did you enjoy it?' Jamie went on.

'Ask me again later,' said Tom, handing his luggage tag over to a volunteer, who retrieved his rucksack from the vast pile on the wagon which had brought all the racers' belongings from the start line.

'Come on,' said Jamie. 'I left the rest of the team holding a spot in a pub on Piccadilly. Anna can't stop crowing about how much cash we've raised for the refugees.'

Tom hobbled off in pursuit of Jamie, whose pace belied the 26.2 miles he had also put in his legs that morning. Tom fumbled in his bag for his mobile as he walked. 'Happy with your time then,

Jamie?' he asked.

'Yeah, it's ok, I guess,' Jamie replied, with a twist of his mouth. 'No PB, but under three hours will do, given I'm focusing on the Ironman this year.'

Tom laughed. 'Try harder, that's really just not good enough.' Tom enjoyed the banter. He managed a team of six, responsible for an eclectic range of security trading at the bank. Four of them, along with his assistant, Anna, were sat around a high table in the Queen's Head on Piccadilly. They were young, driven and terrifyingly bright, with an amazing grasp on the cyber threats that targeted the bank. Their abilities astonished Tom at times – and he knew his malware well. They cheered when Tom and Jamie approached. Tom brandished his medal. The little crowd offered him their congratulations and clapped him on the back before thrusting a flute of champagne into his hand.

Tom struggled onto a bar stool and sipped the champagne. He glanced at his phone. There were a few messages from friends and family congratulating him, but it was the voicemail from an unknown number that drew his attention.

'Give me a minute,' he said and hobbled into a quieter corner of the pub where he could better hear the message.

'Tom, this is Charlotte Benfield,' said Kat's voice. *'I hope you'll forgive the intrusion on your weekend, but I've just spoken with Steven, and he's champing at the bit to meet you. What do you think to an informal chat tomorrow? You mentioned being keen to expedite the interviews, so I thought this could be pencilled in for Tuesday. Let me know, and I'll get something in the diary with Steven.'*

Excellent, Tom thought. He returned to the table and said to Anna, 'Remind me to call Charlotte Benfield first thing tomorrow.' She nodded and handed back his topped-up glass of champagne.

'To all the Syrian refugees you've saved from suffering,' she toasted, and they clinked their glasses together.

*

Edison returned to his list. '*Health*' glared at him, he felt reproach scowling at him with every cursive curl. Three years ago, Edison had been fit. His field work had demanded a special level of physical prowess, and he'd prided himself in his strength, agility and speed. When he wasn't hiding out in the computer science lab, he had spent his teenage years on the rugby pitch at Harrow. That childhood passion for sport had matured with him, and he'd won his blue at Oxford. He'd also taken up the university's ubiquitous sport of rowing for his college. He'd left education a lithe, muscular twenty-two-year-old and sustained that physique until Eloise's diagnosis.

Edison dug around in a chest of drawers and pulled on a pair of jogging bottoms and a T-shirt. He rummaged in the cloakroom and dragged out a dog-eared pair of trainers. He laced them up, grabbed his keys and hurried down to the street before he could question his own resolve.

He made it to Lambeth Bridge at a run, his lungs burning and heart racing. He gave up on his ambitious pace and jogged on to Westminster Bridge. His legs were aching, and he felt like he might cough up a lung. He turned around and shuffled home, consumed with embarrassment at the state of his fitness. What would happen to him in the field in this state, Edison mused as he unlocked the door.

Stepping over the threshold, he was immediately alert. He felt its presence even before he saw the figure at the window. A sixth sense, nearly two decades in the development, was a little sluggish but tingling. His eyes darted to the top draw in the hallway cabinet. The short entrance corridor led into the living area. His line of sight from the front door was unbroken to where a woman stood with her back to him. Edison's hackles relaxed and heartbeat began to slow as he recognised Tanya Willis, his former boss.

'So that's where you keep it?' the figure said and turned to face Edison, looking stern.

'It's fully registered,' Edison protested.

'The Remington hunting rifle is, but I don't think you're keeping that in the telephone table. The Glock 26 that's been missing from the armoury for the last year and a bit, on the other hand, would fit neatly into that draw.'

'If you knew I had it, why didn't you come and get it?' Edison challenged, approaching cautiously.

Tanya shrugged. 'It was legitimately written off in the Folkestone sting – you orchestrated that well. You were always the cleverest officer I ever worked with.' Dismissing the discussion around Edison's ill-gotten firearms, she turned her attention back to the view from the window. There was a prolonged silence as Tanya's focus seemed to be consumed with the surveillance of the boats nosing about below. Tanya was the first black woman to be promoted to her rank in MI5. She was in her mid-forties, tall and slim, meticulously dressed in a trouser suit with her wild black hair scraped back from her forehead. Standing, looking out over London, she cut a majestic figure. She looked as fierce as her reputation of being a no-nonsense head of section, unflappable and seemingly unstoppable in her rise through the ranks at Five. Although these traits often made working for her uncomfortable, as she demanded such a high level of dedication from her team, unmatched elsewhere in the Service, they were amongst the many reasons why Edison had enjoyed reporting to her. She inspired fierce loyalty in her team and returned it in equal, if not greater, measure.

'Why are you here?' Edison ventured. 'And how did you get

in?' It was protocol that active officers kept a house key at Thames House in the event of an emergency, but on leaving the Service, one of the first things that Edison had done had been to change his access codes and locks.

Tanya gave him a look that suggested he should know better than to ask such questions. 'I haven't always been a paper pusher, Edison. Before I spent my days managing the higher-ups such that they don't meddle too much with you lot getting on with your day jobs, I wasn't a bad field officer myself. I can occasionally dig a little tradecraft out of my memory when I need it.'

Edison knew better than to press the issue but made a mental note to examine the flat's access points critically before remembering that he would be moving out the following day.

As if reading his thoughts, she said, 'I understand you're moving.' Turning away from the window and crossing toward the kitchen, she added, 'Aren't you going to offer me a cup of tea?'

'Just dropping in for a cuppa, are you?' Edison filled up the kettle.

'Not exactly,' Tanya said but didn't elaborate. 'I'm sure Tony's excited that you're moving in.'

'Excited to share the bills with someone.'

Tanya laughed and slid onto one of the breakfast bar stools. 'Inspired by today's race?' she continued to make conversation, with a nod toward Edison's attire.

'Something like that,' said Edison, throwing teabags into the two cups that he'd got out of the cupboard. He reached for the sugar, remembering how Tanya took her tea. She waved a hand at him.

'I'm cutting back,' she told him. 'You don't look very packed?' Tanya went on, looking around at the kitchenware that still littered the surfaces.

'I won't need it. I'm sure Ellie's mother will find a suitable home for it all.' Edison did his best to sustain his interest in the small talk whilst he ran over in his mind the possible reasons why Tanya, his former boss who he hadn't seen for over a year, had secured access to his flat while he was out and was waiting, some might say menacingly, on his return. She wasn't vetting Tony's new flatmate. For analysts, although some checking of their background was required, vetting certainly wouldn't be undertaken in person and definitely not by someone of Tanya's rank. He fished about for other reasons. The gun was a possibility, but she had passed over that subject with surprising casualness. He was flummoxed.

'As delightful as it is to see you, Tanya, I suspect this isn't a social visit.'

Tanya adopted a pose of businesslike formality, pulling a khaki-coloured folder toward her. Edison hadn't spotted it, although it had been lying on the breakfast bar since before he'd got back from his run. Tanya noticed Edison's almost imperceptible shake of his head as he berated himself for poor observation. 'What's wrong?' she asked him.

'I can't believe I didn't see that there.'

'You're out of practice. It'll soon come back to you.' Edison digested what she'd said, passing her a cup of tea, pulling a stool in beside her and looking at the folder. She's bringing me back, he realised.

'I have a job. And I think you're the only person who can pull off the level of deep cover required.' Tanya opened the folder to reveal a sheaf of papers, cuttings and photographs. She checked herself and looked hard at her former star officer. 'Edison, are you ready for this?'

'To go undercover? Absolutely.' Edison wasn't convinced he believed his own words, but he wasn't going to give anything away to Tanya. He turned his attention to the contents of the khaki folder. 'What's the op?' He reached for the paperwork, and Tanya pulled it away from him defensively.

'I'm bringing you onto this op unofficially.'

'What do you mean, unofficially?'

Tanya chose her words carefully, 'There are people at Thames House who would rather you didn't get involved in matters of national security—'

'For fear of what else I might work out about the rotten core of the machine and its bent operators?' Edison felt slighted. It had been a huge personal sacrifice to expose Sir Donald Hughes.

'No,' Tanya spat back immediately. 'The management takes the death of an informant very seriously, and very few are willing to offer second chances. They are especially unforgiving of an agent runner who is getting blind drunk whilst his operator is reaching out for help.'

Edison couldn't argue with her on that point. His personal and professional failings haunted him. Tanya fixed him with a stern gaze. 'This is all off the record,' she said, paused then went on. 'Your involvement is off the record. You are off the record.'

'I will go on record and assert that my involvement is off the record,' Edison attempted a joke, trying to lighten the mood.

'Don't. I'm deadly serious.' Her choice of adverb was deliberate. If things went south, she was asking Edison to put his life on the line without any of the protections enjoyed by fully on-boarded agents.

A kernel of a feeling began to germinate inside Edison. It was the thrill of being back inside the covert world of espionage. His heartbeat quickened. He took a deep breath and said, 'What do I need to know?'

'Operation HAPSBURG. We've had eyes on a sleeper cell of

jihadi sympathisers – we call them VIPERSNEST – in Vienna for some time now, after links to one of the 7/7 bombers surfaced. In fact, they would have been on our radar before you left but you wouldn't have been read in on it.' Edison winced. He'd suspected he'd been handled with kid gloves for months before he'd left, but this was the first time it had been confirmed that he had been purposefully kept in the dark on live operations. 'Separately, the Met has been keeping tabs on a bunch of drug runners bringing merchandise from Afghanistan via the Middle East and through to ports in Northern Europe for shipment to the UK on fishing trawlers. The goods ended up at Billingsgate and were sold on from there.'

'Drug trafficking,' Edison interrupted. 'Hardly a matter of national security.'

'True, unless the proceeds of such sales are going toward purchasing weapons and explosives for terrorist groups in Northern Syria. Which was our working hypothesis at the time.'

'Probably a good bet.'

'Do you remember about a year ago, a dismembered body was discovered at Billingsgate?'

'Vaguely, delivered in a packing crate wasn't it?'

'Yes. Everything went quiet after that on both the drug route and with our cell. Until a few weeks ago when Six picked up chatter on the wires that the same trawler is back in business. It all looks like a perfectly legitimate fishing operation on the surface, but our assets tell us there are men being shipped over too.'

'So, the body was linked to this operation? HAPSBURG did you say it was called?'

'Yes, HAPSBURG. We haven't been able to dig up the link, but we have to assume there is one.'

'Tell me about the corpse.'

'He was identified as Metin Dastan, a Syrian national who had applied for a visa just before Christmas the previous year. It was declined.'

'Why?' Edison's brain was whirring, and he was carefully filing the details of the operation into his memory.

'Dastan had a brother. Kerem Dastan, who emigrated to the UK five years ago. He was a naturalised Turk. He was well known to the Met.'

'A criminal record?'

'Yes, nothing desperately exciting. Some money laundering, he was almost done for intent to supply on a couple of occasions, sources suggest he was involved in a bit of forgery too. More than enough for a red flag to pop up when brother Metin tried to get his visa. The same happened to his sister and two children three months before.'

'What happened to Mr Dastan, the one with a pulse?'

'He's completely disappeared.'

'How convenient.'

'Indeed. We know VIPERSNEST is on the move. We think the shipping channel is being resurrected but for transporting human cargo not just white powder.'

Edison whistled. 'What's the threat level?'

'Severe.'

'So VIPERSNEST is now in the UK. We need to find them. Where do you need me undercover?'

'At a boutique investment bank in Canary Wharf, Penwill & Mallinson.'

'How do we get from North Sea drug runners to high finance?'

'Another of Six's officers in Vienna reported an uptick in their activity a month ago. More comings and goings and a few new faces making appearances. Transiting through. All this costs money.

They've increased their income somehow. Have you heard of cryptocurrency?'

'You mean like Bitcoin?'

'Exactly like Bitcoin, but there are a couple of others which are less well known and, as a result, more difficult to track. We managed to drop an asset into the heart of their operation in Vienna, and he reported that they were receiving income in Ethereum from an unknown source in London. They'd been using that to fund training camps, weapons and transport.'

'And this links to the bank how?'

'Penwill & Mallinson operate the only Ethereum exchange in Europe.'

'Can't they mine this stuff themselves? There's no guarantee that they're using an exchange to buy the currency,' Edison asked, digging into his memory for newspaper reports he'd read about the development of digital currencies. There had been a time when he would have lapped up news of any digital developments such as this, but his brain had been on low power mode for months and he'd only occasionally dipped into the financial and technology press.

'True, but our source thinks this is a wire transfer. They don't have the computing facilities to be mining it themselves, and there are suggestions of a link to a more mainstream Bitcoin income from their online drug sales.'

'The Silk Road,' Edison muttered, remembering his own covert forays onto the Dark Web's illicit e-Commerce platform, when he had been tracking down drug dealers, gangsters and porn barons as part of MI5 ops. 'So why do you need me?'

'We know enough, thanks to our techies, to be sure that the transfers are not coming directly from the bank. The cryptocurrency market has really heated up in recent months though – unbelievable exchange rates, and we think that might have encouraged our guy back into action.'

'Do we still have our man inside the sleeper cell?'

Tanya shook her head. Edison didn't press what might have happened to the officer.

'So, someone is moving the money "legitimately",' Edison air-quoted the word for emphasis, 'and then out of the country by some other means. But it all has to be done digitally. Surely we can track it?'

'You'd be amazed how easy it is to hide on the Dark Web.'

'Yes, Tanya, of course *I* know how easy it is to hide on the Dark Web.' At MI5, Edison had spent all the time he wasn't in the field navigating the shadier corners of the internet, rooting out communications between terrorists, right-wing activists and anarchists. 'What I mean is, *I* can track it.' Edison's heart beat slightly quicker, and he felt a prickle of goosebumps on his bare arms. He tried to squash the sense of excitement he felt under another question. 'So, what are we dealing with at Penwill & Mallinson?'

Tanya shuffled through the papers to find a glossy brochure. It profiled the investment capabilities of the small investment bank. 'Boutique bank,' she said. 'Mostly concerned with fund management but creating a profitable niche in the emerging world of digital currency and blockchain payments.' She paused. 'You know about this stuff?'

'Yes, distributed ledger technology, cryptocurrencies, it's gone pretty mainstream lately.'

'You'll need to swot up on it. Colin pulled some homework together for you.' Colin headed up the research team within counter-terrorism and spent his time, among other things, preparing plausible cover stories and pulling together background for officers about to head into the field.

'So, what's my legend?'

'You are Steven Edwards. You've worked at the Bank of England for the last six years where, latterly, you were responsible for identifying and implementing regulation for digital currencies. Before that, you were a digital payments specialist at a small start-up and even further back on a graduate scheme at Lehman Brothers. Kat has been working undercover as a recruitment specialist and has an initial meeting with the MD, Tom Woodward, pencilled in for you tomorrow. They will call you to confirm the details.'

Mention of his team prompted a further question from Edison. 'Who knows I'm back? Who's assigned to HAPSBURG?'

'Kat is the team lead. She's also got Colin. Jock and Natalie are on surveillance. Mo is her junior intelligence officer.' All but one of them had been on Edison's team. Mo was new to him, and he felt a strange sense of loss that they had been reassigned to a new team lead.

'Not Tony?'

'No, not Tony.'

'Tell me more about the bank set-up.'

Edison eyed the collection of photographs on the table. They had been printed from the firm's website and showed expensively dressed young men and women, mostly in their late twenties and early thirties. Tanya pulled them forward, one by one, reading off a short biography for each as she did so. 'Emma Pearson – fund manager. Twenty-nine. British. Lives in Greenwich with her boyfriend and cat. Christoph Langer – fund manager. Thirty-four. Austrian – originally from Innsbruck but studied in Vienna.' Edison made a note of the Viennese link. He had, as Tanya had been speaking, semi-consciously pulled the notepad, that was still on the table from yesterday's list-making, toward him and started scribbling key points down. 'He lives with the office manager, Anna on the Isle of Dogs.'

'Are they an item?'

'Not that we can tell from the usual social media trawl. Just roommates.'

'Tariq Mahmoud.' Tanya pulled forward a photograph of a dark-skinned man with almond eyes that shone as brightly as the broad smile he wore. 'Muslim. Third-generation son of Pakistani shopkeepers from Bradford. His parents wanted him to be a medic. He's twenty-four and a trainee fund manager.'

'No known links?' Edison asked, referring to the network of mosques in Bradford with well-publicised connections to some of the most prolific terrorist organisations known to the security services.

'None that we can dig up, and we have looked very hard.'

'So, who are the techies?' Edison asked, looking at the remaining three photographs and carefully laying them out in front of him.

Tanya pointed at the first, 'Billy – William – de Santos, Brazilian – has lived in Stockwell for a couple of years since he moved over from Sao Paulo. He's a payments expert and oversees all the technical aspects of the team's currency trading. Both the other two work for him. Maria Zinovyeva.' Tanya dabbed a finger on the picture of a blonde-haired woman. She wore heavy make-up which accentuated her fine features. Her lips parted in a broad smile to reveal a set of perfect white teeth.

'Russian?' Edison asked.

'Yes,' Tanya replied. 'Moved from Moscow to study Econometrics at the LSE before studying a computer sciences masters at Imperial. By all accounts, the sharpest of a pretty bright bunch.'

'Anything we need to be worried about?'

'We don't think so. Her family have links to the oligarchy but aren't particularly active politically. Her cousin's a diplomat in Scandinavia. No red flags although Six were a bit cagey about him.'

'And this guy?'

'Jamie Dunn. Brit. Brought up on a council estate in South London. Self-taught programmer. Self-taught everything really. Didn't go to university. Got the job winning a hackathon in the city that he went along to during his lunch break from his job as a barista. Real rags to riches story. And that's your lot,' Tanya concluded, gathering the photographs together and sliding them back into the folder.

'What do I need to know about Tom?'

Tanya shuffled through the pictures, fanning them out like a card deck and pulling the familiar face of Tom Woodward from the pack. 'Tom Woodward. Originally from Newbury in Buckinghamshire. Privately educated at Eton before studying natural sciences at Cambridge. Went into fund management straight out of university and held down a series of jobs around the City and Canary Wharf before joining the leadership team at Penwill's almost three years ago with responsibility for building up their digital currency capabilities. He also oversees some minor emerging market currency trading and an infrastructure portfolio. It's a boutique bank, so he's one of three directors who sit below the CEO.'

Edison considered the dossier he had in front of him. 'It's not desperately thorough, is it? I could have just printed this from the firm's website.'

'That's why I'm sending you in, Edison. Get under their skin. Find out who might be syphoning off funds to Islamic extremists. Dig into the code and get me some answers.'

Edison nodded.

'A couple more things – we also need insight on the investors. See what you can get once you're in, and Colin can take a look at it.' She thrust an encrypted USB stick into Edison's outstretched hand.

'You said a couple more things.'

'We're still keeping an eye on Billingsgate should our men return. Their drop day was Thursday, but Jock's had a member of his ops team there every week for the past month ever since the volume went up on the chatter.' Edison whistled. Such commitment to surveillance meant this was serious. 'You should go along on Thursday. Take a look.'

'I'll be there.'

Tanya looked pointedly at Edison's left hand. 'Steven Edwards is not married.'

Edison twisted his wedding ring and nodded, acknowledging what was required of him.

'I had better move,' Tanya said, looking at her watch.

In the hallway, before opening the door, Edison said, 'There's one thing I need from you if I'm going to do this.'

'Are we negotiating, Edison?'

'Yes, we're negotiating. I believe you said I'm the only one capable of going undercover at the bank. I need some security.' Edison explained what he wanted.

Tanya conceded the point with a subtle tilt of her head then disappeared down the corridor.

*

Edison closed the door softly behind him and stood with his back to it. He was shaking. The adrenalin that had been coursing through his veins was beginning to subside, and he felt cold, his clammy skin still caked with sweat from his run.

He breathed deeply and moved across the room slowly to the drinks cabinet on which stood a photograph in a slim silver frame.

Eloise grinned at him from the glossy surface, her hair tousled and flying in the breeze. She was dancing barefoot across a sandy beach, her jeans rolled up around her knees. Edison recognised the beach at Tynemouth in the blurry background. It had been freezing that day. Edison remembered every moment of that trip – it had been the first time he had taken Eloise home to meet his mother. They had boarded the Metro from Byker out to the coast to escape the claustrophobia of his mother's council flat. Despite the arctic temperatures, Ellie had insisted on dipping her toes into the icy North Sea. Much to the amusement of the dog walkers, the only other people on the beach in mid-February, Ellie had danced in and out of the surf, squealing with delight as the waves chased her up the beach. Looking at her in that photograph, she oozed life, she always did. Edison smiled. 'What do you think, Elle? Am I mad?' he asked the photograph. Silence hung in the air. 'I should pack, shouldn't I Elle? We'll worry about HAPSBURG and VIPERSNESTs once that's done.'

In the main bedroom, Edison considered the task at hand. After Ellie's death, Edison had tossed restlessly, and very occasionally slept, in the spare room – a cramped and desolate space, furnished only with the futon on which Edison had begged sleep to release him from the torment of consciousness. In contrast, the bedroom he'd shared with his wife was luxuriously furnished, reflecting his wife's talent for design and love for textiles. The vast bed was lavished with cushions and throws in muted, neutral tones. He padded, in his socks, across the whitewashed floorboards to the enormous built-in cupboards that had once housed Ellie's fashionable, expensive wardrobe. In what was, on the surface at least, an act of compassion, Jane had sorted through the flat shortly after the funeral on one of her many visits to London and packed away all her daughter's belongings – which amounted to the majority of the flat's contents. Edison was a man of frugal tastes. Jane's enthusiasm for decluttering had, in fact, been spurred on by her desire to sell the flat. The de Courcy's did not need the money, but displacing the heartbroken son-in-law, of whom she had never approved, was too good an opportunity to miss for Jane. Edison had won a stay of execution, thanks to the London housing market taking a dive in the aftermath of the financial crisis. Although Jane tried to press on with the sale, Gauthier convinced his wife that they would be mad to try to liquidate the asset at the time, although his true motive was to keep a roof over his son-in-law's head whilst he struggled through his grief.

Edison opened the wardrobe and stretched up to pull down a large holdall and a dusty camping rucksack. He spent the remainder of the day moving around the flat, half-heartedly packing his few possessions. He tipped draws of socks and underwear directly into the holdall. His jeans and shirts hanging in the wardrobe went in a single armful into the rucksack.

Dusk began to gather, and Edison was compelled to turn on the lights. He looked around the barren flat that had been his home for so long. He wandered in and out of each of the rooms, checking that he had packed everything he wanted to take with him. All that was left were his laptops.

He found the two computers, a Dell Alienware laptop and an early model ThinkPad in the dresser, where he'd stashed them over a year ago. He ran his hand over the cold metal lid of the ThinkPad. He ran his thumb along the edge and pushed the button that released the screen, and the machine unfolded in his hand. He toyed with the power button. All afternoon, the conversation with Tanya had been preying on his mind. He was itching to dig into the detail of the case. That would involve reacquainting himself with the shady message boards and illegal retail sites that operated on the dark side of the web. The thought excited and terrified him.

'So, Elle,' he looked over at the photograph, 'what do you think?'

Silence hung in the air. A dull ache blossomed around his sternum and radiated through his chest. Carefully, he put down the laptop before he dropped it. Even after all this time, he couldn't understand how these tidal waves of grief emerged out of such calm waters. He gazed through teary eyes at the picture. He wondered whether he would ever feel whole again. Her absence was as powerful as her presence had been in life. The weight of what he was about to do hit him hard. Would leaving their home lessen that sense that he was missing a part of him in any way? He couldn't bear the idea of losing even more of her.

He went to the drinks cabinet and poured himself a large measure of whisky. The feel of the cut-glass tumbler in his hand had a reassuring and familiar weight. He went to the window and surveyed London as it lit up in the gathering gloom, drinking in the view for the last time. He poured himself another generous helping and proceeded to get steadily more drunk, drowning in his melancholy.

Chapter Four

0825, Monday 26ᵗʰ June, St George's Wharf, Vauxhall, London
The tuneless ringtone on a mobile phone cut through Edison's torrid dreams. He ignored it, not wanting to open his eyes, sure that doing so would only make the pounding in his head worse. It rang again, demanding attention. Edison tested his theory and was proven right. Pain roared through his head, and he struggled to focus on the screen of the phone. He rubbed his eyes and was able to read the caller ID on the iPhone that Tanya had handed him the previous day. It served a number set up for his alias, Steven Edwards. Steven Edwards has a truly abominable taste in ringtones, Edison thought before exclaiming, 'Shit,' seeing Tom Woodward's name, his soon-to-be boss, written large across the screen just as the phone rang off for a second time. The curse caught in his throat. His mouth was painfully dry. With a superhuman effort, he hauled himself off the futon and, ignoring the drumming behind his temples, staggered toward the kitchen where he gulped down three glasses of water in an attempt to smooth the sandpaper adhered to his gullet. He retched as he tried to force down a further glass. Spitting out the bile and remnants of whisky still sloshing in his stomach, he turned his attention back to his phone and fumbled through the missed call log. His haste made him clumsy, and he twice dialled the voicemail before he lighted upon Tom's number. Tom picked up the phone within a couple of rings, giving Edison very little time to compose himself.

'Steven,' said Tom, his tone was warm.

'Tom,' Edison attempted, but his greeting came out crackly and muffled. He swallowed, wetted his lips and tried again with a cough, 'Tom, sorry, got a bit of a frog in my throat. Sorry I missed you.' He fished for a plausible excuse and was thankful that Tom cut in before he offered a barefaced lie. Jeez, Edison thought to himself, you're a former MI5 intelligence officer, you lied for a living. But, he admonished himself, you were always crap at subterfuge on a hangover. It's why you are no longer a spy.

'How are you?' said Tom.

'Pretty good thanks,' Edison lied as convincingly as he could. 'You?'

'Oh, wee bit sore. A couple of my team tricked me into running a marathon yesterday. They're a bunch of fitness nutters in this office. Hope you can keep up,' he laughed. 'Listen, Steven, I'm dashing into another meeting. Could you come to the Wharf for a drink later today? A bit of a "getting to know one another" exercise.'

'Sure, what time?'

Tom consulted one of the four screens he had in front of him. 'I'll be tied up 'til seven-ish. Could we put seven thirty in the diary? We could grab a bite.'

'Sure,' Edison said again.

'Awesome,' Tom enthused. 'Anna will book somewhere and send you a location. Gotta run. See you then.'

Edison wondered how late he had slept if Tom was already between meetings. He consulted his phone for the time. It was half-past eight. He double-checked it. Yes, only eight thirty. I guess that's the world of high finance and twenty-four-hour business. Not unlike agent running, mused Edison looking reproachfully at the empty whisky bottle on the countertop. It had left a sticky imprint on his list from the previous day. Things were just about falling into place, he thought.

*

Barely an hour later, Edison was crossing the river at Vauxhall. All that he owned was crammed into the rucksack and holdall that he had packed yesterday. He had showered before loading up the final few items, carefully packing away his computers.

Ellie smiled at him from the silver-framed photograph on the drink's cabinet. He looked at her and fiddled with his wedding ring. His heart tumbled over itself in his chest as he remembered what Tanya had told him the previous day. *Steven Edwards isn't married.* The words echoed in his head. With some difficulty, he manipulated the silver wedding band up his finger. The pain he felt as the ring pressed against his knuckle, refusing to budge, was unmatched by the agony he experienced when eventually he liberated the jewellery from his hand. He slipped the ring into his pocket and offered Ellie's photograph an apologetic smile. 'I still love you,' he told her and packed the frame into his holdall.

He left the keys on the kitchen island for Jane to recover when she arrived later that week. Hurriedly, he left the flat, choosing not to look back at the memories he was leaving behind.

Arriving at Thames House, Edison pulled out his mobile to dial Tony's number. As he did so, two familiar figures approached from the direction of Lambeth Bridge.

'Hello stranger,' said Colin. 'What brings you here?' Holding out his hand and shaking Edison's warmly. Colin was a friendly Welshman, and Edison liked him. He was dedicated to his job, and Edison knew he could rely on Colin to investigate quickly when he needed intelligence. He had four children with his partner, Pete, which kept him exceptionally busy when he wasn't working all hours of the day behind his computer at Five, so didn't often join the pub-goers. Edison hadn't seen him since he'd left the Service. His companion was Kat, and Edison felt himself redden in her presence, but she seemed the picture of cool, despite Edison's unexpected appearance.

'Just meeting Tony,' Edison said. 'I'm renting his spare room for a while.'

'Good for you,' Colin said. 'About time you stopped rattling around in that flat.'

'Shall we tell him you're here?' asked Kat.

'That would be great, thanks,' said Edison.

'I'll do it,' offered Colin. He disappeared into the imposing building behind them before either Kat or Edison had a chance to protest.

Edison shifted uneasily, recognising the face of an analyst from counter-espionage who was emerging from the building behind them with a co-worker. He caught Edison's eye and nudged his companion. 'That's Scott Edison,' he heard him say. They both stared wide-eyed.

'The best hacker ever employed by the Service.' Edison cringed, he hated the term 'hacker'.

'And field officer. Did you ever meet him?'

The second analyst shook his head in response. 'I heard he had a nervous breakdown.' Edison rolled his eyes and turned his back to the two desk monkeys, and they hurried away. The last he heard one of them say was, 'Do you think he's back? He looks dreadful.'

'How are you?' Kat asked, smiling at him.

'Good thanks, contrary to what they might say.'

'You do look a bit tired.'

'Thanks.' They stood silently for a moment before Tony appeared out of the double doors, breathless from his hasty descent from the upper floors.

'I'll leave you to it,' said Kat, disappearing through the same doors before Edison had a chance to say goodbye. Tony eyed Kat lecherously as she left then turned to Edison.

'Hey, here you go,' Tony said, thrusting a bunch of keys in Edison's direction. Carefully, he picked up the first of the three keys that dangled from the keyring. 'This one's for the downstairs door. Main door deadlock.' He picked up a second key, 'And this one's for the Yale lock,' indicating the final key. 'Ok?' Edison nodded. 'Your room is the first left on the landing. The other bedroom is empty, but you can't use that one as it's above mine, and I don't like the noise.' His brow furrowed at the thought of Edison's heavy footsteps overhead. 'Make yourself at home.'

'Thanks,' said Edison.

'Ok, better go. See you later.' The perfunctory exchange over, Tony scuttled back up the steps into Thames House. Edison pocketed the keys and trudged off toward to tube station at Westminster.

*

1921, Monday 26th June, Canary Wharf, London

Shortly before 7.30 p.m., Scott Edison emerged from the tube station at Canary Wharf and consulted the email that Tom's secretary had sent, providing directions to the brasserie restaurant Tom defaulted to for informal evening engagements. Edison gave Tom's name to a beaming concierge who fussed over taking his coat before escorting him to a table near the bar. 'This is Mr Woodward's favourite spot,' she explained. 'Can I bring you a drink whilst you wait? We have a fine selection of craft beers on offer, or if you'd prefer to review the wine list ...'

'Just a water for now, please,' replied Edison.

'Ok sir, that will be right with you.' She smiled and backed away, stopping to relay Edison's drink order to one of her colleagues. The colleague appeared moments later with a bottle of water and poured a large glass. He sipped it as he looked around. The restaurant was filling with bankers and lawyers escaping from a long day in the office, greasing the wheels of capitalism. There was a crowd of young men and women opening a bottle of champagne at the bar, loudly celebrating the closing of a big deal. Elsewhere, a couple sat in awkward silence at a high-top table. A first date gone horribly wrong, Edison mused. He surveyed the room and spotted Tom striding toward him, smiling.

'So sorry I've made you wait,' he said warmly, reaching out a hand and shaking Edison's.

'I haven't been here long,' Edison reassured him. Tom took a seat and scanned the wine menu.

'What are you drinking?' he asked, then spotted Edison's water glass. 'Will you join me for a drink?' he ventured.

'Just the one,' Edison replied, promising himself that he would maintain his sobriety.

'Ok,' said Tom to the waitress who had served Edison his water. 'We'll have a bottle of the Burgundy. Thank you.'

Edison smirked at the wine choice. His companion looked at him quizzically, and Edison was about to explain that that that particular vineyard neighboured his father-in-law's estate when he remembered that he was Steven Edwards, home counties born and bred, not Scott Edison with the tragic personal life.

Once the ceremony of tasting and accepting the wine had been completed and the waitress had furnished them both with generous helpings in their oversized glasses, Tom sat back in his chair and said, 'So, I understand from Charlotte that you're the best of the best.'

'She's paid to say that, but I do know my way round a distributed ledger.'

'You collaborated with Luke Patterson on the blockchain working group at the Bank of England, right?'

Edison knew the name of the central bank's lead on

cryptocurrency regulation from his speed read of his cover story notes on the tube. 'Indirectly,' he said evasively. The banking community was a small one and he couldn't risk Tom mentioning his name to Luke or members of his team expecting them to recognise him.

'I need to make sure our systems are adhering to and keeping up with the changes in regulation. It's becoming a very profitable part of the business, but if the FCA chose to crack down on cryptocurrency, like they did in New York, we might have some issues. I think, with someone like you on board, we can stay one step ahead. You may even be able to help spot some opportunities. We're already managing some bilateral trade transactions over our in-house blockchain, all hard-currency stuff at this stage but could quickly evolve to altcoins – would be good to get your view on those.' Tom continued to talk excitedly about the opportunities available at the bank whilst Edison purposefully metered the consumption of his wine and interjected occasionally with a soundbite from the literature he had memorised that afternoon.

They ordered, and as they ate, Edison steered the conversation toward gathering further intelligence on Tom's employees. 'So, tell me about the team … you said they tricked you into running a marathon.'

Tom laughed. 'Yes, I've been hobbling around all day, thanks to losing a bet to Jamie last summer. I'd rather just stick to my bike, but I think he'll be pushing me to join him on his next ultra or ironman or whatever it is that he and Tariq are doing.'

'Tariq?'

'Tariq Mahmoud, he's one of the fund managers along with Emma and Christoph.' Tom rattled off the names and job titles of the rest of the team, adding nothing to the picture Tanya had painted earlier that day.

'What about fundraising? Does that sit with your team?'

'No,' Tom explained, shaking his head. 'Sales sit centrally. A handful of relationship managers report to a guy called David Murray. They're pretty good at bringing the cash in. But you won't have much to do with them,' he finished, dismissing the topic. He looked at his watch. 'I need to go, I'm afraid. Could you come in for a formal interview tomorrow? Tick the HR box and just run through some of the more technical stuff. I need you in place as soon as possible, so hopefully, this is just a formality, and we can expedite the paperwork. I'll get Anna to get a time in the diary.' He pulled out an iPhone and dashed off an email.

*

Edison made his way to the bus stop, having seen Tom onto the tube. On the bus, Edison combed through all the information he'd gleaned from the conversation, he carefully evaluated each piece of intelligence and made a mental note of lines of enquiry he would pursue. He would have to get under the skin of Emma and Jamie's algorithm. That wouldn't be easy, fund managers are notoriously cagey about disclosing their investment strategies. Jamie would likely be the better source there. He guessed that Jamie, the marathon-running triathlete and self-made man, might be keen to show off to the new boy in the office.

He reached Tony's dingy maisonette buzzing. The mystery of an operation was like a drug to Edison. He felt energised. In his small bedroom, he sat at the table onto which he'd unpacked his laptops earlier. Reverently he lifted the lid of the ThinkPad.

His fingers trembled a little as they hovered above the keys. The black screen offered him a reflection of a man he didn't recognise. His ragged features looked back at him, his cheeks sagged and the bags beneath his eyes aged him by a decade. He shook his head, banishing the thoughts of his physical demise and reached for the power button. The machine whirred into life. Spidery white writing shuttled across the screen, and as if on autopilot, Edison typed in the commands that would take him to the Tails operating system on the external hard drive he'd plugged into the USB port. He needed to work with total anonymity, and The Amnesic Incognito Live System, Tails for short, was the best way of guaranteeing nobody could track what he was doing online.

He pulled up the Tor browser that would transport him into the darknet. He paused. Was he ready to re-enter the shadowy underworld of the internet? Largely frequented by hackers, drug dealers and peddlers of child pornography, once inside the maze of unindexed sites, he was always just one click away from something disturbing or illegal. As if preparing for a free dive, Edison took a deep breath and plunged into the murky waters.

Carefully, he typed in a seemingly random string of letters and numbers followed by '*.onion*', the top-level site suffix reserved for the anonymous side of the internet known as the Dark Web. He waited. Patience was a virtue when navigating this hidden digital world. Every move needed to be pinged through a host of Tor servers. It took time, but it was essential for remaining untraceable.

Time ticked by as the message board loaded, and Edison's thoughts drifted. He worried about whether any of his multiple aliases would be remembered. For years, he had tended to the false identities, creating voices for a gamut of characters, identified online by their different handles. They all had questionable motives, from an outspoken member of the alt-right to a cypherpunk supporter of small government, total digital freedom and requisite anonymity. He'd been a terrorist sympathiser, a desperate junkie and a member of the dissident group, Anonymous. Over time, he had retired some usernames and birthed others, depending on the needs of the operation. He'd come to know the denizens of countless online hangouts well. He wondered, as he scrolled through various message boards, whether he would be able to slot back into this nefarious world.

He skimmed over the trolling and flaming that made up most of the chatter on the boards until he found the conversation he was looking for on a dedicated hacker forum known as *0Day*. He typed a message into the Internet Relay Chat and waited. Nothing. For an hour, Edison distracted himself, digging around his old haunts on the Dark Web as he waited, hoping for a reply. The night was deepening around him. The dull thud of Tony's computer game soundtrack stopped at just gone midnight, and silence descended on the flat in Bethnal Green.

Edison was about to give up for the night when the IRC chat box glowed, indicating a reply.

<MadDog> OMG Rumpelstiltskins alive!

Another message followed almost immediately.

<m1ck> lol missed u rumpy

<MadDog> Where u been

Edison considered his reply. Rumpelstiltskin had been a black-hat hacker for hire, willing to sell his services to the highest bidder. An arrest and a prison stay were a feasible explanation for an extended absence from the chat boards, but Edison didn't want to undermine his credibility.

<Rumpelstiltskin> stuff happened IRL

IRL meant 'in real life'. Edison's use of the jargon was rusty. Before MadDog or m1ck had a chance to challenge him any further, another user joined the conversation. Edison recognised the username of another hacker renowned for sophisticated ransomware attacks.

<4hire> omgomgomgomg rumpelstiltskin

<4hire> missed u

<Rumpelstiltskin> lol

As Edison chatted, his fingers started to fly across the keyboard. Being back on IRC was like riding a bicycle or speaking a mother tongue after years living in another country, tricky at first but as he immersed himself further in the Dark Web's counterculture, his fluency returned. The clock in the bottom right of his screen read 3.00 a.m. when the conversation began to dry up. He itched to probe his contacts about cryptocurrency but knew better than to look too curious so early in his return.

<Rumpelstiltskin> G2G

Reluctantly, he shut down the computer before anyone had a chance to reply.

Chapter Five

0227, Wednesday 28th June, Internet Relay Chat

<Rumpelstiltskin> So whats new round here
<4hire> always something new.
<4hire> What u interested in these days?
<Rumpelstiltskin> my guys want crypto stuff. Ether. BitCoin.
<MadDog> everyone wants crypto
<m1ck> Everyone thinks there the next Dread Pirate
<Rumpelstiltskin> Silk Road 2.0
<4hire> yeah came across some guy
<4hire> crowing about hacking an exchange or something
<Rumpelstiltskin> ??
<4hire> wouldn't touch it
<m1ck> Feds love that stuff
<Rumpelstiltskin> Sounds like the guys got skillz
<4hire> mhhm
<4hire> u wd like him rumpy
<Rumpelstiltskin> name?
<4hire> RubiksKube
<MadDog> remember that guy. He's not in it for the lulz
<m1ck> rofl

*

0515, Thursday 29th June, Nelson Gardens, Bethnal Green, London

'Early start?' Tony startled Edison, who was about to leave the flat at quarter past five on Thursday morning. Edison had one hand on the latch of the front door but turned to look at Tony, adopting an air of nonchalance.

'First day,' Edison said to appease his suspicious flatmate, whose ratty features were arranged into an expression of curiosity and distrust. 'Can't sleep. So, thought I'd get some air and head to the Wharf early. You're up early.'

'I could hear you tramping around up there,' Tony accused him. 'Rather than a walk, you could have a coffee with me, now I'm up.'

'Thanks, but if it's all the same to you, the air will do me good. Settle the nerves.' Tony shrugged and scuttled into the kitchen where he busied himself, filling the jug on the filter coffee machine whilst Edison made his escape.

The warm light of a mid-summer morning was just beginning to wash over East London as Edison made his way to the bus stop and boarded the empty D6. He watched the world go by through hazy eyes, still half asleep, and was startled when the tinny voice announced over the bus's PA system that the next stop would be Billingsgate. 'Pull it together, man,' he muttered to himself as he stepped off the bus. He needed to have his wits about him as he headed into the field for the first time in over a year. He strode off in the direction of the fish market, where he was met by Mo, the agent Kat had told him to expect.

Kat had been in touch with Edison the previous day. Their conversation had been perfunctory and functional. Mo, a relatively new field operative, would be staking the possible drugs drop that Thursday morning. His cover was as a buyer for a West London hotel, Edison would be his boss, along for the ride after a bad batch of langoustine the previous week, if anyone asked. 'Which they won't,' Kat assured him. 'If they do make an appearance, we don't interfere,' Kat explained. 'We just observe.'

'All right,' Mo greeted Edison with a wary handshake. 'We'll head inside, walk the floor and see what merchandise is on offer. I think our punters might like a bit of monkfish this week, and there's a few guys with stalls near our target, if they're there, which I doubt, who sell that. Let's go.'

Edison's smart brogues shuffled through the slush of melting ice as the pair of spies made their way past the stalls of produce. Mo came to a halt. Edison saw a near imperceptible widening of his eyes before the young man collected himself and studied a selection of red snapper, inviting Edison to bow his head over the display of fish with a wave of his hand.

'Opposite side of the aisle, two stalls down,' Mo said urgently, positioning himself so Edison could see two young men tending an understocked stall. 'They're back.' Edison felt a shot of adrenalin course through him. Surreptitiously, he eyed the men on the stall. He caught his breath. Of the two men busying themselves around the stall, one was familiar to Edison. He recognised the single earring, and the man was wearing a gold chain round his left wrist, just as the shadowy figure in the pub in Clapham had been. The guy with two mobile handsets, thought Edison. It's definitely him, he thought, eyeing the target as best he could without drawing unwanted attention.

'Anything I can help you with gentlemen?' the thickly accented voice of the stall owner spoke to them. He spoke like he'd never left the Isle of Dogs; his East London accent took a bit of deciphering.

'Any monkfish?' Mo asked, seemingly ignoring the activity of their marks.

'Not today, mate, but there's some fine halibut,' the fishmonger encouraged him, manhandling a large fillet of white fish out of the polystyrene box in front of him and proffering it to Mo for closer inspection. He considered it carefully before shaking his head.

'Thanks mate, but it has to be monkfish today,' with a nod to

Edison who was slowly making his way toward the next stall. 'Boss's orders.'

'Good luck, there's not been a good landing of monkfish for a while.'

Mo followed Edison, who had moved off, perusing the wares of the market holders as he went. A large crate had arrived, wheeled on a pallet, at the stand where their marks were busying themselves with a crowbar to get the top off. Edison observed them covertly.

'Do we know who those two are?' said Edison quietly, jerking his head in the direction of their targets.

'I recognise them from the e-fits the drugs squad provided us. They reckon they're petty criminals. Pawns. Call them what you will.' Both men looked back toward their marks, they were busying themselves with the humdrum routine of regular stallholders.

'So, they aren't members of VIPERSNEST.'

Mo shook his head.

The pair moved off. Edison cast a furtive glance back at the man with the earring. Once they were out of earshot, Mo said, 'I need to phone this in. Get everyone mobilised.' He disappeared into the crowds.

Edison turned toward Canary Wharf, lost in a whirlwind of thoughts. He couldn't shake a sense of unease that centred around the identity of the stranger who, in a city of seven million people, had crossed his path twice in less than a week.

*

0753, Thursday 29th June, Canary Wharf, London

He didn't have long to contemplate the stranger with the earring. He was late for the team scrum. Edison arrived in the foyer of the soaring office building that housed Penwill & Mallinson, breathless and sweating, at three minutes to eight. His journey had been hindered by the crowds of people, and he had dodged his way through the throng at a jog to begin with before his lack of fitness caught up with him, and he slowed to a walk, weaving in and out of the commuters with their heads buried in their smartphones and plugged into their headphones. A smartly dressed woman greeted him. 'Steven,' she addressed him with a forced smile as she looked him up and down. Edison glanced down to see his dishevelled appearance. His shirt was stained with sweat where his overweight midriff strained against the buttons, and his shoes were splashed with fishy residue. He felt embarrassed and promised himself for the umpteenth time in the last three days that he would lose the extra weight he was carrying and get fit.

'Anna,' he said, slipping into the skin of Steven Edwards. He held out a hand and offered Tom's secretary a broad smile, 'A pleasure to see you again.' The woman who'd greeted him took it gingerly, returning none of Edison's warmth. She was blonde and impeccably dressed in a tailored trouser suit. They had met for the first time two days earlier when Edison had come into the office for his formal interview, and she had been just as unfriendly then.

'I have your security pass ready, so we can go straight up. This way.'

Edison followed Anna as she led him to a bank of lifts which took them up to the fifteenth floor. They hurried past the bank's reception desk, past a well-appointed kitchen, where some of the staff were chatting over their morning coffee, and into an enormous open-plan office, walled on two sides with floor-to-ceiling windows, flooding the space with light and offering far-reaching views over to the City of London in the west, and south across the river to Greenwich.

'Don't get used to the view,' Anna said. 'They're building office blocks at a rate of knots, it feels like, and one will pop up there before you know it. We're probably funding it.' She laughed at her own joke. Edison smiled, glad that the icy reception he'd received downstairs was beginning to thaw. A good relationship with the office admin staff was key for any intelligence-gathering – secretaries and assistants know everything about everything. 'The team sits over there,' she indicated three banks of desks at the far end of the office, flanked by a fishbowl office on one side and windows on the other. 'That's Tom's office, where you had your interview.' Anna pointed at the fishbowl. 'I sit just outside. I'll give you a proper tour after the scrum. This way.' She led him across the office where, against one of the two walls not made of glass, there was an open space, sparsely furnished and a few people milling around a large LCD screen. Edison recognised some of the faces from Tanya's brief.

'Boys and girls,' said Anna, commanding their attention, 'this is Steven Edwards. I'll leave you to introduce yourselves.' She put a folder she had been carrying on a high-top table next to the screen before disappearing.

Edison smiled self-consciously as his new colleagues gathered around him. He recognised Tariq, Maria and Emma. Billy and Christoph appeared moments later, both clutching coffee and relieved to discover that Tom hadn't arrived yet. 'He cannot abide lateness,' Billy explained to Edison. 'Jamie will be late though. He's always seven minutes late for everything.'

'Gets away with it too,' Maria said. Edison sensed a note of jealousy in her tone, carefully concealed under her jovial manner. She spoke with a clipped, cultivated accent, no doubt acquired at an expensive boarding school, but she was clearly Russian. And very beautiful, Edison thought, before admonishing himself – although he wasn't sure whether that was out of deference for his dead wife or the complicated relationship he had with Kat.

'Who gets away with what?' Tom said, striding in and greeting

Edison warmly. 'Hey, Steven, welcome, I hope they're all making you feel at home.' He paused, pulling a face of mock horror. 'You don't have a drink, they really aren't looking after you.' Anna reappeared with an enormous cup of coffee, the mug adorned with the words '*The Boss*', which she handed to Tom. Later, Edison spotted a matching cup with the words '*The Real Boss*' emblazoned on it, sat on Anna's desk, which made him chuckle. 'Anna – thank you. Please could you sort Steven out with a coffee?'

'Sure,' Anna said. Turning to Edison she asked, 'How do you take it?'

'Any chance of a tea?'

'Of course. Green, chai, chamomile, English Breakfast, you name it we probably have it.'

'Regularly bog-standard breakfast tea, please. White, no sugar. Could you leave the bag in?'

The tea appeared just before Jamie came sauntering across the room. Edison checked his watch. 8.07 a.m. as predicted.

'Thank you for joining us, Jamie,' said Tom to the latecomer and then, turning to the rest of the team, he said, 'Could someone please update Jamie's calendar? I believe this meeting has somehow ended up in his diary for eight fifteen.'

Jamie grinned, ignoring the sarcasm dripping from Tom's tongue. 'Struggled to find a spot in the bike park.' He turned to Edison. 'Jamie Dunn,' he said, holding out a hand.

'Steven Edwards.' Jamie conducted himself with a confident swagger, and Edison was glad that his predictions, so far, had been proved correct. He was looking forward to getting to know him a bit better. He was sure he would learn a lot from him.

'All right, let's get started,' Tom said, positioning himself at the high-top where his secretary had dropped his briefing file. He consulted it then went on, 'You've all met Steven, the newest member of the team. He's mostly going to be working on the security around our trading systems and ensuring they're adhering to whatever new straitjacket the FCA are lumbering us with. Make sure you're working with him, not against him.' The meeting continued with updates on trading positions from the fund managers and news of a cash injection coming from the sales team who had closed a round of fundraising for the third iteration of the bank's alternative fund which seemed to get everyone excited. Edison was reminded of Tanya's request to find out who was invested and began to formulate a plan to secure that information.

His phone had been buzzing occasionally in his pocket throughout the meeting, but as the time ticked on, it vibrated more insistently against his leg. Finally, after Anna delivered an update on the grand total raised by the team at the weekend's marathon – 'That's nearly five thousand pounds for the plight of the refugees,' she told the team with tears in her eyes. 'You guys really do care. Unlike some of our politicians.' – Tom released the team to their desks and accompanied Edison back to his office. 'Tom, where are the bathrooms?' Edison asked, searching for an excuse to check his mobile messages in private.

'Has no one shown you?' Tom said, genuinely concerned about the warmth of Edison's reception and the impression it might be leaving on his newest recruit.

'Oh, don't worry,' Edison assured him, 'I was a bit later than I would have liked to be. Anna promised me a full tour after the scrum.'

'Back past the kitchen, toward the lifts, on the left,' said Tom. 'Come back to my office once you're done, and I'll brief you on what needs doing.'

Once safely tucked away in the privacy of one of the cubicles, Edison retrieved his phone from his pocket. There were three missed calls and five voicemails, all were from his mother-in-law. Three of the messages on his answerphone were date-stamped from two days ago. Another the day before. In the excitement of the last few days, Edison had forgotten about the de Courcys' imminent arrival in London.

He listened to the voice messages in order. The first explained that she and Gauthier would be in London for a little over a week to arrange for the sale of the flat. She'd requested that they arrange a time when he would be out for the agents to take the promotional photographs. She'd also asked how long it might take for Edison to make arrangements to move out. Her messages had become increasingly frustrated in tone as Edison continued to blank her. Her final message the previous day had changed tack, and she'd affected concern, saying she was worried about him and that she understood that he may be finding the sale of the flat difficult, but she would really appreciate an acknowledgement, if nothing else, just to let her and Gauthier know he was ok. That message had ended with Jane telling him that she and Gauthier would be arriving in London on the last Eurostar that evening (Wednesday) and would get to the flat to meet the first agent at 8.00 a.m. on Thursday.

This morning's voicemail had been left at 8.45 a.m. '*Edison,*' Jane's voice said. '*We have arrived at the flat. Am I to understand from your absence, the keys left on the table and the fact that I cannot see any of your personal effects, that you have already made arrangements to find alternative accommodation? Please let me know.*' The faux concern of the prior evening had evaporated, the message was full of venom. Her son-in-law had outsmarted her. He had deprived her of the satisfaction of evicting him in person.

Edison sent a text message. *Yes, moved out. Good luck with the sale.* Jane did not like text messages. She insisted on calling them SMS and never used the verb 'to text'.

Edison turned his attention back to his work and read the text message from Kat. *Edison,* it read, *need to debrief on Billingsgate ASAP. Be at the Star & Garter on The Narrow at 8pm.*

Edison shot off a reply confirming he'd be there.

Back in Tom's office, he explained Edison's priorities for the coming days. After twenty minutes, during which time Edison had taken copious notes on Tom's expectations for him, Tom drew breath and said, 'I think that should keep you busy for a day or two.' Edison thought that Tom's instructions could keep him busy for a month but didn't say anything. The meeting was concluded, and Edison retreated to his desk to consider how best to approach the mountain of work expected of him whilst pursuing his other lines of enquiry.

*

'Fancy lunch?' A voice interrupted Edison's focus. He had spent the hours since his meeting with Tom familiarising himself with the technical set-up at the bank. It wasn't a complex system. But it was elegantly built by someone who knew what they were doing.

'Lunch?' the voice said again. Edison had been digging around the security profile of the trading system. He looked up from his screen to realise he was being addressed by Jamie.

'Sure,' said Edison, 'but I'm on a diet.'

Jamie looked him up and down critically, and his eyes lit up. 'Getting in shape for something?' he asked and bowled on without waiting for a reply. 'I can help you. I know a bit about nutrition and could even sort a training programme out. I managed to get this guy round a marathon at the weekend you know.' He slapped Tom on the shoulder, who had made his way out of his office.

'I still haven't forgiven him for that,' Tom said. 'Have you seen Emma?'

'Gone for a sandwich, I think,' said Jamie. 'Joining us for

lunch?'

'No time today,' said Tom, retreating into his office.

'Come on, Steve.' Jamie said. 'There's a good place for salads. High protein, low carbs. That's what you need, I reckon. Did you say you were training for something?'

'No, nothing. Just getting back in shape. Eat less, move more,' said Edison.

'All right,' Jamie continued as they accelerated down to the foyer in the lift. 'Bring some kit in tomorrow. I can show you some good running routes round here. You'll soon be back in shape. With a bit of help.' Jamie winked and Edison grinned at him, building rapport with targets had been a key part of Edison's role as an intelligence officer, and he'd developed a chameleon-like ability to adopt multiple personalities to inveigle his way into people's trust.

They settled down to lunch, tucking into superfood salads served in cardboard cartons with plastic cutlery.

'How long have you been with Penwill's?' Edison took the opportunity to probe Jamie.

'A year and a half,' said Jamie through a mouthful of kale and pumpkin seeds.

'And you work for Billy?'

'Yeah, sort of. Mostly I work with the PMs, sorting them out with programs to run their trading strategies.'

'PMs?' Edison queried.

'Portfolio Managers,' Jamie explained. 'Mostly Emma 'cos she does the cool crypto stuff. But Christoph too. He's a dullard when it comes to programming.'

'Tom mentioned you and Emma had built a crypto hedging algorithm which was proving pretty successful.'

'Ha, yes, you could say that. It's working really well. We're delivering in excess of twenty basis points on that strategy. Some days, it pushes thirty.'

'Tom asked me to take a look at it,' Edison lied, picking at his salad with distaste. 'Make sure it's watertight from a regulatory point of view. Could you take me through it?'

'Happily. How's your C++? I'm pretty busy, so it would be better if I sent it to you to get under the skin of.'

'Pretty proficient.'

'Good, the last guy seemed to think he could get by calling himself a developer on just Java.'

'Hmmmm.' Edison wondered whether the 'last guy's' lack of programming knowledge might explain someone's ability to syphon off funds from the trading algorithm unchecked. 'Send over access to the repository, and I'll let you know if I have any questions.'

'Sorted. Will send it to you as soon as I'm back at my desk.' Jamie washed his lunch down with a green juice that smelt vile. They returned to the office, Jamie chatting incessantly, explaining his triathlon training in a level of detail that bamboozled Edison.

At Tom's behest, Anna had filled Edison's diary with introductory meetings with each of the team. Edison would bait the conversation to see if he could tease out any possible connections to the terrorist ring or the mysterious money moves. Edison speculated that it was quite possible for the perpetrator of the fraud to have no knowledge of the wider web of criminality that wove its way out from their actions. Edison's first conversation with Maria proved benign. She briefed Edison in the bank's investment strategies and the expectations of their clients. There was no denying her razor-sharp intelligence. They talked amiably about the relative merits of python programming for scaling algorithms versus C++.

'Why would you use something so static for your API?' she exclaimed. She was an attractive woman and tossed her blonde hair over her shoulders as she argued.

'But the python system will inevitably fall over at higher trading volumes, and what about the volatility?' Edison said.

'Pah. We're not talking high trading volumes in these currencies. There is only a small pool of counterparties for these trades. And as for the volatility, that is what we want. It is all a volatility play. Emma and Jamie have a beautiful program that works around the volatility on the Bitcoin/Ethereum exchange. Very stylish.' Her eyes lit up, and she spoke in a tone most others would reserve for great works of art or music.

'Do you ever edit that code?'

'The crypto algorithm. No, but I occasionally take a look at it. Just to see what new ideas they are trying. Jamie is always tinkering with it.' Maria looked wistful. Edison smiled. This woman was consumed in the intellectual challenge of her work. He thought it very unlikely she would be tapping off funds to bankroll jihadis.

The mention of Jamie's algorithm reminded him that the triathlete hadn't sent him the access he'd promised at lunch. He wound up the meeting with Maria. She made him promise that they might resume this argument. 'Perhaps over a glass of wine,' she suggested, a coy gleam in her dark-rimmed, blue eyes.

'Sure,' Edison responded automatically, only to realise afterwards that the beautiful Russian had been flirting with him. Fuck, he thought to himself, as he went to find Jamie, what had he just agreed to?

Clad in Lycra, Jamie was leaning over his desk, shutting down his computer. The screen went black just as Edison arrived. 'You were going to sort out an access log,' he said as Jamie pulled on a bicycle helmet.

'Sorry mate. I completely forgot. Tomorrow?' Something in the way that Jamie shifted his weight drew Edison's attention. The young man's gaze didn't quite meet his. Jamie hurried away, and without looking back, he said, 'First thing tomorrow, promise. Got to dash tonight.'

'Ok, have a good evening,' said Edison to Jamie's retreating figure.

'He's always dashing off for some gym session or other.' Edison turned to see the broad, smiling face of Tariq Mahmoud. 'How's your first day been?'

'Bit of a whirlwind to be honest,' said Edison.

'Fancy a quick drink?'

'Sure.'

'Let's see if Billy fancies it.'

Moments later, the three men were seated in a wine bar in the basement of the building, all three with pints of beer. Tariq's faith no longer played a big part in his life, Edison determined. Tariq lifted the beer to his lips and confirmed Edison's suspicions by saying, 'My parents would be horrified.'

'I'll drink to that,' replied Billy. 'Nothing but a disappointment to my parents.' He went on to explain. 'They thought I'd be home after six months, ideally with a wife in tow. Not sure what my boyfriend would have to say about that. What's your story, Steven? Let your old man down by not taking over the family business? Not given your mum enough grandchildren yet?' Edison felt the questions land like sucker punches. He'd not really known his father, one of the last workers in the North East's docks before they finally closed in the eighties, plunging the area deeper into economic gloom and his family into a financial plight from which they would not recover. Scott Edison Senior had spent most of the meagre benefits the Thatcher government gave them at the bar of the working men's club in Byker before eventually walking out on Edison and his mother when Edison was only nine years old.

Edison couldn't begin to contemplate answering either of the questions honestly and took a long draft of his pint, buying himself time to compose himself and work out if Steven Edwards might have any skeletons in his closet. He laughed and said, 'Something like that. But tell me, what do I really need to know? You know, in the office?'

Billy looked at him and laughed. 'Tariq,' adopting an exaggerated tone and nudging Tariq conspiratorially, 'he wants the gossip.'

'Well,' said Tariq, furrowing his brow in mock seriousness, 'Emma makes the most excellent brownies.'

'Christoph is very, very serious.' Billy picked up on the jest and adopted a mock German accent, 'We shall not joke about ze infrastructure fund, ja?'

'And I'm fairly sure that Anna is having an affair with one of the sales team, given how much time she spends on the fourteenth floor,' Tariq finished with a flourish. He and Billy fell about laughing, and Edison joined in.

'In all seriousness,' Billy said, composing himself, 'all you really need to know is not to take anything Jamie says too seriously. He thinks he's God's gift to programming—'

'And women,' Tariq interrupted.

'And triathlons. But really, he's harmless.'

'Noted,' said Edison with a grin. He checked his watch. 'I need to get going. Can I buy you guys another before I shoot off?'

Both Tariq and Billy declined the offer, and the three men left the bar together before setting off in different directions. Edison made his way to the DLR, deep in thought. His mind ran over the conversation with Maria. Should he be reading more into her flirtations? Is Jamie as harmless as his colleagues consider him to be? Was the delay in him sending access to the trading program through a genuine memory lapse or something more sinister? There was something about Jamie that didn't quite add up, but Edison couldn't put his finger on it. He was out of practice.

Chapter Six

1028, Thursday 29th June, Moniedubh Estate, nr North Ballachulish, Lochaber

The phone rang in Sir Donald Hughes' study a little before half-past ten. Angus, who was snoozing on the sofa after an energetic romp over the hills with his master that morning, lifted an eyelid as Hughes picked up the handset.

'Colchester just dispatched a unit to Grimsby,' a breathless voice on the other end of the line told Hughes. He felt his blood boil.

'You shouldn't be calling on this line, Waring,' Hughes admonished the informant, although he was glad to have the information.

'I thought you should know.' The junior Met police officer sounded meek. 'I thought it was the right thing to do.'

Hughes was about to launch into a tirade about protocol and security but thought better of it. He had been worried about reopening the Grimsby import route and had been proven right. He could have guessed that the police would be watching Billingsgate even after all this time. 'Ok, Waring, thank you for letting me know. That will be all.' He hung up and dialled another number immediately.

'Hello, my love,' he said when a woman picked up the phone.

'Donny, you shouldn't call me at work.'

'I had to speak to you. I was right to be worried. The police are crawling all over Grimsby. I don't—'

She interrupted him, 'Give me a minute whilst I run

downstairs. Find a little privacy. I'll call you back in just a moment.'

Whilst Donald waited for the phone to ring, he wondered what options were available to him now the Grimsby to Billingsgate route had been burned.

'My darling,' her tones were soothing when she finally called back. 'What's worrying you?'

'The Met has sent the sniffer dogs to Grimsby.'

'So?' Hughes could hear the shrug in her voice. 'We tried and it didn't work out. It would have been nice to have a little more money in the bank, but we can still go ahead with our plans, no?'

Donald looked longingly at the details for a flat in Knightsbridge he'd received from an estate agent the previous day and bit his tongue. He was going to struggle to afford such a love nest and had been relying on a few more successful shipments to stock up the coffers.

'I'm sure we can make it work. But what if the police find something?'

'They won't, my darling. You were ever so careful. It will be impossible for them to track the drugs back to you.' The stroking of his ego went some way to reassuring Hughes, and he sighed. 'I must go, my love. And you must not worry so much. Everything's going to be fine.'

'Let's speak again tomorrow.'

'Yes, of course,' she promised and hung up.

For some time after the call, Hughes stood in a meditative state watching the clouds race over the horizon. His thoughts turned to Edison. If it hadn't been for him, he thought, he wouldn't be in this god-awful position. He wondered whether there was any truth in the rumours that Tanya Willis was going to recall him to active service. He dragged his gaze away from the grey-green mountains that rolled away from the study window and fired up his computer.

He dashed off an encrypted email – *What is your flatmate doing for work? Has he been at Thames House?*

*

Like many of the analysts at Thames House, Tony harboured dreams of promotion to the vaunted ranks of field operative. Prior to Hughes' departure from the Service, his career development had looked more assured, as the head of the Service had taken a special interest in his ambitions. They had gone for the occasional coffee. Hughes seemed particularly concerned by Tony's financial position and alluded to his potential for advancement within the Service. His departure had been a bitter blow for Tony. Hughes had explained what a huge misunderstanding it had all been, in their last conversation prior to Sir Donald's departure.

They'd been nursing a coffee in their usual haunt when Hughes had said, 'Tony, things might hot up for me a bit over the next few weeks. I'm likely to have to leave the Service.' Tony's shock had shown on his face. He'd been counting on the promotion Hughes had promised to be able to remortgage the flat. 'Don't worry,' Hughes had assured him, 'I still have a lot of friends in the Service, and I'm sure I can continue to help you. However,' he'd leaned in closer, 'I will need a little bit of help in return.' Tony's eyes widened. 'All good experience for you, of course, if you're going to work in the field.'

Hughes had continued, 'I have a few covert operations still live, matters of national security, rather hush-hush, not many people read in.' Tony had nodded, not really understanding. 'Might need you to report a few things in to me, old boy.'

'Of course,' Tony had agreed without a second thought.

*

Tony received the message from Hughes and opened it eagerly. Dutifully he tapped out a response –

No sign of physicist at Thames House other than to pick up key from me. He has job working on security at a bank in Canary Wharf, I think. Hasn't told me much about it. Tony ran the message through an encryption key, watching with satisfaction as the prose transformed into a string of meaningless letters and numbers. He pressed send then turned his attention back to the dead-end task of trawling through wiretap transcripts from a call centre in Birmingham. A middle-ranking intelligence officer had taken a dislike to a young Pakistani worshipping at one of his team's 'hot' mosques and tasked Tony with the job of digging through the conversations he had, all day, every day, in case he was using his position as a telesales executive to proselytise and recruit. Tony yawned and hoped Hughes would reply with further instructions for him soon. He was enjoying his foray into the world of covert surveillance.

*

The police are crawling all over Grimsby. It was always a risk going back to Billingsgate, but it doesn't matter. Our purpose is no longer to profit from their weakness. We no longer need to supply the infidels with coke and crack to lubricate their immorality.

The mujahideen are here. They are in London. They prepare themselves for their greatest and most glorious sacrifice.

But there is work still to do. I must cover up our tracks. There are men who must be dealt with. Men who could reveal too much if the police get to them before I do. So, I am on my way to Grimsby to ensure the silence of the captain. He has served his useful purpose, and now he must take my secrets to the grave.

Brother Metin, the day of vengeance draws nearer. We will be united once more in paradise, once I have seen justice done for you, Samar and Houda on this earth.

Chapter Seven

2008, Thursday 29th June, The Star & Garter, Wapping, London
Shortly after 8.00 p.m., Edison arrived at The Star & Garter, a small pub tucked away on the edge of Wapping. Kat wasn't there yet, so he settled himself in a corner nook with a pint of beer.

She arrived ten minutes later, looking as close to flustered as the unflappable Kat ever did. She slid in next to Edison and picked up the drink he'd ordered for her. 'You are a star,' she said, taking a big gulp. Edison shifted uncomfortably as he felt Kat's leg brush against his in the tight confines of the nook. He was conscious of their relationship away from work, the relationship that meant he knew that she only ever drank malt whisky on the rocks. 'Everything ok?' Kat asked, eyeing him suspiciously. Earlier in the week, before Edison had gone undercover at the bank, they had met for a brief chat about the operation's objectives and the Billingsgate observation. Kat had kept the conversation professional, and the subject of their affair hadn't arisen. That had been over a sandwich in Westminster. Here, in the more familiar surroundings of the pub, Edison felt the line between personal and professional begin to blur and wasn't sure how to react. Kat placed a hand on his leg. 'It's ok, Edison,' she said. 'I can deal with this. But if you can't—'

Edison interrupted her, 'You can't take me off this because of us.' The reluctance to be drawn back into the covert world of espionage that had dogged him for the first forty-eight hours after Tanya's visit had evaporated with the thrill of the observation at the fish market that morning and the challenge of the undercover operation at the bank. He panicked that Kat might convince Tanya that he wasn't up to the job, and the thought horrified him.

'Let me finish,' Kat said. She was calm and metered out her words carefully, 'But if you can't handle it, we don't have to keep fucking.' She said it matter-of-factly as if she were suggesting she could change her nail colour if Edison didn't like it. 'Tanya wouldn't let me take you off this. She's convinced you're the sole reason we'll get to the bottom of this.' She took a sip of wine and smiled at Edison, 'Teacher's pet.'

'Do you think she knows?' Edison ignored the jibe.

'Probably. Tanya knows everything. And she brought you onto the op anyway, so we had better get on with it.'

'Yes,' said Edison, sitting up straighter and looking at Kat seriously. 'What's the fallout from Billingsgate? I guess that's clear evidence that our importers are back in business. What happens now? Will you go up to Grimsby?'

'One question at a time,' said Kat, lowering her voice. The pub was busy, and the pair could easily maintain their conversation at a volume that wouldn't be overheard. 'I'm heading up to Grimsby tomorrow with Mo. If our theories are right, in recent weeks, the white stuff wasn't the only thing that came off the ship. Our band of terrorists are making bigger moves. We're moving into the end game.'

Edison felt a prickle of excitement at the words. 'So, what's our next move?'

'Tricky. The drugs are technically Organised Crime's purview, but thankfully, the commissioner saw fit to read in SO15 when we highlighted the possible terrorism links.'

'Who's managing the investigation for the Met?' Edison silently prayed that Kat would tell him that Charlie was the lead officer for counter-terrorism.

'Colchester.' Edison's heart sank at the mention of

Superintendent Michael Colchester, whose loyalties lay firmly with their friends across the river at Vauxhall Cross. His disdain for the domestic Security Service was well known.

'Any chance we can get Charlie subbed?' Edison knew the question was futile.

Kat shook her head. 'Colchester's got his teeth stuck into this and isn't letting go. He was lead on the body in the box last year. And you know what he's like. He's obviously sensed that MI5 are sniffing around and worked out it's got potential to be high profile.'

Edison sighed, and his shoulders slumped, knowing that any cooperation from the Met on that side of the investigation had evaporated. 'So where do we go from here?'

Kat raised an eyebrow. '*We* aren't going anywhere unless, of course, you fancy coming back to mine tonight?' She laughed. Edison admired her confidence. Nothing seemed to phase Kat. 'You are at the bank indefinitely. The finances are the key to unlocking this. I'll be heading up to Grimsby tomorrow.'

'With Colchester?'

'Probably not. Tanya's working on getting an officer onto his team, but it isn't easy.'

'Anything else I should know?'

'You should know that I'd like another one of these,' she said indicating her empty tumbler. Edison obligingly went to the bar to secure top-ups for them both. As they enjoyed their drinks, Edison filled Kat in on his first day at Penwill's before the conversation moved to non-operational subjects. They chatted amiably about the office and Kat's sister's forthcoming wedding. Edison was enjoying the slightly hazy effects of three pints of beer when last orders were called.

Without really thinking about it, he accompanied Kat back to her apartment where he stayed the night, waking early and dashing to Bethnal Green. He tiptoed into the flat a little before six, hoping not to disturb Tony. The ancient boiler rattled into life whilst Edison showered, and by the time he headed out the door thirty minutes later, there was a sliver of light under his flatmate's door.

*

0501, Friday 30th June, Penn Street, Hoxton, London

Kat had an early start, and she'd woken Edison at five. Once he'd gone, she showered and prepared for a day on the road. By the time Mo pulled his modern Mini into the car park, she had furnished herself with a large coffee to go. She'd dressed in jeans, sturdy walking boots and a thick jumper, over which she pulled a gilet. Mo sent her a text announcing his arrival, although she'd already seen the junior officer smoking a cigarette, leaning against his car as she'd busied herself in the kitchen. She pulled her hair into a ponytail and slipped a cereal bar into her pocket on the way out. Coffee in one hand, she grabbed a beanie hat with the other and quietly pulled the door shut behind her.

'Good morning,' she greeted Mo and look disparagingly at him as he stubbed out the cigarette under his foot. 'They'll kill you, you know.'

Mo shrugged. 'So will these bloody terrorists. I'll take my chances.' He slid into the driver's seat. Kat got in on the passenger side and settled herself.

'How long will it take us to get to Grimsby?' Kat asked.

'Satnav reckons three hours thirty. I think we can make it in under three.'

'We better get moving then.' Mo took Kat at her word and put his foot down. They sped through streets of north London, which were fairly quiet at that time of day, and were on the M1 in no time. On the motorway, Mo pushed the boundaries of the speed limit, and true to his promise, they were in sight of the Humber estuary shortly after eight fifteen.

They parked the car a short walk from the main port building. Mo eyed the snack van hopefully. 'Go on then,' said Kat. Mo scurried off to join the short queue of workmen waiting for their bacon butties. 'Mine's white, no sugar,' she called after him. Whilst she waited, Kat watched as vans and lorries manoeuvred out of the port. There were a few trawlermen returning from the night's voyage, but most of the activity was from the engineers arriving to service the vast wind farms that now served as the main industry in what had once been the world's largest fishing port.

Mo returned with two steaming Styrofoam cups, and Kat accepted hers gratefully. 'So,' she said. 'What do we know?' They had made their way to the harbour wall and rested their drinks on it, looking out over the water.

'The trawler is the *Boston Jubilee*.'

'What do we know about the crew?'

'Same crew as was interviewed after the body in the box. I went through the notes from the murder investigation which concluded that the crew had no idea what they were carrying in that crate.'

'But Organised Crime was up here yesterday to talk to them about the drugs, right?'

'Yes, with our friend, Colchester, too, apparently. The drugs squad brought them in – three men, all local, yesterday. That accounts for the crew but not the captain, a guy by the name of Jack Fleming.'

'He's disappeared?'

Mo nodded. 'From what I've heard, which isn't much, I don't have much of an in on Colchester's team, very little has come from the interviews. They're as ignorant about the drugs as they were about the body.'

'Well,' said Kat, draining her coffee and tossing the cup into a nearby bin, 'let's see what we can find out. We'll split up. I'll take a look at the main market. You head down to the docks and see what you can see.'

Mo walked off in the opposite direction, humming the children's nursery rhyme, *A Sailor Went To Sea*. Kat made her way casually through the fish market. There wasn't much activity. 'Can I help you, love?' A grizzled dock worker approached Kat.

Kat turned her most charming smile on him, 'Oh yes, I'm a reporter for the *Yorkshire Star*. I'm doing a follow-up piece – *One Year On From The Body In The Box*.' She motioned bunny ears for dramatic effect. 'I was hoping to speak to Jack Fleming.'

'Really, do you have to go stirring all that up again? He's only just gone back to sea, a few weeks back. Poor bloke.'

Kat pulled a small notepad from her back pocket and fixed her interlocutor with an intense look. 'How awful. That long out of work. When exactly did he and the crew go back to sea?'

'Well, where are we now? End of June. Must have been late May. It was a funny business that, with the *Boston*.'

Kat sensed that her companion wanted to gossip, despite his earlier protestation, and offered him an inquisitive expression and said, 'Oh yes?'

'Since they relaunched, they always seem to be picking up a new apprentice over in Europe. Every week, Jack is bringing another new face in.' He paused assessing his audience, 'They are always foreign. Pakis generally. Never see the same face twice.'

'Can you tell me more about Jack?' Kat encouraged him to go on.

'Jack's been skippering the *Boston* for years. Works with a fishery in Denmark, I think. He's not been himself since his missus got ill a couple of years ago. Cancer, you know. She can't work. They're short of cash, that's for sure. I think the apprenticeships might bring a bit extra. But he always looks on edge.'

'How many apprentices do you think they've had?' Kat asked.

'The first one must have arrived about three weeks back, and since then, there has been a handful.'

'How many is a handful?' Kat pressed.

He didn't seem troubled by Kat's curiosity and said, 'Three, maybe four. Not sure what the deal was with their paperwork, but no one round here's going to ask too many questions.'

'The police were here yesterday?'

'Yes. Couple of posh tossers from London,' he said with venom in his voice. 'Talking about drugs now. After all that with the murder a year ago, now they want to pin drugs on Jack and the *Boston*.'

'Did they speak to you?' asked Kat. 'The police.'

'Yeah, spoke to everyone, didn't they? Not good for business. Poor old Jack. Sure, he had nothing to do with it, but it doesn't look good does it?' Kat shook her head. 'Anyway, they'll be landing soon, so you'll excuse me if I get on.' He headed off in the direction of the docks.

Kat gave her new friend a good head start to get down to the docks and then followed. There was much more of a buzz of activity than when she and Mo had arrived. The weather was bright, and the wind had picked up whilst she'd been inside. The dock workers were congregating in anticipation of the incoming fleet. Kat shielded her eyes against the sun and spotted Mo coming away from the water, battling against the offshore wind.

'Find the *Boston Jubilee*?' Kat asked.

'Yes, couldn't get too close. Surrounded by police tape and a local plod on guard,' Mo said. 'Not been in the force long. Had a quick chat.' Mo grinned. 'Most exciting thing that's happened here in years, notwithstanding the body last year, so he was desperate to fill me in.'

'And?'

'He said a chief inspector from London was up here yesterday, assume that's Colchester, with another of his officers. They brought in the crew, but not Fleming who, in his words, "has done a runner". Colchester spent much of yesterday questioning the crew. They've all three been remanded in custody.'

'He arrested them?'

'On some drugs charge, he couldn't remember the specifics.'

'Anything else?'

'There's an "all ports" out on Jack Fleming, but they don't think he's gone far. Apparently, his wife's in a hospice and hasn't got long. You get anything useful?'

'Possibly. Let's go see how the catch comes in.' The two officers set off and watched from a distance as trawler after trawler nosed into the dock. As each approached the landing stage, a noisy exchange erupted between the onboard crew and the workers stood on the dockside, pulling in ropes. Some boats unloaded crates of fish. The bigger vessels craned their cargo onto pallets, which were deftly manoeuvred on forklifts. Most of the crates went to the market building where Kat had just been. A few boxes were delivered straight onto waiting vans, which sped off as soon as their doors were closed.

'So,' Kat looked thoughtful. 'Our theory is that the *Boston* was pressed back into action to smuggle in people has been corroborated.' She relayed the headlines of her conversation with the dockhand to Mo. 'So, we have to assume that these men, our "*apprentices*",' Kat found herself using bunny ears for emphasis again, 'are making their way to London from here. I can't imagine they're just hopping on a train.'

'I guess they could have been collected.'

'Yes, and my money's on one of those vans' drivers.' Kat indicated the fleet of transits into which box after box of fish were being loaded.

'So, we need to find the driver,' Mo said.

Kat spotted the dockhand with whom she'd struck up a rapport earlier. He was hefting a crate of floundering fish onto the quayside. She skipped over to him, slipping back into character as a precocious reporter for a regional newspaper.

'I'd really like to talk to some of John's colleagues if I can.'

He scowled at her. 'You really shouldn't be here. It's not safe.'

'Who took John's cargo off his hands?' Kat carried on, following him as he trudged back toward a pile of lobster cages.

'You should have a chat with Damien. He usually took John's stuff down to London for him. He's parked up over there.' He waved in the direction of an empty Ford Transit van, parked on the far side of the loading bay.

Kat beamed at him. 'Thank you so much.'

*

Mo stubbed out his half-smoked cigarette as Kat approached the Mini. 'Ok, we need to talk to Damien. The driver of that Ford Transit.'

'Shall I get Colin to sort us out with an address?' Mo pulled out his phone and began tapping out a message with the registration number.

'Ok, thanks, but I need you back in London with the Met. I'll take the train home.'

Mo nodded. He wasn't enjoying the Met police liaison role he seemed to have been landed with. Colchester was notoriously tight-lipped and unhelpful on joint investigations.

Kat looked at her watch. 'How about a bite to eat and then you head back to London?'

'Fish and chips?' said Mo, his eyes brightening.

Kat rolled her eyes, 'When in Rome,' and they set off in search of lunch.

*

After wolfing down lunch, Mo dropped Kat off at the address Colin had sent through. It was a bland, terraced house with paint peeling from the window frames and a cheap uPVC front door. Kat was relieved to see the Ford Transit parked on the opposite side of the street. She pressed the doorbell and heard a metallic rendering of Greensleeves announcing her arrival. A dog barked in one of the neighbouring houses. The door was opened by a man in his late twenties who offered Kat a wary smile. 'Can I help you?' Damien thrust his hands deep into the pockets of his bleached, ripped jeans as he spoke.

'Might I come in, Mr Clough?'

'Are you police?'

'Yes,' Kat lied and hoped that would be enough to gain admittance to Damien's home. If he asked to see a warrant card, she was stuck. To her relief, he shuffled out of her way and indicated that she should come in.

The front door opened into a living room, a moth-eaten three-piece suite crowded around a faux brick fireplace. On the mantlepiece, Kat observed pictures of the three young children. Colin had included a limited profile in the brief he'd sent along with the address. In some of the photographs, there was also a woman, Damien's common-law wife, Tracy. Kat took a seat on the three-seater sofa without invitation and Damien perched on the edge of an armchair opposite.

'Is this about the *Boston*?'

'Yes, I understand you transport their deliveries to Billingsgate in London.'

'That's right, but I had no idea that Jack was involved with the drugs stuff.'

He was anxious in the way that innocent people are nervous in the presence of law enforcement. Kat doubted it was a double-bluff and offered him a conciliatory smile. Deep cover hostile agents were trained to divert suspicion with such behaviour. Colin had dug up too much history on Damien Clough, Grimsby born and bred, to suggest he was anyone other than who he claimed to be. Kat pressed on, 'I'm more interested in some of the passengers that have arrived in recent weeks.' She let the statement hang in the air.

'The refugees? What about them?'

'How many men have you taken to London in the last month?'

'Listen,' Damien's began to look agitated and his eyes flicked to the pictures on the mantlepiece, 'I haven't done anything wrong. I didn't know anything about those drugs. And those men, well, I was just doing a favour for an old friend.'

'For Jack?'

'Yeah, for Jack. He just asked me to take these guys, refugees, he said they were, to London. Drop them at an address where they would be looked after by a charity. I didn't like to ask too many questions. Jack's been having a rough time lately with his missus being so poorly and … well … you know …' He trailed off.

'And if he was making a bit of money on the side, who were you to question it, right, Damien?'

'Listen, that business last year nearly finished him off. Your lot did everything they could to pin the murder on him. It's taken him nearly a year to get back on the water.'

'I'll need the address you took the refugees to. Just to corroborate your story.'

'Of course.' Damien pushed himself off the sofa and hurried into the kitchen. Kat followed, just in case he made a run for it out the back. He pulled a dog-eared piece of paper out of a drawer and thrust it at Kat. He glanced over Kat's shoulder to the front door. He looked like he was hoping she would be leaving, but she had a few more questions.

'Thank you for this. A couple more questions. Who did Jack Fleming get these addresses from?'

'Damned if I know. He just gave me the address, and each time I would pick a guy up at the harbour and drive him to London. I'd drop him there,' he nodded at the crumpled paper in Kat's hand.

'Then you would come back to Grimsby? You didn't go on to Billingsgate?'

'No. There hasn't been any merch bound for London in the last month. The stuff I dropped yesterday morning was the first shipment since last June.'

'How many men?'

'Three.'

'Did you talk to them?'

'Not sure they spoke much English.'

'Could you describe them?'

Damien shrugged. 'I guess. They all had brown skin, black hair, one of 'em had a beard.'

Kat sighed. It was a generic description. She would get someone up here to attempt a facial reconstruction but didn't hold out much hope. Maybe she could twist the Met's arm to take care of that. She fingered the piece of paper in her hand. This, on the other hand, she thought, was cause for optimism. It was the first firm lead she had to VIPERSNEST's location in the UK. She needed to get back to London. Quickly.

'Thank you, Damien. One of my colleagues will be in touch.' She turned toward the door and with one hand on the handle, added, 'When did you last see Jack Fleming?'

'Two days ago, when I picked up the merchandise for the delivery to London.'

Kat left in the direction of the train station, pulling out her phone and sending an encrypted message through to Colin with the address. She itched to go and find the *Boston Jubilee's* captain and interrogate him on the identity of his paymasters, but the address in her pocket would lead her team to the ticking time bomb. And the security of the thousands of Londoners vulnerable to a terrorist attack took precedence. Every time. The bigger picture would have to wait. VIPERSNEST was in London, and she had to find them before all hell was let loose.

*

Damien Clough closed the door behind Kat and dialled Jack Fleming. There was no answer. He decided to leave a message. 'Jack, listen, I've had the police here. They're asking about those refugees this time. Not the drugs. Might be best if you make yourself scarce for a bit.'

He hung up.

On the other side of Grimsby, the man in possession of Jack Fleming's mobile phone dialled the voicemail and listened with growing anger. He deleted the message, removed the SIM card and threw the handset into the cold waters of the North Sea. The SIM followed the mobile into the icy depths. The man then made another phone call over a secure VOIP line. 'Time to move,' was all he said when the phone was answered. There was no reply.

Chapter Eight

0658, Friday 30th June, Canary Wharf, London

After his early start, Edison had chosen to walk the three miles to the office. It was bright, and there was warmth in the sun. Edison enjoyed the journey. It was an opportunity to think. He began trying to unpick the conversation with Kat from the previous evening. He was hopeful that she would call later. Edison realised that it wasn't just an update on her visit to Grimsby he was hoping for. He found himself longing to hear her voice and to know what she had been up to. Edison shook his head with surprise. Something was changing in their relationship. He wasn't sure it was a good thing.

Canary Wharf rose out of the Thames, a gleaming icon of capitalism, and Edison's thoughts turned to the day that lay ahead of him. As a matter of priority, he needed to meet Christoph and Emma, secure a copy of Jamie's algorithm and get hold of a list of the fund's investors.

When he arrived on the fifteenth floor, Christoph, Tariq and Billy were already hunched over their desks. Tom was pacing his office with an earpiece in. On seeing Edison look over, he waved a greeting and mouthed the words, 'Hong Kong.'

'He has a weekly with the reps in Hong Kong,' Tariq said.

Edison nodded and sat down at his desk. 'He works long hours.'

'Nonstop,' said Christoph, he spoke in a clipped German accent, over-pronouncing every syllable. 'We didn't really meet properly yesterday, for which I apologise. Can I buy you breakfast?' Christoph offered with a smile.

'That would be nice,' said Edison, casting his eye over his inbox. There were three emails from Tom, with further instructions, and one from Anna, arranging an introductory meeting with the head of sales, David Murray, for the following Wednesday. There was a note apologising for the delayed date of the meeting. David was on the road until the middle of next week.

Christoph led the way out of the building in silence. The next words he spoke to Edison were once they were standing in the queue at a nearby coffee shop, 'What would you like?'

Edison looked longingly at the pastries but remembered his resolve to get fit and ordered the granola and yoghurt. 'To drink?' asked Christoph.

'Tea, please. Shall I grab us a table?'

'Yes.' Edison was growing accustomed to Christoph's curt responses. He found them a spot in a quiet corner of the café and waited. His companion set down a tray a moment later and took a seat.

'So,' said Christoph. 'Steven, you are here to make sure we're playing by the rules?'

Edison evaluated his colleague. He didn't detect a hint of irony in the question but decided to counter with some of his own. 'Yes, *are* you playing by the rules? It would make my life a lot easier if you could just own up to all your indiscretions now.'

'My fund is totally compliant,' Christoph said, his tone hard and serious.

'In which case, we will get along swimmingly.'

'Where did you work before? Your LinkedIn profile was a little sparse.'

Edison didn't miss a beat. It was a tricky balancing act for the team at Thames House when creating legends in a world where everyone had such a comprehensive digital footprint across social media. An analyst would have been tasked with creating Edison's digital cover as Steven Edwards. A LinkedIn profile would have been written with just enough information to be plausible without enough detail to allow someone intent on snooping to find the holes. 'Ah yes, LinkedIn.' He grinned. 'I've always been a bit rubbish at the whole social media thing.'

Christoph's expression didn't change. 'That is clear. Your Facebook does not give much away either.'

'You've been checking up on me.' Edison sounded light-hearted but was beginning to wonder whether Christoph's interest in him had more sinister motives. Did he have reason to be cautious? Was he in some way caught up in the fraud? He was not a technical member of the team, and he thought it unlikely he had access to the trading code. Jamie had said that the Austrian had little skill when it came to computers.

'I like to know who my colleagues are. So where did you work before?'

'I worked in the Home Office but was seconded to the Bank of England to work on their cryptocurrency working group.'

'So, you are a technology person?'

'That's me. I understand you manage the infrastructure fund?' Edison wrenched the conversation away from his personal history.

'Yes, I prefer bridges and tunnels to bytes and blockchains.' For the first time a smile crept around Christoph's lips and he chortled at his own wit. Edison humoured him with a hearty laugh.

'You're from Austria, aren't you?' Edison steered the conversation toward Christoph's background.

'Yes,' came the monosyllabic answer.

'Whereabouts?'

'Innsbruck.'

'Did you study there?' Edison wondered whether Christoph

was being evasive or whether he was tacit by nature. It was impossible to tell.

'No, I studied in Vienna,' Christoph replied then added, without prompting, 'Economics.'

Perhaps he's warming up, thought Edison, filing the mention of Vienna and the possible link to HAPSBURG. 'Beautiful city. Do you go back often?'

'Yes, I have some business interests there.'

'Oh yes? What kind of business interests?' Edison kept his tone light and conversational, but Christoph's face immediately clouded over.

'Nothing of interest to you,' he said abruptly and drained his coffee. 'I must return to the office. Are you complete?'

Edison nodded. He had eaten the granola in only a few mouthfuls and was already wondering how he would make it until lunchtime. He picked up his paper cup of questionable-strength tea and followed Christoph back to the office.

The floor was a hive of activity as the rest of Tom's team had arrived. Jamie grinned at Edison. 'Morning,' he said. 'How was Christoph's sparkling repartee this morning? I'm sure he's told you his life story, and you couldn't get a word in edgeways.' Christoph glared at the young programmer and plugged himself into a large pair of headphones. 'Did you bring your running kit?' Jamie went on.

Edison cursed himself for forgetting and missing the opportunity to get to know Jamie better. 'Oh, sorry mate, I completely forgot.' Edison chose his words carefully, mimicking Jamie's from the day before.

'How convenient,' Jamie laughed. 'Not to worry. Monday?'

'Sure.' Edison turned his attention to the computer screens in front of him and immersed himself in the humdrum activity of his day job, trying not to get distracted by thoughts of the case.

Edison worked industriously through Tom's instructions until late afternoon. 'Jamie,' he said.

'Yes mate.'

'I don't suppose you've had a chance to send me that access to the repository?'

'You read my mind,' he replied. He clicked his mouse with a dramatic flourish. 'There'll be an email in your inbox in seconds with a username and password. Be gentle with it. It's making us a fortune.'

Edison laughed. 'Will do. Thanks.' He opened the email and snorted. '*Game of Thrones* user names, really?'

'It's a bit of a laugh. Do you not fancy being a Greyjoy?'

'I'm more worried about what the regulators might think.'

Jamie shrugged.

'I assume you're a Lanaster,' Edison went on.

'Naturally. And Maria's a Targaryen and Billy's a Baratheon.'

'And it's only the tech team who have access to the repository and log?'

'No. The FMs have users too. Em's a Tyrell, Christoph Arryn and Tariq's a Martell. They dabble with coding occasionally, particularly for their client's front-end portals although, more often than not, I have to come in and tidy up the mess they've made.' He laughed whilst Christoph glowered at him. Edison figured his headphones were only for effect, the Austrian was evidently listening to everything that was happening on the office floor. 'We make sure they can't touch the trading codes, access is carefully audited,' Jamie went on obsequiously. 'That should satisfy the FCA even if they're not keen on our avatars.'

Edison ignored the comment and turned his attention to his computer. He navigated to a secure web browser and pulled up the full script for the trading algorithm. The screen filled with letters, numbers and symbols. Edison scrolled through the code and let out a deep breath.

On hearing that, Jamie looked up at him, 'Bit dense, isn't it?'

'I'll say. Definitely calls for a cuppa.' Edison locked his computer and pushed his chair back. 'Anyone else?' Everyone around him declined the offer, and Edison made his way to the kitchen to make himself a very strong cup of tea. He texted Charlie – *Drink tonight?* The reply came back before he was a back at his desk – *9 at the Red Lion?*

Edison confirmed he'd be there. The location gave away that Charlie was at New Scotland Yard and Edison thought it unlikely that his friend had managed to manoeuvre himself onto the reopened Billingsgate investigation. He hoped Charlie would at least have some intel to share.

Sipping at his scalding tea, Edison focused on the pages of code on his computer screen. Following the master branch, he found the section for the crypto algorithm. It was going to take him time to dissect the reams of code, work out the mechanics of it, before he investigated the log repository for any discrepancies. It was late in the day, and the team were starting to drift off. Billy interrupted his focus and asked if he wanted to join them in the pub. 'No thanks,' Edison declined.

'Don't work too hard,' Jamie said, shutting down his computer and following Billy and Tariq toward the lifts.

'Are you sure you won't join us?' asked Maria with a seductive smile a few minutes later. 'We'll be in Davy's if you want to come later.'

'Thanks, but you know what it's like when you're new,' Edison said. 'Loads to get on top of. I just need to get my head down for a bit longer.'

Maria offered him a sympathetic smile and picked up her expensive handbag. 'Well, you know where we are.'

Edison returned her smile and watched her leave. He looked around the office. Christoph, his headphones still firmly wedged over his ears, was pecking at his keyboard using two index fingers to laboriously tap out an email. Behind Edison, Anna was shuffling papers into a file that she dropped into her out tray with a satisfied sigh. 'Home time,' she said. 'Chris, are you done?'

Edison remembered that the colleagues lived together and imagined that Anna's commute home was unlikely to be filled with engaging conversation. Christoph pulled off his headphones and nodded. They left the office together. Edison observed their retreat. There were none of the tell-tale signs of a clandestine affair. He turned back to his computer screens. Only Tom was left, still hammering away at his keyboard in his fishbowl. He was glad that he could work without worrying about anyone looking over his shoulder.

On one monitor, he had the algorithm in all its complexity. On the other, he pulled up the IRC where 4hire had told him he'd last heard from RubiksKube. At the bottom of a thread in which RubiksKube had got into an argument about the most effective way to launch a phishing scam on a high-street bank, Edison posted, using a newly created alias:

<ares> why bother with phishing? It's just hit and hope. ddos campaign would bring down system in jiffy

He left the bait and focused back on the trading algorithm, combing through the code with all his concentration. Half an hour later, an alert pinged on the message board. Gotcha, thought Edison and he swivelled on his chair to read what his folly had to say.

<RubiksKube> You may choose DDOS if you're an anarchic dissident, by all means. It is not sophisticated. Nor will it provide access to any key data

sets. That is where the value is.

Edison had spotted the unusually precise language in RubiksKube's plethora of previous posts. In the early days of Usenet, when it was emerging from its service to academics in the late eighties, pedantry around spelling and grammar had been a popular rouse for trolls wanting to keep the boards exclusive. Since then, Usenet, BBS and 4Chan had been the birthplace of the acronyms and emojis familiar to anyone with a messaging service on their phone. Spelling and punctuation had become a lot more fluid in favour of speed. Edison began to craft a reply when another message popped up.

<RubiksKube> *Who is the n00b?*

Edison ignored the slight but noticed his adversary did stoop to using the board's recognised jargon. N00bs were users new to a message board and typically the target of a sustained harassment campaign to test their mettle in the hostile environment. He typed:

<ares> *the levels of encryption make any sustained malware attack unlikely to work*

<RubiksKube> *there are always ways*

<ares> *such as?*

No reply. Damn it, thought Edison and returned his focus to the crypto algorithm.

When Tom emerged from his office, a gloomy twilight had descended on the silent fifteenth flour. 'Steven, hi.' Tom was taken aback to find his newest recruit still hunched over his workstation so late on a Friday. The interruption brought Edison abruptly out of his digital wormhole. He looked up, startled. 'I would have thought you would have been in the pub with the others long ago,' Tom went on, rummaging in a cupboard for his jacket and throwing it over his shoulders.

'Just trying to tick a few things off before the weekend,' replied

Edison.

'Same here.' Tom waved expansively at the paperwork still strewn across his desk, 'But it's half eight, and the wife will be wondering where I am if I don't get away soon.'

'Half eight?' Edison looked at his watch, finding it difficult to believe where the time had gone. 'I'm due in Westminster in half an hour.'

'You better get a move on,' Tom said over his shoulder as he moved toward the lifts. 'Have a good weekend.'

'You too,' Edison called after him, his focus back on his screens. His hand hovered over his mouse. He was tempted to delve back into the code for another ten minutes and beg Charlie's forgiveness for being late. His fingers itched to comb the log of repository. There was something in the code that had caught his attention, like an errant fingerprint at a carefully cleaned crime scene, and he was eager to investigate it further. Perhaps he could come in over the weekend? No, that would draw too much attention to himself if anyone were to find out. Perhaps he could pretend to be a keen new starter, desperate to get ahead of his workload and impress the boss. No, still too risky. The puzzle would have to wait until Monday. Reluctantly, he shut down the computer.

*

2100, Friday 30th June, The Red Lion, Westminster, London

By nine o'clock on a Friday evening, the Red Lion in Westminster was beginning to empty. Post-work drinkers were slinking off to their homes or in search of dinner. Edison arrived to find Charlie at the bar, paying for two pints of beer and a glass of wine. Edison eyed the red wine with suspicion. Charlie gestured toward the back of the pub, where Tanya was sitting watching them both. 'I didn't know we had company,' Edison said to his friend, ducking behind Charlie so Tanya couldn't interpret what he was saying. Anyone with a history in the field was an expert lip-reader.

Charlie, who had his back to where Edison's boss sat, said, 'She called to ask after the Billingsgate affair. I mentioned I was seeing you, so she invited herself along. I could hardly say no, could I?'

Edison shrugged and picked up his pint. He took a small sip to prevent too much of the amber liquid sloshing onto the floor as he negotiated his way through the thinning crowd.

'Good evening,' said Tanya as he approached.

'Hello, how are you?'

'Very well, thank you,' said Tanya, accepting the glass of wine from Charlie. He and Edison both perched on stools. Tanya was seated on a wooden chair with curving armrests. The stools were significantly lower than the chair and the two men looked like naughty schoolboys in the presence of the headmistress. 'How have the first few days been?'

'Uneventful,' said Edison. 'Pursuing a couple of possible leads but nothing obvious.'

'It'll take a bit of time. You always were impatient.' Tanya turned to Charlie, 'Speaking of impatience, my own, that is, your esteemed colleague, Superintendent Colchester is being typically unresponsive.'

'He's been orchestrating a merry band of junior officers all day from what I can see,' Charlie said. 'I had a quick look at the incident board before I came out.'

'Anything on the address my officer passed on? Or the "refugees"?' she air-quoted with her fingers.

'What refugees?' Edison pounced on the titbit of information about the case.

Tanya's face hardened, knowing that she'd already said more than her agent's security clearance permitted him to know. Cagily, Tanya recounted Kat's report from Grimsby, sparing as much detail as possible to assuage her own conscience. 'I was dashing into the Joint Intelligence Committee, which is why I'm a bit light on detail,' she concluded.

'Anything interesting come up at the JIC?' Edison pressed. Traditionally, it was the Service's director general alone who attended the meetings, but John Featherstone, who had succeeded Sir Donald Hughes after his departure, liked to give his senior team exposure to what he called 'the rusty wheels of democracy' and attended meetings accompanied by a member of his top team each time.

'HAPSBURG was originally just a footnote in the meeting's minutes but had been moved up the agenda after yesterday.' Tanya was warming up a little. She'd missed having Edison in her inner circle and was secretly relishing the top-class operative's return to the field. 'I stressed the need for cooperation between the police, National Crime Agency and us, given the suspected links to the Met's still-open murder investigation.'

'I'm sure Commander Gambles,' Edison referred to the Head of Counter Terrorism Command, 'made all the right conciliatory noises about information sharing being of the highest priority.'

'Quite. I pulled him aside at the end of the meeting to confirm that I'd be seconding Mo to the Met, but he was too worried about tailgating the Home Secretary from the room to pay much attention. Keen to have a cosy drink in the members' bar with the Right Honourable Timothy Johnson, I'm sure.'

'I wonder what particular problem Gambles wanted fixing. Johnson's good at getting people out of scrapes,' Edison spoke viciously. It was an open secret that Johnson had been the one to ensure the accusations against Hughes led to nothing more than a dismissal. By all rights, the man should be withering away in jail.

Tanya shot Edison a warning look. 'Best not to get into that,

Edison. Anyway,' she slipped seamlessly back onto the previous topic, 'letting Commander Gambles know that Mo would be shadowing the investigation had been a courtesy. He was already at New Scotland Yard. Colchester had agreed, grudgingly, I'd point out, to his participation on the operational team re-investigating the Billingsgate body and the links to VIPERSNEST.' She turned to Charlie, 'You said you'd looked in on the investigation. Any news on the cell? What about the captain?'

Charlie had no information on the missing captain, and Tanya soon realised that she could glean nothing further from him. 'I better head home,' she said. 'Thanks for the drink, Charlie.'

The two men watched as Tanya left. She was a tall woman and towered above many of the punters still milling around the bar. She looked back at them once she reached the door and waved before disappearing into the night.

Edison breathed out heavily, and Charlie looked at him warily. 'Everything ok, Eddie?'

His friend meditated on the response for a while, staring into his near-empty glass as if the answer to the question would be found in the amber liquid that swilled there. 'I'm fine.' He paused. 'But there's something big afoot here, Charlie. I don't feel as though I have a grip on it.'

The pub was emptying quickly as the last orders bell sounded. The hubbub of evening drinkers was dying down, and Charlie evaluated how private their conversation was likely to be. 'Shall we walk?'

'Sure.' Edison swallowed the last mouthful of his pint, and Charlie drained his glass.

Summer had arrived in London, and the evening was warm. The two friends turned left out of the pub and passed under the shadow of the palace of Westminster, its sandy turrets lit up in the gloom. A uniformed police officer patrolled the pavement, and Charlie greeted him, as was his habit, 'Good evening, Sergeant Jennings.'

'Good evening, sir,' came the reply. Edison always marvelled at Charlie's knowledge of the Met's junior ranks.

They walked in silence until they reached Lambeth Bridge where Charlie picked up the conversation exactly where Edison had left it in the Red Lion. 'You don't need to have a grip on it, Eddie. You're a field agent. Just a field agent, tasked with securing information. The bigger picture doesn't concern you.' He spoke softly and kindly, but his words were serious. Ever since his friend's recall to the Service, he'd been worrying about the responsibility Tanya had foisted on Edison. Charlie knew that Edison would consume himself with the operation and potentially put himself in danger. His appetite for defending his nation was only matched by his passion for solving puzzles, and he had a track record of doing that by any means possible, often at the expense of his own personal safety.

'I know, Charlie.' Charlie looked sideways at his friend, Edison's jaw was locked and there was tension written all over his face. 'Whoever these people are,' Edison went on, 'they're not just smuggling drugs. They're bringing in people too. That guy, last year, he must have been one of their pawns. There's big money changing hands. And we haven't got a clue what their end game is. That's not good Charlie. It's really not good.' He slowed and leaned against the wall, looking out over the river. The tide was high, and the reflections of the lights on Chelsea Bridge danced across the water, lapping against the concrete embankment.

Charlie turned his back to the water, 'Eddie, you're doing your bit. You're part of a big team. And you know there couldn't be a better team on this.'

Edison acknowledged the truth in what he said with a grudging nod. Charlie pressed on, 'You have to be part of that machine. You can't be the hero every time.' They were cautionary words, borne of thirty years' insight of his friend's psyche. 'It's the weekend. You need to get some rest. There's nothing you can do until Monday, so go home, get some sleep, relax.'

The pair retraced their steps to Westminster in companionable silence, and Charlie saw Edison onto an eastbound train before he headed south to Clapham to be greeted by his wife, who was fussing about the countdown to their family holiday in the Highlands.

Edison rattled back toward East London. He pulled out his phone and sent a text to Kat – *Fancy a drink over the weekend?* He wanted to see her and not just because he hoped to learn more about the case. At Whitechapel, Edison turned his back on the busy Whitechapel Road and cut through the back streets to Bethnal Green. He observed the flat from a distance. It was shrouded in darkness but for a blueish light flickering around the drawn curtains of Tony's room.

He slipped his key noiselessly into the door, hoping to avoid conversation. He was tiptoeing up the stairs when he heard Tony's door creak open. 'Long day, Edison?' came a voice from below. The television in Tony's room was on and hummed in the background.

'Yeah,' said Edison, hoping to shut down the conversation. 'Sorry if I woke you this morning.'

Tony shrugged. 'That's ok. Where were you last night?'

'Stayed with a friend. It's late – I'm going to hit the sack.'

'Do you have plans this weekend?' Tony wasn't ready to let Edison go.

'No – need some rest. Will make it a quiet one.' Edison paused then added, 'What about you?'

'Probably ought to see the kids. Maybe take them bowling.'

'That'll be nice.' Edison didn't know what else to say. 'Well, sleep well.' He turned and continued up the stairs. He didn't relish spending the weekend holed up in the flat with Tony. There was something very odd about him, and Edison couldn't quite put his finger on it. He was furtive, and Edison couldn't help but feel like the murine man was watching his every move.

'You too,' Tony called after him.

Edison closed his bedroom door, threw the contents of his pockets onto the table beside the bed and slumped onto it. His phone buzzed, and he juggled it in one hand, unbuttoning his shirt with the other. *Sorry, Edison* – he read the message from Kat with disappointment – *Working all weekend. Need sleep when I can.* Edison's heart sank. He finished undressing and lay on the bed staring up at the ceiling. The flat was in a state of disrepair, and there was a damp patch expanding across the bedroom ceiling. Edison lay there for a while, trying to untangle the complicated mix of feelings knotted in his stomach. He wanted information about the case. He wasn't sure he could wait until an unfixed date for that. But more than that, he wanted to see Kat. To hear her laugh and enjoy her company. Something stirred in his boxers. He rolled over and Ellie looked back at him. Guilt flooded his body, and tears pricked in his eyes. He crawled under the duvet and begged sleep to consume him. Eventually, after tossing in and out of dreams where his dead wife morphed into his present-day lover, Edison fell into a deep, dreamless sleep.

Chapter Nine

1709, Friday 30th June, Brooks Road, West Ham, London

Mo had passed on Kat's intelligence to a sulky female PC. She had been overlooked for field work by her commanding officer for the fourth operation in a row. She had been left with responsibility for managing the incident room, and she wasn't happy about it.

'I'll get the address to one of our street teams,' she told him, without looking up from her computer screen.

'I'll need to know which team, please,' replied Mo, trying not to let his frustration get the better of him. After the long drive back from Grimsby, he was feeling crotchety, the early start and four-hundred-mile round trip catching up with him. The malaise that met him when he arrived at the Met's headquarters did little to improve his mood. The policewoman raised her eyebrows as she reached for a radio. Mo listened as she rattled off a series of call signs and instructions. The radio crackled as they both waited for a response. Moments later, a disembodied voice replied, confirming receipt of the address and that his unit was moving there now. The brief exchange ended with the police constable spitting the words, 'Nothing more. Out,' into the handset and turning to look at Mo.

'Detective Sergeants Hulme and Walsh are expecting you. They'll be in an unmarked surveillance vehicle.' She scribbled a number plate on a Post-it which she thrust in Mo's general direction. As he hurried from the incident room, Mo considered her reticence to expand on his brief. It was most likely due to the institutional distrust for MI5 that Colchester carefully nurtured within his teams. This was going to be a tough gig, he thought.

*

Brooks Road was a short walk from Plaistow tube station, past an Indian takeaway, dry cleaners and small supermarket. There was a terrace of 1970s brick-built houses on one side and a more modern development of low-rise flats on the other. At the far end of the street, a high-rise block of council flats rose seventeen storeys into the sky. Cars were parked occasionally along the length of the road on both sides. Among them, about halfway down, was a grey Ford transit van. Mo checked the number plate against the one the taciturn PC had given him, which confirmed that this was from where the surveillance team were conducting their observations. He shoved his hands deep into his pockets and affected the swagger of a local. He walked up to the van and banged on the door, careful to mark out the very specific signal he'd been given to identify himself. After a short pause, the door slid back wide enough for Mo to get inside but not far enough for any bystanders to observe the raft of surveillance equipment packed into the back of the van. Mo was met by two plainclothes policemen.

'You must be the spook,' said one, his tone was friendly, and he held out a hand to Mo.

Mo shook it and, matching the other man's hushed tones, said, 'That's me. Mo Hussein.'

'Doug Hulme,' the first policeman replied, and twisting in the cramped conditions, he indicated his colleague, who had a pair of headphones on and was watching a computer monitor intently. 'This is Nick Walsh.'

Nick didn't take his eyes off the screen but raised a hand by way of greeting.

'So, what do we know?' said Mo.

'Absolutely sweet FA at this stage,' said Doug, his frustration evident. 'We weren't far off when your tip-off came in, so we've already been here nearly an hour.'

Nick sat back from the screen and removed his headphones, which he threw down in exasperation in front of him. 'There's no one there, I'm sure of it. Looks like you wasted a trip, Double-O Seven.'

Mo shrugged and leaned over Nick's shoulder to take a look at the screen. It showed a wide-angle view of the street outside the van, the picture centred on number eighteen. 'What do you know about the neighbours?'

'Not much,' said Doug. 'We saw the family who live at number sixteen arrive home from the school run about half an hour ago – think it was probably grandma in charge, older Indian lady with two kids in tow. At a guess, they must have been seven and nine. On the other side, a city type arrived in a suit and left in gym gear ten minutes later.'

'Maybe grandma can tell us some more about who lives at number eighteen?' Mo wondered aloud.

'Our instructions are to wait for backup before we access the property. The chief is still waiting for a final bit of paperwork.'

Mo pulled the door open and hopped out, saying, 'I'll be back in a bit.' He disappeared down the road.

Mo returned twenty minutes later, carrying a large brown paper bag and pretended to look closely at the numbers on the houses as he made his way along Brooks Road.

'What is he playing at?' said Nick to Doug, spotting Mo on the monitor screen. Nick shrugged and watched as Mo made his way up to the front door of number eighteen, where he knocked and waited for a while. When he couldn't rouse anyone, he walked the short distance to number sixteen and rang the doorbell.

The door was answered by an elderly woman matching the description Doug had given him. 'Oh hello,' said Mo. 'Sorry to disturb you, love, but I have a delivery for number eighteen.'

The woman looked at him and offered him a gummy smile. 'I'm sorry, this is number sixteen. But are you sure it's number eighteen you're delivering to?'

'Pretty sure,' replied Mo, pulling a receipt from the brown paper bag, already stained with grease, on the top of which he had scribbled a few, illegible numbers.

'Because they packed up and left in a bit of a hurry earlier today. Around lunchtime it was. A real racket they made, too. Woke the baby up. I couldn't get her back down for hours.'

'Oh, how strange. A biriyani and two kormas, garlic naan, pilau rice, the works they've ordered.'

'Sounds like a lot for just the three of them, although they needed feeding up.' The woman spoke with the ease of someone who spends their days in their own company, and Mo didn't discourage her. 'I wondered whether they were refugees when they arrived. They didn't speak much English. Not that I spoke to them really, but I did run into one of them in the corner shop. He was buying them out of candles. I wondered whether they had the electric cut off. They weren't here long, maybe a month.'

Mo shifted the paper bag in his grasp and looked again at the receipt. 'Oh, you know what, it's my boss's dreadful handwriting – this says twenty-eight, not eighteen.'

'Ahhhh, that explains it.'

'So sorry again to have troubled you, love,' Mo apologised again and headed up the road. The grandma at number sixteen watched him go before closing the door. Confident he was well out of the line of sight from her sitting room window, Mo crossed the road and returned to the transit van.

The door opened as he approached, and he hopped in to be met by Doug and Nick who looked at him, waiting for an explanation. 'House is definitely empty. Three residents made a hasty departure earlier today.'

'Shit. We just missed them,' said Nick. 'Impressive detective work though, Bond.'

'What's more impressive is that you've managed to bring us dinner,' said Doug, eyeing the brown paper bag, from which the smells of an Indian curry were beginning to permeate the van.

'Help yourselves,' snapped Mo, perturbed that Doug didn't seem more concerned that a group of suspected terrorists had slipped through their fingers. 'Just pass me that receipt for my expenses.' As they tucked into the takeaway, Mo asked, 'When are you expecting backup?'

Doug looked at his watch, 'Around six thirty. It's just gone six, so not long.'

Nick had half an eye on the CCTV, and as they polished off the last of the poppadums, a large police van swung around the corner and pulled up outside number eighteen. 'Looks like the cavalry's here,' said Nick and pulled back the door as the first of the armed officers descended from the newly arrived van.

Mo watched the black-and-white pictures from the van as Nick briefed the head of the armed unit. A further four armed police, all wearing substantial body armour, emerged and swiftly positioned themselves around the entrance to number eighteen. Mo spotted his new friend at number sixteen drawing back her net curtains and peering out. With a firm kick, one of the officers broke down the door, and they trooped into the house. From the safety of the van, Mo watched the drama play out without sound, but could imagine the shouts of, '*Armed police, stay back!*' that would precede each move. The lead officer reappeared minutes later and spoke to Nick. Nick looked round to the van and beckoned to Doug. Mo followed him over the road and saw all the colour had drained from Nick's face.

Doug introduced the armed unit head to Mo as Sergeant Jake Ducker.

'Your lot are going to have a field day with this,' Ducker said. 'You're clear to come in. Forensics are on their way.'

Mo filed in after Doug and Nick. The house was dimly illuminate by the light that filtered through the grime-ridden net curtains. The party moved through the front room which was sparsely furnished with a dilapidated sofa, a television propped up on a crate and a single rug that Mo recognised, based on its odd angle, as a prayer mat, positioned to face Mecca. No one had turned on the lights, and Mo quickly realised why as his eyes became accustomed to the gloom. In the kitchen, into which they had come, stood a large table. On the table were boxes of nails and screws, a dozen boxes of candles, batteries and packets of gelatine. To the uninitiated, it looked like a random selection of homeware, but Mo knew immediately that they had discovered a bomb factory.

'They must have taken most of the stuff with them when they left,' said Ducker, shining a torch at the items on the table. 'There's no sign of any detonators or other explosives, but we shouldn't risk a spark from the lights. They've left the stuff that's easy to get hold of.'

Mo slipped out of the kitchen and up the stairs. There was little to see. Off the cramped landing were two bedrooms, one with a single mattress, the other a double, and a bathroom. A copy of the Quran lay next to one of the mattresses, but there was nothing else that would help identify the occupants of number eighteen Brooks Road.

Nick leapt up the stairs just as Mo came out of the bathroom. 'Find anything, Double-O Seven?'

'They may have left in a hurry, but they've left very little behind,' said Mo.

'I'm sure forensics will be able to find something,' said Nick. 'Not sure there's much more we can do until they've got their swabs into the place. Doug and I are calling it a day. I'd suggest you do the same. You look dead on your feet.'

Mo caught sight of his reflection in the mirror above the sink. Nick was right. He looked terrible – exhausted with dark bags under his eyes.

'When do you think we'll have a report from forensics?'

'Mid-morning at the earliest, I suspect. I'll give you a call when we have it.'

'Thanks.'

The two men descended the stairs. Outside on the pavement, the bright evening light caused Mo to blink after the gloom of the house. Another police car had arrived, out of which spilled two forensic investigators, already suited up in their blue protective garments. They ignored Doug and Mo as they hurried into the house.

'I guess I'll see you tomorrow,' said Doug.

'See you then,' replied Mo. He moved off in the direction of the tube station. He looked up as he passed number sixteen to see the grandma he had spoken to earlier, staring at him wide-eyed. He smiled at her, a tacit apology for his earlier deception, but she quickly dropped the net curtain and scurried away from the window.

Chapter Ten

1233, Friday 30th June, Moniedubh Estate, nr. North Ballachulish, Lochaber

Donald huffed his way up the side of the ben. He had escaped the mausoleum early, shortly after the dawn light had crept across the moorland. He looked innocuous enough, albeit slightly anachronistic in his tweeds, knee-high socks and flat cap, which contrasted with the Gortex'ed and Lycra'd hikers, climbers and trail runners who frequented the tracks and passes of the Highlands. He whistled, and the lurcher loped across the hillside toward him. The sun was threatening to break through the rug of light grey cloud, and the air was heavily scented with a Highland summer. He breathed deeply, catching his breath after the climb. There were certain things, like that heady smell and this magnificent view, he would miss when he left. But they were small sacrifices.

Standing at the peak of the ben, he remembered, with a jolt, that the last time he'd been up there was with Edison. It had been the moment when everything had changed.

Ahead of a hunting party he was hosting for some of his most important contacts, he had invited his protégé to the family estate a day before his distinguished guests' arrival. It had felt like the right time to bring Edison into the family business. The business had started as a modest affair. Some years earlier, Donald had seen an opportunity to realise his long-held ambition to unshackle himself from Elizabeth and her family's money. Trade had been brisk, and he soon found himself struggling to meet demand. He needed additional support to continue servicing the voracious appetites of his clients. There seemed no end to their hunger for drugs, amongst other things, and his own pool of agents abroad couldn't service the demand. He needed Edison's help, well connected as he was in the Middle and Far East and having a huge network of contacts. Plus, he had the technical wizardry to support the furtherance of the business. Hughes needed his surrogate son's encyclopaedic knowledge of the Dark Web to keep up with demand.

In the early morning light, Hughes and Edison had left Moniedubh and hiked to the top of the hill that overlooked the estate. There, he'd poured two drams of his favourite whisky from his hip flask, offering one to Edison. He was hoping to toast their new venture together, but as he had recounted his business operations to the young man, to his horror, Edison's body language had changed. The trusting warmth that had existed between them since their first meeting in Oxford, more than a decade earlier, evaporated into the cold Scottish air. He had begun to back away from Hughes, the tin cup of whisky spilling its contents onto the heather as his arms fell slack at his sides, and disbelief consumed him.

He had followed Edison back to the manor house, trying to recant, suggesting the whole story had been a ploy to test Edison's commitment to the Service as he embarked on the next stage of his career. He had recently been promoted and was on a fast track for a head of section role. But he knew at the time that Edison wasn't buying it. He would have to rely on the young man's affection for him. He spent the whole of the weekend reminding Edison of his role in shaping his illustrious career at MI5 as he introduced him to the ambassadors, politicians and senior civil servants who descended on his home that weekend.

It had been a subdued party as Hughes struggled to cover his tracks.

'What the hell is going on?' he recalled being asked by the Turkish ambassador, as he'd pulled him aside to express his frustration at the lack of the hospitality he'd become accustomed to at Moniedubh. 'I'm only in the country a few times a year, and I didn't bring my god-daughter here for the pleasure of your company alone.'

It had been the first time he'd met her. Wonderful and beguiling, she had been the only good thing to come from that ill-fated weekend. The memory of meeting her drew him back to the present. He was due a phone call from her any moment and before they spoke, he needed space to think. To take stock of the circumstances.

The events of Thursday at Billingsgate hadn't made the twenty-four-hour news channels. However, it had drawn unwanted attention to his business activities, according to one of his contacts at the Met. He was confident that his involvement couldn't be traced, but he was worried about his plans, the wheels for which were well in motion, being derailed. He needed the money from the imports. He was desperate to get out of Scotland to join her in London. He had his eye on a mansion flat in Knightsbridge, recently listed on a property website, but it came at a price. His phone rang and he felt his spirits lift, recognising her number.

'Hello, my love,' he answered.

'Well, hello, sexy,' the voice on the other end of the phone breathed.

'I miss you, my darling. Did you get my gift?'

'Yes, roses! My favourite. You really do spoil me.'

'I'm worried, my dear. I think reopening the route has drawn more attention to us than expected.'

'Oh Donny, we discussed this already, don't worry about that. They can't trace you, and even if they do, you can fix it, can't you?'

'Of course.' Donald answered confidently, but sometimes he wondered how many more favours he could call in from his high-flying friends, no matter how debauched the dirt he had on them.

'Anyway, it was important. We cannot exfiltrate you,' she giggled at the use of the word – Donald knew how sexy she thought being a spy was, 'without the money.'

'Yes, of course.' Donald's confidence swelled as she spoke of his escape from Elizabeth and the life in which he felt so trapped. 'But what about the collateral? The captain?'

'I can assure you he has been dealt with.'

'Do you know how?'

'Money, probably, it's usually money. You should know that, my darling.' She laughed, a tinkling, seductive laugh that Donald couldn't resist.

'Yes, yes, of course.'

'There is one thing that worries me though,' she said. Donald could imagine her pretty brow furrowing.

'What is that my darling?'

'This Steven Edwards. The new employee at the bank. He seems to be snooping around the Ethereum trading platform with a little too much interest.'

'What does he look like, this Steven Edwards?' Donald asked seeing an opportunity to corroborate the story he had received from Tony on Scott Edison's new job.

'Very tall, broad-shouldered, messy dark hair, his eyes are …' she broke off to consider her description.

'Intelligent, piercing, blue?' Donald suggested.

'Yes, exactly.'

Donald drew a long breath.

'Do you know this man, my love?'

'Only too well. He works for MI5.'

She squeaked on the other end of the line. 'We must do something. They are coming after you *again*, my darling!'

'No, no, there is nothing to worry about. I'm just an investor in the fund. That's perfectly legitimate. As you said, we have covered our tracks well elsewhere.'

'I am sure I might know someone who could sort that problem for us,' she urged him.

'What on earth do you mean?'

'I could ask someone to, well, stop him from digging around in our affairs.'

Donald was taken aback by the subtext implicit in her proposal. He hated Scott Edison for all that had passed between them, for his betrayal and the way he had let him down. He wanted the man to suffer, certainly, but the suggestion that one of her contacts might orchestrate a hit on him was a step too far. 'No, no, my love, that would be a very bad idea. Play it cool with Mr Edwards, but don't let on that you know who he is. That could be very dangerous. Very dangerous indeed.'

'Ok, my darling Donald. You always know what's best. I must go, my love.'

'Let's speak a little longer, my darling. Let's speak of cheerier things.'

'No, no, I must get back to work.'

Donald let her go as pangs of hunger were beginning to stab at his gut. He regretted setting out that morning in such a rush. The anticipation of speaking with her had driven him from the house without breakfast. Looking out over the moors, shafts of sunlight picked out the path he would take. It would bring him down into Ballachulish, where he would have lunch.

Sir Hughes contemplated the view before him. The beauty of Scotland never failed to astound him. He still had some lingering concerns about the captain of the trawler, even though he had been assured that the risk had been contained. He was a liability, no matter how much money her contacts had supplied.

Donald whistled, a high-pitched sound that brought Angus bounding to his heels. 'Come on, my lad,' he said to the dog and set off in the direction of the village where he hoped a cheddar ploughman's and a pint would be waiting for him in the pub. 'I think we're back on track, Angus,' Donald said, and the dog looked up at him, wagged his tail and trotted along beside him until they reached the sleepy village of Ballachulish on the shores of Loch Leven.

Chapter Eleven

2356, Saturday 1st July, Internet Relay Chat
<RubiksKube> Ares? God of war.
<RubiksKube> What is your chosen battle?
<ares> big government, surveillance, right to privacy
<RubiksKube> a principled dissident
<ares> are you not?
<RubiksKube> no
<RubiksKube> I like puzzles. I enjoy games. Of course, war is a game.
<ares> Tru
<ares> I am fighting the war against the governments who want to take ownership of our cryptocurrency
<RubiksKube> this is a worthy fight. Can I assist you?
<ares> yes, but not here.
<ares> do you use telegram?
<RubiksKube> of course

*

1526, Sunday 2nd July, New Scotland Yard, Westminster, London
Mo's weekend had been tedious. Dutifully, he'd arrived at Scotland Yard each day, as instructed by Kat, to keep tabs on the investigation. There was a tangible sense of unease growing in the incident room. The discovery of the bomb factory had put everyone on edge. Nick, having recently become a father, had somehow wangled a weekend's leave and Doug, back under the watchful eye of his commanding officer, was a lot less friendly toward Mo than he had been when they'd met in the West Ham van. The whole team

were looking into the West Ham address, extra bodies had been drafted in from other units to help with the investigation, but even with the inflation in manpower, they weren't getting very far.

Michael Colchester wafted in and out, barking requests for new information every few hours. The updates provided were limited, and the lack of progress was testing Colchester's patience. He became increasingly snappy as the weekend bore on. On Sunday, his frustrations boiled over.

'Who the hell are you?' he shouted across the incident room. Mo looked up startled by the verbal assault.

'Mo Hussein, MI5.'

'Oh, for fuck's sake. Do your lot think we need babysitting through *this*?' Members of the investigatory team who'd been focused on their computer screens surreptitiously raised their heads to observe the altercation. Colchester crossed the incident room, eyes bulging and leaning in to speak, he brought his large nose uncomfortably close to Mo's. 'I will advise at the earliest opportunity should anything pertinent to your enquiries arise,' he said through gritted teeth.

'Thank you. But I'm happy to observe and save you the additional hassle of providing updates to my service.'

Colchester bristled. 'Thank you, *sir*, are the words you're looking for, I think.'

Mo kept his mouth shut, thinking a discussion on whether rank was transferrable between services would not be good politics. Colchester shrugged, the wind taken out of his argument by Mo's silence. He looked round at his team. 'I'm going home,' he said to no one in particular. 'Buzz me immediately if you find anything.'

Nothing happened that warranted calling the commanding officer nor to arouse Mo's interest. He headed home, worried that his brief to shadow the Met was not going to add anything to the investigation as a whole. He felt impotent in the face of the threat that hung over London like a guillotine's blade waiting to fall.

*

The incident room was bubbling with excitement when Mo arrived on Monday morning. Looking around, it was clear that Colchester wasn't there yet. 'What's going on?' Mo asked Doug.

'Good news,' Doug said. 'We've got a lead on where the cell might have moved to and …' he caught himself before ploughing on.

'Nice. So,' said Mo, 'tell me everything.'

Doug was about to launch into the news when he appeared to think better of it. 'Sorry mate, the super hasn't been briefed yet. Probably shouldn't …' he trailed off, embarrassed, but Mo knew it was more than his job was worth to undermine Colchester's command of the case.

'When will he be in?' Mo asked.

Doug looked at his watch. 'Likely another half an hour.'

'Time for a coffee and some breakfast then.' Downstairs, in the cafeteria, as he waited in the short queue for a stale croissant and a strong cup of coffee, he sent a message to Kat.

On my way – came the reply within moments.

Having polished off his meagre breakfast, Mo went to the reception area where he hovered, waiting for Kat. She arrived a few moments later, unruffled by the dash from Thames House along a blustery Embankment, although he did detect hints of grey bags starting to develop beneath her eyes. She flashed her ID at the reception desk and was ushered through the security system.

'So, what do you know?' she asked as they hurried through the maze of corridors into the heart of the building.

'Nothing. Colchester isn't in yet. How was your weekend?'

'Uh, don't ask. I've called on every officer with agents

embedded in extremist groups across the country for intelligence and drawn a blank at every turn. We're combing CCTV from the docks for any sign of our targets arriving. Nothing.'

From a distance behind them, a voice familiar to Mo bellowed, 'Oh God, the spies are multiplying.' Kat and Mo turned to see Colchester bearing down on them. He reached them in a few strides, falling in step beside them. He looked down his nose at Kat as they all kept walking, 'And who are you?'

'Kat Cox,' replied Kat coolly. 'Lead Intelligence Officer, Counter-terrorism, MI5.'

Colchester grunted and said to Mo, 'She's your boss then.'

Kat replied, used to the institutional sexism prevalent in the upper ranks of the Met, 'Yes, Mo is one of my officers.' She carefully stressed the fact that Mo was one of a bigger team for which she was responsible. She was not, as Mo recognised, saying this in an egotistical way. She was simply and carefully asserting her authority with the senior police officer.

'Well if you are the boss, then you had both better join the briefing,' was Colchester's curt repost. They turned the final few corners in silence before arriving in the incident room. On their entrance, the noise subsided. About a dozen officers and investigators turned expectantly to greet the superintendent. A few cast a quizzical glance at Kat.

'What have you got for me, Sergeant Hulme?' said Colchester.

Doug Hulme cleared his throat, 'Well, sir, the squat we discovered on Friday is owned by a management company. The registered address for the firm, Barinak Holdings, according to Companies House, is in Wood Green. It's run by two Turks – Murat Yousuf and Hakan Gurbuz. We haven't got much information on their property inventory as yet, but the guys are working on it.' He nodded at the men and women hunched over computer screens behind them.

The assembled company were silent for a moment, each of them turning these developments over in their minds, trying to spot the critical connection. Colchester was the first to speak, 'We need to find the other properties to work out where the bomb factory has been moved to. We can get a warrant quickly enough.'

'We need to be careful though,' said Kat. 'We don't want to spook them.'

Colchester snorted, 'Rich, coming from a spook. They know we're onto them. That's clear from their hasty relocation at the end of last week.'

'Yes,' said Kat, her voice steady, but her frustration at the Met officer's arrogant attitude was mounting, 'but we don't want to back them into a corner, force them to play their hand.'

'You mean blow central London sky-high. Of course not. We stop them first.' Colchester looked at his watch. 'I have a meeting with the commissioner. Good work, Doug. You'll excuse me.' He addressed Kat, ignored Mo, and left.

'Thank you, Doug,' said Kat, smiling. 'Mo will stick around and keep us informed.' Doug nodded. 'Coffee at Thames House Mo, before they forget what you look like?'

Kat's joke broke the tension that Colchester had created. 'Let's go,' said Mo, then turned to Doug, 'I'll be back shortly.' Doug nodded again and set about updating the incident board with the information that he had just shared.

*

As Mo and Kat made their way out of the building, a voice called after them. They turned to see Charlie haring down the corridor. He was carrying a buff-coloured folder. On reaching them, he said, catching his breath, 'Glad to see you're still here.' He looked around, but the corridor was empty. 'Let me walk you out.'

The front desk staff greeted Charlie with warmth and smiles, which he returned as he ushered the MI5 team from the building. Kat turned to him as they reached the pavement, but Charlie took her arm and guided her to start walking toward Thames House. 'Make as if you're leaving,' he said under his breath. They acted casually, although Mo, the least experienced of the three, was visibly agitated and kept glancing back at the exit of New Scotland Yard from which they had just come.

At the corner, opposite the Houses of Parliament, they merged with the crowds of tourists that milled around the famous site, and Charlie slowed his pace. He handed the folder he'd been carrying to Kat, 'You've just been with Colchester, correct?'

'Yes,' Kat confirmed.

'Did he tell you Yorkshire police have found the skipper?'

'No,' they exclaimed in unison and Kat felt her face flush with anger.

'When?' Kat asked.

'Saturday morning.'

'No way,' Mo protested, looking from Charlie to Kat in disbelief. 'There's no way that news came in on Saturday. I was with the operational team all weekend.' Kat rested a hand on Mo's arm to calm him and assure him that she believed that her officer hadn't missed anything whilst he'd been shadowing the police.

'I had a suspicion Colchester might have been choosing to be economical with his information sharing,' Charlie spoke as much to reassure the distraught Mo as he was imparting information, 'so I thought I'd check in on the inquiry this morning. One of the guys let slip that Colchester had explicitly told them that this file was not for sharing.'

'Why the hell would he cover this up?' Kat spat out her words.

'He wasn't keen on how quickly you got the information about the inhabitants of the West Ham flat is my working theory,' Charlie nodded at Mo who was simmering, going back over his memory of the tedious hours wasted in the operation room at the weekend.

'Thanks, Charlie. So, what do we have here?' Kat said. She opened the folder. It contained a handful of glossy photographs. She looked closely at the one on the top and saw the prostrate body of a man, draped over the steering wheel of a car. The image was artificially lit with the bright white light from the photographer's flash. She thumbed through the images to one taken from further back from the scene. The body, for the man was evidently dead, was in a red Ford Escort which was parked in a cluttered garage. Another image showed the pipe running from the exhaust and in through the nearly closed driver side window of the Ford. There were further pathology images of rooms inside a frugally furnished home. One of the photographs captured a collection of empty pill bottles.

'Jack Fleming killed himself.' Kat's shoulders slumped. She had been hopeful that they might be able to use the skipper to their advantage. She'd reasoned that a Yorkshire fisherman in his early sixties was highly unlikely to be working with a terrorist cell driven by motives of idolatry. He needed the money, was her working theory. Perhaps he'd been promised funding for treatment of his sick wife. It was a common trope for coercion. It was possible he didn't even know who he was working for. With some careful questioning, she'd hoped he would have given up a huge amount of useful information pertinent to Operation HAPSBURG.

Charlie raised his eyebrows. 'I don't know the circumstances well, but I'd hazard a guess that his demise may not be wholly self-inflicted.'

Kat was skimming the notes in the file and was rereading the house's inventory, she looked up, 'You might be right, no note. And the stomach contents don't match the empty packets found in the house. Just a few over-the-counter painkillers as opposed to the cocktail of anti-emetics and narcotics pictured. What does Colchester think?'

'A professional hit that he's unlikely to be able to track down.'

'Unfortunately, he's probably right.'

The great bells of Big Ben began to chime above them. 'Listen, I have to go. I'll keep my ear to the ground on the investigation, but my suspicion is that you lot are set up to run with it from here.'

Kat looked after the retreating figure. 'Charlie,' she called after him as he weaved in and out of the tourists with their camera phones trained on the chiming clock. Charlie looked back. 'Thank you,' Kat mouthed. He gave her a thumbs-up and disappeared into the crowd.

Turning to Mo, Kat said, 'I know I promised you a coffee, but I think it might be best if you got back to the Yard.'

Mo nodded. 'You'll put someone on the landlords?'

'I'll give that to Colin. We should be able to track down where the cell has moved to that way.'

'I just hope you find them before Colchester's trigger-happy mob do.' Kat nodded. 'And the skipper?'

'That's got institutional hit written all over it.' Mo looked at her blankly. 'Probably a hitman, hired by whoever's behind this. They will have covered their tracks fastidiously,' Kat explained and Mo looked crestfallen. 'Disappointment is part of this job,' Kat counselled the junior officer, as members of the public skirted around them, oblivious to their role in keeping them safe. 'Finding VIPERSNEST is top priority, and that's not going to happen with you moping along the Embankment.' Kat spoke confidently but she felt overwhelmed. The loss of the captain as a potential intelligence source was a major blow. 'Stay focused on whatever's in the works,' she said to Mo as a parting missive and ushered him in the direction of New Scotland Yard.

*

0025, Monday 3rd July, Telegram Messaging Service

<RubiksKube> how can I help you?

<ares> coding for a version dark wallet

<ares> the encryption on the open source code is shit

<ares> The advanced encryption standard with 256 bit key :(

<RubiksKube> I agree. I have worked on this. I will send you a suggestion.

*

0806, Monday 3rd July, Penwill & Mallinson, Canary Wharf, London

Edison's weekend had been uneventful. Other than a few titbits of information he'd been able to glean about the mysterious RubiksKube, his progress on the case had been limited. He had been for a couple of short jogs and was beginning to recognise some of the benefits of the active regimen. He was no longer quite so breathless on arriving at the top of the three flights of stairs at the flat. Tony had watched him incredulously but didn't comment on his flatmate's routine. Swallowing his pride, on Saturday evening, Edison had knocked on Tony's bedroom door and suggested to his reclusive flatmate that they might get some pizza. He looked shocked by the proposal. Edison's intrusion had come at a particularly sensitive point in his online multiplayer game. Despite this, he made his excuses to his fellow players, firing off multiple messages in quick succession and followed him into the sitting room. The pair had watched a terrible film and consumed three large pizzas. Tony had offered Edison some of the beers he kept in the fridge, and the evening had ticked over pleasantly. On Sunday, Edison had had the flat to himself as his flatmate went to visit his children. And so it was, that on Monday morning, Edison arrived at the office in good spirits and well rested.

He opened the code repository and skimmed through it. Billy looked over. 'How are you getting on with that?'

'Not bad. There are a few syntax issues that are taking a little bit of translating, but I think I'm getting there.'

'Is there anything you need in particular? I'm sure Jamie could point you to the right bit of the script if necessary.'

As if summoned, Jamie appeared on the fifteenth floor, clad head to toe in Lycra and carrying a bike helmet. 'What was that?' he said, having just caught his name as he arrived.

'Oh nothing,' Edison interjected, who didn't want to be pressed on his views on the code by Jamie. 'You cycled in today?'

'Yeah,' Jamie said, placing his helmet on his desk and rummaging around in the drawers below to retrieve a washbag. 'It's hard to work up a sweat between the lights but you can get up a decent speed coming along the cycle highway.' Jamie turned and started to make his way toward the lifts that would take him to the showers. 'You and I need to go for that run,' he said to Edison as he left.

'Definitely tomorrow,' Edison promised as the young man disappeared. 'I might know what questions I want to ask you by then, with a bit of luck,' he added under his breath. Edison turned his attention back to the screen, on which lines and lines of spidery white script appeared against a black background.

It took Edison most of Monday through to the following morning to find the section of the algorithm he was looking for. The associated database was equally impenetrable. It recorded every position taken by the bank and traded, on average, once every three minutes. The volume of information was staggering, but Edison persevered and eventually unpicked the mechanics of the trading strategy. By early afternoon on Tuesday, Edison felt confident in challenging Jamie on some of the detail. 'Hey Jamie,' Edison said.

'Yup,' said Jamie.

'Could you clarify something for me on your algorithm?'

'Sure.' Jamie pushed himself away from his workstation, and without getting out of his wheeled chair, scooted himself to Edison's side.

'So,' Edison said, waving the cursor at a section of code, 'am I right in thinking that this is a volatility play? Buying BitCoin and selling Ethereum almost simultaneously? The return is on the difference between the two currencies?'

'Bingo, you got it,' said Jamie. 'FCA shouldn't have a problem with that, right?'

Edison pretended to ponder the question. 'As long as the system registers the spot price for each trade, no.'

Did Edison detect a slight shift in Jamie's confidence? There was a hint of a flush in the young man's face and he swallowed audibly. He needed to dig deeper. Jamie's composure had slipped only momentarily, and he was back to his usual confident self. 'Spot prices are all recorded and backed up in the primary database, you can see them here,' he said, snatching the mouse from Edison and pulling up a list of numbers, each coded to a particular trade. 'No issues!' Hurriedly, he wheeled himself back to his desk.

Edison put his head down but observed his mark as Jamie began to pack his things. He pulled a USB stick from his own machine, burying it in his rucksack. Within five minutes of their conversation, Jamie stood up and announced, to no one in particular, that he wasn't feeling great and was getting away early.

Edison watched him retreat to the lifts. He walked with the familiar gait of someone who was trying to disguise his haste. What was he up to? He was certainly acting like a man with something to hide.

Edison focused and entered his password. He may have lost Jamie for the day, but he still needed to identify exactly what he was up to. That would take a few more hours of sieving through the original data on the server and digging into the commit history, the log indicating every time a change was made to the code, by whom and what they did. He also wanted to make a few subtle changes of his own in the system, and that was going to require every bit of his intellectual might to pull off without raising suspicions.

Before he immersed himself in the task, he shot a text to Tanya – *Think I know where the money is coming from.* The head of section picked up Edison's message an hour later, having emerged from a tedious meeting about budgeting. She smiled at the news. 'Good old Edison, he really is a genius,' she said to herself and her empty office. She replied to Edison and then went to find Kat. They would meet Edison for a debrief that evening.

The notification of Tanya's summons to Thames House drew Edison out of his focus with a start. He looked down at the vibrating mobile phone on the desk as if it were an alien creature and he had no idea how it had ended up there, so deeply engrossed was he in the programming language. Thames House, Edison thought to himself, maybe his exile was over, and he would be permitted onto the Grid for their discussion.

With plenty of time to cross London, Edison shut down his computer and packed his few belongings into the messenger bag he'd taken to carrying.

As the Jubilee line train rumbled through the darkness, Edison wondered where Jamie had gone in such a hurry. There were strict rules about removing information and data from the building. Any home working was done from a carefully monitored, secure remote desktop system. Who wanted what was on that USB key? Was he meeting someone? Was it a missed opportunity not trailing him today? It would have been impossible without blowing his cover completely.

*

Edison navigated through the tourists around the Houses of Parliament and made his way along the Embankment to Thames House. He was surprised to find both Tanya and Kat waiting outside.

'Lovely evening isn't it,' was Tanya's greeting as Edison approached.

'Lovely evening for a walk along the river,' added Kat, it sounded rehearsed.

'I thought we'd meet upstairs. Could do with the loo,' said Edison.

Kat returned a sympathetic look and Tanya said, 'You know I can't register you onsite, Edison.' She crossed the road, and Kat followed. They both turned to look at Edison, his shoulders slumped, the picture of dejection. He was struggling with being on the edge of the team. He missed the buzz of the Grid; the team's headquarters, where they could retreat, regroup and kick ideas around. He was battling too with a sense that he wasn't getting to the bottom of the mystery of the Penwill & Mallinson's hacker quickly enough.

He crossed the road to join the two women, painting a picture of defiance on his face. 'Do you really need to use the bathroom?' Kat whispered. Edison smiled despite himself.

'Of course not,' he said.

The three of them set off in the direction of Vauxhall Bridge. Edison thought back to his recent chat with Charlie, covering similar ground and his friend's counsel to embrace his unofficial status on the operational team.

'So, what do you know?' asked Kat.

Edison took a deep breath. 'The core trading strategy relies on the volatility in the altcoin's exchange rates. There's an algorithm that's trading BitCoin into Ethereum and back again, sometimes. The money's made on the difference between the exchange rates.' He was walking between Kat and Tanya. He paused briefly and shot a look at his companions for confirmation that they were following him. They both looked slightly vacant. He wished he was in the comfort of the office, with a whiteboard, pen in hand, scrawling diagrams to help his audience get to grips with this. Instead, the wind ruffled his clothes and blew Kat's long hair into her face, forcing her to occasionally pull long strands of it from her eyes and her mouth.

'So,' he went on, 'if you have ten BitCoin, the algorithm will trade that into Ethereum at a given spot price. Let's say, for the sake of argument, every BitCoin buys you two Ethereum. So, you end up with twenty Ethereum.' Tanya and Kat nodded. Edison went on, 'On the next trade, the exchange rate has shifted such that every BitCoin is worth one point five Ethereum, so you end up with fifteen BitCoin. Gives you a return of five BitCoin.' Edison had gained momentum and pressed on, 'It's an arbitrage on the relative spot values of the given digital currency at that point. It's all set up to execute automatically and trades every three minutes, pulling the exchange rates from the Ethereum exchange.'

The two women nodded. Kat asked, 'What if the price goes against them?'

'There's a choke switch built into the trading mechanism. If the exchange rate goes against the bank's position, they don't trade.'

'So that's the basics,' Tanya said. 'Where's our money coming from then?'

'It's rather elegant really,' said Edison.

Tanya raised her eyebrows. 'I'm not sure I'd call aiding and abetting terrorism elegant.'

Edison ignored her. 'There's a loop in the algorithm, or at least there was.'

'Was?' Kat queried.

'Yes, the code on the server was clean. Even when I dug into the code repository, it appeared totally clean. Nothing out of the ordinary in the commit log.'

'The what log?' asked Tanya.

Edison didn't fancy delivering a full tutorial on Git, the distributed version control system used by all tech developers to track their projects. 'Whenever a developer makes a change to the code of a program, he or she has to make what is called a "commit" which is logged. If the code is changed or merged in some way, there will always be a copy of what it was like before in the repository.'

'So, we're still at square one.' Kat couldn't hide her frustration as she pulled a chunk of hair from her mouth and spluttered in disgust.

'Not at all. Last Friday morning, there was a reset of the master branch. Lannister rewrote the repository.'

'Who's Lannister?'

'That's Jamie's username and avatar on the system.'

'I thought his name was Dunn.' Tanya's brow furrowed.

'Lannister is a house in *Game of Thrones*.' The creases in the head of section's forehead deepened. She opened her mouth to ask another question, but Edison interrupted, irritated by the diversion, 'The pseudonyms the team use on their system isn't relevant. What is important is that Jamie has been changing the code and then covering his tracks by rewriting the log repository. And not just last Friday. A little forensic analysis on the server proves someone has done the same thing twice this week, late in the evening, really late.'

Kat's eyes flashed with concern, and she interrupted Edison's flow, 'Such behaviour suggests your cover is compromised. Surely, we should pull you out. Jamie has worked out that you are looking for something.'

'Of course they've worked out that I'm looking for something. That's my cover,' Edison scoffed and immediately regretted it when Kat shot him a hurt look. He nearly reached out for her hand by way of apology but stopped himself when he spotted Tanya observing their interaction keenly.

She raised her expressive eyebrows and spoke calmly, 'Edison, do you have any reason to suspect that your cover could be blown?'

'Not my cover. Jamie, I think, has worked out that I might have, in my capacity covering a security and regulatory audit on the systems, sussed that he's syphoning off funds.'

'How's he doing it?' asked Tanya.

'So, I'm not one hundred per cent sure because the malicious code has been erased. But I've …' Edison hesitated. When he had been an MI5 officer, his methods for tracking criminality on the Dark Web were considered risky, tiptoeing along a fine line of legality. His head of section had largely turned a blind eye to his questionable practices, focusing on his astounding results instead. On the rare occasions that a red flag was raised by a senior officer, Donald Hughes' patronage had come to his rescue, and the flag was always hastily lowered again. Now though, thought Edison, as a regular citizen, recruited as an agent without any of the official or unofficial protections he'd grown used to over his fifteen years at Thames House, he needed to tread more carefully.

'You've what?' Tanya pressed.

'I've an inkling of how it's being done. I'm guessing in the malicious code, the foreign exchange rates were fixed at ten per cent lower than the spot rates. That ten per cent was digitally transferred into an offline wallet. I don't know where that is, but my guess is that it lives locally on Jamie's machine, and he's moving that out of the bank on a lowly USB stick.'

'So, who *is* Jamie?' asked Kat.

'He's a techie. Twenty-four years old. He's been behaving rather oddly, and I think that's down to me showing up.' Kat looked at him as he paused, her next question was implicit. 'I can't see him being mixed up in Jihad,' he said. 'Someone is pulling his strings.'

'So,' said Tanya, 'he's taking the USB stick home and transferring the money from there. We can get the team to check that. We know where he lives.'

'I think it unlikely he's executing from home.'

'Why's that?'

'Although he's probably using an encrypted browser, the connection is still linked to his identity via the ISP.'

'Do you think you've spooked him entirely?' said Kat.

'Not sure. My guess is that he'll leave things running kosher for a few days before changing it back and pocketing his percentage. Leave it with me.'

Tanya looked perplexed. 'You mustn't deviate from your brief, Edison. If you need backup or surveillance, I can set up a detail on Jamie.'

'I don't think that's necessary.'

'If there's a risk your cover is blown, we should pull you out,' Kat tried again.

'No,' Edison said, firmly. 'We don't have the list of investors. We need to know where Jamie's moving the money and on whose orders.'

'The first question, you can answer. Your cover story means you're ideally positioned to secure that information. The second gets into much riskier ground.'

Edison looked at Tanya defiantly. Tanya sighed and turned back the way they had come. She began walking. She raised a hand and waved. With her back to them, 'I'll leave you to agree where we go from here.' Edison detected a hint of irony in her voice. 'Be careful, Edison.'

Once her boss was out of earshot, Kat turned to Edison. 'I really think we should put a surveillance detail on Jamie. At least at his home. We can dig into his internet history too. See what we can find out.'

Edison shrugged. 'If you think that's the best use of resources,' he said. 'But you know I can find him much more efficiently.'

'How?' Kat challenged him.

'If I told you that, I'd have ...' Edison didn't have the opportunity to deliver his punchline as Kat landed a hefty punch on his upper right arm that knocked him sideways.

'For fuck's sake Edison. This is my investigation. I need to know what's going on.' They had stopped walking and were standing facing one another. Kat bristled, fixing Edison with an angry stare.

Edison softened. 'Kat,' he reached out for one of her hands that were planted firmly on her hips. She stepped away from him shrugging off his advance. A jogger approached and looked at them curiously. He slowed, wondering whether he ought to intervene in the altercation. Kat forced a smile, and with a look of relief, he sped up again and disappeared into the night.

'It really is better if I don't tell you the detail,' Edison said. He saw Kat's shoulders slump and knew he'd won that mini battle. They walked in silence for a while before Edison ventured, 'Anything else new on the case?'

Kat glanced at him. 'I'm really not sure I should tell you too much.'

Edison didn't respond. He let the silence hang between them. He was confident she would crack.

'The captain committed suicide,' Kat conceded after five minutes of frosty silence had passed between them.

'Shit. Really?'

'I think it was a hit.'

The conversation continued in a staccato fashion as Kat slowly recounted details of the brief she'd received at New Scotland Yard. Edison absorbed all the information, asking the occasional question.

'It's difficult to see how these two link up, isn't it?' was his conclusion as they reached Thames House.

Kat nodded and looked at Edison affectionately. 'I've probably told you way more than your security clearance allows.'

'What security clearance?' Edison joked, and they both laughed.

*

Less than one week to go. My brothers, my new brothers, have settled into their new home and everything is set. It was unfortunate that we had to move. But they still have time to prepare themselves and their materials.

*A few more payments yet. The money is important. They tell me what the weapons cost. She tells me we will have a couple more payments. Her puppet, for that is the most appropriate word, is working hard for us. But **he** expects his reward in this life, not the next, as I do. It is a significant burden to pay for such skills, but it matters. It will be done. She can deal with that soon.*

I must focus on the end. The purpose. My own calling.

Just seven days now until we bring Dar al-Harb. The lands of war will reach these British shores once more. And I have led the mujahideen here. I feel alive. I have a purpose once more. For all those years living amongst the kaffir, these unbelievers, following their customs, their culture, ignorant to their hatred of me and my brothers. I regret this. But I shall avenge my own shortcomings as I shall avenge my family. How could I have forgotten? Allāhu akbar.

Chapter Twelve

0303, Tuesday 4th July, Telegram Messaging Service

<ares> thank you for the suggestions
<ares> may I send you my version for your thoughts
<RubiksKube> of course
<ares> 134Bndh87.exe
<ares> it is clever and serves my purpose well
<RubiksKube> I will review this later. I am busy now. For now, are you complete?
<ares> yes, good night

*

0945, Wednesday 5th July, Penwill & Mallinson, Canary Wharf, London

Before he had left her flat the following morning, Kat and Edison agreed that he would shadow Jamie if he moved that afternoon. As they'd lain in bed before dawn, they'd run scenarios together. 'What if he's on his bike?' Kat had asked. He had already, without consulting Kat, made an excuse to Tony about needing to get to a meeting on the other side of London quickly and arranged to borrow his moped. Kat hadn't argued, but Edison knew, from the way her body lay tense beside him in the silence that followed, that she wasn't particularly happy. The way in which Edison's role in the investigation had moved from the relative safety of a desk-based surveillance job to a fully active operative in the space of just a few days meant she was not only worrying about the escalating threat levels on HAPSBURG but also for the safety of the man she was developing deeper affection for every day.

'And you'll get Colin read in on the flagged Ethereum so he can track it?' Edison had asked her earnestly as he'd laced up his shoes.

'Yes. Are you sure everything he needs is in here?' She was scrolling through her device to find the instructions that Edison had written up, hunched over her laptop at three o'clock that morning after they'd had sex. He'd taken the opportunity to exchange some messages with the mysterious RubiksKube whilst Kat lay dozing. He was finding it hard to believe that whoever was on the other end of the chat was Jamie, but the trap he'd left in the executable file he'd sent over might go some way to smoking out whoever lay behind the avatar.

'Colin will understand every word, I promise,' replied Edison, thinking back to the years of working with the Welshman, whose knowledge of complex programming languages was unmatched by anyone at MI5 except Edison. He brushed a kiss across Kat's lips and retreated into the dawn.

On his way back to Bethnal Green in the early hours, to shower, shave and collect Tony's moped, Edison had mulled over whether Kat's concern was purely a professional one. He didn't allow himself to admit to hoping that she was worried for his safety on a personal level too.

*

Jamie arrived in the office even later than normal. He looked pale and sported bags around his eyes. Despite this, he conducted himself with his usual bravado.

'Are you feeling better?' Billy asked when Jamie first turned up in the office.

Jamie shrugged. 'Must have been something I ate. Still feeling a bit dodgy.'

'You didn't cycle today then?' Billy went on. Edison had already spotted the absence of a bicycle helmet on Jamie's desk and wondered whether he'd chosen to leave the bike at home. Edison was hopeful, this would make his plan easier to execute. His hand went instinctively to his inside leg, and he patted it reassuringly.

'Nah,' Jamie went on. 'Couldn't face it when I got up this morning. Stomach was still churning, and I'm not sure I fancied leaving my breakfast on the cycle path.'

Billy half-laughed, 'Well, I'm glad you're feeling well enough to come in, at least. I need you to take a look at some of Chris' back office stuff.'

'Sure. I'm sure it will be a morning packed full of banter and laughs. Where is the Schnitzel?'

'I am here,' a voice boomed. Christoph had materialised at the end of the bank of desks. Anna was hovering behind him. 'I do not appreciate your jokes. We will work on my machine.'

Jamie turned to Billy and shot him a comical look, twisting his mouth into a mock expression of fear before wheeling himself over to Christoph's workstation. He came to an abrupt halt next to the Austrian.

Edison, who had been eavesdropping on the conversation from the cover of his double monitor opposite Billy's desk, heard Christoph announce, 'I have the server login open ready for you to enter your password.' He watched Jamie do so with a flourish as Christoph scribbled in his notebook.

'You two play nice,' said Anna, leaning over the two of them as Jamie typed.

'Does Christoph often need tech's help with his system?' Edison asked Billy quietly.

'Maybe once or twice a week,' Billy replied. 'It's funny. You'd think he wouldn't want to work with Jamie, but he always requests that it's him who sorts out his stuff.'

A calendar alert flashed up on the left-hand screen on which he kept his email. His meeting with David Murray, the head of sales, was imminent.

'Anna,' he spoke to Tom's assistant. The fair-haired secretary peered round her screen, her blue eyes looked at him through heavy rimmed, trendy glasses. 'Where does David sit?'

'Down one floor to the fourteenth, and you'll see the sales team – you can't miss them for all the racket they make. The team sit directly below us, and David's desk is here.' She waved in the direction of Tom's office behind her.

'Thanks.'

*

The fourteenth floor was filled with noise, as members of the enthusiastic sales team shouted into their telephones to be heard above the cacophony. As Edison navigated his way through the desks, he caught snippets of their patter. 'Great returns, outstripping the base rate by in excess of a hundred points,' one man was telling a client on the other end of the phone – he was dressed in a sharp dark grey suit, aggressively tailored, and a slimline tie.

'If you want to offer your clients something a little different, I'd highly recommend the crypto fund. There's a minimum sale of fifty for high-net-worth clients but I would have thought that your crowd might be looking at something closer to three figures, no?' A woman was speaking animatedly into her headset. She was pacing confidently back and forth as she spoke, towering over her desk in skyscraper heels. 'Ok, great, great, Michael, I knew it would appeal,' she went on, a broad smile expanding across her spray-tanned face. 'I'll put you down for a hundred and fifty,' she paused, and the smile contracted slightly, as Michael on the other end of the phone interrupted her. 'Of course, of course, Michael, I appreciate it's only a tentative commitment at this stage. I'll send through the KYC stuff later for you to review. I must stress though, we have a hard stop at the end of the month, and this round of fundraising is already significantly oversubscribed.'

Edison found David. His desk was an imposing L-shaped affair that set him apart from the rest of his team, who were confined to single units. He was on the phone when Edison approached. 'Listen, I have a meeting to get to. It'll be ok. Tell him I'll sort it out later,' David said and slammed the receiver into its cradle. 'Are you married?' he asked Edison. Edison opened his mouth to explain his widower status but quickly remembered his cover and just shook his head.

'Good man,' David said. 'More trouble than they're worth sometimes.' Edison felt a familiar ache tugging at him as David went on, 'All she had to do was get the builders to move the outlet six inches to the right to fit the cistern *she* had chosen. If she changes her mind on the bloody bathroom suite one more time, I swear I'm going to have a meltdown.' The tirade brought memories flooding back for Edison. Ellie had called him at the office when he had been working late one summer. The air-conditioning unit was on the blink, and somehow, the thermostat had got stuck at thirty-two degrees. She'd been sweltering in the sauna-like flat all evening, but rather than calling a plumber, she'd tried to fix it, which had resulted in the electrics blowing completely. Not only was the flat a furnace, but now there was no light. Edison had calmed her down and found the number for a twenty-four-hour plumber on the internet, who had come out, at great expense, to fix the situation. Edison felt angry that this man could be so callous, speaking ill of his own wife in front of a complete stranger. What Edison would have given to be dealing with the challenges of Ellie's domestic shortcomings. Edison blinked hard in an attempt to rid his head of the ghost of his wife.

'Anyway,' David said, 'enough of my issues. You must be Steven Edwards.' He held out his hand and Edison shook it. 'Why don't we see if there's a meeting room free? I understand I'm to give you a full introduction to the sales function.'

'Yes, please,' said Edison, trying to hide his cool feelings toward David. He was struggling to rid himself of lingering thoughts of Ellie, 'And a list of all the investors in each fund, please.'

'Of course, I'll get the admin to print that for you.'

As they walked across the floor to a bank of empty meeting rooms, Edison wondered if the admin had a name. David addressed a young man who looked barely old enough to have left school, 'Sort me out with a copy of all the investors by fund.' The young man cowed slightly at being spoken to and nodded.

'He's new,' David explained. 'He wasn't here when I left for Switzerland last week. There seems to be a new admin every other week. Hardly seems worth learning their names.'

In the cosy meeting room, David indicated for Edison to take a seat with his back to the door and positioned himself opposite, leaning back in the chair and crossing his arms. 'So, Steven, before I start, is there anything in particular you need me to highlight. I understand you're checking that our credentials stack up for the FCA, so it'll save an awful lot of both of our time if you could just let me know what, in particular, you'd like to know.'

The admin knocked timidly on the door and David waved him in.

'Are these all the names?' David asked, taking a sheaf of paper, stapled in one corner, from the young man's sweaty hand and leafing through them.

'Yes,' he replied, his voice barely more than a whisper.

David placed the papers on the table and slid them across to Edison. The admin retreated quickly from the room. 'Thank you,'

Edison called after him.

'So, fire away,' said David.

'Can you tell me about your team structure?' Edison began.

'Sure. I have six salesmen covering all global territories. Four are based here. One in New York and another in Hong Kong.'

'And who are the typical investors?'

'That depends on the product.'

'The infrastructure fund, for example.'

'Only institutional investors in that fund. Pension funds, insurance companies and so on. There's quite a hefty price tag, minimum investment is north of 100k.'

'And the crypto fund?'

'Now that's a lot more fun. We can go out to the private banks and family offices with that one. We're mostly talking new money here. The old family wealth doesn't like the smell of anything too techie – more fool them. They'd rather stick with mines in Sierra Leone than the spoils of a bit of crypto mining.' David paused and chuckled at his own pun. Edison raised a smile in response. 'Of course there are some exceptions, but mostly, I'm selling that fund to ultra-high-net-worths who've made their money from finance or even in Silicon Valley.'

'So, it's you who cover those relationships?'

'For that particular fund, yes. It's a relatively complex product, so I like to make sure I brief the clients personally. That should tick your little "know your customer" box.'

Edison didn't allow himself to rise to the other man's baiting. Calmly, he paused and flicked through the papers the poor admin had brought through. He looked up and continued, 'And the anti-money laundering box, how do you go about ticking that little box?'

'Compliance deal with that,' David said, reddening a little.

Edison felt his phone vibrate in his pocket, and his thoughts flew to the trap he'd hidden in the trading algorithm for Colin to monitor. 'Ok,' Edison picked up the papers, and tapping them on the table, 'I think that's all clear.' David looked taken aback by the abrupt conclusion to the meeting. 'I'll let you get back to your cistern issues.'

In the men's bathrooms, Edison dialled Thames House. 'What have you got for me?' he asked when Colin answered.

'Two hundred and thirty-seven Ethereum landed in an offline wallet just moments ago. Things have gone dark, but I'll let you know as soon as anything changes.'

'Cheers.' Edison hung up, tingling with excitement. The game was afoot. The hacker hadn't spotted his carefully camouflaged code when he'd copied and edited it. He needed to get onto the server.

Edison slipped back into Steven Edward's shoes as he arrived on the fifteenth floor, affecting an air of calm although his heart was racing. He logged onto his machine and began to dig into the log repository. Clean. 'Damn,' he muttered.

'Everything ok?' Anna said.

'Oh, sorry. Yeah, just missed a call from a former colleague who was going to give the low-down on what's changing with the regulation of autonomous trading strategies.'

'I'm sure he'll call back,' was Anna's vanilla response.

With some effort, Edison banished the thoughts of where the Ethereum would surface – there was nothing he could do until either Jamie made a move or Colin called him back – and made himself a strong cup of tea before turning his attention to the reams of names and numbers on the papers David's put-upon admin had printed.

Listed were all the positions on each of the four funds that Tom's team managed. Next to each name was a column with a two or three-figure value in it. Edison checked the column header and confirmed that the number was the value in thousands of pounds of that investment. Next, there was a column with a date, indicating the age of the commitment. Edison started by skimming through the infrastructure, emerging market currency and alternatives fund investors but found nothing noteworthy amongst the names of familiar pension funds, insurance companies and private banks. With a more forensic eye, he began to comb through the list of investors for the crypto fund. The list was longer and the investments smaller. As he went, he highlighted any names that could possibly link to the case. At the end of each page, he ran them through Google. They all returned a legitimate private bank or family office in Dubai, Riyadh or Qatar.

He completed his first pass and looked up to catch Anna peering at him from behind her screen. She looked away quickly then, feigning a thought coming to her, she said, 'I knew there was something I wanted to ask you, Steven. I'm organising a team dinner on Thursday. An amazing Turkish restaurant just off Brick Lane. Let me know if you can make it.'

'Oh, ok, will do,' Edison replied.

'I'll send you an email,' Anna said, then added as much to herself as to Edison. 'Email seems to be the only way to get anyone's attention round here.'

Edison turned his attention back to the list and decided to take another look. He let out a long breath. On the third page was a familiar name. How had he missed it first time around? He underlined the name three times and stared at it. His mind raced. This couldn't be a coincidence. He felt his body shiver. What had he got himself into?

His inner debate was interrupted as Jamie announced to no one in particular, 'I'm really not feeling too well still, I'm going to shoot off.' Hastily he buried a memory drive into the rucksack at his feet, just like the previous day, and swung it onto his back. He surveyed his colleagues sheepishly as though waiting for one of them to stop him, and when no one did, he hurried toward the lifts.

Billy looked after him. 'Feel better,' he said before returning his attention to the problem that had been absorbing him all day.

Edison watched Jamie leave and pulled up the departure times for the outbound trains on both the Jubilee Line and DLR. If Jamie were to head home, he would most likely board the Jubilee line west. Edison calculated the walk to the station would take between four and six minutes. He thought it unlikely that Jamie would risk a run. If he did, Edison's efforts to track him were doomed for the second day in a row. As it would be if he didn't take the Jubilee line, but he tried to bury thoughts of failure and losing his mark. Jamie would miss the next two trains, by Edison's reckoning, which gave him eleven minutes to get down to the platform.

Edison retreated to the men's toilets where that morning, he had stuffed a holdall. His heart beating fast, he exchanged his smart brogues for a pair of comfortable trainers. He retrieved a black baseball cap and lightweight jacket from the bag and was reminded of David's wife as he shoved it back behind the cistern. He slipped out of the toilets, feeling glad that there was no direct line of sight from the team's desks, and made his way to the fire exit that led to the stairwell. He leapt down the stairs two at a time, feeling the comfortable weight of his Glock 26 against his inside thigh.

Appreciating the cover that his training shoes and cap afforded him, he ran to the tube station. As he crossed Canada Square, he pulled out his mobile and speed-dialled Kat over a secure VOIP line. To Edison, it felt like she answered before the call had even connected, let alone rung.

'Edison,' she said, there was a glimmer of concern, a slight quiver, in her familiar, businesslike tone, 'is he on the move?'

Edison sprinted toward the yawning entrance of the tube station, talking to Kat as he went. 'Yes, he left the office about five minutes ago. I'm tracking him to the tube.'

'He's not on his bike then?'

'No, thankfully. Is Colin keeping tabs on the money?'

'Listen,' Kat spoke matter-of-factly and with a menacing authority. She ignored Edison's question. 'You're to keep your distance, Edison. Advise on his destination as soon as it's clear, and I'll have a team with you.'

'Kat, don't worry about the obs team.' Edison let exasperation creep into his voice. The two of them had run this scenario multiple times earlier in the day. 'All I'm likely to need is one of the guys ready to run traces on the money. Is Colin keeping an eye on my flags?'

At Thames House, Kat looked over to where Colin was manipulating browser windows and reams of code across three different screens. He gave her a thumbs up. 'Yes, he's all set.'

Edison had reached the bank of escalators that would take him underground to the cavernous ticket hall. 'Keep me updated. Got to go, Kat,' he said without breaking step.

'Edison do not …' the signal cut out before Edison found out what Kat was forbidding him from doing.

The week of dieting had made some difference, and he moved quickly but still arrived at the ticket barrier breathless. He waved his Oyster Card, and the gates parted. At the top of the next set of escalators, Edison heard a train rattle into the station. He sprinted, taking the steps two at a time. The train doors opened as Edison stepped off the escalator. The platform was sparsely populated. He looked around. A woman with a buggy, two builders and a handful of office workers waited patiently. At the front of the train, he spotted Jamie, looking agitated as a few passengers pushed past him to make their way off the train. He barged his way on before the last of the alighting passengers had made the platform and disappeared from view. Edison was confident that his mark hadn't spotted him, but he zipped up the jacket and pulled the collar up around his neck anyway.

There was a beep of the closing doors, and Edison hurried along the platform – his target being the penultimate carriage, one along from where Jamie had boarded. Edison just made it through the doors as they swooshed shut behind him. A tinny recorded voice came over the PA system, advising passengers that the train would terminate at Stanmore. The next station would be Canada Water. Edison swayed his way down the aisle to position himself as close to the end window as he dared. His mark had taken a seat in the next carriage.

Jamie, his rucksack on his lap, clasped closely to his chest, looked impatient. His knee jiggled, his head bowed. At each stop, he looked up before returning his gaze to the floor.

At London Bridge, he quickly stood up and jumped off the train, elbowing his way through the crowds of people waiting to get on. Edison got off and pretended to consider the plethora of exit options signposted whilst Jamie made a beeline in the direction of the Northern Line. To be expected, thought Edison, if he's on his way home. Edison jostled his way through the crowds, his height affording him a good view of his retreating target over the heads of the throngs of tourists and office workers. As Jamie ascended the stairs, he paused momentarily and looked back, scanning the crowds below. Edison buried his chin in his chest, relieved when Jamie turned and ploughed on.

Edison lost Jamie in the crowds that were surging toward the Northern Line. A train was arriving at the southbound platform as

Edison made his way down the stairs. He didn't know whether Jamie had gone left or right. Left, and he would be boarding the southbound train in moments. Right, and Edison would find him waiting on the platform. Edison gambled that Jamie was still heading home and turned left. He arrived on the platform in time to see Jamie stepping onto a carriage in the centre of the train. Edison jumped through the nearest doors and was on board just as they slid closed.

Contravening the instructions pasted on the windows, he opened the interconnecting doors between the carriages and moved through the train. Eventually, he was in the carriage next to Jamie, and observed him from behind a copy of the *Metro* he'd grabbed on his way through London Bridge.

At Elephant & Castle, as Edison predicted, Jamie alighted the train. He took the lift to street level whilst Edison puffed his way up one hundred and seventeen stairs. A wall of sound hit Edison as he emerged at the top of the echoing spiral staircase. The traffic screamed past the exit of the tube station, and the pavement was busy with people waiting for one of the many buses that stopped there.

Edison looked about, orienting himself. He was on the south side of Elephant & Castle. Behind him was the 1980s monolithic shopping centre that was always on the brink of being demolished but never seemed to meet the bulldozers. Edison was just through the ticket barriers when two things happened at once. His phone vibrated in his pocket, and the lift carrying Jamie arrived at the ticket hall. A tidal wave of people spilled out and filed toward the ticket barriers.

Edison ducked behind a pillar and buried his nose in his phone as Jamie made his way, blinking into the daylight. He barely paused as he exited the station, turning right and striding purposefully through the crowds.

Edison fired off a message to Kat. The buzzing had been her urgent requests for updates, arriving as his phone reconnected to the 3G network. *At Elephant & Castle. Suspect going home.* – he advised her. He knew Jamie rented a flat in one of the new developments on Newington Causeway. He had left the station in that direction. Having hopefully satisfied Kat's need for an update, he looked up in time to see Jamie disappearing around the corner.

The day was overcast, and heavy clouds threatened rain. Edison dashed to where he'd last seen his mark, unsuspecting pedestrians skittled out of his way as he ploughed through the crowds.

At a crossing, Edison clocked Jamie, walking down the road opposite. He glanced left and right before hurrying out in front of the oncoming traffic. He ignored the expletives from irate drivers. A lorry's horn screamed at him when it narrowly avoided hitting him. Edison held his breath, focused on Jamie, praying the kafuffle hadn't drawn his attention. But he continued to trudge in the direction of a new-build block of flats.

At the entrance, Jamie swiped a key fob, and the sliding doors parted. He went inside.

Edison pulled out his phone and dialled. 'Where are you?' Kat said without a greeting.

'Outside his flat. Did you get the floor plans?'

'Yes,' Kat said, referring to the architect's plans sourced from the council's website earlier that morning. 'He's on the third floor, flat 3C. I reckon you should have a view of his main room from Gaunt Street.'

'Thanks. Heading there now.'

'I'm on my way.'

'Anything else from Colin?' Edison asked hopefully.

'Not yet, but if Jamie's only just got back, he's not likely to have logged on yet.'

Edison grunted a non-committal response. 'I'll see you on Gaunt Street then.'

'Yes.' Kat hung up. Edison found a spot across the road from Jamie's block of flats from where he had a view directly into Jamie's kitchenliving room. The young man whom Edison had tailed across London appeared in the room, switching on the light. He dropped his bag by the door, removed his shoes and padded around the kitchen island in his socks. He pulled a beer from the fridge, opened it then returned to his rucksack to retrieve the memory stick. Edison held his breath. Was he wrong? Was the memory stick hosting an offline wallet stuffed full of illicitly gained Ethereum? Swigging his beer and twiddling the drive between his fingers, he crossed the room and picked up a laptop. Edison watched him power-up then slip the USB drive into one of the ports.

Edison held his breath. The blue light flickered across Jamie's face. He took a swig of the beer held in one hand and manipulated the trackpad on the laptop with the other. Edison's phone vibrated with an incoming secure line call.

'Edison, it's Colin,' Colin said when Edison answered.

'Our target's just gone online. Has the Ethereum surfaced?' Edison asked, glancing up at figure with a laptop on his lap in the flat.

'Uh huh, two hundred and thirty-seven Ethereum came back online about three minutes ago.'

'That's a result. Can you confirm where?'

'Tracing it now. Needless to say, the IP has been bounced around a lot.'

Edison fidgeted as he waited for Colin. He pictured the scene on the Grid now. The office he'd shared with Natalie, Kat and

Colin. A big screen dominated one wall which they rarely used. They preferred the whiteboard, on the opposite side of the room, to record their movements on operations the old-fashioned way. Colin sat behind three enormous monitors, he would now be hunched over his keyboard, tapping furiously, trying to trace the port where the money had reconnected with the blockchain.

'Yes,' Colin hissed into his headset. 'Gotcha.'

'Where?'

'Interesting,' Colin mused.

'Come on, Colin.' Edison replied, his patience waning.

'Not far from you.'

'But not Jamie's flat?'

'Sorry, Ed. It's reconnected somewhere in the Elephant & Castle shopping centre.'

'Shit, he's not our man. Can you pinpoint it any more than that?' Edison had already abandoned his post watching Jamie and was moving in a long, loping run, back in the direction of the shopping centre.

'All right, I've managed to locate their router,' Colin said, 'but it's heavily protected. Three levels of encryption and a firewall, the kind of thing you'd expect from your average investment bank.'

'Can you get into the firmware?' Edison asked, taking a short flight of stairs two at a time. He found himself among market stalls selling fruit, vegetables and knock-off DVDs.

'It's taking time, I'm almost there,' Colin reassured him.

Edison willed Colin to get through the complicated process as he wended his way through the tightly packed stalls. Fingers of light shone through the makeshift awnings. The stallholders haggled with customers and shouted their wares loudly to passers-by. Edison stuck a finger in the ear that wasn't clamped to his mobile phone. 'There must be a way in,' Edison muttered. 'Nothing is watertight, no matter how hard you try.'

There was silence on the line as Edison headed toward the shopping centre which towered above the market stalls. He pulled open a grubby glass door and entered a wide corridor, lined on either side with discount stores. 'Open sesame!' Colin said. 'I'm in. Ok, ok, bear with me.' He heard Colin's fingers clattering across the keyboard.

'Listen, Colin, I'm in the mall. Cross-reference the Wi-Fi network with the GPS data. That should give me a location to within about ten metres.'

'Ok, pinging that to you now.'

'Thanks. I'm going to have to go.'

'Ok, Edison. Stay safe.'

'Will do. I'll call for an update on the money once I know what's going on here.' Edison navigated, via his map app, to the red pin Colin had sent him. He passed a greasy spoon which was the source of the smell of frying that pervaded the place and came to a halt opposite the café. He had stopped where the parade of shops intersected another at a T-junction. A staircase led shoppers to the upper floor and, as a faded sign promised, to the bowling alley. Edison evaluated each of the concessions nearby, but nothing jumped out at him as being the likely hub for the digital transfer of the cryptocurrency.

The noise of the bowling alley echoed through the shopping centre and got louder as Edison climbed the stairs. He stopped at the top, adopting a nonchalant pose of a bored shopper. He observed a dark blue sign, picked out in garish green lettering, hanging above a grimy window that made up the frontage of a small store. It read *'Continental Internet Café'*. The window was bedecked with handwritten notices and offers promising punters *'Superfast conneshions'*, *'State of the art computer's'* and *'Best Turkish coffee'*.

'Bingo!' Edison muttered and took stock of his surroundings. He ducked into another greasy spoon and took a seat in the window which offered good sight lines to the internet café.

A buxom waitress bustled over, brandishing a laminated menu card. 'Can I get you anything to drink, luv?' she asked, throwing the card on the table. It slid across the glossy surface and came to rest against an unbranded bottle of red sauce.

'Tea, please,' Edison said, glancing up at her. She scribbled in her notebook and turned on her rubber heels.

Through the haze of grime, Edison could just about make out the arrangement of desks in the front of the shop. There were three tables, sporting ancient desktop computers, and there was no sign of any customers. The man behind the counter was the only person in the shop. He was tall and slim and, Edison reckoned, of the same ethnicity as the coffee advertised in the window.

Edison pulled out his phone and was about to dial Colin's number when a call came in. It was Kat. 'Where are you?' She sounded livid. Edison told her. 'Why are you there? I thought you were staking Gaunt Street, but I'm here and there's no sign of you.'

The waitress returned with his tea. A silver metal pot and milk jug, accompanied by a thick china mug, was placed before him. 'Will you be eating, luv?' the waitress asked, ignoring the phone pressed against Edison's ear. Edison shook his head, and she leaned across the table, her ample bosom passing uncomfortably close to his face as she retrieved the menu. She bustled away, and Edison turned his full focus back to the surveillance of the shopfront opposite.

'Things moved on whilst you were in transit.'

'Care to fill me in. I'm only the lead officer on this case.'

'Might be best if you join me here. There's nothing to see at Jamie's place.'

'So I see. When I arrived, he was slouched on his sofa one hand on a bottle of beer, the other one down his pants. I'm on my way.'

Edison hung up. He shot off a message to Colin – *Any movement?* The reply came back in seconds – *Nothing. The money's sitting in a wallet in Vienna. I reckon they're done for today. What's happening OTG?* On the ground, thought Edison, reading the once-familiar acronym. I'm OTG in a key clandestine operation for the Security Service. Sourcing intelligence vital for the protection of the nation. After the chase across London and the thrill of tracking the hub for the cryptocurrency, the enormity of the situation hit Edison. He drew a deep breath and swallowed a mouthful of tea. *All quiet* – he replied to Colin.

The shop's proprietor perched himself on a stool behind the bar at the back of the shop and scrolled through his phone. Edison watched patiently, nursing his tea. As he waited, his mind drifted back to the list of investors he'd been given earlier that day. He would have to tell Kat about the mysterious name on the list. As if the thought had conjured her, she appeared in the doorway of the greasy spoon. She was dressed in jeans, Converse trainers and a leather jacket. Her hair was pulled up in a high ponytail, revealing ears heavy set with costume jewellery. The get-up allowed her to blend into London's streets from Elephant & Castle to Whitechapel.

She slid onto the bench opposite him. 'Black coffee,' she said before the waitress had got within three feet of the table.

'Anything to eat, luv?'

Kat shook her head.

'Fill me in and quickly.'

Edison did as he was asked. As he came breathlessly to the end of his recount of the afternoon's events, Kat leaned back in her chair and landed a fist on the table. 'So, Jamie isn't our man at the bank, and whoever is managed to get in here and out again without us noticing. Fan-bloody-tastic.'

Edison didn't have a chance to reply to her outburst before their attention was drawn back to the Continental. The man in the shop had moved from his perch and was switching off all the lights. He backed out of the door, locked it and scurried off in the direction of the Old Kent Road.

'Doesn't look like we're going to get much more out of today here,' Kat said, draining her coffee and throwing a five-pound note on the table. 'Let's get back to the Grid.'

Two hours after he'd tracked Jamie through the crowds at the tube station, Edison and Kat walked in silence through the hordes of commuters negotiating their way onto the tube. Emerging at Westminster, Edison raised the thorny issue of his access to the Grid.

'Bugger,' Kat said in response. She'd forgotten that Edison's revised security clearance meant she couldn't bring her former colleague up to the office. She dialled Colin and arranged for him to meet them in the Morpeth Arms.

*

'I think we should make a habit of debriefing in the pub,' said Colin with a grin as Kat and Edison arrived. He'd secured a table away from the busy bar area, and on it sat two pints and a whisky. Edison took a long draft as he sat down, and Kat smiled gratefully as she swallowed the measure in one. 'So, it all kicked off after you guys went underground,' Colin said, flipping up the lid of his laptop which was perched precariously on the crowded table.

'Tell us,' Kat said. Edison was intrigued.

'So, the crypto had landed in a wallet, and I assumed that that was that for today. But about ten minutes later, it was traded out via a mainstream exchange into good ol' Great British Pounds.'

Edison whistled, knowing that was the end of his track on the altcoins.

'Do you know where it's gone from there?' Kat asked.

'Into a bank account with the HSBC. A business bank account.' Colin's eyes sparkled. 'A bank account we know well. Indeed, our friends at the Met might want to know about this bank account too.' Colin was enjoying the suspense and rapt attention of his boss and his former boss.

'Ok, enough of the amateur dramatics,' said Kat, her patience tested to its limits. 'Spit it out.'

'It's the bank account belonging to the property management company, Barinak Holdings, that owns the West Ham squat.'

Kat and Edison simultaneously sat back in their chairs. Colin looked from one to the other.

'Excellent work,' Kat spoke first.

'What now?' said Edison.

'That is a very, very good question,' replied Kat.

The three of them sat in silence, each of them consumed with their own thoughts. Edison added what Colin had told them to the case details he already had stored in his head. People-smuggling across the continent through a Yorkshire fishing town via a boat skippered by a now dead captain, the circumstances of his demise still open to interpretation. A bomb factory in East London abandoned. VIPERSNEST, Edison assumed, had been moved to another of the properties owned by the Turkish property company. Layered on top of that, the laundering of money from Penwill & Mallinson, syphoned into a bank account owned by the same property company to finance the operations of the terrorist cell.

Edison imagined the words that would be plastered across the top of the whiteboard in Thames House – *What? Who? When? Where? Why?* – the five questions underpinning any investigation. They were making progress on the 'who', but the other questions were eluding the team, and it was frustrating Edison.

It was clearly exasperating Kat too, as she released a pained noise and pummelled her fists on the table. The glasses wobbled and chinked. 'They're planning something, and we don't know when or where.' It was the biggest challenge of the job, and time was of the essence. Innocent people's lives were in their hands, and the feeling that the enemy was one step ahead of them was overwhelming. The immediacy of the questions of when and where an attack might take place always took precedence for the operational team. But answering the 'why' question could often lead them to the perpetrators much more quickly, as the army of psychoanalysts, that the Service engaged from the private sector at great expense, liked to remind them regularly.

Edison looked at Kat. She ran her hands over her hair three times. He recognised the familiar tic which betrayed her stress levels. She was young to be leading such a complex operation, and in that moment, Edison's heart contracted, and instinctively, he laid a hand over hers. Momentarily, she allowed the warmth and weight of Edison's hand to rest before pulling her hand away and looking at Colin. He hadn't noticed the affectionate exchange; his attention was on his laptop screen.

'We're working through the property company's portfolio, but it's huge – they've got over a hundred flats and houses across East London and another handful further south. Mo tells me the Met are working through them too.'

'Anything on the internet café?' Kat asked, her composure returning.

Colin shook his head. 'You know everything I do at this stage. I have to go, I'm afraid. The twins have got ballet tonight. Is there anything else?'

'I don't think so, Colin,' Kat said. 'I'll see you tomorrow, good work today.'

'Thanks.' Colin snapped his laptop closed and left, rushing home to his family. Kat and Edison watched their colleague retreat.

Once Colin had gone, Kat's face crumpled. Edison shuffled his chair over and put his arm around her. 'This is nuts,' she breathed, leaning into his embrace. 'Every time we think we make some progress, there's another dead end. What do you think Jamie was up to with that memory stick that made him so nervous?'

'It looked to me like he had downloaded a bunch of boxsets on the bank's bandwidth.'

'Oh, come on, Edison. You said he was jumpier than a flea in the office. He must be tied up with this one way or another. Maybe he's sharing his login details with someone?'

'It's possible, I suppose,' Edison mused. His mind was elsewhere, itching to get back online.

'Edison? Edison?' Kat was waving a hand in front of his glassy eyes. He snapped his focus back to her. 'I could really do with your help on this, and it would be a good start if you could stay in the room with me.'

'Sorry,' Edison muttered. Parking the suspicion that had started to develop in his mind. 'What do we know?'

'A cell of jihadis are at large in the city. We found enough evidence of bomb-making at the squat in West Ham to blow the roof off Westminster Abbey. There's a link to P&M through the financing and Barinak Holdings. But who's the connection between Barinak and P&M?'

'What about targets?'

'Targets, targets, targets …' Kat ruminated.

'It could be anywhere.'

'The big summer sporting events? Silverstone? Wimbledon? There's a test at the Oval.'

'All good possibilities.' He found himself parroting his own mentor, Hughes, who had guided him through many difficult cases over the years.

'The list is endless.' Kat wrung her hands together and studied her empty glass. She jerked to her feet. 'I need another one.'

'Something interesting came up this morning,' Edison said when she returned from the bar.

Kat's eyes filled with hope that this might be the piece of the puzzle that would bring the full picture into focus.

'I got the list of investors earlier today,' Edison explained. 'There's a name very familiar to us invested in the crypto fund.'

'Who?' Kat asked.

'Lady Elizabeth Hughes has a significant stake in the fund. Invested really early on. One of the seed investors would be my guess.' Edison delivered this intelligence with a triumphant smile, but it faded quickly as Kat's face didn't light up with the excitement he'd expected. 'You don't look like this is news to you – did you already know Hughes was involved in this?'

'Don't be daft, Edison,' Kat said, scoffing. 'He's not involved in this.'

'He's invested in the fund in a big way,' Edison protested. 'Surely that puts him squarely in the frame for some kind of involvement.'

Kat sighed. 'How many other filthy rich individuals were there on that list?'

Edison shrugged. 'A dozen,' he offered.

'Exactly. Hughes is a very rich man. Or at least his wife is. I suspect if we dug into the investor list of half of London's asset managers, we'd find some of his family money.'

Edison's shoulders sagged. 'It's a bit of a coincidence, isn't it? A seed investor? Such a big stake?'

'But why, Edison?' Kat pushed him. 'Let's say, for the sake of argument, Hughes is somehow involved, what's his motivation? Tell me why?'

'There's the drugs link,' Edison offered, referring to the reason why Hughes had been dismissed. Edison would never forget the sense of falling he felt while standing on the mountain, listening, open-mouthed, as Hughes laid out their future together. The deliveries had been coming in pure, via Turkey, and the product was then being distributed to Hughes's network of right honourable friends, and now it was Edison's turn. He had watched as his mentor and friend crowed. The two of them would be rich, Hughes had said, and the bottom had dropped out of Edison's world.

Edison could see the look on Kat's face as the steam leaked out of his argument against Hughes, and he began to wonder whether it *was* just a coincidence that he'd come across the former Head of MI5's wife's name on the list of investors.

Kat shook her head, 'Too tenuous.' She then looked hard at Edison. 'I know you hate him,' Edison's close circle suspected that Edison had not been the sole architect of his departure from MI5, 'but there's no way he's involved in a plot against the country.'

'We should at least have a chat with him?' The idea of seeing Hughes again filled him with a sort of sick fascination. 'Perhaps his involvement is purely monetary. If we can't work out the connection between Penwill & Mallinson and VIPERSNEST, then maybe he hasn't either?' Edison played his final card, knowing it was hopeless.

'Do you have the full list?' Edison pulled the papers from his pocket that David Murray had given him earlier and handed them to Kat. 'I'll have Colin run this tomorrow.' It was a conciliatory promise, Edison knew, but there was nothing he could do to push the issue further.

'Home time, I think,' Kat said. 'It's been a long day.' Edison nodded. 'I'll let you know what the plan is from here.'

'Ok,' Edison said, although he hadn't really heard her. His mind was still focused on Hughes. He left Kat on the pavement outside the pub. She gave him a good head start to reach the tube station, recognising he needed space.

*

Back in Bethnal Green, Edison collapsed at the kitchen table. The muffled boom of a shoot-'em-up computer game came from Tony's room. He pulled out the photocopy of the list he'd taken before leaving the office and stared at where he'd underlined Lady Elizabeth Hughes. Edison felt exhausted and drained. His mind was racing. The conversation in the pub had stirred up a painful cocktail of emotions. His own failings. His wife's death.

As Ellie had been dying, he'd travelled to Scotland for a weekend with his mentor. Hughes had invited him to get out of the city. He was having a hunting party with some friends, and he thought that it would do Edison good to get away for a few days. The revelations of that weekend had knocked Edison for six. As he'd stood on the summit of the ben, he could scarcely believe what the man who he'd come to respect like a father was telling him. He had been using his own agents to smuggle drugs into the country. Supplying the upper classes with the finest cocaine and extorting vast sums of money out of some of the country's most senior civil servants, politicians and government officials. Hughes had spent the weekend back-peddling and reminding him of how indebted he should feel to the man who had orchestrated his career. Edison had travelled back to London, to his ailing wife, feeling miserable and conflicted. After six months of soul searching, during which time Ellie's condition worsened, he'd submitted what he knew to the whistle-blowing service. Ellie had died the day Hughes was formally cleared of all charges. He recalled standing on the steps of Thames House as Hughes had been driven away. Across the river, in St Thomas' hospital, his wife drew her last breath without him.

The memory haunted him.

This wasn't a coincidence. Edison was sure of it. He would have to do something.

*

Later that night, Edison lay awake on his bed, unable to sleep. It was one o'clock in the morning when his phone rattled on his bedside table, announcing a message from Kat – *No action other than ongoing surveillance. Maintain your cover at bank.*

What about Hughes? Edison replied. It was an incendiary question, he knew, but he knew Hughes better than anyone, and there was no chance he'd have cut all nefarious ties after his dismissal from Five.

The phone rang. The caller wasn't identified, which meant that Kat was still in the office despite the hour. He ignored the call.

*

The morning light crept through the window, waking Edison. He was fully clothed, and he hadn't drawn the curtains before collapsing onto his bed the previous night. He looked around for his mobile and spotted it, nestled amongst the duvet, where he'd discarded it. He checked the time on the screen. It told him that it was a little before 5.00 a.m. and that Kat had tried to call him four times and left two voicemails. Reluctantly, he dialled his voicemail.

'*Edison,*' Kat spoke to him, her tone was stern, bordering on angry, '*you need to take your personal issues with Hughes off the table. He's a rich man and has lots of investments. Add to that that he's a tech fiend and the likes of the crypto fund are going to be right up his street. I really think you're reading far too much into this. We need to focus on the property company and what the funds are being used for.*' She hung up.

'*Edison,*' her tone was more conciliatory in the second message, '*please don't get caught up on the Hughes issue. I really don't think it's relevant. The guys will run the investor list. I really need you at the bank, keeping an eye on whoever it really is who's messing with the trading algorithm and maintaining your cover. Call me in the morning, will you?*'

Edison rolled over to place his phone on his nightstand. Ellie looked back at him from the photograph propped there. 'This isn't a coincidence,' he told her. He knew what he had to do. 'Just one thing to check at the bank in the morning, and then it's time for a trip up north, Ellie,' he said and fell back into a heavy sleep.

Chapter Thirteen

0655, Thursday 6th July, Thames House, Westminster, London

Kat returned to Thames House barely five hours after she had left it. She had fallen into bed at just after two in the morning, to be woken what felt like seconds later by her alarm. She'd had a cold shower, allowing the freezing stream to bring her to full consciousness. She'd travelled on a near-empty tube to the headquarters of MI5, deep in thought on her team's next steps in this complex operation.

Colin handed her a strong black coffee as she arrived. She took a long, grateful gulp and felt the coffee push away the last remnants of sluggishness. Mo arrived, followed almost immediately by Natalie and Jock. By 7.30 a.m., Kat had her full team gathered around the board in their office. They waited for her to speak.

'You've all read your briefing on the intelligence we gathered from our field asset yesterday?' Kat felt odd referring to Edison as a field agent – he was one of the best intelligence officers in MI5's recent history. He should be here, in this room, running this operation. He would know what the next steps should be. Kat felt woefully ill-equipped to direct the team, but the need to act was increasingly urgent, she knew. Her sixth sense was tingling. It was the sense the Service's recruiters can spot in you within the first hour of interview. The rest of the day is spent stress testing for the ability to keep secrets. They dug deep into indiscretions of your past, finding out anything that might leave you vulnerable to a potential blackmail or worse.

The team confirmed they'd all read the encrypted summary file

Colin had sent to them the night before.

'Mo, I need you at Scotland Yard. Keep an eye on Colchester's directives. I'm worried he'll compromise any potential sting with his heroics.' Mo nodded. 'Are they pursuing the captain's supposed suicide?'

Mo shook his head, 'No. The forensics came back and were pretty scant on detail. If it was a hit, it was very professionally done. Nothing in the path report indicated other than a suicide.' Mo paused, 'Do *we* definitely think it was a hit?'

Kat was taken aback by the challenge but composed herself. 'Here's my take on things. Our suspect, or suspects, whoever's pulling the strings when it comes to VIPERSNEST's movements, had eyes and ears on Fleming. My conversation with Damien Clough precipitated a call to the captain which our man picked up on. Either a tap on the line or, more likely, he had hold of Fleming's phone. It was conspicuously missing from Fleming's home when they found him. Hearing that the police were sniffing around again, he moves the cell and makes sure that Fleming is no longer a risk.'

Mo nodded. 'What about the drugs? Getting rid of the captain means the drug running is over.'

'Another indication we're moving into the end game. We know their main source of income is coming from the bank. They were using the fishing route to bring their men over.'

'What about the rest of the crew? They knew nothing about the drugs or the people-smuggling?' Natalie pitched into the conversation.

'They, all three, knew about the drugs,' Mo confirmed. 'One of them admitted to receiving a tidy payout for each shipment. But on the illicit delivery of wannabe jihadis to British shores, they were quite certainly kept in the dark.'

'So, we can only speculate on Fleming's demise,' Kat

continued. 'Where are Colchester's efforts focused, Mo?' She looked at her watch, 'Give us the abridged version; you need to get going.'

'The property company. There are eighty-six flats and houses, according to the land registry, owned by the business.' Kat looked to Colin for confirmation. He nodded. 'Colchester's doing a door-to-door.'

'That'll take a month of Sundays,' Natalie pointed out.

'Which is probably a good thing,' said Kat. 'Means we can pursue that line of enquiry a bit more efficiently without stepping on anyone's toes. I'm going to bring Yousuf and Gurbuz in for a little chat. Whilst they're out of the way, Natalie, I thought you might take a look around their offices?'

'No problem. Anything in particular you're looking for?'

'Use your imagination. Rental details, tenancy references, that kind of thing. Can you see what you can find?'

'Sure. You're going to bring them both here?'

'No, I've dug out a safe house in Leyton that should be nice and secure.'

'What if the police strike lucky?' asked Mo.

'It will be difficult to justify not going in if Colchester's men find the cell, even with the risk of lost intelligence on the broader network. We'll cross that bridge if and when we come to it.'

'Before I go, what are we doing at the bank?' Mo asked. 'We should speak to this Jamie character, right? Even with what happened yesterday, he's still the prime suspect.'

Kat had been musing on the best course of action with Jamie, and her decision not to pick him up was haunting her. She'd batted the options around late last night, arguing each one through with her own inner critic. Through the fog of exhaustion, at one o'clock this morning, she'd resolved not to arrest Jamie immediately. He was either ignorant to what was being done under his cover on the system or working in tandem with another operative. Whether the perpetrator of the bank fraud was an accomplice or not, arresting Jamie would risk spooking his paymasters. VIPERSNEST are definitely working toward an attack. Bringing Jamie in would either accelerate their plans or they would go to ground completely, setting HAPSBURG back months. 'No,' Kat explained to Mo, 'I'm keeping him and the operation at the bank under close surveillance but nothing more at this stage. If we need to, we can arrest him on suspicion of money laundering, but for now, I think we need him in the field to smoke out the real hacker. There may be more money moves, so best not to cut off VIPERSNEST's blood supply at this stage.'

Mo looked sceptical but didn't object.

'Speaking of the money moves,' Kat went on, 'Jock, can you sort out surveillance on the internet café? I'm pretty sure they're still in the dark on how close we are to them, so will likely continue to use that hub.'

'Sure,' Jock, the head of the mobile surveillance team, said. 'That'll be a job for me and Nat tonight.'

'Right, Mo, time to get out of here. I don't want Colchester to think we've lost interest,' Kat instructed Mo, who gathered his things and left.

Kat ran through her mental checklist. She'd arranged surveillance on the internet café, set in motion a sting on Barinak Holdings, and she still had Edison in Canary Wharf to smoke out the hacker. At the thought of Edison, her eyes flicked to her mobile. She hadn't heard from him all morning. She tried to push aside his obsession with Sir Donald Hughes and put her growing affection for him out of her mind. He was just a field agent, supplying information on a particular part of the operation. She wrestled her focus back to the action points on her list. 'Colin – are you looking at the investor list?'

'The team is running it now for red flags,' Colin replied. He looked down at his laptop – he was never seen without it – and scrolled across the screen. 'Nothing as yet.'

'Ok, keep me posted.' Kat turned her attention to her nearly empty coffee cup. She was still contemplating the dregs of liquid when Tanya appeared outside the office and tapped on the glass wall. All four sets of eyes turned to her. Tanya looked stern and indicated for Kat to meet her in her office.

'Ok. Everyone know what's needed of them?' Kat snapped, wondering what her boss wanted.

Jock, Colin and Natalie nodded, taken aback by Kat's uncharacteristic tone. Kat hurried out of the room to follow Tanya.

*

0756, Thursday 6th, Nelson Gardens, Bethnal Green, London
When Edison woke again, his body felt heavy with exhaustion. The full light of day was pouring in through the window. 'Fuck,' he said out loud. He focused on the red glow of the digital clock by his bed. It told him it was just before eight o'clock. 'Bloody hell!' He hauled himself off the bed – there was no time for lengthy ablutions. He sprayed deodorant liberally, hoping that would go some way to masking the stale smell of sweat that hung about him, and pulled on a clean, unironed shirt. He brushed his teeth as he moved about the kitchen, making a cup of tea. Eight minutes after he'd discovered the lateness of the hour, he was leaving the flat, a large ceramic mug steaming in his hand.

He willed the bus through the rush-hour traffic. His mug garnering curious looks from the other commuters who were clutching paper cups bearing the garish logos of high-street chains. Edison arrived at the office just as the Thursday morning meeting was wrapping up.

Tom gave him a disapproving look, pointedly looking at his watch. Edison muttered an apology. Tom simply said, 'One of the guys will fill you in on what you've missed,' before disappearing into his fishbowl.

'You ok?' Billy looked concerned. 'You look like death.'

'Thanks,' said Edison ironically. 'To be honest, I'm really not feeling great.' He was feeling a lot better for the litre of tea he'd drunk on the bus, but the illusion of ill health was important for the plan he had formulated en route into the office.

'Maybe you've got what Jamie's had,' Billy went on, nodding at Jamie, who was nursing a triple espresso in the corner. Jamie looked up at them and offered a weak smile. He looked pale, as if he hadn't had much sleep either.

'Yes,' said Edison, seizing on the opportunity to consolidate his subterfuge, 'there's definitely something going around. I'm not sure how long I'll last today.'

At his desk, Edison pulled up a command prompt and logged onto the bank's server. Rather than navigating to the crypto trading algorithm, as he had done every day for a week, he logged into the management database for the infrastructure fund. Half an hour later, and with a cache of code downloaded for future reference, he was satisfied he had what he needed to tie up the loose ends at the bank. He turned his attention to searching for trains. He was scribbling times in his notebook when Anna spoke to him. 'Are you coming for dinner this evening, then?'

'Dinner?' Edison looked at her blankly.

'Yes, team dinner tonight,' Christoph chimed in. 'Anna knows all the best Turkish restaurants in the city. This is probably in the top three. It is an unassuming-looking place in Edgware, but the best doner kebab on this side of the Bosphorous.'

'I really don't think I'm going to be up to it,' Edison made his excuses. 'In fact, I think I'm going to have to go home. I feel dreadful.'

'That's a shame. Feel better,' Anna said. She exchanged a meaningful glance with Christoph, but he didn't notice as he was thrusting belongings into his satchel ready for his escape. Edison quietly made his way off the fifteenth floor and headed home.

*

0915, Thursday 6th July, Thames House, Westminster, London
Kat spent an hour with Tanya, relaying the detail of the previous day's events and providing a comprehensive summary of her plan of action. She stopped Kat in her monologue when she spoke of the appearance of Lady Hughes on the investor list for the crypto fund at Penwill & Mallinson's.

'That's interesting, isn't it?' she said.

Kat was surprised that Tanya should pick on this minor detail, she had only included it because of the connection to Edison. 'I don't think it's relevant,' Kat replied. 'The Hugheses must be invested all over the place.'

'You're probably right.'

'Although,' Kat paused, wondering how to broach the subject of Edison's fixation with the former director general, 'Edison's got himself wound up about it.'

Tanya looked uncomfortable. 'What is the latest from Edison?'

Kat gritted her teeth. 'I haven't heard from him since we debriefed yesterday evening.'

'What?' Tanya exploded. 'What do you mean you haven't heard from him? He still hasn't got to the bottom of who's pulling the strings at the bank. I would expect him to be submitting hourly reports!'

Kat felt angry. He's your agent, she thought. 'It wasn't my

choice to bring him onto this investigation,' Kat blurted out, regretting it almost immediately.

Tanya seethed but collected herself. 'I need you to focus on the investigation, Kat.' She spoke sternly. 'As you say, it was my call to bring Scott Edison back as a field agent, and it was his decision to accept the opportunity. Please let me know as soon as we have anything on the property search. I will deal with Edison.'

Kat bowed her head in acknowledgement of the instruction. 'Is there anything else?' she asked.

'Not currently,' Tanya replied, a menacing staccato applied to every syllable.

Kat left the office as quickly as she could without running and made for the ladies' toilets, thankful to discover them empty. She barricaded herself in one of the cubicles and let out a long breath. She took out her phone and dialled Edison, promising herself that this would be the last time she would check up on him.

He didn't answer.

She returned the phone to her pocket and, true to her promise to herself, pushed the thought of Scott Edison from her mind.

*

Tanya made a call of her own after Kat left her office.

'Hello,' Charlie answered his phone after a number of rings. Over a crackly line, Tanya could hear young children squealing in the background.

'Charlie, it's Tanya.'

'Oh, hello.' His voice was deadpan but the infinitesimal pause between the 'oh' and 'hello' told Tanya that Charlie had been put on edge by her call. 'What's up?' He was trying to sound calm.

'I was wondering if you'd heard from Edison lately?'

'No, I'm on holiday with the family. What's happened?' His voice cracked with concern. Tanya could feel the blame already creeping into his tone.

'Nothing.' Tanya tried to sound reassuring, 'Can't tell you too much. It was a tough day yesterday, and he hasn't checked in this morning.'

Tanya could hear the noise of the children receding as Charlie moved away from his family. Safely out of earshot, he said, 'For fuck's sake, Tanya. There is more than the defence of the realm and your career trajectory at stake here. He's pushed himself too far, hasn't he? Beyond his brief as a field agent, and that's got him into trouble?' Tanya tried to interrupt Charlie's tirade, but he was on a roll, 'He couldn't stand not being fully read in. You can't expect a man of Edison's experience to stick to run-of-the-mill intelligence gathering.' Charlie finally ran out of steam. A pregnant silence hung on the line.

'What do you mean, Charlie? What has he told you?'

'Nothing that's in breach of the official secrets act,' Charlie spat back. 'Don't worry.'

Tanya could sense that she was getting nowhere. 'Charlie,' she adopted a soothing tone, more in hope than expectation that it would calm Charlie, 'if you hear from him, could you let me know?'

'Daddy, Daddy,' a child called in the background, 'can we have ice cream, please?'

'I have to go, Tanya.'

'Will you call me if you hear from him?' Tanya pressed.

'I'm not making any promises,' Charlie replied and hung up, turning to the youngest of his three children, who was looking at him with hungry eyes. 'Chocolate or strawberry?' Charlie said, lifting the small boy into his arms and carrying him back to where his brothers and Layla waited. The little boy pondered the question carefully, a furrow forming in his brow beneath his shock of curly, ginger hair.

'Chocolate,' he said seriously.

Charlie set the little boy down and turned to his wife, 'Layla, I have to make another call – could you sort these monkeys out with ice cream if they promise to be good for the rest of the day?'

'Do you promise boys?' Layla asked, and the three children nodded in unison. Addressing Charlie under her voice, 'Everything ok? You look upset.'

'Just work,' he replied and moved away from her.

Charlie dialled Edison and willed him to pick up.

In the flat in Bethnal Green, Edison glanced at the phone as it rang, expecting to see an unknown number. He was surprised to see Charlie's caller ID on the screen, and he grabbed the phone, answering it just before it went to voicemail, 'Charlie.'

'Eddie, everything ok?'

'Yeah, why wouldn't it be?'

'Had Tanya on the phone.'

'Really?' Edison was incredulous. 'They're using you to check up on me?'

'Something like that.'

'I'm fine.' Edison tried to shut down the conversation. 'You can report that back.'

'I'm not reporting back to anyone. Are you sure everything's ok?'

Edison softened, recognising the genuine concern from his friend. He let his guard drop a little to reassure him. 'I'm ok, it's all been a bit much, and I'm tired. Going to take a few days off, I think.' He was careful not to reveal his true motives for abandoning his post at the bank. He did not think anyone, even Charlie, would understand what he needed to do.

'We've got a sofa bed at the holiday let – why don't you come up here? If you can put up with the kids – they would love to see you.'

'Charlie – that would be amazing. I might pop in on me mam on the way.'

Charlie chuckled.

'What's so funny?' Edison asked.

'Eddie – the only time you'd ever know you were from Newcastle is when you talk about your mother. Listen, I have to get back to the family. Get the train to Inverness and I'll pick you up. See you tomorrow?'

Edison's brain worked quickly, considering his plans, 'I might not make it up until Saturday.'

'No problem, just let me know when you're on your way. Love to your "mam".'

'Ha ha. See you soon.'

'Eddie,' Charlie said as an afterthought, 'just let Tanya know you're ok, will you?'

'Sure.' Edison made the hollow promise easily and hung up.

Briefly, Charlie considered calling Tanya but decided that affording Edison a break from the pressure cooker he'd found himself in lately was more important. He pushed the conflict from his mind as his middle son charged at him, a clown's mouth of chocolate decorating his face. 'Come on, Daddy,' he cried, tugging at his sleeve, 'we're going to the top of that mountain over there to see if we can spot the Loch Ness Monster.' Charlie followed his son, putting the worries of London out of his mind as best he could.

In Bethnal Green, Edison's stomach was churning. Ellie's photograph looked up at him reproachfully as he shoved a change of clothes in a holdall. What would you be saying, he wondered as he retrieved his Glock from his sock drawer.

'*I'd be telling you not to go, Eddie.*' Her voice in his head was so loud that Edison caught himself looking round, believing she might be standing at his shoulder. '*You're needed here*,' his dead wife went on.

'I know Elle,' Edison addressed the photograph, 'but what if he's up to something? Or what if he doesn't realise what on earth he's got himself mixed up in?'

'*He won't thank you for it. He'll make your life miserable.*'

'More miserable than it already is?' Edison looked around at the dilapidated room he called home.

You know I don't trust him, not one little bit. Edison remembered the words his wife had said years earlier. She was right about so many things. But I have to go, he thought. If I owe that man anything, I need to go, he concluded, wrapping the gun carefully in a T-shirt before burying it right at the bottom of his bag.

By mid-afternoon, he was making his way through the crowds at Kings Cross, his holdall slung over one shoulder. He purchased a ticket that would take him as far as Newcastle. He settled himself on a train that would get him there shortly before half-past six. A wave of exhaustion washed over him. He closed his eyes and slept most of the way to the city of his childhood.

*

1835, Thursday 6th July, Central Station, Newcastle-upon-Tyne

Edison descended to the platform at Newcastle Central Station. The two-coach Metrolink train was pulling out of its dedicated platform, ferrying shoppers to the Metrocentre, an indoor shopping complex that was once the largest mall in Europe. The people of Newcastle took their shopping almost as seriously as they did their football. It was an overcast evening, but the pubs around the station were busy with drinkers spilling out onto the pavements. Edison had left London bathing in late-July warmth, but up north, there was a distinct chill in the air. Scantily clad women tottered about on high heels whilst short-sleeved men with aggressive tattoos bought them vodkas and cokes.

It was a familiar panorama for Edison but one he felt disconnected from. He felt no affinity with the city of his birth. Other than his ageing mother, there was nothing here for him. Sometimes, he wondered whether his real father was still living in the city. But now, and for many years, everything he cared about, or had cared about, was in London.

Outside the station, he clambered into a waiting taxi and gave the driver his mother's address. 'Alreet mate.' The taxi driver spoke with a thick Geordie accent, 'You local, like?'

'Sort of,' Edison replied trying to soften the public-school inflection he had refined since he was eleven years old.

'Been a rough ol' time in Byker lately, some of the kids 'ave been causing a ruck. Knives an' all. Y'oughta be careful, mate. You don'sactly blend in.'

'Thanks, I'll be careful.'

They pulled up alongside the Byker Wall, its familiar bright blue vents ascending into the grey skies. The vast block of council flats stretched before him, and Edison took a deep breath before releasing his seatbelt. He handed the driver a ten-pound note and instructed him to keep the change. It was almost double the fare on the meter. 'Thanks, mate, tek care o' yousel'.'

'Aye mate, I will.' Edison replied, letting some of the dialect creep in. He opened the door and stepped onto the pavement. He immediately regretted his decision to take a taxi.

'Who gets a taxi t'Byker?' a dishevelled-looking middle-aged man called from the opposite side of the road. He was smoking a roll-up cigarette and carrying a can of supermarket own-brand lager. Edison looked around to see whether he was addressing anyone in particular. He wasn't, but the crowd of teenagers clustered around a dilapidated children's playground looked over and sniggered. Taxis were an attention-seeking extravagance on Newcastle's most famous social housing estate. Edison pulled his collar up around his face and strode toward the communal entrance that led to his mother's flat.

'Nice jacket,' one of the youths commented as he passed. He was languishing on a swing, the rusty chains crunched against the frame from which paint flecked and fluttered to the ground with every movement.

Edison dug his keys out of his pocket, swiped the key fob and slipped inside the musty corridor. A woman was bumping a buggy down the stairs. She reached the ground floor, and Edison stood aside, holding the door open. The woman looked up at him as she passed. 'Ta,' she said before stopping. 'If it isn't wee Scotty Edison?'

Edison was taken aback. The woman was in her early fifties and was clearly grandmother to the toddler in the buggy. He smiled. 'Eee, you got big, din't ya,' she went on. 'Betcha canny remember me.'

'Sorry,' Edison mumbled.

'Nah, ye never visited much affer you went t' tha' posh school. Mary was so proud of ye. Ye gannin up to see ye mam?' Edison nodded. 'Try to check in on her most days, I do, but this one keeps me busy.' She waved at the toddler, ''Is mam's working all hours. I'm Tracy Cole. Lived at number twenty-three.' Edison nodded and smiled in a pretence of recognition. 'Bes' be off, love to ya mam, Scotty.' The woman hustled off.

On the third floor, he paused outside the familiar front door, the brass number twenty-five was faded and tarnished. He had not been home since Ellie's death. His mother had been unable to travel to the funeral because of her deteriorating health. Since then, he'd wallowed in the misery of losing first Hughes, then his wife and finally his job. His mother had been so proud of everything her son had achieved, and it had all evaporated in the space of months. He carried the burden of feeling he'd let her down, and that had prevented him from visiting in over a year.

He wondered what he might find on the other side of the door. He wondered whether her health would have grown even worse in the time he'd been absent. Edison shook off the wave of guilt that washed over him. He buried the thoughts of turning around and leaving, took a deep breath and slipped the key into the lock.

The front door opened onto a small, dingy hallway. Edison stepped through it in three strides and pushed open the door into the living room. The room was dark – the only light filtered through dirty net curtains hanging in the small window. He looked around at the décor and furniture that hadn't changed since his childhood. The chintzy three-piece suite was squashed into an area designated as the lounge, and a large dining table that could have comfortably seated six took up the other half of the room. The TV-dinner-tray table next to the occupied armchair served as evidence that the table was surplus to requirements – Edison considered it was probably two decades since anyone had sat round that table for a meal. Even when he and Ellie had visited, they had eaten fish and chips from their laps in front of the television. The television was playing on a low volume, showing the BBC's coverage of the Wimbledon women's semi-finals.

Mary Edison turned a gaunt and wizened face away from the screen to look at Edison. There was a moment's hesitation before recognition swept over her grey features. A smile broke on Edison's mother's face – thin lips parted to reveal a perfect set of white teeth, and a sparkle lit in her rheumy eyes. She opened her mouth to speak, but something caught in her throat. She coughed, and her voice crackled like someone who hadn't spoken to another human soul for some time. 'Scotty,' she said. 'My canny lad.' Edison crossed the room and crouched to kiss his mother's cheek. 'What a luvly surprise. I must put the kettle on.' She spoke with none of the malice that Edison would have forgiven her for. Arthritic fingers curled around the armrests as she braced herself to stand.

'No, no, Mam,' Edison protested, resting a hand gently on his mother's gnarled hand, 'I'll sort it.' He stood up and went through to the kitchen. Dust moats caught in the grey light and settled on the surfaces. But for the evidence of a well-used microwave oven, the small galley kitchen didn't look like it was regularly used. Acting on autopilot, he pulled open a cupboard where he knew he would find the mugs.

'No, Scott,' a voice admonished him from the doorway. He turned to see the diminutive figure of his mother leaning heavily on a walking stick. 'Let's have the decent china. Next cupboard along. I don't get much chance to use it these days.' She said it matter-of-factly without a hint of self-pity. Edison's heart flipped.

'Ok, Mam, you go sit down.'

'Ok, luv. Don't forget some biscuits,' she instructed, turning slowly and painfully and disappearing from view.

Edison busied himself, setting a chipped, enamelled tray with the 'good' china. He filled the yellowed, brittle plastic kettle and waited as the furred-up element worked hard to heat the water. As the kettle laboured, he stuck his head round the door to find this mother sitting at the dining table, her hands crossed in a pose of practised patience. 'Where are these biscuits then, Mam?' he asked, and she jumped, unused to having company.

'The biscuit tin, luv,' she said, 'where else? On the shelf with the tea.'

Edison found the tin and put a handful of supermarket knock-off Twix and KitKat bars on a prettily decorated china plate. He was glad to find fresh milk in the fridge.

The kettle eventually boiled, and he poured the water over the teabags in the teapot. He surveyed the tray and carried it through to the sitting room.

'I better serve yours before it gets too strong for you, Mam,' he said and poured her a cup of pale yellow liquid that she doused generously with milk, splashing some from her unsteady hand onto the saucer.

'Glad you can remember how I take it. It's been a while since you've made your mam a cuppa.'

'That's true.' He was about to apologise when his mother interrupted him.

'So, luv, how are you getting on? I haven't heard much from you since …' her eyes brimmed with tears as she spoke, 'since Ellie,' she forced the words out.

Edison could feel a lump forming in his throat. 'I've been doing ok, Mam,' he tried to reassure her, smiling through his grief.

'And are you working, luv? I think you said that you were having trouble with your work, but that must have been over a year ago now.'

'Yes, Mam, I'm still working.'

'For the government?'

'Kind of.'

'Oh good.' She looked pleased. 'Not going anywhere, the government. Not like the shipbuilding and the car building.' She sipped at her tea and reached a shaky hand for a biscuit. 'And what about Charlie? How is he? He's such a luvly lad. And a policeman – that's a good job. Although there are those round here who don't like 'em.'

She struggled with the wrapper on the biscuit, trying to work her claw-like fingers around the paper. Gently, Edison manipulated it from her grasp and opened it. 'I told Charlie I was visiting, he sends his love.' His mother smiled. Satisfied the tea had reached a drinkable strength, Edison poured himself a cup. The conversation turned to the mundane detail of life on the estate, discussions of the weather and who Mary wanted to win the men's Wimbledon final on Sunday – 'That dishy Swiss man – he's very good, isn't he?'

The carriage clock on the mantlepiece chimed. It was nine o'clock.

'Have you had any tea, luv?' Mary said, looking concerned.

'Yes, Mam,' Edison lied.

'Will you be staying?'

'I best be going, I think, Mam.' He needed to get out of there. There was too much of his past crammed into this tiny home. The photograph on the wall of his wedding day, the memories of Ellie, sat cross-legged on the sofa, making her mother laugh over some anecdote about a model at the fashion magazine, and the spectre of his runaway father haunted the place.

Edison felt desperate to escape the claustrophobic flat, but as he stood at the door, his mother embraced him so tightly that tears sprang into his eyes. Mary's diminished figure pulled away and looked up at him. 'I love you, son, you know where I am.'

'Yes, Mam,' Edison turned quickly, picking up his holdall and descended the stairs.

Outside, the clouds had given way to a bright, clear evening. Early July, and the sun was lingering in the sky. The youths had disappeared, and a young mother was pushing a small child on the swing.

Edison walked back into Newcastle city centre, avoiding the ignominy of a taxi and the darkness of the Metro. Passing the handful of mattress shops at Manors then crossing the Central Motorway, he left behind him the rundown, inner-city housing estate and former industrial buildings which lay derelict between Byker and the river, waiting patiently for the inevitable creep of gentrification that would transform them into trendy apartment blocks and lofty wine bars. The buzz of the metropolitan city centre engulfed him, and he dived into the Tyneside Cinema Café and ordered a pint of craft beer.

Kat had called him once at around 8.00 p.m. and followed it up with a text message – *Just let me know you're ok*. Softened by the afternoon spent with his mother, Edison sent a short reply – *All ok. Please don't worry. Might head up to visit Charlie for the weekend in Scotland*. The reply arrived almost immediately – *Thank you x* – was all it said. Edison knew there was very little more he could glean from the surveillance at the bank. He had stalked the perpetrator through the Dark Web and had him cornered. He would fill Kat in on all that as soon as he returned to London. It was far more important that he confront Hughes.

Sipping the bitter amber beer, Edison scrolled through the handful of other messages that had arrived that afternoon. There was one from Charlie, saying he was looking forward to seeing him and another from Maria, which surprised him.

She had sent a photograph of the Penwill team, seated at a table laden with dozens of dishes of Turkish food. He zoomed into the picture and studied it more closely. He wondered if he could spot any hint of the hacker. Billy, Tariq and Maria were all grinning wildly, having made the most of the restaurant's bring-your-own policy. Edison noted Tom's absence. He was most likely still in the office. Jamie looked on edge. Neither Anna nor Christoph were looking at the camera, engrossed in conversation. And Emma was looking at Jamie and seemed to be midway through moving to comfort him in some way. Maria's message asked after how he was feeling and told him that the whole team were missing him. Edison smiled. He was genuinely pleased to have assimilated so quickly into the close-knit crowd, and he was equally happy to know that his cover was still intact.

He replied to Maria, thanking her for her concern, telling her that he was so sorry to be missing the meal and making his excuses for his continued absence from the office the following day.

Whilst he still had his phone in hand, he opened an online shopping app and tapped in an order. Next, he searched for a suitably cheap hotel in which he could stay, checked the times of the trains to Inverness the following morning and the details of his planned onward journey from there.

The sun had long dipped beneath the horizon, but there was still light in the midsummer northern sky when Edison made his way to his hotel room and crawled under the duvet.

*

1123, Thursday 6th July, Westbury Ave, Wood Green, London

After the briefing at Thames House, Kat drove with Natalie to Wood Green and parked on Westbury Avenue. The address took them to a terrace of shops, and they found the offices of Barinak Holdings, sandwiched between a bookmakers and a beauty salon. A peeling sign clung above heavily shuttered windows. *Barinak Holdings: Lettings, Property & Building Management Services* it announced. Natalie took up her post on the opposite side of the road, talking animatedly into her mobile phone. Kat knocked.

Minutes passed before a key turned in the lock, and the door opened to reveal a short, round man with a balding head and a shy smile. Kat judged he was probably in his late sixties. 'May I help you?' he said, shading his eyes from the sunlight now flooding through the door.

'Mr Yousuf?' Kat ventured.

'I'm afraid Murat is abroad. I am is his business partner, Hakan

Gurbuz. Can I help you at all?' He held out a squashy hand, and Kat shook it.

'Mr Gurbuz, I am with the police.' She flashed her fake ID as she spoke. 'I need to speak with you about your property inventory. Would you mind coming with me?'

Gurbuz's brow wrinkled into a frown, and Kat braced herself in the doorway should he attempt to run. 'Of course, of course. I do hope everything's in order. I'll be as much help as I possibly can, but I must admit that I have not been that involved in the business lately. Murat, that's Mr Yousuf, has been managing the day-to-day affairs. I'm not getting any younger, and it would be nice to retire one day.'

Kat directed Gurbuz to the car and watched in her rear-view mirror as Natalie, still rabbiting away, crossed the road. Kat drove to the Service's nearest safe house, a tired 1970s terrace with views over Tottenham cemetery. She ushered a startled Gurbuz into the living room. 'I … I … would have expected to go to a police station,' he stammered, looking fearful.

'Mr Gurbuz,' Kat took a risk, 'I work for the government.' She watched for any hardening in the man's demeanour, a hint that he was playing the game. His expression didn't change from one of bewilderment. 'Your property in Brooks Road was recently discovered to have been housing terrorists.' The old man's face slackened, and he opened his mouth to speak. Kat ploughed on, 'We believe these men intend to commit mass murder.'

'In London?' Gurbuz croaked, his mouth dry.

'Yes.' Kat watched him carefully.

'I … I … I don't know what to say …' He swallowed hard and licked his lips. Kat handed him a bottle of water that he sipped gratefully.

'You had absolutely no idea that the three men living at Brooks

Road—'

'Three men,' he interrupted her, 'at Brooks Road? But that property has been empty for nearly a year. They found asbestos in the roof, and Murat assured me he was dealing with it. He was finding it hard to secure a contractor for the work.'

'Mr Gurbuz, where did you say Mr Yousuf had travelled to?'

'I'm not entirely sure. Most likely he's visiting family in Turkey.'

'And when did you last see him?'

'What are we now? Thursday? Exactly a week ago. That was when he was last in the office.'

'How long have you worked with Murat Yousuf?'

'He joined the business about a year ago. This really does not make any sense. Why would you ask after Murat? I'm sure he knows nothing about all this? Maybe these men, the terrorists,' he spat the words out, stood up and quickly took another sip of water, 'were squatting. What proof do you have that Murat is involved?'

Kat changed tack. 'How often do you check on the accounts for the business, Mr Gurbuz?'

'The accounts? Are you suggesting these men were paying rent?' He was becoming more agitated, and Kat was worried she wouldn't be able to keep him here too much longer.

'Please, just answer the question,' she said calmly. Hakan, who had been pacing back and forth in front of her, sank into one of the armchairs, deflated.

'I can't believe this,' he muttered, holding his head in his hands. 'I just can't believe it.'

'Mr Gurbuz, the accounts,' Kat pressed.

A pair of sorrowful eyes rose to meet Kat's. He shook his bald head and clasped his hands together. 'I don't think I have looked at the business accounts since just after Murat joined the firm. He seemed to have everything under control.'

'Do you have a home address for him?' As Gurbuz scribbled an address in Palmers Green onto a piece of paper, Kat's thoughts flew to Natalie. She hoped that she had given her enough time. She escorted Hakan Gurbuz back to the car, and they drove in silence back to Wood Green. As they turned onto Westbury Avenue, Kat was relieved to see Natalie, examining her nails, waiting nonchalantly at the bus stop as they had agreed.

Kat followed Gurbuz into the letting agency, watching carefully for any sign that he might have spotted the intrusion. He laid a shaking hand on the door that led up to his flat above the shop.

'You will call me if you hear from Yousuf.' Kat held out a blank card with a number on.

Gurbuz nodded. Kat turned her back on the old man and went back to the car.

*

'Did you put the tap on the line?' she asked Natalie as soon as she slid into the passenger seat.

'Yep.' Natalie dialled a secure connection into Thames House. Colin picked up. She put him on speaker. 'Anything on the tap?' She had spent her time in the offices of Barinak Holdings, methodically installing bugs in the front office, a smaller room at the back, packed with a flimsy desk and filing cabinets, and the bedsit upstairs.

'Not a peep,' Colin replied.

'Nothing through on the mic either?'

'No, and he definitely hasn't left the flat.'

'He was about as genuine as they come,' Kat pitched in. 'I think I seeded enough doubt in his mind about his business partner that I'd have been very surprised if he had been straight on the phone to Yousuf.'

'What did you get from the files, Natalie?' Colin asked.

'I managed to clone their hard drive, but judging from the size of the files on there, there's very little digital record keeping going on. The office had three massive filing cabinets, thankfully pretty well organised. There are only three properties that aren't currently occupied. The property at Brooks Road. Another in Hackney on Danesdale Road, just off Victoria Park, I think, and one in Stratford on Carpenter's Road.'

'Colin, get those addresses out to Mo straight away.'

'On it.'

'Anything else of interest?'

'Yeah, one thing. There were a couple of photographs on the walls. One of Yousuf and Gurbuz shaking hands. It's weird, but Yousuf looks really familiar, but I can't put my finger on why I recognise him. I took a snap of the picture.'

'We'll get it up on the board as soon as we're back and see if anyone else thinks they know the mysterious Yousuf. Colin, you still there?'

'Yes, I'm all ears.'

'Gurbuz thought that Yousuf had gone to Turkey to visit family. Can you run a scan on departures for the last week? Cross-reference facial recognition with the picture Natalie's sending through.'

'Sure. Will get onto that too.'

'Thanks. We'll be back on the Grid in half an hour.'

Kat hung up and cursed as they ran into a traffic jam and crawled back to Thames House.

Chapter Fourteen

2130, Thursday 6ᵗʰ July, Thames House, Westminster, London

Jock McDermid had worked for the domestic Security Service MI5 for more than a quarter of a century. He was recruited in the early 1990s when his computer science degree set him apart as special, and the appeal of a career at a tech firm wasn't the distraction it was now. He had skilfully enlisted a gifted team of technical whizz-kids over the years. Such talent was proving more and more difficult to secure as big salaries on London's Silicon Roundabout beckoned.

Three years prior, he'd convinced Natalie Freeman to turn down an offer to work for an up-and-coming social media start-up in favour of protecting the country, with a role in the surveillance team at MI5. 'It may pay significantly less, but you'll be adequately compensated in job satisfaction,' he'd told her in her final interview. 'You just won't be able to tell anyone about it.'

She'd laughed and accepted the job without a second thought. Even when the start-up, in which she would have had a stake had she accepted the offer, was sold to Facebook for an eye-watering sum of money, Natalie didn't regret the decision she'd made.

Natalie and Jock loaded up the panniers on Jock's motorbike with the technical kit they needed for their night's work. From their vantage point, they could just see the clock of Big Ben peeking over the top of the Houses of Parliament. It told them it was nine thirty in the evening. They would reach the shopping centre at Elephant and Castle shortly before ten.

'Punters should be safely out of the way. Parked in the pub for the evening, I hope,' said Jock. Despite thirty years in London, his

Scottish accent hadn't diminished. 'Got some insight from a friend of a friend who's on security there. He reckons, but for a few people still floating around the bowling alleys, it'll be pretty deserted by this time of night.'

Natalie nodded and tucked another set of router intercept devices into the top of the panniers. It was a source of constant amazement for her the web of connections Jock had managed to weave around London. She wondered how she would ever achieve the same.

Jock zipped up the front of his biker jacket, 'Good to go?'

'Let's do it.' Jock laid his hand out, and Natalie brought hers down in a low-five gesture that marked the beginning of an op. It was a tradition that Jock observed with religious levels of superstition, and he'd taught her the ritual on her very first day in the job.

Jock threw his leg over his motorbike, Natalie pulled on her helmet and positioned herself behind him. Jock released the throttle, and they roared away in the direction of Lambeth Bridge. They swung left across the river and along a deserted Lambeth Walk. The bike sped past the Imperial War Museum, looking majestic in the evening gloom. At the shopping centre, Jock parked the bike in a back road. Natalie unclipped the top of the pannier and retrieved the rucksack she'd stashed in there. Jock shouldered another bag, and they walked silently toward the shopping centre.

Their appearance was carefully considered to be as innocuous as possible. Both wore jeans. Jock wore a baseball cap in addition to his casual leather jacket. Natalie had her long auburn hair loose about her face and had her chin buried in a voluminous scarf. At the entrance to the shopping centre, Jock greeted one of the security guards, a young man, not much older than twenty, in an oversized uniform. 'We good to go?' Jock asked him. A look of fear crossed the young man's face. 'It's ok, nothing to worry about,' Jock paused and added, 'for now.'

The security guard swallowed hard. In a faltering voice, he said, 'He left two hours ago. All clear.'

'Thank you.' Jock smiled at him as he and Natalie set off across the shopping precinct.

'Why was he so afraid?' Natalie whispered.

'Always good to have a little leverage when you're asking people for assistance,' Jock replied, a glint in his eye. He stopped opposite the darkened shopfront of the Continental Internet Café, adopting a pose of practised nonchalance, his nose buried in his phone.

'What's your leverage?'

'He's got a criminal record,' Jock muttered, not taking his eyes from the mobile handset. 'Pulled up for carrying a concealed weapon when he was sixteen. Needless to say, he didn't disclose this in his job application.'

Natalie felt a brief pang of guilt at such manipulative tactics. She looked back to the slim figure of the security guard who was casting occasional furtive glances in their direction. 'Who does he think we are? Police?'

Jock nodded. He slipped his phone into his pocket and pulled out a keyring, loaded with bits of wire and skeleton keys. 'You're on lookout,' he told Natalie as they approached their target.

Natalie positioned herself in front of Jock as he jiggled wires in the Yale lock. The precinct was deserted, but Natalie's heart pounded loudly in her chest. Moments later, the door swung back, and Jock breathed, 'Bingo.'

He produced a pencil-thin torch from his pocket and crossed the darkened shop floor. Expertly, he disabled the alarm. He had visited the café earlier in the day under the guise of a customer. He had been grateful to discover a standard model of intruder alarm and no evidence of any closed-circuit television. The extensive digital security Colin had reported did not extend to the café's physical boundaries.

The pair worked quickly by the light of their torches. Natalie pulled out the tools they would need and handed a small drill to Jock. He stood up on one of the counters and made a tiny hole in the wall, right by the ceiling. Into the hole, he threaded a camera. At the counter, Natalie checked the picture and sight lines on a laptop. She gave him the thumbs up, and he repeated the operation in the back office. Finally, Natalie fixed a bugging device to each of the computers and another to the Wi-Fi router. They would not know how successful they were until the following day when the systems were fired up.

Jock stood back, satisfied. 'No matter where on the web they're working, that should tell us what they're up to.'

They were both in the back of the shop, packing up, when they heard a noise. Natalie froze. Jock indicated for her to move toward the door. She stood on one side of the doorway and pressed her back against the wall. Jock did the same on the other side. Someone was moving about in the shop. A broad torch beam swept across the floor. 'Who's there?' a gruff voice demanded. 'Police,' the voice went on. 'Show yourself, hands where I can see them.'

Natalie saw Jock's head fall back in exasperation. 'For fuck's sake,' he mouthed at her then jerked his head indicating that she should follow his lead.

'All right officer,' Jock said, he waved both his hands in the empty doorway and walked out, squinting in the glare of the uniformed policeman's torch.

Natalie did the same, shaking violently. She'd completed dozens of this type of operation and never had there been a confrontation like this. The policeman looked at them both. 'Don't move,' he said then reached for his radio.

'Officer,' Jock said, standing still in the torchlight, he spoke with an urgency that made the policeman look up before he'd pressed the radio's transmission button, 'we are members of the Security Service. Please do not radio this in.'

The policeman looked taken aback then he sniggered, 'Pull the other one.'

Jock went on in a stern voice, 'I am deadly serious. This is a matter of national security. You can call Chief Superintendent Harrington-Smith in Counter Terrorism for confirmation.'

Jock's urgency of tone and the mention of a highly ranked counter-terrorism officer had the desired effect, and the police constable dropped his radio. 'Don't move,' he warned them and pulled out a phone. He stepped out of the shop and out of earshot. Jock and Natalie watched from the darkness of the shop as he made a call and spoke briefly, glancing up at the two MI5 officers.

'You're to come and wait in the car with me,' the police constable told them when he returned.

'I'm going to secure the shop,' Jock told him in a tone that couldn't be argued with. He grabbed the few remaining tools still strewn on the counter. Next, he reset the alarm system and once all three of them were outside, he pulled the door closed and locked it.

'Come on,' the policeman said, grumpily. 'Superintendent Harrington's on holiday apparently. Superintendent Colchester is on his way. I'm to wait for instructions in the car.'

'Shit,' Natalie heard Jock mutter under his breath.

The trio was walking toward a squad car that was parked behind the shopping centre when the policeman received a phone call. He listened, nodding and making affirmative noises, as a voice on the other end of the line dished out instructions.

'I'm to let you go,' he said to Jock and Natalie once he'd hung up.

Natalie couldn't help but release a long breath that she felt had been trapped in her body for the last twenty minutes. The police constable looked deflated. 'You don't look like spies,' he said as Jock and Natalie walked away.

'Best not to in our line of work,' Jock replied with a wave.

They rounded the corner and Jock volleyed off a stream of expletives. 'They're not going to be happy on the Grid. I'd better call Kat.' He pulled out his mobile to discover an incoming call. He answered it.

'Jock,' it was Colin. 'Everything ok? All hell's broken loose here.'

'We're fine. Tell me the worst.'

'Tanya's on the rampage. Apparently, Colchester called her at home. She's on her way in. I think he's coming too.'

'Shit.'

'Exactly – it's really hitting the fan. You need to get back here.'

'On our way.'

'What went wrong?'

'Nothing. Just really bad luck.'

'Ok, see you both soon.'

Colin hung up and Jock looked at Natalie. 'Brace yourself,' he said. They both mounted the motorbike and sped back to Thames House.

*

1123, Thursday 6th July, Thames House, Westminster, London

Jock and Natalie arrived at Thames House. Although night had fully descended on London, the fifth floor was ablaze with lights and activity. Kat intercepted Jock as he made his way across the floor. 'Tanya's on her way in,' she said, steering him by the elbow to a corner of the office.

'I heard.'

'And Colchester's on the rampage.'

'I heard that too.'

Over Jock's shoulder, Kat saw Tanya appear behind the glass doors that separated the open-plan floor from the lifts. She was looking harassed. Behind her, loomed the imposing figure of Michael Colchester, wearing a face of thunder. She pushed through the glass doors, Colchester tailing her as if, if he gave her an extra inch, she might give him the slip. She was saying loudly, 'I'm sure we can get to the bottom of this.'

Colchester blustered about 'proper process' and 'full cooperation' in response.

'Kat, Jock,' Tanya snapped. 'My office.'

They exchanged looks and followed the police superintendent and their boss. Tanya held open the door as everyone filed in and then turned to the main office, addressing no one in particular, 'Could someone sort out some coffee?'

Colin and Natalie had been watching from a safe distance. 'I'll do it,' said Colin, getting up from his desk. Despite the late hour, the floor was busy with analysts, almost all were working the periphery of HAPSBURG. They were ploughing through the investor list or scanning border control itineraries to spot Yousuf's departure or analysing intelligence reports for hints on the attack location.

In Tanya's office, Jock and Kat hovered near the door. Tanya threw herself into her high-backed chair at the conference table. Colchester took the seat opposite her, positioning himself to maximise the feeling of confrontation. He glowered, 'What the hell was your team doing, bugging an internet café at Elephant & Castle?'

Tanya raised her eyebrows and turned to Kat, 'Can you enlighten us?'

'Routine surveillance. We discovered a link to our investigation yesterday.'

'What link?' Colchester growled.

Kat shifted from one foot to the other. 'It's possible our targets are moving money through the Continental.'

Colchester's eyebrows shot up. 'Why wasn't I informed of this new information?'

'Probably for the same reason you didn't advise us of the death of Jack Fleming,' Kat shot back without thinking.

Colchester bristled but didn't reply.

Tanya intervened. 'Kat, please could you brief the Chief Superintendent in full now.'

Kat swallowed hard and provided an abridged version of their discoveries, the use of Jamie's account on git hub to manipulate the coding history, tailing Jamie from the bank the previous day and his possible involvement in diverting funds out of Penwill & Mallinson into the account of Barinak Holdings. She didn't mention Edison. She concluded with, 'We felt it necessary to monitor any further traffic coming through the internet café.'

'And I assume you have all the necessary permits for such surveillance?' Colchester spat.

The tension in the room was interrupted by Colin's arrival with a large cafetière of coffee and four mugs.

'Thank you, Colin,' Tanya said, and he retreated quickly.

'What a merry little dance you lead here,' Colchester said, as the door closed behind Colin. 'Why hasn't this Jamie been collected?'

'We felt it would be more beneficial to continue to collect intelligence. We believe he is a scapegoat. He's under close surveillance,' Tanya said. Kat shifted uncomfortably, knowing that

Edison had not been in the office at Penwill & Mallinson for most of the day.

'Not good enough, Tanya,' Colchester roared and slammed his fist on the table. The mugs rattled and coffee spilled from the spout of the generously filled cafetière. 'We need to bring this joker in. If he has information, we need it. And we need it yesterday.'

'We don't think he's the operator. He's probably just a puppet. What if it forces the hand of this organisation and they rush an attack? We don't have any idea as to what they're targeting or when. It's too risky,' Tanya countered, her accent colouring with a West Indian twang.

'*Probably* ... *We don't think* ... No. No more waiting. There's enough evidence. You said he was caught red-handed, removing digital material from the bank. We have to bring him in.' Colchester's face was set in a grim expression, his jaw hard, his teeth grinding.

'No,' Kat pleaded. She sensed her grip on the case loosening. 'He didn't go to the internet café.'

'He could have passed the flash drive on to another operator. A brush drop. Isn't that right up your alley as spooks?'

'He's not our man.' She wished Edison had told her more about his suspicions, wherever and however he was uncovering his information. At least then she would have been able to make a more coherent argument for leaving Jamie in the field. Instead, she flailed helplessly, 'It's not him. We know it's not him.'

Colchester ignored her and spoke to Tanya, 'We'll move first thing in the morning. Perhaps that chap who's been twiddling his thumbs, getting under my team's feet all week would like to observe the interrogation for you.'

Tanya ignored the Met officer's jibe, 'He's busy in the field. Kat is the senior investigating officer. If you must go ahead, please let her know when you have your suspect in custody, and she will join you at the Yard.'

Colchester nodded, 'Ok.'

'Will that be all?' Tanya asked.

Colchester looked at his watch. 'I don't think now is the time to discuss the appalling lack of cooperation we're receiving on this case. I shall speak to the commander in the morning.'

His threat delivered, Colchester stood up and stalked out of the office.

Tanya watched him go then turned on Jock and Kat, her face set in stone. They both squirmed under her gaze, waiting for the tirade that would inevitably come. She looked tired and not just because of the early hour of the morning. For the first time, Kat saw signs of severe strain on her boss's face. There were tight lines developing at the edge of her mouth and dark bags under her eyes, betraying a lack of sleep. 'I can't afford many more mistakes like that,' she said. Jock and Kat felt the full force of her authority. 'The JIC is really worried about the lack of intelligence we have on what is considered to be a significant existential threat to national security, and they believe, as do we all, that an attack is imminent.'

Jock nodded and opened his mouth, preparing to defend what his boss had labelled a mistake but decided against it.

'I don't think there's any doubt that the DG will hear from the commander tomorrow morning,' Tanya went on. 'Make sure you're playing by all the rules for the next few days, at least, and keep the Met well apprised of our intelligence. Is Mo still on site with them?'

Kat nodded.

'He'll be in for the morning briefing though?'

Kat nodded again.

'Ok – I'll be there.' Kat felt every bit of the criticism being levied was directed at her personally. She didn't relish the idea of her boss attending her morning case briefing and worried about her credibility in front of her team.

'That'll be all,' Tanya dismissed them.

*

Back in the open-plan office, she slumped at her desk. Jock, Natalie and Colin seemed to materialise from nowhere and huddled round her. 'Guys, go home,' she insisted. 'It's late, and tomorrow's going to be a hell of a day.' The assembled company made their protests but eventually started to dissipate.

As Natalie was picking up her handbag and preparing to leave, Kat turned to her, 'See you in the morning, chief's taking the brief.'

Natalie smiled, 'You're heading home too, aren't you?'

'Definitely.' Kat picked up her own bag to prove the point and watched the others leaving the building. As the last of her team disappeared into the lift, she collapsed into a chair and turned her attention to the HAPSBURG board. Since the morning, new information had been added from Natalie's visit to Barinak Holdings. The two hot-property addresses were written up in Colin's familiar hand – carefully articulated capital letters: *FLAT THIRTEEN, ST JOSEPH'S COURT, CARPENTER'S ROAD* and *TWENTY DANESDALE ROAD*. Nothing new had come in that afternoon from Mo. He had been stuck at New Scotland Yard for the day, and his surveillance unit had got caught in the same traffic she had crawled through that afternoon. He'd assured her that they would be at the first property at dawn.

Kat stood up to examine the photographs. The man she'd met that day was shaking hands with his business partner, standing in front of the shop, both beaming into the camera lens. Murat Yousuf was a tall, wiry man with a long face and a sharp jawline. His dark hair was sprinkled with grey flecks. The hand held by Hakan had slender fingers, tipped with neatly shaped nails. Like Natalie, she felt as though she'd seen Murat Yousuf somewhere before. How did she know him? It was from another photograph, she was sure they hadn't met in person. She willed her mind to work as she dug desperately into her memory. Where had she seen that man before?

After twenty minutes staring at the picture, a kernel of an idea wormed its way into her head, and she snatched open a cabinet where the team kept files from earlier in the investigation. She sifted through the exhausted leads and evidence from countless dead ends.

In triumph, she pulled out the photograph she was looking for. Kerim Dastan. The brother of Metin Dastan, the body in the box at Billingsgate, discovered last year. The body delivered on the same shipping line used by the HAPSBURG drugs pushers. The same route that VIPERSNEST had used to enter the country. The team had toiled for months, trying to dig up the connection between the body and HAPSBURG. And here it was, smiling back at her from beneath the Barinak Holdings sign.

'But why?' Kat asked the empty room. If Kerim's brother had met his end at the hands of a terrorist cell, why would he be working with them? And she was still missing a link to the bank. 'Damn it,' she cried and slammed her palm against the picture of Hakan Gurbuz and Murat Yousuf. She composed herself and pinned the grainy image of Kerim Dastan, a passport photograph blown up to A4 size, onto the board.

It was three o'clock in the morning when Kat made her way out into the dark and hailed a taxi. Half an hour later, she was lying on her bed, staring at the ceiling, her thoughts racing. Twice, she pulled out her phone and considered calling Edison. All she wanted was to hear a friendly, familiar voice. Someone to listen as she vented her frustrations and to sympathise, encourage and advise. But Edison wasn't and couldn't be that person. There were too many layers of complication. His dead wife. His remarkable recall to unofficial active duty with the Service. His gonzo behaviour – dashing off to Scotland, abandoning his surveillance post. The fact that he used to do her job and did it so much better than her. Finally, she dozed off and managed to sleep for the full two and a half hours until her alarm went off, summoning her back to Thames House.

*

She tells me they have taken the bait. That was a clever idea of hers to ensure we had what the English call a scapegoat. They are so stupid. To arrest a man who has simply been set up. But I do not care. The plans are working, and whilst they are looking the other way, we shall strike. Less than three days now. As they sip their champagne and eat their strawberries, we will rain down on them the full power of our rage. In the moment, they will not know what has hit them. But as the dust settles, as my brothers enter paradise, they will know the name Dastan, and they will know that they should not have crossed my family. I will follow my brothers, I will follow them then, and we shall know the glory of martyrdom.

Chapter Fifteen

0738, Friday 7th July, The East Coast mainline, between Newcastle and Edinburgh

Shortly after the 7.30 a.m. train, carrying Edison, drew out of Newcastle Central Station, bound for Scotland, the postman buzzed at flat number twenty-five and delivered a brand-new kettle to Mary Edison with a message attached. '*I love you, Mam,*' was all it said. Mary Edison placed the note carefully on the mantlepiece beside the cheaply framed photograph of her only child in his Harrow uniform.

Edison was dozing in his seat when a notification of the delivery came through. 'The wonder of the internet,' he muttered to himself, pocketing his phone and hauling himself into the aisle. 'If only its uses were limited to next-day deliveries.' He swayed through the train to the buffet car where he ordered a cup of tea and surveyed the breakfast options. With little enthusiasm, he settled on a bacon bap and watched with horror as the attendant heated it up in a microwave.

Back in his seat, he nibbled on the sweaty sandwich whilst flicking through the street atlas of the UK that he'd bought at the WHSmith's on the station. He found the page showing Inverness and turned over a couple more pages to find his intended destination. The navigation would be straightforward, although the roads appeared twisty and narrow.

In Edinburgh, he changed trains and continued his journey north, watching as the countryside that sped past the window transformed from the arable farmland of the lowlands to wild, moss-covered crags. The moorland stretched away endlessly toward a blue horizon, occasionally broken by woodland of majestic fir trees. It would be an inhospitable place in winter, but today, the sun was shining, and the countryside was bathed in bright summer light that picked out the spectrum of yellows, greens and purples in the heather.

He had made this trip with Ellie when they had travelled to Moniedubh, on Hughes' invitation, and they had mused together, as they'd travelled, what it would be like to leave London behind and live a quieter, rural life in Scotland.

As the train laboured further north, Edison lost himself in a fantasy, imagining chasing a cluster of small children across the vast open countryside. The children weren't Charlie's three boys, they were his own with Ellie, and they were squealing with delight as they skipped over the heather, lost in a game. Edison gathered them to him, hoisting the smallest onto his shoulders. The little girl had ribbons tied neatly around her pigtails. Everyone said she looked like Edison, but to him, she was the stamp of her mother. Edison held the hands of the other two children, both boys, as they returned to the picnic mat, where, in Edison's mind's eye, Ellie, resplendent in the sunshine, was waiting for them with sandwiches, lovingly wrapped in brown paper and salty crisps and tea, poured from a huge thermos flask.

The train drew to a stop, and Edison was catapulted from his daydream by the guard announcing their arrival in Aviemore. Edison wiped tears from his eyes and smiled at an elderly lady who had taken a seat across the aisle from him and was offering him a tissue in a warm Scottish accent.

'Oh, no thank you,' Edison said, waving her away.

'I'll just leave it here,' the kind stranger replied, placing the folded tissue on the open tray table in front of Edison and patting it.

Edison blushed, 'Thank you.' He turned away from her to hide his embarrassment.

Half an hour later, the train pulled into Inverness. 'This is the end of the line, ladies and gentlemen. This train terminates here,' the train guard announced. 'All change please, all change.'

Edison grabbed his holdall from the overhead rack and hurried from the train. He took his bearings at the station and made a beeline for the car hire booth. He explained to the clerk behind the desk that he wanted an entry level hatchback for a couple of days' sightseeing. He declined the salesperson's attempts to upsell him to a more luxurious model. Having failed to upgrade Edison, the young man behind the counter pushed firmly on the optional extras.

'Your 3G won't be much use up here,' he said, trying to hammer home the value of the satellite navigation system.

Edison brandished his newly purchased road map and replied, 'I'll stick with the old-fashioned methods, thanks.'

The salesman's final attempt to extract more money from Edison involved something to do with not having to return the car with a full petrol tank. At this point, Edison's patience deserted him, and he snapped, 'I explained exactly what I wanted when I first arrived. That was now,' he made a dramatic show of looking at his watch as he paused in his diatribe, 'nearly fifteen minutes ago. Please could you simply furnish me with the keys, direct me to the vehicle assigned to me, and I will be on my way.'

The poor young man mumbled something about 'only trying to help' and pulled open a drawer to retrieve a set of keys. He showed Edison to a silver-grey Peugeot 207 and rattled through the pre-hire vehicle check.

Edison signed the paperwork, slung his holdall onto the back seat and got into the car. The clerk retreated to the safety of his booth, and Edison started the engine. He put the car in gear, briefly consulted the road atlas that was laid open on the passenger seat and set off. The digital clock on the dashboard read eleven fifty. The drive would take the better part of two hours. Edison considered briefly picking up something to eat at the large Tesco he was passing but decided to press on.

Soon, the large roads gave way to country lanes that wended their way along the edges of lochs and around the bottom of mountains. After an hour and a half's driving, Edison pulled into a passing point to collect his thoughts. The familiar landscape was playing havoc with his emotions. He was less than half an hour from the Moniedubh Estate and an audience with Sir Donald Hughes.

*

0645, Friday, 7th July, Thames House, Westminster, London
Kat arrived to a near-empty office. The revelations about the true identity of Murat Yousuf had done little to calm her frayed nerves. The new piece of intelligence seemed to throw up more questions than it answered. She knew she was no closer to identifying the location of the imminent attack, and that had consumed her thoughts as she tried to snatch a couple of hours' sleep. She had fifteen minutes before Tanya would host the morning's briefing. Only Colin was at his desk, who looked up and gave her a welcoming smile. 'Eventful night, huh?' he said. 'This is interesting.' He wagged a finger at the photograph of Kerim Dastan, 'Great spot, Kat.'

Kat turned on her heels. Somehow Colin's praise made her feel worse. In the kitchen, she was glad to see that Colin had fulfilled his duty as first on the Grid to put the filter coffee on. Colin tailed her with his own empty cup in hand.

'Where's Edison?' he asked.

'Taking a bit of time off, visiting Charlie, who's on holiday in the Highlands.' A shadow passed over Kat's brain, like someone walking in front of a projector screen. She tried to grasp whatever it was that was worrying her about Edison, but the shadow eluded her. She brought her focus back to the room, wrenching her thoughts away from the agent. She topped up Colin's cup with coffee before pouring herself some.

'Anything on the investor list, Colin?' she asked.

'Nothing noteworthy,' Colin replied. 'A bunch of pretty clean family offices and private banks.' He paused. 'You know the former director general's wife has got money tied up in the fund?'

'Yes, she's minted, probably invested in half the funds in London.'

'True,' Colin agreed. 'It was all her money, wasn't it? Even if Hughes likes to pretend he's landed gentry. That great big estate up in the Highlands is Lady Elizabeth's family home.'

'Hughes loved playing lord of the manor, as if he wasn't just a bright lad from the East End who got lucky. He was always hosting politicians and industry CEOs for hunting parties. I think Edison went to a few—' Kat stopped speaking abruptly. It hit her. Edison's dash to Scotland. His insistence that the former director general was somehow mixed up in HAPSBURG. 'Shit. Shit. Shit.' She bolted back to her desk, coffee sloshing from her mug. She ignored the splatters of hot liquid peppering her hand.

Colin followed her, matching her pace, 'What's up, Kat?'

'Edison. Shit. Edison.' Kat ignored him and scrabbled for her phone. She dialled. 'Straight to voicemail. He's got no signal. Damn it.'

'Kat,' Colin caught her slender arm and spun her round her to look at him. 'What is going on?'

'Edison's not going to visit Charlie. He's going to confront Hughes about all this!' She gestured wildly at the wall where every detail of the HAPSBURG was plastered.

'He can't be involved, can he?'

'He's a lying, cheating, greedy bastard, but he's patriotic. He can't. He can't be …'

'What can we do?'

Over Colin's shoulder, Kat saw the lights in Tanya's office flickering. 'Put an analyst on calling Edison's number non-stop, with strict instructions that I'm to be buzzed the second it connects. We best get moving. Tanya's hosting this morning's briefing.' The pair, grasping their full mugs, made their way to Tanya's office where Jock, Mo and Natalie were waiting for them.

*

0715, Friday, 7th July, New Scotland Yard, Embankment, London
Sergeant Nick Walsh gulped down his third coffee of the morning, but his eyes still felt heavy. He had left home at 6.00 a.m., leaving his wife to fend for herself with their crotchety six-month-old. Nick had not slept for the best part of a week, as teeth pushed painfully on his baby's inflamed gums. Despite her current sleep-deprived monster status, Florence had been all that the besotted father, Nick, could think about. A picture of her smiling face, framed with curly blonde hair, served as his screen saver – a reminder of the most joyful day of his twenty-eight-year life.

Doug gave him a friendly slap on the back as he arrived in the canteen. 'You look like you haven't slept in a week,' he said and pulled out a chair to sit opposite his friend and colleague.

'I haven't,' Nick confirmed. 'Flo's teething, Shelley's exhausted …' he trailed off, realising the futility of trying to explain to his childless, bachelor friend what it was like at home.

'So, are we still trawling through those bloody addresses?'

'Mo's lot have a lead on two of them. They narrowed it down somehow.' Up to that point, with limited information with which to whittle down the search, it had been a manual process of visiting and surveilling each address in Barinak Holdings' inventory. They had worked in order of proximity to the Brooks Road squat. They had got nothing from the first forty-one properties on their list and had already covered the areas of West Ham, East Ham and Canning Town.

'Ahhhh, James Bond strikes again,' Doug quipped. 'We had better get going then, hadn't we?' Doug shoved the remainder of a ham and cheese croissant into his mouth, and chewing vigorously, he got up. Nick pulled himself to his feet wearily.

Mo arrived in the canteen looking harassed. 'Sorry guys,' he said, breathlessly, 'I was held up in a briefing.'

The morning meeting had been a bit of a circus. Mo hadn't been aware of the previous night's events until he'd arrived at Thames House and Natalie had given him a whistle-stop account of everything that had happened following her and Jock's close call with the police in Elephant & Castle. The Grid was gripped in a frenzy of activity when Mo arrived, and it took some time for Tanya, who, to Mo's surprise, was chairing the morning's meeting, to get through all the briefing notes.

He was relieved to see that Doug and Nick hadn't hit the road without him. Although he knew that the two policemen themselves were not vindictive, Mo wouldn't have put it past Colchester to engineer things such that Mo was left twiddling his thumbs in the incident room for another day, especially after everything that had happened overnight. Since Monday's tense meeting with Kat and Colchester, Mo's week had been tedious. He'd been out on the surveillance operation on Tuesday and Wednesday, but the previous day had missed his ride, having been waylaid by Kat's morning brief and spent a monotonous day at a desk in the incident room, trying to work out a better way of prioritising the property search.

'Any news from your lot?' Doug asked as the three men made their way to the car park.

'No, not really.'

'Not really,' Nick repeated, and nudged Doug with an elbow. 'That's James Bond-speak for there is some news but nothing he can divulge to mere plods like us.'

Mo laughed it off. He was a little surprised to discover that neither Nick nor Doug knew of the issues that had arisen between their institutions overnight or that a major arrest was planned for the coming afternoon. Mo marvelled at Colchester's management style and felt grateful for Kat and Tanya's enlightened approach, whereby, notwithstanding security clearance levels, the team, from lowly analyst upward, were kept apprised of all operational developments. 'You never know where a good idea might come from,' Tanya always said. 'Just because you've been at your desk the longest doesn't mean your eyes are any better.'

That afternoon promised to be a busy one, and Mo was already anxious to learn of the outcome of Jamie's arrest. Like the rest of F-section, he harboured doubts on whether it was the right move. He turned his focus to the first address secured from Barinak Holdings and tried to put thoughts of Jamie's arrest out of his mind. 'St Joseph's Court, Carpenter's Road,' he instructed Doug. He put the car in gear, and as he pulled out of the car park, Mo grasped the two policemen on the shoulder and said, 'This is it, lads. Today's the day we find the buggers.'

They crawled through traffic on the A11 for forty-five minutes and arrived at the first property well after 10.00 a.m.

*

1156, Friday 7th July, Thames House, Westminster, London

Kat threw her phone across her desk in disgust. 'What's the news?' Colin asked, not taking his eyes off his screen.

'They went ahead with the arrest.' She'd just hung up the phone on a junior officer in Colchester's team, who had been instructed to let Kat know that Colchester would be interrogating the suspect once he'd had some lunch.

'Did they go with the money laundering charge?'

'Yes, thank goodness. But I doubt our true targets have fallen for that cover story.' Kat perched on the desk next to Colin. 'Since I've got a bit of time whilst Colchester enjoys his lunch, what have you got for me on Yousuf?'

'I can confidently say that Yousuf is the pseudonym for Kerim Dastan. We know that Dastan had a line in forged documents, it was one of the reasons for denying his brother a visa. He definitely hasn't left the country by traditional means under either identity, and there's no reports on the wires of anyone matching his description arriving in Skagen which would be the most likely unofficial route out for him.'

'I don't think he's gone far though if he's running VIPERSNEST. Keep an eye on that bank account for activity. And start scanning CCTV around the Barinak office and the home address Gurbuz gave us. Let's see if we can't build a picture of his movements. Gurbuz said he'd last seen him on Thursday, a week ago.'

Colin nodded and scribbled himself a note. 'On it.'

'Right, I'm off. Let's see what Jamie has to say. Maybe we've got it all wrong, and he'll confess it *all* and give us the attack location.'

'I wouldn't mind being wrong if that were the case.'

As she walked to Scotland Yard, Kat dialled Edison for the umpteenth time without success.

*

1245, Friday 7th July, New Scotland Yard, Westminster, London

Kat crowded into the anteroom with Colchester and two detective constables. The one-way glass revealed their suspect, Jamie Dunn, his head was bowed, and his hands were clasped around the top of his head. He cut a dejected figure.

'Has he been advised of the revised charges?' Colchester asked.

'Yes,' replied one of the constables who'd been introduced to Kat as Jason Morley.

'Did he say anything when you told him about the terrorism charges?' Kat queried.

'His eyeballs nearly fell out of his head. He said something about messed-up code.'

'We had better get on with it then.' Colchester sounded gleeful. He rubbed his hands. 'Time we let this little shit know just how much trouble he's in.'

'Michael,' Kat interjected, Colchester's hand was already on the door handle, ready to enter the interview room. He looked down his nose at her, surprised to be addressed by his first name. Kat ploughed on, 'We need information. If he has any, we *really* can't afford for him to clam up.'

'Are you trying to tell me how to conduct this interview, young lady?'

'Not at all.' Kat pulled her shoulders back unwilling to be intimidated by the senior policeman.

'Good. Let's go, Morley.' He pulled open the door and Kat watched through the glass as he strode into the room. Jamie looked up as he entered. His eyes were red, and his face was drained of all colour. The observers saw Colchester mouth an introduction.

'Can we get some sound?' Kat said.

The policeman fiddled with the control panel, and they heard Colchester and Morley introducing themselves for the purposes of the tape. Colchester pulled back a chair noisily, sat down and leaned back, his arms crossed in a practised pose. Detective Morley took the seat next to him, placing a khaki folder on the table in front of him and sitting forward, his fingers laced together in front of him. 'Please could the suspect confirm his name for the tape?'

'Jamie Dunn,' Jamie muttered. The detective asked him to confirm his address, and Jamie gave the address in Elephant & Castle that Edison had watched him go back to three days ago. Reminded of the events of earlier in the week, Kat wondered how only a few days had passed. She took a long draught of the coffee she'd managed to secure from the canteen.

'Thank you.' Detective Morley went on, 'At this point, I'd like to remind you that you do not have to say anything, but it may harm your defence if you do not mention, when questioned, something which you later rely on in court. Anything you do say may be given in evidence. Do you understand?'

Jamie nodded.

'I must ask you to confirm your understanding verbally, Mr Dunn.'

'Yes,' Jamie croaked, fresh tears welling up in his eyes. To Kat, he looked younger than his twenty-four years. The interview room had diminished him from the cocky, self-assured young man Edison had described.

'Jamie Dunn, you have been arrested on suspicion of financing terrorism acts and money laundering in relation to terrorism acts.'

Jamie shook his head violently and opened his mouth, 'I've no idea what you're talking about.'

From his reclined pose, Colchester fixed his eyes on Jamie. 'I find that very hard to believe, Jamie.' Colchester paused, leant forward and jammed a finger on the folder that lay in front of Morley. 'In here, I have the details of every trade made at Penwill &

Mallinson. Every time BitCoin left the fund. Every time Ethereum arrived in the accounts. Dates. Times. All neatly recorded on an immutable ledger. Very neat. Now, I can cross-reference those transactions with the accounts for the fund. What do you think I will find, Jamie?'

More silence from across the table. Jamie looked, aghast, from one police officer to the other and back again.

Colchester took a deep breath. 'You see, Jamie, it's possible that you had no idea why you were syphoning off the money with your fancy algorithm.' Colchester eyed his suspect who was staring at the table, his shoulders were rounded.

'I don't know anything,' a whisper escaped Jamie's lips.

He's terrified, thought Kat. He's been stitched up. Damn it, Edison, couldn't you have worked out who was pulling his strings already?

Colchester pounced. His tone softened slightly, 'That's what I thought. You didn't know what the money was being used for. Is that right?'

Silence on the other side of the table.

'Someone paid you a decent wad of cash to sort all this out, and you were seduced by the money on offer. I don't blame you there, didn't ask any questions. Is that right?'

More silence.

'What I need to know is who asked you to do this?'

Finally, Jamie snapped. 'I have no idea what you're talking about! My code was a mess. Something kept on going wrong. Every time I tried to clean it up, the bottom fell out of it again. I really don't know what you're talking about … syphoning off funds … financing terrorists … I just don't know what the hell you're talking about.'

Colchester stood up suddenly, slamming his palms on the table.

Everyone around the table jumped. 'Listen,' Colchester roared. 'I'm not buying that. What a load of bullshit. Believe me, the charges we will bring against you will see you behind bars for the rest of your life.'

Jamie looked disorientated. It was as though the parties in the interrogation room were having two different conversations. He looked around as if seeking someone who might listen to him.

'It was just … I didn't want anyone to know I couldn't fix it. I pulled copies. Took it home to try to get to the bottom of what was going on. But every time I uploaded it again, there was another bug … another glitch … I can't … I don't see … how …'

On the other side of the glass, Kat muttered, 'I'm wasting my time.'

As she left the room, she heard, over the tinny intercom, Morley clearing his throat and saying, 'Interview paused at fifteen forty-seven.'

A junior police constable entered the room and escorted Jamie back to a cell. Colchester swept through the anteroom without stopping. 'Don't think we'll get anything more from him today,' Kat heard him say to Morley as they retreated down the corridor.

You're not going to get anything more from him, full stop, she thought.

As she left the building, she switched on her phone. It rang immediately.

'Kat, it's Colin.' He sounded breathless and excited, 'We've got a lead on Yousuf.'

Chapter Sixteen

1343, Friday, 7th July, Moniedubh Estate, nr. North Ballachulish, Lochaber

The sign for the Moniedubh Estate was faded and almost totally obscured by moss, but Edison didn't need it. He turned onto the familiar potholed drive on auto-pilot. On one side of the track, the land banked steeply upwards, but on the other, the heathered hillside sloped gently toward the main road from where he'd come. The land disappeared over a ridge a few hundred yards away, and beyond, Edison could see the water of Loch Leven, cold and grey, reflecting the menacing ash-coloured skies above. He could feel his heart beating faster.

Edison's hire car bounced over the uneven surface. Occasionally, he had to swerve to avoid the sheep that galloped out in front of him without warning. Having driven for about three miles, he rounded a bend and saw, some way up the road, a squat, stone-built house, topped by a chimney pot from which a spire of smoke came. Edison briefly considered reversing back around the corner and out of sight to continue his journey on foot, but the thought came to him too late as a man, dressed in heavy khaki trousers, an oilskin jacket and sturdy boots, appeared from the front door of the little house.

Edison pulled the car up a short distance from where the man stood. He hauled himself out of the car and pulled his jacket around him against the breeze. It was cold, and the morning's bright sunshine in Inverness had given way to a blanket of cloud as Edison had driven west. He took a deep breath. The smell of the peat fire filled his lungs, and a fierce wind whipped at his hair. The man made no move to greet Edison as he approached. Edison tried desperately to remember his name.

'Mr Edison. You're here to visit Sir Donald, I don't doubt?' the man said once Edison was close enough for the words to reach him without being lost to the wind.

'Macarthur, yes, is he home?' Edison replied, the gatekeeper's name rolled off Edison's tongue, dragged from the depths of his memory. He tried to keep his face neutral. Only for the first time considering the possibility that the man he had travelled the length of the country to visit might not be in.

'Aye, doesn't get away much these days,' the man replied.

'How are you keeping?'

'It's been awful quiet of late.' The two men considered each other briefly. 'You're up from London then? He doesn't get many visitors. Just the occasional suit comes through. Business affairs, apparently.' A phone sounded from the depths of the gatekeeper's cottage, and Edison's opportunity to press for more information on Hughes' business associates evaporated. Macarthur hurried back into the lodge, and the shrill noise stopped. He reappeared soon afterwards. 'He says he's been expecting you.'

Edison felt his blood freeze in his veins as a jolt of adrenalin shot through him. He felt light-headed. How did he know he was coming?

The gatekeeper laughed when he saw Edison's horrified expression. 'He's got a mighty strong pair of binoculars, you know. You can see the house from here.' He pointed up the road to where Edison could just make out a large familiar building. 'But with those binoculars, he spies on the goings on for miles around.'

Edison relaxed a little, but the shock was enough to remind him to be on his guard. The binoculars were a perfectly reasonable explanation, but it was quite possible that Hughes was keeping tabs on Edison's movements.

'Right, you best not keep his lordship waiting, as you well know,' the gatekeeper insisted and ushered Edison back into his hire car.

Edison wound down the window before pulling away, 'Is the Drovers Inn still the best pub in the village?'

'Aye,' Macarthur eyed him warily. 'I would avoid anywhere further up the loch, tends to be a bit touristy.' Edison filed the information carefully away and put the car in gear. He approached the house with trepidation.

*

Hughes was standing, straight-backed and head held high, in the shadow of the imposing mansion. He was flanked by two large dogs – one lay at his feet whilst the other sat back on its haunches, looking as proud as his master. The enormous double doors, one of which was slightly ajar, rose behind him, framing the portrait.

From Edison's vantage point behind the wheel, he could see Sir Donald Hughes watching his approach. He killed the engine and opened the door, not taking his gaze from the man in front of the house. He was now approaching, the two dogs trotting obediently at his side. When the lurchers saw who it was they broke rank and threw themselves affectionately at Edison. He squatted down and fondled them.

'Eddie,' Sir Donald Hughes said, with what appeared to be genuine enthusiasm, 'what a truly delightful surprise. If you had called ahead, I would have made sure your welcome was a little warmer, but as it is, I've just returned from a romp with the hounds, so you will have to forgive my appearance.'

'Well, I was visiting Charlie – he's on holiday near Inverness – and I couldn't not drop in, Don.' Responding to Hughes' effusions,

Edison threw on a cover act and prayed his bravado looked authentic. He had steeled himself for a cool reception, filled with suspicion. Was it possible, Edison wondered, that Hughes didn't know that he was the whistle-blower? Surely not.

Hughes winced at the nickname. 'It's a long journey,' Donald went on, 'come along inside.' He put a strong arm around Edison's shoulders and steered him in the direction of the house. Edison felt the grip of the older man's hand on his shoulder and an almost imperceptible squeeze, full of menace and control.

Inside a cavernous hallway, Donald pulled off his green Hunter wellies, and there was silence between the two men. His boots shod, he pulled on a pair of brogues. 'Elizabeth,' he called. When he got no response, he tried again more loudly, 'Elizabeth!' Nothing. 'Where is she?' Hughes muttered to himself.

From somewhere in the depths of the house, Lady Elizabeth appeared, looking flustered. 'Yes dear,' she said before she spotted Edison, standing awkwardly by the front door. 'Edison,' she cried, and a smile played across her thin lips, 'I had no idea you were visiting.'

'A bit of a last-minute thing, Lady Elizabeth,' Edison replied, beginning to relax into his subterfuge. If there was a game afoot, he needed to play it.

'I missed you the last time you were here as I was away. So it must be three years since I last saw you. That lovely dinner when we were still in the Chelsea house and before your beautiful w … oh … I am sorry. Always putting my foot in it.'

'Before my wife died,' Edison finished Lady Elizabeth's sentence for her. He remembered the evening she mentioned. At the end of it, as he and Ellie had got into bed together, she'd turned to him, full of earnest, and uttered the words that had come back to him only the previous day, 'I don't trust him. Not one bit,' she'd said.

'Don't be daft Ellie,' Edison had defended Hughes.

'Seriously, Eddie, there's something off about him. You really must be careful.' When she wouldn't drop the matter, they had argued, and the topic of Donald Hughes' trustworthiness was never raised again. Ellie had dutifully accompanied her husband to Scotland occasionally and made small talk with Edison's mentor at functions. How right you were, Ellie, he thought.

'Are you still with the Service, dear?' Lady Elizabeth went on, trying to bury her conversational faux-pas without realising she was committing another.

'No,' Edison spoke to Lady Elizabeth, but his eyes flicked to her husband, who was watching the exchange, his face passive. Edison couldn't read him. 'I left shortly after Sir Donald.'

'Oh, what a shame. Donald always spoke so highly of you and your potential.'

'Yes, indeed,' Sir Donald interrupted. 'He had the potential to go right to the top, but mistakes can be so costly on that fragile ladder.' Elizabeth looked at him blankly. 'Elizabeth, we shouldn't keep our esteemed guest waiting in the hallway. We get so few visitors these days, but my memory is that the decorous thing to do is to offer tea to a weary traveller on their arrival.'

'Yes, yes, I shall speak to Maggie. Will you be in the study?'

'Indeed. Follow me, Edison. We have a lot to catch up on.'

They entered the study, and a lurcher immediately colonised one of the sofas. 'You will have to tell me all the news from Thames House.' Hughes spoke smoothly, but Edison could feel the undercurrents.

Edison didn't miss a beat, 'Like I said Don, I'm not with the Service anymore.'

'Do take a seat.' Edison did, and Hughes busied himself

emptying his pockets into a desk drawer. Edison noticed two mobile handsets being slipped in before Hughes closed and locked it.

'So, you *are* no longer with Five? I did hear such a rumour, but I must say I was a little surprised, I wouldn't have expected them to let such a talent go. But then I did hear another rumour that someone matching your description is working in Canary Wharf. Why would you use a cover name, I wonder, if you're not in the employ of the Security Service?' Donald stood up and crossed to the drinks stand.

'You *do* keep your ear to the ground,' Edison tried to sound nonchalant.

'A very dear friend of mine works there. Indeed, you met her, I think, the last time you were here.' A frisson of tension hung in the air between them at the mention of the weekend it had all changed between them.

'Oh?' Edison wracked his brains. He would have recognised one of the bank's staff if he'd met them before, surely?

'Anna Graham, the Turkish Ambassador's god-daughter, she's one of the MD's secretaries.'

Edison reeled. Had he met Anna before? Edison combed through his memories of that ill-fated weekend. 'I ... I don't remember meeting her,' he admitted, his veneer slipping slightly.

Donald revelled in the younger man's discomfort. 'No?' Donald waved his hand as if dismissing the topic, 'You did rather rush off that weekend, maybe she arrived after you'd gone.' Hughes crossed the room to the drinks trolley. 'The tea will be here shortly, I am sure, but could I offer you something a little stronger first?' Edison nodded. 'And yes,' Donald turned sharply and thrust a generous measure of whisky in a cut-glass tumbler into Edison's hand, 'I do keep my ear to the ground, as you put it. I hired you, Edison. Handpicked from a crop of very talented young men at

Oxford. You may understand, one day, the bond between a mentor and his protégé.'

Edison felt his stomach lurch. The debt of gratitude he had felt toward Hughes for recruiting him as a graduate had meant he had sat on his findings for months before reporting the director general, feeling the full weight of the personal treachery when he did so. He took a long swig of whisky and let the warmth of the alcohol seep through his body. He collected his thoughts. Could Anna be the missing link in all of this? Was her connection to Hughes another coincidence? What had Hughes got himself mixed up in, and was he aware of the disastrous consequences?

'The wires tell me there's been an arrest at Penwill & Mallinson,' Hughes went on. 'Nasty business. Some poor chap caught up in money laundering.'

Edison's eyes widened and his mind raced. Jamie had been arrested.

'You hadn't heard?' Hughes said smoothly. 'I would have thought you would have been at the centre of that little storm.'

'Do you have any idea what kind of a storm *you're* caught up in, Don?' Edison exploded.

'What on earth are you talking about, dear boy?'

'The money,' Edison rolled on breathlessly, 'you've got at Penwill's. Your friend, Anna. There's going to be an attack. Terrorists. You need to get out. Whatever it is you're doing, get out.'

'What on earth are you talking about? Are you accusing me of something, son?' The last word shot through him like a bullet. Memories of the time they'd spent together, the relationship they'd shared, akin to the one Edison had longed for as a child growing up with an absent father.

Donald moved over to where Edison sat, clasping his tumbler in both hands to stop himself from shaking. He laid a hand on

Edison's shoulder, and the younger man felt its menacing weight. 'You and I are the same, Eddie. Both dragged ourselves up from nothing, married ourselves into better families …'

'You and I are nothing alike, Don,' Edison growled.

There was a knock on the door, signalling the arrival of the tea, borne in by the housekeeper. The tray was deposited on the coffee table. Edison sat in a leather bucket chair on one side of the table whilst Sir Donald loomed over him. He hadn't removed his hand. The housekeeper carefully poured two cups of tea into the fine bone china and without speaking, offered Edison the silver milk jug. He took it and poured a minuscule amount of milk into the tea. He watched it swirl into the brown, hot water. 'Thank you,' he muttered. The housekeeper bobbed her head in response and turned to Sir Donald.

'Thank you,' Donald said once they were both furnished with tea and generous slices of fruit cake. The housekeeper retreated from the room.

Donald released Edison's shoulder and sat down in the leather wingback chair opposite Edison. He picked up his teacup and fixed Edison with a piercing gaze. 'So, what is all this Edison? You're back working for the Service. There are arrests at the bank where you are, I assume, working undercover and then, out of the blue, you show up here, in my home, bandying accusations of terrorism at me.'

Edison flailed under the gaze of the older man. He was twenty-three again, desperate to impress the senior spy.

'Maybe you really weren't ready to return to the field, Eddie.'

The allegation seemed to focus Edison's mind. He decided to appeal to Donald Hughes' compassion. It must be buried in there somewhere, he thought. He sat up straight and met Donald's eye. 'You may have the morality of a snake, Don, when it comes to some of the decisions you have made, in both the distant and recent past.

That is what sets us apart. But the one thing we do have in common is that we're patriots, and whatever you're mixed up in, you need to get out of it. I am telling you that in deference to everything you did for me. Before.'

'How dare you come into my house and talk of deference,' Hughes snarled. 'You have accused me once, with disastrous consequences for us both. And now you have the audacity to do so again.'

'I am not accusing you.' Edison gritted his teeth. 'I am offering you a warning.'

Edison knew the words had fallen on deaf ears even before Hughes spoke again. 'I think it would be best, Scott Edison, if you were to leave my home. I do not believe we have anything more to say to one another.'

Edison bowed his head and shook it.

Sir Donald smiled a hyena's smile and got to his feet. 'It was a pleasure to see you Edison. The news of Eloise's death and the circumstances under which you left the Service really did break my heart.' It was as though the conversation that had passed between them had never occurred. The two men walked through the house, back to the front door. Both dogs followed obediently, and Donald ruffled Angus's ears fondly.

'It is strange,' Donald said as they paused in the hallway, one hand on the front door, ready to open it, 'how life goes. How bad luck befalls people.' He was speaking wistfully but his gaze was trained on Edison, making him feel uncomfortable. 'One does wonder sometimes, what you might have done to deserve such luck.' Sir Donald opened the door, and with his words ringing in his ears, Edison bolted for his car.

He saw Sir Donald Hughes in his rear-view mirror as he accelerated along the potholed driveway, still in the doorway, his hand raised in a regal wave. Edison urged the car to go faster. When he looked again, Donald was gone.

*

Donald Hughes peeled the forced smile from his face and allowed a thunderous scowl to arrange itself in its place. He stomped through the hallway, ignoring his wife who was wafting down the stairs in the hope of some news of their departed guest.

'Donald,' Lady Elizabeth ventured, trying to engage her husband in conversation. But the heavy oak door to the study slammed as she reached the bottom of the stairs, and she retreated to the garden room.

But for the ticking of the carriage clock, the room was silent. Donald found himself shaking. He crossed the room to the drinks trolley. The glass stopper tinkled against the decanter as his tremulous hand removed it and he sloshed a sizable measure into a glass. Holding it to his lips, the golden liquid vanished in a single gulp, and he poured another. He jumped when Angus' wet nose nuzzled his hand. His nerves were on edge. Edison's visit had rattled him. The best spy he had ever worked with was on his trail. But what on earth was he talking about? Terrorist threats to London linked to the crypto fund at Penwill's – it beggared belief. Anna couldn't be caught up in something so dangerous. All they wanted, she and him, was the money. For him to escape the shackles of his marriage and begin a new life together. If that meant a few illicit imports of very profitable collateral, so be it. He'd only invested in the fund because she'd asked him to. He needed to protect his own interests. Divert Scott Edison's considerable intellect away from him and his business affairs.

'It's not like it's hurting anyone,' Donald muttered. 'Time to call in a favour.'

Donald picked up the telephone. He didn't need a secure line for this particular call – he didn't mind if this conversation was broadcast to the world – it was time to cause Scott Edison a good amount of discomfort. He dialled.

Chapter Seventeen

1546, Friday 7th July, Thames House, Westminster, London

'Tell me everything,' Kat demanded of Colin as she flew through the doors at Thames House.

'Anna Graham,' Colin said, his eyes shining, 'was picked up as she tried to access the Barinak Holdings account at an ATM in Canary Wharf.' He tailed Kat across the floor to the investigation board, which she surveyed with her hands on her hips.

'We don't have a picture of her.' She pointed at the collection of mugshots of the Penwill & Mallinson's team, clustered at one side of the board.

'Can Edison tell us anything about her?'

'Has the analyst you put on calling him got through to him?' she spat at him with a degree of vehemence she regretted immediately. Edison's disappearance was playing havoc with her emotions.

Colin held his hands up in mock surrender, 'We've not managed to get through to him.'

'Sorry,' Kat muttered. She looked up to see Tanya advancing across the floor, weaving her way purposefully through the banks of analysts. She looked livid – her mouth set in a grim line, her eyes narrow. Kat turned to Colin and reeled off instructions, 'Get in touch with Colchester, and tell him I'll be there for the interview. Get me a picture of Anna up here too, and start digging into any possible links with Yousuf.'

'My office, now.' Tanya towered over Kat, delivered her missive and turned on her heels to stalk back to her office. Kat followed, thinking, what now?

*

1723, Friday 7th July, Carpenter's Road, Stratford, London

Mo yawned loudly – the warm fug in the back of the car was almost overwhelming. The sweltering July day was slipping into a sweaty, claustrophobic evening. Early that morning, he, Nick and Doug had arrived at Carpenter's Road, the first of the two addresses Kat had phoned through from Barinak Holdings.

'Is this it?' Mo asked as they pulled into the car park. He craned his neck to look up at the block of flats.

'Yup,' Doug said.

'We're interested in flat thirteen.' Mo opened the door and hopped out, 'I'll go take a look.'

He strode across the car park toward the entrance of the tower block. He was examining the buzzer system when a young man pushed open the door from the inside. 'Doesn't work, bruv,' he told Mo and held the door open for him to enter.

'Thanks,' Mo replied and went inside. He glanced around. The communal area was shabby and smelt faintly of urine. The brick staircase led up to a balcony, open to the elements, that wrapped around the building. Off the balcony, Mo counted five front doors. The second floor was a carbon copy, so Mo expected to find his target address on the next level.

The flat in question didn't offer much to differentiate it from its neighbours. The paint on the front door was peeling, the windows were grimy, and Mo, not wanting to draw attention to himself, only took a cursory glance through them as he passed. The place was in darkness, and the curtains were pulled. Mo moved past the flat and kept on ascending, affecting the air of someone in search of a particular address. He considered the drawn curtains as he climbed the next flight of stairs. Would an empty flat have drawn curtains?

On the sixth floor, Mo shrugged for the benefit of any onlookers, to all intents and purposes, he had not found the address he was looking for, turned and jogged back down the stairs.

He got back in the car. Doug had been to a corner shop and handed Mo a coke. 'Thanks,' Mo said and took a long swig.

'Anything?' Doug asked.

'No, the curtains are drawn. Pretty empty up there. Didn't see anyone. If we pull round to the other side of the building, we can keep an eye on the door.' Nick did as Mo recommended and parked the car in a shaded spot with sight lines to number thirteen, and the neighbours at number twelve, on the third floor.

'And so, we wait,' Nick said, sitting back and drawing on his can of Sprite.

But wait for what, Mo wondered. He busied himself, noting the details and plates of the handful of vehicles in the estate's car park. A clapped-out Ford Escort that was almost as old as he was. A couple of hatchbacks. An expensive-looking estate car. And a white Ford Transit van bearing the insignia of an industrial laundry company called 'LaunderLoad'. He called Colin at Thames House and gave him this information' to run through the system, more in hope than expectation that there might be anything noteworthy about them.

Colin picked up his phone. He sounded harassed. 'Everything ok?' Mo asked.

'The shit has well and truly hit the fan here,' Colin replied.

'What's going on?'

'The Home Secretary's on the rampage.'

Mo glanced at his companions, who were listening with interest to his side of the conversation. He got out of the car, unwilling to share the Service's troubles in public, 'What's happened?'

'Tanya was summoned to Whitehall with the DG not long ago …' Mo heard Kat's harried voice in the background and a reply from Colin. He came back on the line. 'Listen, I have to go. Patch over those details, and I'll see what I can do, but I'm not making any promises.'

Mo hung up the phone and shot an email with the vehicle details over to Colin with no expectation that he would be able to look at them.

From their roasting vantage point, the three men watched a handful of school-uniformed children arrive home at about 4.00 p.m. Shortly afterwards, a few of them reappeared, uniform shed in favour of jeans and football shirts, and kicked a ball around in the car park for a while. An hour later, from a lofty floor, a woman screeched a summons, and two of the boys disappeared inside, in search of their supper.

Each time a car arrived or left the car park, Mo noted the time and information. If it was a new vehicle, he sent it through to Colin but got no response.

Doug was dozing fitfully in the front seat, and Mo was scrolling on his mobile when Nick said, 'All right boys, we have movement.'

'Finally,' Mo said.

All three of them trained their eyes on the door to number thirteen which had opened. A bearded man appeared and lit a cigarette. A second, clean-shaven man came onto the balcony beside him. The first offered the second the cigarette, who took a drag, breathing the smoke out into the summer evening air. Both men were of Middle Eastern colouring. They spoke sparingly to one another as they shared the cigarette. Barely ten minutes after their appearance on the balcony, both men went back into the flat.

All three men in the car let out a long sigh.

'Well that was worth waiting for,' Doug voiced what they were all thinking.

'The flat isn't *supposed* to be occupied,' Mo pointed out.

'Hang on.' Nick clutched at his partner's arm and gestured to the apartment. The door had opened again, and the clean-shaven man was heaving three large sacks onto the walkway. He hoisted one onto his shoulder and made for the stairs. The man with the beard added a further three sacks to the pile on the walkway. He, too, shouldered a bag. A third man left the flat. Locking the door behind him, he followed his flatmates.

They moved to the Ford Transit van and threw their loads into the back.

'Launderers,' Mo muttered.

They watched the men make two more trips to the third floor, loading the laundry into the back to the van. They shared another cigarette, leaning against the parked transit. Mo took a few photographs but felt that this was another dead end on what was increasingly becoming fruitless line of enquiry. From what Kat had told him, the man she'd met yesterday at Barinak Holdings had very little grasp of what was going on with the property letting company. Maybe the files weren't up to date. Maybe these men were letting the property legitimately.

The clean-shaven man got into the driver's seat and the other two clambered into the cab on the passenger side. They drove away just as Mo's phone buzzed in his lap.

'All right, Mo,' Colin said when he answered. He sounded more relaxed, 'Sorry it's taken me a while to get back to you on this.'

'Don't worry,' Mo said. 'Have thing's calmed down a bit?'

'Sort of. Tanya's back on the Grid but has been holed up in her office all afternoon. The DG, Featherstone, was there for a while. Kat's just back from the Dunn interview at the Met but was straight in with Tanya the second she got through the door.'

Mo whistled. 'What's going on?'

'Your guess is as good as mine, mate.' Colin paused as if he was trying to remember why he'd called, 'Oh yes, those vehicles. Nothing noteworthy really, except for that Transit.'

'Yeah?' Mo's ears pricked up, and he sat up straighter, 'What about it?'

'Well, it was reported stolen from the premises of the laundry company this morning.'

'Shit.'

'Something in that then?'

'Three guys left one of our hot properties in that van ten minutes ago.'

'We can probably track it down on CCTV,' Colin offered.

'Can you get onto that now?' Mo replied.

'Ok, I'll let you know if ANPR picks anything up.' Colin hung up and Mo relayed the detail of the conversation to his companions.

'Come on then,' Nick said, starting the engine, 'let's track 'em down. How far can they have got?'

'Which way did they go?' Mo asked. Both Doug and Nick shook their heads. 'Wild goose chase. Let's see what the cameras pick up.'

The three men waited impatiently as five minutes ticked by before Mo's phone rang again.

'They've been picked up on the south side of the Rotherhithe Tunnel,' Colin said. 'We tracked them as best we could but lost them somewhere around London Bridge.'

'Bugger.' The two men in the front of the car looked defeated, knowing they had lost their lead. 'Thanks, Colin. I'll come in.'

'Ok, Mo. See you in a bit.'

Dispirited, Nick, Doug and Mo drove back into the city and said their farewells at Scotland Yard.

'See you in the morning,' Nick feigned cheeriness.

'At least we've made some progress,' Mo tried to offer a positive light on their day's endeavours.

'And let the buggers slip through our fingers. It's two steps forward, one step back in this job,' Doug growled. 'I'm going to the pub. Either of you fancy it?'

'Better get home,' Nick replied.

'Ah yes, Mrs Walsh will be waiting for you. Bond?' Doug turned to Mo hopefully.

'Sorry, got to check in back at base. This is looking pretty ominous don't you think?'

*

2010, Friday 7th July, Thames House, Westminster, London

Mo scanned through the security doors that opened onto the open-plan floor, where Tanya's section operated. There were a dozen officers and analysts still working diligently at their desks. He was surprised to find the usually buzzing section in near silence. He scanned the office for Colin and found him leaning over the desk of a graduate analyst – Mo thought her name was Hannah – speaking to her in hushed tones. The young woman looked uneasy. Colin looked up at Mo's approach. 'Keep running the ANPR scans, and let me know if anything comes up for that van,' he instructed the graduate. She placed shaking hands back on her keyboard. Colin nodded to Mo, indicating they should meet in the men's toilets.

The door had barely swung shut behind the two men when Mo exploded, 'What the hell's been going on here? It's like a morgue.'

Colin puffed out his cheeks and let out a long breath. 'Edison's gone rogue,' he said.

'What do you mean? Gone rogue?'

'Donald Hughes has been onto the Home Secretary. They're still best chums, despite everything. Apparently, Edison took it upon himself to go to his home and accuse him of involvement in this operation.'

'What?!' Mo was absorbing everything that Colin was saying. It had been a very long day, cooped up in the sauna of a surveillance vehicle. 'Where on earth did he get the idea that Hughes was somehow involved?'

'His wife is invested in the Ethereum fund.'

'There are a lot of people invested in that fund.'

'Exactly, but you know there's history between Hughes and Edison? Edison blames Hughes for having him kicked out of the Service. And vice versa. We can't track Edison down,' Colin went on. He was leaning on the edge of the basin, his head bowed. He looked exhausted. 'He's gone completely dark. Somewhere in the Highlands. All that Tanya's worried about is finding him. I'm lucky I've got Helen to pursue the van lead.'

'Helen not Hannah,' Mo said.

'What?' Colin lifted his head and looked, via the mirror, at his colleague.

'I thought her name was Hannah.'

'No, it's Helen,' Colin seemed irritated by the diversion, 'and if she hadn't been working late, I'd have to leave the van – which is well and truly the only real lead we have on HAPSBURG at the moment.'

The door swung open, and Kat came in. Both men looked nonplussed. 'This is the men's,' Mo pointed out.

'I saw you come in here earlier,' she explained, her voice deadpan, 'and maybe, just maybe, she won't find me in here.' Kat put her back against the wall, slid down to sit on the floor and put her head in her hands. 'I've never known her to be so unreasonable. Apparently, this is all my fault.'

'How can it possibly be your fault?' Colin asked. Both men

looked at their boss with concern.

'Good question,' Kat snapped. 'It was *her* call to bring Edison in as an agent. It was *her* risk, and she said she'd run him. I'm not his minder. I'm trying to manage the biggest operation of my life. There are three men at large, running around London with Semtex packed into their pockets. We've just picked up a hot suspect. I should be interrogating *her*, not babysitting a rogue agent that I didn't even recruit.'

'You haven't heard anything from him?' Mo said, softly. Kat and Edison's relationship was an open secret amongst the team.

All the tension in Kat's body flooded out of her, and she burst into tears. 'No,' she breathed through her tears. 'I'm so worried.'

Mo shifted awkwardly from one foot to another, horrified that he'd moved the senior officer to tears. Colin moved over and crouched on his haunches next to Kat's distraught figure. He placed a tender hand on her shoulder, and Kat leaned into his subtle embrace.

'What do we need to do?' Colin asked.

'*I* need to speak to Anna. *We* need to find that van. And if, whilst we're doing that, we could also find Edison, well that would be grand.' Mo, Kat and Colin fell silent as they contemplated the challenge of locating their errant friend and colleague when he clearly didn't want to be found.

Kat stood up, crossed to the sinks and examined herself in the mirror, delicately rubbing a smudge of mascara away from the corner of her eye. Her eyes lit up as a thought struck her. 'Charlie's on holiday in the Highlands with his kids. Edison told me he was taking a bit of time out to visit him. So, he can help us find Edison.'

'We're talking thirty thousand square miles, Kat,' Colin pointed out. 'How do we know where to tell Charlie to start looking.'

'Hughes' wife's family home, the Moniedubh Estate, is near

Glencoe – I think the closest village is Ballachulish,' her tongue struggled round the Gaelic words. 'What time is it?'

Mo looked at his watch. 'Half-past eight.'

'There will be a handful of pubs, and Edison will be in one of them,' Kat concluded confidently, looking a lot cheerier than she had a little while earlier. Mo and Colin nodded, acknowledging the plan. 'Ok,' Kat went on. She gripped the edge of the sink, steeling herself for emerging onto the office floor. 'I'll call Charlie.' She was well and truly back in the zone now, the emotional crisis of the past few minutes carefully boxed and put away in a recess of her mind. 'When are Colchester's lot going into the Carpenter's Road flat?'

'At first light with the bomb squad.'

'Can you be there?'

'Wouldn't miss it.'

'In which case, get out of here. It's late.' Mo didn't look like he wanted to go, keen to stick with the team in a moment of crisis. Kat noted his hesitation. 'Go,' she insisted. 'That's an order.'

Mo nodded and shuffled off. With the departure of the junior officer, Kat's veneer of confidence drifted a little. Colin had worked with Kat since she'd joined the Service, and he felt protective toward her. 'We better get on with it.'

'Kat,' Colin said, putting an arm around her small frame, 'you're doing everything you can. You couldn't be doing any more.' He paused as Kat's dark-rimmed eyes filled with tears again, 'And Edison is Tanya's agent. She's running him.'

'But it's *my* investigation,' Kat protested.

'Then let's get to the bottom of it.'

She smiled at him, pulled her shoulders back and walked confidently out the door.

*

Kat picked up her mobile and dug out Charlie's number. She dialled.

'Harrington-Smith,' a voice answered the phone after a single ring. Charlie sounded distant which, along with the faint hum of an engine, gave away the use of a hands-free set.

'Charlie, it's Kat.'

'I haven't found him yet.' There was an unfamiliar hardness in his tone.

'Who called you?'

'Tanya. An hour and a half ago.'

'Oh.'

'So, Tanya Willis' world famous open communication is breaking down,' Charlie went on, his words dripping with sarcasm. 'I'm going to find him. I should be in Ballachulish in under twenty minutes. I can't believe this has happened.'

'Listen, Charlie, I can't get into this. Edison is Tanya's agent. My only concern is for his safety.'

'I'll call you when I've found him,' was all Charlie said before he hung up.

Kat lowered the phone and looked around the office, much emptier than it had been earlier, Colin and Helen were the only people left. 'Anything on the van?' she asked.

'Nothing,' Helen said and added as an afterthought, 'yet.'

Chapter Eighteen

1826, Friday 7th July, Drovers Arms, Ballachulish, Lochaber

Edison pulled up outside the Drovers Arms and switched off the engine. In the silence, he sat in the driver's seat of the little car, collecting his thoughts. His heart was beating fast, and his hands felt clammy as they gripped the steering wheel, his knuckles white. For all that the conversation with Hughes had left him rattled, bringing back painful memories, it was the news of Jamie's arrest that gave him the most concern. And Anna … where did the unassuming secretary fit into all of this? She wasn't the hacker. He knew that much. Edison knew that Jamie had been set up as the scapegoat. He was close to unmasking the true culprit at the bank but not quite. He wanted to get online, smoke him out, but first, he needed a drink. He breathed deeply, picked up his wallet and mobile and got out of the car.

The clouds lay heavy and ashen atop the mountains. The village of Ballachulish sat on the edge of the sea loch which, in the early evening light, was reflecting the colour of the sky. When Edison entered the pub, the few men, already installed with pints around the edges of the public bar, looked up to evaluate the new arrival. They offered suspicious glances and muttered to one another before falling back into silence. Edison took a seat at the bar. Having taken his time to finish the conversation with a regular, the publican approached him, his mouth set in a grim scowl.

'What can I get you?' he growled.

Edison scanned the bottles behind him and selected one from a nearby distillery. He handed over a large note. The barman handed him the whisky and returned to his conversation without offering him any change.

Edison opened his mouth to challenge the barman on the price of the dram but the energy for the confrontation deserted him. He studied the golden liquid in his glass, lost in his thoughts. His phone vibrated on the bar. he ignored it. It vibrated again and again and again, the screen lighting up repeatedly as notifications for a day's worth of messages and missed calls arrived. The pub offered a rare network hotspot, and Edison had been out of signal range since he left Inverness that morning. Edison considered the notifications. Dozens of missed calls from withheld numbers and a couple from Charlie. The final message was from Maria – *Edison* – it read – *Jamie has been arrested. We are worried.* Scared they might come after the rest of us. *x*.

He gulped down the remainder of the whisky, and the surly barman topped up his glass. Edison nodded and pushed more money in his direction. He glanced back at the phone screen once more as it vibrated on the bar. He saw Charlie's caller ID flash up just as the screen went black and the battery died.

He heard the door open to admit another punter.

'Mr Edison,' a familiar voice said, and he felt a clap on his shoulder, 'how was tea with the lord of the manor?'

Edison turned to see the grinning face of Robert Macarthur. Without invitation, the gatekeeper pulled himself onto the vacant bar stool beside Edison. Robert nodded to the barman, 'Two more, Andy.'

The publican obliged with two more whiskies and sheepishly pushed a generous handful of change on a small trivet toward Edison. His companion gulped down the double measure and held the glass up to inspect it. 'They don't make it like that anywhere else in the world,' he said. When Robert set the glass down again, the barman poured another substantial measure. 'Will you have one yourself, Andy?'

The barman paused long enough to suggest a pretence that he might decline, before saying, 'Aye, it is Friday after a long week.' The local he'd been speaking to slunk off to take up a seat elsewhere, and Andy, whisky in one hand, held out his other and said, 'Pleasure to meet you.'

Edison shook the proffered hand.

'You look like a man who's had a rough week. What brings you to meet our honourable laird? You seem a little English compared to his usual guests.'

'What do you mean?' Edison's curiosity was aroused.

Andy gave Edison a conspiratorial look, 'He's often getting foreign visitors.'

'What kind of foreign?'

'A fair few Russians and some wealthy Arabs.'

'Not that they come in here,' Robert added, 'but we see them sweep through in their expensive cars. That's if they don't come by helicopter.'

'Do you know what business they have with Sir Donald?' Edison asked Robert.

'I cannae tell you. But he wines and dines them something proper when they are here.'

'I don't suppose you recognise any of them?'

'No, not the foreign ones. The Brits I know from the TV. Mr Timothy Johnson for one.'

'The Home Secretary?'

'Aye, but you know that, Mr Edison. They've been firm pals for years. You came to a fair few of those parties yourself.'

Edison drained his glass, toying with this new intelligence.

'But you haven't told us why *you* were visiting, Mr Edison,'

Andy pushed him whilst he poured an ever more generous measure of whisky.

Robert gave his friend a knowing look, 'Sir Donald and Mr Edison here used to work together.'

'Ohhhh,' Andy's eyes lit up, 'so you're in the sneaky beaky line of work too then?'

'Used to be,' Edison said shortly, trying to shut down the exchange as it crept into treacherous waters.

'Did you get booted out too?' the barman wasn't going to let it go. 'Our Sir Hughes, up there on the hill, wears it as some sort of a badge of honour. Wrongfully accused of misdemeanours. Valiantly defending the honour of his friends. Falling on his sword such that others' livelihoods would not be affected.'

Edison had no response to this. The details of Sir Donald Hughes' departure from the Security Service had never, and would never, be released to the media. Edison had been assured that there were only a handful of people that knew of his involvement. The case against Hughes had been predicated on Edison's anonymous evidence. It had been strong enough to evict him from his position as director general but, notionally, not sufficient to bring criminal charges. Edison blamed himself for this, having been unable to pull together enough intelligence to back up his hearsay evidence in time. The truth of it was that Hughes had some very influential friends, and Edison suspected the disgraced director general had dossiers of dirt on some very senior figures in British politics. Timothy Johnson, Edison believed, had pulled the necessary strings to exonerate his friend in the eyes of the law.

The pub was beginning to fill up, and Andy was called into action to prepare a large round for a rowdy group of men who looked like they'd just come off a boat. 'Down from Mallaig, lads?' Andy asked.

'Aye,' one of them replied. 'Back for the first sailings tomorrow morning.'

Robert excused himself, spotting a friend on the other side of the bar, and left Edison to his thoughts. They were filled with Hughes and Anna and stowaway terrorists. The ill effects of the whisky were causing these thoughts to muddle uncomfortably in his head. He knew he needed to speak to Kat. 'Andy,' he summoned his new friend, who looked at him, expecting another drinks order. 'Any chance you could find me some juice for this?' Edison waved his dead phone in the air.

'Aye, give it here.' The publican plugged a charging cable into the handset, and Edison saw it glow. He left it for twenty minutes before deeming there was enough battery to make the call.

'I need to speak to Kat,' he slurred when the phone was answered at Thames House.

'Edison, is that you?' Colin had answered the phone.

'Colin, I need to speak to Kat,' Edison repeated, trying to sound urgent.

'She's gone downstairs for an interrogation.'

'Of Jamie? Waste of time, he doesn't know anything. Scapegoat.' The last word came out as 'scaygo'.

'It's a different suspect,' Colin said cagily.

'Who?'

Colin didn't reply.

'Who Colin? Who?'

'Edison, I'm not sure I should be talking to you. You're *persona non grata* round here at the moment.'

'What do you mean? I told Kat I was taking a couple of days off.'

'Yes, but you didn't tell her you were going to see Sir Donald Hughes and accuse him of treachery, did you?' Colin exploded.

'I didn't accuse him, I just needed to talk to him,' Edison objected. He was reeling from Colin's uncharacteristic outburst. He was always so calm. In the fifteen years they'd known one another, Edison didn't think he'd heard more than a handful of cross words uttered by the Welshman. 'Anyway, how do you know where I've been?'

'He called the Home Secretary, Edison.' Colin was losing patience.

Edison was dumbstruck. Moments passed in silence before Edison pulled himself together. 'Listen, Colin, I've screwed up. I know I have, but there's no time to lose on this. You know that arresting Jamie was a really stupid thing to do, right?' Edison could feel the influence of the whisky waning as if he were shedding a skin.

Colin muttered his almost inaudible agreement.

'And you know I'm more use to you on the inside of the fence than the outside, right?'

Colin mumbled again.

'Who is Kat interviewing?'

'We brought in Anna earlier this evening.'

'Anna? Why?' Edison's mind ran back over the conversation he'd had with Hughes and the mentioned of the Turkish Ambassador's god-daughter.

'She was pulling cash from the Barinak Holdings account.'

Edison whistled as the door of the pub burst open, and a familiar figure appeared, silhouetted against the light outside. The pub had few windows and was dimly lit by a handful of electric lights. Despite the hour, outside, the mid-summer late-evening sunshine of the Highlands was still illuminating the sky.

Recognising the figure, Edison volleyed instructions at Colin, 'Colin, I need you to get Kat to call me *before* she speaks to Anna.

And I need Jock to go to the flat she shares with Christoph. Get hold of any laptops or computers there.' Charlie was standing next to him now, glowering at his friend. 'Also, track down Christoph Langer, if it's not too late.'

'On it,' Colin said, all his earlier anger having dissolved.

'I need to go. Get Kat to call me *before* she speaks to Anna.'

'Bloody hell, Eddie,' Charlie hissed as he hung up the phone and placed a firm grip around his arm.

Robert appeared at Charlie's shoulder, looking merry. He grinned widely and said, 'Friend of yours, Mr Edison? Should we sort him out with a drink?'

'That won't be necessary,' Charlie snarled.

Robert cowered at Charlie's ferocious glare and slinked back across the room to where his friends were pretending not to stare at the unfolding scene.

'Let's go,' Charlie said in Edison's ear.

'I'm fine, Charlie,' Edison protested as he was manhandled off the barstool.

Edison stumbled to the door, following his friend out into the tiny car park. There was only one car other than Edison's hatchback parked there, and Charlie guided his friend toward it firmly. He opened the passenger door with his free hand and bundled Edison in. Charlie dug in his pocket for his phone and eventually liberated it. Against the backdrop of the loch and imposing mountains, Edison observed him raise his phone in the air and twist around, staring at the screen. 'Not even one bar,' he grumbled.

'Who are you trying to call? There's signal in the pub,' Edison offered. 'I just checked in with the Grid.'

'What? They've had me drive virtually the breadth of the country to find you, and you just casually check in.' Charlie made his way round to the other side of the car and got in. 'You've caused quite the furore today, Ed.'

'I've really screwed things up, I know.' Charlie started the engine. 'Woah, woah, woah, I need to take the car. I need to get back to London tonight.'

'You're not driving anywhere in this state.' Charlie reversed onto the main road. Edison looked worried as he glanced back at the hire car stood in the car park. 'I'll bring you to pick it up tomorrow, Eddie, don't worry.'

'I need to get back to London tonight,' Edison repeated.

Charlie ignored him. They drove on in silence as dusk started to descend on the glen. Charlie flicked on his main beams to pick out the unlit road. Edison toyed with his phone for the entire journey, praying that Kat would call as they drove through a rare window of signal. When they eventually reached the holiday let, she still hadn't called, and he was despairing.

Through the gloom, he could make out that they were parked in front of a small, single storey, wooden cabin. There was a light on in one of the rooms, but the rest of the building was in darkness. 'The boys will be asleep. But it looks like Layla waited up,' said Charlie. Edison nodded, acknowledging the need for quiet so as not to disturb the children.

He and Charlie crunched across the gravel driveway to the door, which opened as they approached, and Layla, wrapped in a dressing gown, stood aside to let them in. They entered an open-plan room. A huge kitchen table stood in front of glass doors on the opposite side. A log burner, unlit, served as the focal point, around which a mismatch of armchairs and a comfortable-looking sofa were arranged.

'I'll put the kettle on,' were Layla's first, whispered words, and she padded on bare feet to the sideboard and filled the kettle. With those words, Edison felt the weight of the world lift from his shoulders. He dropped his holdall next to the sofa and followed Charlie across the room.

At just gone midnight, Charlie, Layla and Edison sat around the dining table with hot cups of tea. Edison, seated closest to the socket where he'd plugged his phone in, still willing Kat to call. Layla spoke first, 'Are you ok, Edison?'

'I think so,' Edison replied.

'What possessed you to visit him?' Charlie asked.

Edison paused, considering the question as he watched the steam rising from his mug, 'I'm sure he's involved in all of this.'

'The HAPSBURG operation?' Charlie asked.

Edison glanced at Layla – she was one of the few people in the world who had known what Edison had done for a living since leaving university. He had assumed that Charlie would have told her about Edison's recall to the Service as a freelance agent but felt, although he trusted Layla as implicitly as he did Charlie, she probably shouldn't be privy to the minutiae of the operation. She took her cue and stood up. 'I'm exhausted, I must get to bed. You two would be wise to do the same. There's linen in the cupboard by the bathroom.' She made her way to where a corridor led to the cabin's two bedrooms. She turned back to them. 'It's good to see you, Edison.' Her eyes were filled with kindness, and Edison felt his shoulders drop as he relaxed a little more.

Once she was gone, Charlie said, 'Why do you think he's involved?'

Edison explained about the investments in the fund at Penwill & Mallinson.

'It's a coincidence, Eddie. I know we don't hold much truck with coincidences, but for once, I think this might be one.'

'But here's what's interesting,' Edison went on. 'The gatekeeper told me that Hughes entertains all sorts of foreign visitors. The property company we're dealing with is run by Turks.'

Charlie gave his friend sympathetic look. 'Spuriouser and spuriouser,' he said, and they both laughed.

'But there's one more thing. Anna, the secretary at the bank, who's just been picked up as a suspect by the team in London, what were the exact words he used?' Edison trawled through his memory of the conversation with Hughes, '*She's a very dear friend of mine.*'

'Five have just picked her up?'

Edison nodded. Charlie looked thoughtful. 'Is she your hacker?'

Edison shook his head. 'Do you have a laptop up here? Wi-Fi?'

'Sorry, it's a digital detox kind of a place.'

Edison's fingers itched to get online, to see what Christoph was up to.

'Do you think Hughes could have got himself mixed up in all this without knowing the full picture?' Charlie suggested.

Edison sighed, 'It's possible. Maybe you're right, maybe I'm desperate, jumping to conclusions. He got away with so much. He's up here, rolling around that estate, living in the lap of luxury when he should be rotting in jail.'

'You shouldn't blame yourself. You did everything you could. What you need is some sleep, Eddie,' Charlie informed him. 'You'll have some questions to answer when you get back to London.'

Edison grimaced. 'Who called you?'

'Tanya first. Kat later.'

'God knows what accusations Hughes has levied at me.'

'I think you need to assume the worst. But for all his friends in high places, there's still a cloud over his name.'

'Unfortunately, there's an equally dark one over mine.'

Whilst Charlie busied himself pulling out bedding and setting up the sofa bed for Edison, he thought for a while about what to say to Tanya. In the end, he opted for the truth – *Tanya, it's Edison. I fucked up. Let my history with Hughes cloud my judgement. I'm with Charlie. Will debrief with Kat when I get back to London tomorrow.*

It felt like he'd barely pressed send before a single-line response from Tanya arrived – *Fucked up may be the understatement of the century.* Edison's stomach lurched, and a wave of nausea, mainly caused by the whisky, washed over him. The phone buzzed at him again, and he was surprised to see an incoming call. He answered.

'Edison,' Kat's voice sounded shaky, 'I'm so glad you're ok. I ... I ...' she faltered and gulped. Edison thought she might be on the edge of tears.

'I'm ok,' he said softly. He'd never heard Kat, always so calm, even under the most immense pressure, sound so unhinged.

'I was so worried,' she breathed.

'I'm sorry.' A silence hung between them. Edison pulled himself together, 'You've brought in Anna?'

'I got your message,' Kat replied sounding more businesslike.

'Have you interviewed her?'

'Not yet. I'm waiting for Colchester. I think it'll be tomorrow morning now.'

Edison rolled his eyes. 'And have you picked up Christoph?'

'He's disappeared off the other end of the Eurostar. Colin ran a trace on all ports the second he was off the phone with you. He took a train at just gone half-past three, it couldn't have been more than half an hour after Anna was arrested. He could be anywhere by now.'

'Shit. I suppose that was inevitable.'

'Do you really think Christoph's the hacker?'

'I'm sure of it. And him scarpering rather frames him doesn't it? Has Jock gone to collect the kit?'

'He and Natalie are going in in the morning.'

'What else?'

'I need you back in London.'

'I'll take the first flight tomorrow.'

'I'll meet you.'

There was another long silence.

'I can't believe you went to see him,' Kat returned to the subject of Hughes.

'It was a stupid thing to do,' Edison admitted.

'I don't think stupid even covers it.'

Edison looked up to see that Charlie had disappeared. 'I'm sorry,' he said again.

There was a long silence as neither of them knew what to say. Edison ventured, 'Get some sleep.'

'You too.'

'Good night,' Edison offered, and the line went dead. He looked up to discover a small boy standing in the doorway.

'Hello, Uncle Edison,' Charlie's middle son, Henry, said.

'Hello, Henry, shouldn't you be in bed?'

Henry ignored the question and came toward him. He looked up at Edison. Even seated, Edison towered over the eight-year-old. 'Was that your girlfriend?' he asked.

Edison laughed, 'Sort of. Now, back to bed before you get into trouble.'

'Too late,' said Charlie, reappearing and scooping his son into his arms.

'Good night, Uncle Edison,' Henry said as Charlie carried him back toward the bedroom he was sharing with his brothers.

'Good night,' replied Edison.

'Have you got everything you need, Eddie?' Charlie asked when he returned.

'Yes, thanks.'

'Sleep well.'

'Charlie,' Edison said as his friend retreated, 'thank you.'

'Don't mention it,' Charlie replied, turning out the light as he left the room.

*

0830, Saturday 8th July, Dores, nr Inverness, Inverness-shire
Charlie shepherded the three boys past his sleeping friend the following morning and took them into the nearby village of Dores for breakfast. Tucking into fried bread and American-style pancakes, the boys thought this a treat beyond their wildest dreams. They returned to the cabin a little after ten, bubbling over with excitement. As they burst through the door, Charlie was glad to see Edison, dressed and sitting at the kitchen table.

'Uncle Edison,' exclaimed Thomas. 'You're awake. You missed pancakes.'

Edison smiled at Thomas. 'What a shame. That'll teach me to have a lie-in.'

'Lazy head,' said William, the youngest.

Thomas and Henry fell about laughing. 'You mean lazy bones, silly,' Henry admonished the blushing William.

'Ok, you three,' Charlie took charge, 'go and play outside.'

'Do you want to play with us, Uncle Eddie?' William asked.

'Uncle Eddie and I need to have a chat, boys. Off you go.'

Three ginger heads and freckles tumbled over one another to get to the door. 'Do you think Uncle Eddie's in trouble,' Edison heard Henry ask Thomas, who, as the eldest, was considered to know everything.

Thomas glanced back at the adults, they looked serious, 'I think so.'

'I've looked at flights,' Edison said. 'There's a departure from Inverness at half eleven.'

'What about your hire car?'

'I'm needed in London. HAPSBURG is coming to a head. I'll worry about that another time.'

They sat in silence for a while, watching Charlie's children as they careered about in the garden. Finally, Charlie spoke, 'What are you going to do?'

Edison shrugged. 'I guess I'll see exactly how much trouble I'm in before making a firm plan.'

'Fair enough.'

'This operation really worries me, Charlie.'

'HAPSBURG?'

'Yeah, I feel like I'm so close to it. As though I've got all the pieces. I just need to work out how they fit together.'

'Do you really think that Hughes is involved in some way?' Edison looked up sharply. It was the first time that anyone had entertained the notion with any seriousness.

'It's more of a gut instinct thing.' Edison looked helpless. The Security Service and police, ever more accountable to the public, politicians and the media, didn't deal in hunches and instinct anymore. With budgets stretched to breaking point, suspicions had to be backed by layers and layers of evidence, just to establish the minimum levels of surveillance on an alleged target.

'He won't have got his hands dirty,' Charlie pointed out.

'You're right,' Edison sighed. 'And I need to forget Hughes. Even if he is involved, he's not pulling triggers or detonating bombs. My focus needs to be on what's happening on the ground.' Edison fell silent as his thoughts turned to his return to London. Kat was probably in the interrogation room with Anna as they spoke. The promise of a rendezvous with Kat might go some way to filling in the gaps. 'We had better get going.'

'Layla,' Charlie called to his wife who had enjoyed a rare

childfree lie-in.

Layla appeared in the living room, looking bright-eyed. She was dressed in walking trousers and a cotton top. Her dark, wavy hair falling to her shoulders. 'You boys put the world to rights?' she asked, crossing the room, collecting a waxed gilet and putting it on.

'Almost,' Charlie grinned. 'I'm going to take Eddie to the airport. Are you ok to look after the boys for a couple of hours?'

Layla nodded then looked at Edison. 'Please be careful,' was all she said before turning on her heels and joining her children in the garden.

'Ready?' Charlie asked. He picked up his car keys and walked out to the car. As Edison emerged through the front door, the three boys rocketed across the lawn and threw themselves at him.

'Goodbye, Uncle Eddie,' they chimed.

'Goodbye boys, enjoy the rest of your holiday,' Edison replied smiling, ruffling Henry's hair.

Henry squinted up at him and said, 'I hope your new girlfriend is as nice as Auntie Ellie.' Edison smiled and put an arm around the small boy's shoulders. A lump formed in his throat which he tried, in vain, to swallow. 'I miss her,' the six-year-old went on. The other two boys nodded their agreement.

'I miss her too,' Edison said in a barely audible whisper, the words catching against the knot in his throat.

Charlie, already in the driver's seat of the car, tooted the horn. 'Got to go, boys,' Edison said, collecting himself. 'I'll see you all back in London.'

'Yes,' Layla said, prising William away from Edison. 'We'll sort a date out as soon as we're back.'

He slid into the passenger seat. Charlie made quick work of the winding roads that led to the airport.

'So,' Edison turned to his friend as they both got out of the car at the drop-off area outside the terminal, 'I had better get going.' He shifted from one foot to the other.

Charlie wrapped his arms around his friend, 'You had better be careful, Eddie. I don't want you getting into trouble.'

'When are you back in London?'

'We're leaving at the crack of dawn tomorrow morning. Depending on the traffic, we'll be back mid-afternoon.'

'Take care on the roads.' Edison knew his friend had a passion for fast driving ever since he'd taken the advanced driving course in his early days as a police officer.

'I will. Now, get home safe. No more lone-wolf heroics, interrogating dangerous suspects.'

Chapter Nineteen

0832, Saturday 8th July, Scotland Yard, Westminster, London

Kat followed the familiar route into the depths of Scotland Yard. She was welcomed into the same observation room from where she'd watched the Jamie Dunn interview the previous day. Then, she had been feeling miserable. She had been sure that Jamie's arrest had set them back and that Colchester's insistence on bringing him in had been a monumental waste of time. Now, as she surveyed the scene behind the glass, she felt a palpable sense of excitement and optimism. She was getting somewhere. Jock and Natalie would secure Christoph's computer, and then, on his return to London, Edison would work his magic on that to prove irrefutably that he was the mole at the bank. Anna was clearly an accomplice in all this. Running errands. Providing a link between Christoph's shady digital dealings and the very real VIPERSNEST. All she needed now, was a location of the attack. And a lead on Yousuf. Could Colchester redeem himself and extract that from their suspect?

In the interview room, she observed two women. Anna had blonde hair, neatly cut into a bob. She wore heavy-rimmed glasses and was drumming her coral pink, manicured nails on the table. She looked bored. Beside her sat a slim figure, neatly dressed in a dark grey trouser suit and a pale blue silk blouse. Her fine features were framed by an elegant hijab. She was talking quietly to Anna.

Superintendent Colchester swept through, accompanied by Morley. He nodded at Kat on his way past.

Both women looked up when the policemen entered the room. Morley dutifully administered the formalities that signalled the start of the interview, during which Kat learnt that the solicitor's name was Samina Akram. Then silence descended. At length, Colchester spoke, 'Ms Graham, you understand why you are here?'

Anna's solicitor replied, 'My client understands the charges that have been brought against her, but what we both fail to see, is why you suspect my client of involvement with terrorism.'

'It's ludicrous,' Anna spoke for the first time since confirming her name.

'We have evidence that your client, Ms Akram, has been assisting in manipulating a trading algorithm at the bank where she works, Penwill & Mallinson.'

'I have nothing to do with the trading platforms,' Anna protested. Her solicitor laid a hand on her forearm.

'I will handle this,' she told her client. Akram turned a steely look to Colchester, who took that as an invitation to continue his exposition.

'The money that has been syphoned from the fund has been traced to a bank account belonging to Barinak Holdings. It's the same bank account from which Ms Graham withdrew two hundred and fifty pounds yesterday evening. Can you tell me how you came to be transacting on that particular account?'

Anna shot a look at her solicitor who shook her head. 'I'm advising my client not to answer that question.'

Colchester raised his eyebrows.

'Can you tell me how you know Kerim Dastan? Or perhaps you know him better as Murat Yousuf?'

'Neither of those names are familiar to my client.'

Another long silence.

'And what of your relationship with Christoph Langer? You can't tell me that you aren't familiar with him, Ms Graham?' The way Colchester over-pronounced 'Ms' each time was beginning to grate on Kat.

'He is my flatmate. I'm not sure what that has got to do with this absurd charade.'

'It has everything to do with it, Ms Graham. Is it purely a coincidence that he fled the country just thirty minutes after you were arrested?'

'My client cannot be held accountable for Mr Langer's actions.'

'Well, let's set your relationship with Mr Langer aside for a moment,' Colchester suggested.

Kat held her breath. She knew that Colchester was about to play the strongest card held by any counter-terrorism interrogator. The suspect's response would speak volumes about their motives. You were probably dealing with someone acting on a misplaced but steadfast ideology. A hint of remorse and there was a ray of sunlight.

'Anna,' Morley spoke for the first time since the formalities at the beginning of the interview. 'We believe that there is an imminent attack on London planned.' He paused and offered Anna a sympathetic look. It was met with steel. He and Colchester had rehearsed this good cop/bad cop routine in the moments before the interview. 'Such an attack will likely result in hundreds, if not thousands, of people losing their lives. People like your mum, your brother or your niece.' The detective lowered his voice and said softly, 'You can stop that from happening.'

The words hung in the air. Anna held Morley's gaze. Kat despaired.

A cold, self-satisfied smile crept across Anna's fine features. She hissed, 'I could stop it,' and paused, her fierce gaze fixing on Morley, 'but I won't.'

*

1056, Saturday 8th July, Limeharbour, Isle of Dogs, London
Jock made a circuit of the apartment block and returned to where

Natalie was watching the main entrance. 'There's an entry point where the bins come out at the back and an alarmed fire exit on the west side. What are your thoughts on the front door?'

'It's fob entry. No porter on a Saturday. We could tailgate, but we might be waiting a while. You were gone ten minutes, and no one came or went.'

Natalie was feeling trepidatious about their assignment. The botched job at the internet café had hit her confidence, and Jock had spent most of the journey to the Isle of Dogs on the DLR counselling her. 'Got to get back on the horse, Nat. It's par for the course that occasionally, things go south. Odds are, it won't happen again,' he'd told her as they'd walked from Crossharbour Station to their target address.

'Don't look now,' Jock said, looking over Natalie's shoulder, 'but we may be in luck. Wait here.'

A woman with three bags of shopping was struggling along the road, making a beeline for the block of flats. Jock skipped across the road to arrive at the door just as the woman had set down her bags and begun rummaging in her handbag for her keys. 'Let me help you with those,' Jock said, picking up one of the bags and grasping the door handle. With a grateful smile, the woman swiped her key fob, and Jock held open the door, offering her a gentlemanly bow as she lumbered past him.

'Very kind of you,' she said as Jock followed her into the building and deposited her into the lift.

'I've just moved in,' he explained cheerfully. 'Trying to make friends.' The doors of the lift closed before she had a chance to reply. Jock hot-footed it back to the door and beckoned for Natalie.

'Quit looking like that,' Jock warned her below his breath once he'd let her in.

'Like what?' Natalie hissed back.

'Like we're doing something wrong. You'll draw attention to us, and that's the last thing we need.'

'We're heading for the third floor,' she said, painting a picture of calm on her face as best she could. 'Stairs,' she pointed at a door on the far side of the foyer.

They passed two carbon-copy corridors on their way to the third floor where they were faced with white-painted walls and a hardwearing beige carpet. Doors with silver numbers led into each of the apartments. There was a faint hum of a vacuum cleaner coming from one and the sound of heavily bassed house music got louder as the Jock and Natalie made their way toward their target.

With about ten metres still to travel, Jock placed a hand on Natalie's arm, indicating she should stop. 'Right,' he muttered. 'You go in, and I'll watch. Usual signal if anything untoward, ok?'

'Ok,' Natalie replied as confidently as she could muster. Jock laid his hand out, and she hesitated.

'Come on,' he implored, 'I thought you were tougher than this.'

She forced a smile and dutifully low-fived him. She crept forward and inserted a skeleton key into the lock.

Jock watched her disappear from view before pulling out a screwdriver and bending down to examine a nearby plug socket. One of the neighbours came out onto the corridor, pulling their door shut behind him. He skirted the handyman, giving him a nod then striding off toward the stairs.

Barely thirty seconds later, Jock heard a strangled cry from the apartment Natalie had gone into moments before. He hurtled along the corridor and into the flat. After the gloom of the strip-lit corridor, the bright sunshine pouring into the spacious kitchen-living room caused Jock to blink. Through the blur, he made out the silhouette of a man standing against the window. He had Natalie in a stranglehold, his sinewy arm held tightly across her neck.

Jock's eyes grew accustomed to the brightness. The slimly built, wiry man who held Natalie captive was Murat Yousuf. He needed to think quickly. How to apprehend their prime suspect without risking his partner's life.

Yousuf edged around the room, keeping his back to the wall and his eyes on Jock. Natalie whimpered as the man's arm tightened around her throat. Jock's eyes fell on the knife block by Yousuf's left elbow. He threw himself across the room as Yousuf's grip closed around one of the handles. Jock led with the hand still holding the screwdriver. It was a useless weapon, he realised too late, as blood landed on him. Yousuf had drawn the blade across Natalie's throat. She slumped to the ground. Jock was momentarily paralysed. He couldn't take his eyes from his stricken colleague.

Yousuf was advancing on him, and he dragged his focus back to the confrontation. On the sideboard stood an enormous bouquet of roses in a glass vase. Jock swept his arm across the work surface and the vase toppled to the floor, water cascading everywhere. He reached for the largest shard of glass and turned to face his attacker. He swiped at the man, but he was strong and agile. Jock inflicted just a few grazes with his makeshift weapon before Yousuf knocked him to the floor and plunged the knife into Jock's thigh. Then he ran.

Jock pulled himself up, blood pouring from the gash in his jeans and followed, hopelessly. In the corridor, he saw his quarry throw open the fire exit and disappear. The fire alarm sounded, and residents started to drift into the corridor. Jock turned back to the scene of devastation in the flat. There were trails of blood across the white-tiled floor. Natalie lay motionless where she'd fallen. A laptop sat closed on the breakfast bar.

*

1238, Saturday 8ᵗʰ July, Thames House, Westminster, London

Kat's face turned ghostly pale as she listened to the voice on the other end of the line. Colin looked over as she hung up. She stood, staring into the space in front of her. Colin held his breath, knowing this was not going to be good news.

'Natalie's dead.'

Colin drew a sharp intake of breath.

Kat shook her head and screwed her eyes up. 'This can't be happening,' she whispered. She opened her eyes and looked around her as if she didn't recognise where she was.

'Where's Jock?' Colin ventured.

Kat's gaze finally settled on him. She looked like she was trying to place him. 'In the Royal London Hospital,' she said. There was a disquieting, faraway quality to her voice.

Colin took control, 'We had better get to the hospital then.'

'Yes, that's probably the right thing to do.' She fumbled her phone into her pocket.

Colin steered Kat into a taxi and got in after her. He gave the driver instructions to take them to the East London hospital then took Kat's ringing phone from her. 'That'll be Edison,' Kat said, still in an unnerving, dream-like voice.

'Edison,' Colin answered the phone.

'Colin, is everything ok?'

'Not exactly.'

'What's happened? Is Kat ok?' A bolt of adrenaline shot through Edison who was sitting on a train bound for central London from the airport.

'She's fine, just a bit shaken up. Something's happened, I don't know exactly, but Jock is injured and Natalie is dead.'

Kat turned from where she'd been watching the river as they travelled along the Embankment. 'Tell him to come to the hospital,' she said, her mouth dry, then looked away again.

'Edison, we're on our way to the Royal London – can you meet us there?'

'I'm on my way.'

Once he'd hung up and switched the privacy switch so they couldn't be overheard by the taxi driver, he ventured, 'Kat, can you tell me what you know.'

Kat sighed a shuddering breath. She didn't look at him as she spoke. 'There was someone in the apartment. When they went to pick up the tech. He attacked them. Natalie got a knife in the neck, and Jock has just had his femoral artery stitched up.'

'Jesus.'

'Jock thinks it was Yousuf.'

The taxi skirted round the Victorian building on Whitechapel Road, the golden letters of the hospital name glinting in the heat of the July sun. It pulled up in front of the modern hospital development tucked behind. Kat bolted from the car. Colin paid the driver and followed her at a run toward the main entrance.

'A&E,' Kat demanded of the man staffing the information booth in the foyer.

'Go right along to the end of the corridor. Take a left, and you'll find it on your right.'

Colin reached her just as she was haring off to follow the directions. They ploughed through the double doors that brought them into the melee of the accident and emergency waiting room. Colin spotted Jock first and hurtled toward him, calling his name.

He was sitting a little way apart from the other waiting patients. One leg of his jeans had been cut off around his crotch, and a dressing ran the length of his inside thigh. Blood stained the rest of his clothes. Clutched to his chest was a carrier bag containing something hard and rectangular. His face was ashen and shoulders bowed. Colin was almost on top of him before he looked up. Colin's eyes flicked to the carrier and then to the bandage.

'Twenty-three stitches, courtesy of the paramedics, under there,' he said, his voice deadpan. 'Waiting for a full assessment now.'

Kat threw herself into the plastic seat next to him, and Colin crouched down on his haunches, his eyes level with theirs. The three spooks were silent.

'Do you have any idea where he went?' Kat broke the deadlock.

Jock shook his head and gestured at his injured leg.

'Kat,' someone called from the opposite side of the room, and all three of them looked up to see Edison lumbering through the crowds. 'Shit, Jock, what happened?'

Jock didn't answer the question but thrust the carrier bag at Edison, 'I think you wanted this.'

Edison took it and withdrew a laptop.

'Jock McDermid,' a nurse called from behind a desk. Jock stood and hobbled toward her. Colin, Kat and Edison followed. 'Dr Webb asked me to tell you there's a room available on ward 3F.'

'Thank you.' Jock winced as he turned on his injured leg.

'Can I get you a chair? It's a bit of a hike.'

'I'll manage,' Jock replied gruffly and hobbled toward the door, tailed by his colleagues.

'Who's Dr Webb?' Colin asked.

'Friend of a friend. They want to change this blasted dressing and make sure I haven't got any internal bleeding. Didn't fancy discussing HAPSBURG on an open ward, so I called in a favour when I found out I would need to stay for a bit.'

The team were making slow progress down an empty corridor. 'What about Natalie?' Kat ventured, her voice quivering.

Jock stopped abruptly. 'What about her?' he growled. 'She's

dead. Killed by that bloody man Yousuf. If we don't get to the bottom of this, she isn't going to be the only casualty.' Jock limped on down the corridor and disappeared around the corner.

Colin followed him, leaving Edison and Kat alone. Edison turned to face her. Her shoulders were hunched. The pallor of her skin was grey, and exhaustion was writ large on her delicate features. Without a word, Edison enveloped her in his arms and held her close to him. He could feel the tension in her body. She turned dark-rimmed eyes to look up at him, and their gazes connected briefly before she buried her head back into his chest and tears began to pour down her cheeks. Edison kissed the top of her head and tenderly stroked her dark hair where it fell down her shoulders. On instinct, he whispered, 'Shhhhhh, it's going to be ok.'

The words sent a lightning bolt through Kat's body, which stiffened in his embrace. She drew back. 'It's not going to be ok, Edison,' she said, her voice hard and trembling. He tried to reach for her hand, but she pulled it back. She stood with her arms at her side, her fists clenched. Her mouth set in a grim line. 'It's not going to be ok. There's a bomb, Edison. A bomb. And I don't know where it is.' She burst into tears again, the pressure of recent days erupting into swelling sobs that consumed her small frame.

Edison approached her carefully, and this time, she allowed him to take her hand. Kat turned her tear-stained face toward him, and just for a moment, he was struck by how vulnerable she looked. She wiped away the tears, and the look of helplessness was replaced by one of steely determination. It reminded him of Ellie, who, in the throes of the toxic treatment that was supposed to be extending her life, had adopted a fierce, gritty attitude that had floored him at times. The memory caused him to draw breath.

'What's wrong?' Kat asked, looking concerned. 'You've gone white.'

Edison shook his head, trying to rid himself of the images in his mind of his wife in hospital, her body weakened by the relentless treatment but with that determined look she never lost until the last time he saw her, the day before she died. 'Nothing,' he said, pushing the thoughts to the back of his mind. 'Can you fill me in on what I need to know?'

Kat looked up as a hospital porter rattled past them with an empty gurney. She took a deep breath, and breaking every protocol and the official secrets act, in hushed tones, she told Edison everything that had happened with Operation HAPSBURG in the past two days.

She was midway through recounting Anna's interrogation when her phone rang.

She snatched it from her pocket, 'Yes?'

'Kat?' Mo, on the other end of the line, sounded breathless.

'Mo – what's the news from the raid?' Kat demanded.

'Not good. The bomb squad went in late morning, and they've just finished their full sweep of the property. Clear traces of explosives were found in the kitchen.'

'Shit,' Kat said.

'I took a look after they cleared it for me to go in. It's quite obvious our bombers are not going back there anytime soon.'

'Shit,' Kat repeated. 'Ok,' she pulled herself together after a pause. 'The explosives must be with them in the van. Wherever that is.' She began walking in the direction that Jock and Colin had taken, peering into each room as she passed. Edison followed.

'I'm on my way in,' Mo said.

'Mo,' Kat faltered wondering how she was going to get through breaking the news of Natalie's death to her youngest officer. 'We're at the Royal London. Jock was injured on an op this morning, and Natalie …'

'Kat, what's happened?' Mo asked, reading her tone.

'Mo, Yousuf was in the apartment. He attacked Natalie and Jock. Natalie didn't …'

There was a roar of anguish on the other end of the line then silence.

'Mo? Mo, are you still there?'

'I'm on my way,' said Mo, and the line went dead.

*

In the small, private room, Jock had thrown himself onto the bed. He was still sweating from the effort of the journey when Edison and Kat found him. 'I just spoke to Mo,' Kat told them. 'VIPERSNEST is in the wind with a van full of explosives. Colin, I need anything you've got on that van. Can you get in touch with the Grid?'

Colin and Kat clustered around Jock's bedside, discussing the case and making calls. On the other side of the room, Edison stood by the window and pulled out the laptop Jock had given him. He placed it on the windowsill and ran his hand across its cold, metal case. He lifted the lid and fingered the power key. He pressed it, and the screen flickered into life.

Thanks to the trojan horse malware he'd sent to RubiksKube, Edison logged into the laptop with ease. As soon as he had accessed the home screen, Kat made a beeline for him.

'Anything on the location of the attack?' she pressed, a note of desperation in her voice.

Edison didn't respond as he began to dig through Christoph's email.

'How *did* you know it was Christoph?' she asked, watching Edison manipulate the cursor across the screen, pulling up scripts, message boards and emails in quick succession.

Without taking his eyes off the screen, Edison explained, 'All hackers, all coders have a tell, a voice that comes through in their script – like a writer or an artist's style. Little flourishes that mean you can make a pretty good guess as to who wrote it. Jamie's voice, well, there was a lazy timbre to everything he coded. Our man was ruthlessly efficient. I met him online and matched the syntax to the basic code on the infrastructure fund's front end.'

'But how was he accessing Jamie's user on the system?'

'As simple as watching over his shoulder when he entered his password.'

Kat shook her head. 'What else can you tell us now you've got the laptop?'

'He's quite a prolific agent for hire, is Christoph, if these emails are anything to go by. He uses ProtonMail, smart, it's heavily encrypted, and messages aren't stored on servers and neither are the encryption keys. Our colleagues in Europe would certainly be interested in a number of these operations.'

'We'll pass it all on to Six,' Kat said grimly. 'What about HAPSBURG though. Anything on the attack?'

Edison tapped into the command line interface and brought up the telegram messaging program. 'There's only so much I'll get from this as there's a time-sensitive destruct function on communications.' He was silent as he skimmed through the last message or two. 'These numbers,' he pointed at the screen. 'They look like coordinates to me.' He pulled up the maps app on his phone and typed them in. He and Kat watched as the map zoomed in to South London.

'Wimbledon,' Kat breathed.

*

0553, Sunday 9th July, Nelson Gardens, Bethnal Green, London
Jock had finally been discharged at three o'clock in the morning, after much wrangling with the night shift staff. He was bundled into

a taxi and sent home. Colin, Mo and Kat, with Jock's protestations ringing in their ears, set off to Thames House. Edison, too, was banished. 'You're not operational. We can't risk it,' Kat told him when he argued that he should join the surveillance team on the ground. Edison had sulked all the way home, wondering how he might be able to help the team at this, the most critical part of the mission.

'Hello stranger,' Tony greeted Edison as soon as he walked through the door of their flat in Bethnal Green. Edison dropped his holdall by the foot of the stairs and followed Tony into the kitchen.

'You're up early.'

'I'm picking the kids up to go queue for Wimbledon. They want to sit on the hill to watch the final. The oldest one is tennis mad.'

Edison thought quickly, trying to work out how best to dissuade Tony from his plan. 'Are you sure it's a good idea to take your kids to sit out in the sun all day? It's going to be a scorcher.'

'Hats, water, factor fifty, I think we'll survive.'

Looking out the window, the early morning sunshine was reflecting off the roofs of the parked cars below, and the warmth of the day was already seeping in through the ill-fitting frames. Edison wrestled with his conscience. He couldn't push Tony too hard without compromising the operation. Then a brainwave hit him. 'I haven't got any plans for today. Maybe I could join you?'

Tony looked stunned by the suggestion. 'Well, if your idea of a rock-and-roll Sunday is hanging out with someone else's kids, then be my guest.'

'Great. Have I got time to jump in the shower?'

'Yeah, if we could leave by half-past, that would be good.'

At just after six thirty, Edison was sat in the passenger seat of Tony's clapped-out Ford Escort, the reassuring weight of his Glock hammering against his thigh every time the busted suspension encountered a pothole.

Chapter Twenty

0752, Sunday 9ᵗʰ July, Vauxhall Bridge, Vauxhall, London

Kat and Mo were in Mo's Mini, crossing the river at Vauxhall. Kat had an earpiece in that connected, via Bluetooth, to her phone. 'So, tell me what's going on,' Kat picked up her conversation with Colin where she'd left it moments earlier at Thames House. 'Are they evacuating?'

'No, Colchester thinks that's too risky.'

'Idiot. So, what *is* he doing?'

'He has mobilised the counter-terrorism team. Bomb squad. The works. Nick Walsh, Mo's been working with him, is coordinating on the ground. They're mustering nearby on standby.'

'Anything on the local CCTV?'

'I've got all eyes on it, but as yet, no sign of the van.'

'The final starts at two thirty. Gates open at half-past ten.' Kat looked at her watch, 'Another two and a half hours before everyone's in.'

'There are extra security checks in place on the gates, and every vehicle going in is being taken apart. LaunderLoad is one of a handful of commercial laundry companies used by the championships. Our man Yousuf had really done his research.'

'Were there any vans already on site?'

'Yes, but all clean.'

'Ok. The CCTV is key. Mo will be on the ground and will call in any sightings. Let me know if you get anything?'

As they drove, the concrete towers of South London's council estates had given way to the leafy green of the affluent suburbs of

Wandsworth and Earlsfield. 'I had better go,' Kat said to Colin, bringing her hand up to the earpiece to end the call.

*

0808, Sunday 9th July, The All England Club, Wimbledon, London
'Colin, it's Edison.' He'd left Tony and his children shuffling forward in the queue and gone to scout the nearby side streets. He knew he wouldn't get through security with his concealed weapon and needed space to consider his options for accessing the grounds without raising suspicion. He needed to know what the official movements were so risked putting a call into Colin on the Grid.

'Edison, you know I need to be keeping lines clear.'

'Then let's make this quick. Tell me the plan, and I'll get off the phone.'

'Where are you?'

'In the vicinity. You *know* I couldn't just sit at home watching News24.'

'Christ, Edison. You had better not screw this up for them.'

Edison felt affronted, 'Come on, Colin.'

'We had all hell to pay on Friday after Hughes called his chum, Johnson.'

Edison flushed and steered the conversation away, 'Listen, I've been thinking about Yousuf's motive. Any intelligence on why he'd be targeting Wimbledon?'

'Capacity crowds are pushing forty thousand on site. Isn't that enough?'

'Possibly. But any dignitaries attending? Politicians?'

Colin consulted a list of the ticket holders. 'Speak of the devil. The Home Secretary was supposed to be there but changed his itinerary after Tanya reported the latest to the JIC.'

'The Home Secretary?' Edison mused. They couldn't be targeting the Home Secretary if Hughes *was* involved. They were good friends. It was only the senior cabinet minister's intervention that had saved Hughes from criminal charges. 'Anyone else?'

'A few footballers and one minor royal. Listen, I really need to free up this line.'

'Ok, I'll let you know if I come across anything.'

Colin sighed. 'Edison,' he pleaded with his friend, 'don't do anything you'll regret.'

'It's possible to regret doing nothing more, you know, Colin,' Edison's fierce tone invited no argument. He ended the call. A few stragglers were wending their way toward the grounds, clutching their precious tickets. All Edison wanted to do was scream at them to turn around and go home.

*

1405, Sunday 9th July, The All England Club, Wimbledon, London
'Wow it's hot,' Kat said to no one in particular, fanning herself with a programme and screwing her eyes up against the sun. She was at the top of the stands overlooking Centre Court. She had circuited the whole venue three times in the last hour, finishing at this spot each time. There was now only half an hour until play was due to start, and the stadium was almost full. On the court, a television presenter was doing a piece to camera, ahead of the arrival of the players. The crowd was buzzing with anticipation.

Kat turned her back on the stadium and wended her way through the corridors that took her into the depths of the administrative heart of the championships. She arrived outside a door that opened onto a room occupied by four people, one of whom was Detective Sergeant Nick Walsh. Two of the other men were carrying MP5s. They and Nick were dressed in flak jackets. The fourth, a woman, was dressed in jeans and a T-shirt and was studying a bank of monitors intently.

Earlier in the day, Nick had introduced the two armed

policemen as Sergeant Jake Ducker and Sergeant James Woods. They headed the armed response and bomb disposal units respectively. 'And this is Susie, she's going to be our eyes and ears for the day,' Nick had told her when she'd first arrived at the makeshift operational headquarters.

Nick's attention was fixed on the monitors, looking over Susie's shoulder. 'Are your teams in place, Jake?'

Before responding, Jake spoke into a walkie-talkie. 'All units, confirm.' A response came through an earpiece plugged into the side of the police officer's head. 'Yes,' he answered Nick's question perfunctorily.

Nick turned to Kat. He pointed at one of the monitors. There were three vans parked close to one of the buildings. Kat recognised the insignia of LaunderLoad. 'Is one of those our van?'

'James' team have checked them. Nothing.' Nick replied. 'Right,' he said, putting both his hands on the woman's shoulders, 'Susie, you'll keep us informed?' The woman nodded. 'We're going to take our positions now,' he told Kat.

'And so, we just wait?'

'Afraid so.' Nick opened the door and allowed James and Jake to leave before him. 'Your guy, Mo, is on the streets. He's a good chap,' he said before disappearing down the corridor.

Kat looked at the screens. She watched the three men emerging onto a busy concourse that skirted the building they were in. Nick set off in the direction of the terrace where thousands of fans who didn't have tickets for the main stadium were crammed in to watch the match on the big screen. Jake and James waited in a shady spot. Jake would occasionally speak into his walkie-talkie, checking in with his team distributed across the grounds.

There was a monitor dedicated to the BBC's television feed and Kat could see the first set was well underway. She and Susie watched, their gazes flicking from one monitor to another as the pictures cycled through the many cameras dotted around the grounds.

The first set finished, and Kat was feeling impatient, cooped up in the stuffy security office. 'I'm going to take a look around,' she told her companion who made disparaging noises, wanting to protest but didn't.

Kat emerged into the sunshine. The thoroughfares that conveyed visitors around the grounds were empty. Everyone's attention was focused on the action unfolding on the main show court. It was a set a piece, and the match promised to be a tightly contested affair. Kat moved around the grounds, spotting occasionally a member of Jake's team, positioned with snipers. Ready. Members of the public would be totally oblivious to their presence, but Kat's experience told her where to look. It was quiet but for the punctuation of polite applause after each point. An occasional cheer erupted from the terrace where the sun-drenched fans were enjoying the action.

She arrived on the edge of the terrace and stood in the shade, watching the crowd.

Shouting erupted behind her. She heard an engine being revved.

Chapter Twenty-One

1557, Sunday 9th July, The All England Club, Wimbledon, London
Kat whipped round. A white van was careering down the narrow walkway leading toward the terrace. Out of the van jumped a clean-shaven man. His dark skin glistened with sweat. The sun reflected on something shiny in his right hand. A knife. A second man followed, wielding an automatic rifle held above his head. He fired a handful of rounds. The noise of the gun drew the attention of the crowds on the terrace, and many of them scrambled to their feet, screaming.

The van continued to accelerate. Nick Walsh was running toward it, taking aim at the driver. The first shot grazed the side of the van. And his second shattered the glass of the windscreen. His third round missed the driver, who was wrenching the steering wheel from left to right, a ferocious look on his face. Despite the erratic steering, the van continued to advance on the crowded terrace.

Nick lined up his gun to fire again. One of the men was running toward him. Just as he pulled the trigger, the knife-wielding terrorist descended on him and slashed at him mercilessly. Acting on instinct, Kat sprinted toward the stricken police officer.

The shot had found its target, and the driver slumped over the steering wheel. The van veered off its path and was halted when it crashed into the wall. The sound of folding metal against concrete stopped Kat in her tracks, and she looked over to where the van had wedged itself against the wall. For a terrifying moment, the idea that the impact might set off whatever explosives were being carried in the back flashed across Kat's mind. She held her breath.

All around her, chaos was unfolding. Terrified members of the public swarmed up the hill to get away from the horror below.

The man with the rifle had thrown down his weapon and was shouting in Arabic as he ran back toward the van. He rummaged in his pocket. He retrieved an old-fashioned mobile phone and held it above his head. Kat saw a red dot appear on his chest, there was a popping sound. A moment later, he was slumped over. The mobile phone skittered across the ground.

A dozen men, led by James Woods, hurried over to the van, holding blast shields ahead of them.

Kat turned her attention back to Nick and his assailant. There was an angry gash in Nick's neck and another gaping wound, from which blood was pouring, in his leg.

But the man with the knife was no longer assaulting him. He had dropped his weapon and was hurrying away from Nick, his eyes fixed on something on the ground. Kat followed his gaze. He was making a beeline for the mobile phone.

He grabbed it and, with shaking hands, fumbled with it.

'No!' screamed Kat, starting to run toward the man. He looked up at her, a triumphant gleam in his eyes. He lifted his finger in an exaggerated gesture bringing it down slowly toward the keypad.

There was a loud bang. Another gunshot.

The crowds on the hill screamed. Some crouched down, their hands over their heads. Others continued to push as the throng surged up the hill, attempting to escape the carnage below. The terrorist fell to the ground, grasping his stomach. A large wound had opened up in his abdomen, and blood poured from his mouth.

Kat seized the mobile phone, which landed an arm's length from where she stood. She looked up to see where the shot had come from. Barely five metres behind where the man lay dying stood Edison. His Glock 26 at his side.

Chapter Twenty-Two

1611, Sunday 9th July, The All England Club, Wimbledon, London
Edison had spotted the van just as it plunged through one of the access gates at the edge of the All England Club. His working hypothesis had been that the men would don explosive vests and make their way on foot into the crowds, but to his horror, he watched as the van accelerated through the flimsy barrier that separated the deliveries bay from the rest of the grounds. Edison looked on as it raced toward the hill where thousands of people were watching the men's final unfold.

He was frozen to the spot only for an instant and then, acting on instinct alone, ran. He was followed by the security guard, yelling wildly. The van made quick progress, and all too soon, Edison was many hundreds of metres behind it. He observed two figures jump from the cab. He saw, in the distance, the people on the terrace move, like a wave, away from the carnage. As a round of gunshots was let off from an automatic weapon, the noise level rose exponentially. He willed himself on, his lungs about to explode from the exertion.

Edison halted his approach fifty metres from where the van had been immobilised. He surveyed the arena, forcing himself to think clearly and calmly, before taking another step. He saw the bomb squad making a dash for the van. To his right, a policeman lay stricken, having succumbed to the onslaught of one of the terrorists and his knife. He spotted Kat making a dash toward them, and his heart flipped in his chest. He panned round and saw another man fumbling with a mobile phone. From somewhere, a shot was fired, and the man fell to his knees. The phone he'd been struggling with spilled from his grasp onto the floor.

The knife-wielding assailant realised that their success was now solely in his hands and abandoned his weapon, rushing for the phone. Edison didn't take his eyes off the carnage as he pulled out his gun. He scanned the scene again, walking forward. He lined up his shot. Where had Kat gone? Through the dust and the debris that was falling from the wall, he spotted her. She was running toward the man holding the detonator. Don't get any closer, he begged her under his breath.

The man was raising his hand and bringing it down in an exaggerated gesture toward the mobile phone.

Edison pulled the trigger. The man fell forward, onto his knees, the phone slipping from his grasp just before he crumpled into a heap on the ground. Edison's eyes met Kat's. Relief flooded her face momentarily before she snapped back into action. She turned her back on Edison and hurried over to Nick. The policeman was pale, and his eyelids were fluttering as he drifted in and out of consciousness.

A small army of flak-jacketed policemen descended. 'I need a paramedic now,' Kat commanded of one of them as she tore off her jacket and stuffed it into the wound on Nick's neck. 'Nick, this is Kat, I need you to listen to me,' she said urgently to the man lying at her feet. 'We're getting the paramedics now.' She kept on talking to him until another police officer arrived to relieve her.

Edison retreated into the shadows and watched as James Woods' team created a clearance area around the van. Carefully, one of the officers opened the doors. The space at the back was empty but for a small, boarded crate. Very slowly, the crate was shuffled forward and inspected. The specially trained officer, cautiously wielding a pair of wire cutters, removed the detonator, and there was a collective sigh of relief when he raised his thumb.

Up on the terrace, distraught members of the public were being corralled and calmed by the police. There were a few injuries sustained in the crush to escape, and a handful of paramedics moved among the shell-shocked crowd.

Kat caught up with Jake Ducker who was speaking into his radio. 'Your team did well,' she said.

'Let's hope those three,' he replied, nodding toward the bodies, which had been hastily covered with blankets, 'were the only casualties. We just couldn't get a safe shot away on the guy who was attacking Nick.'

'Let's hope so,' she replied as the stricken Nick Walsh was wheeled past them toward a waiting ambulance.

'Do you know who our rogue gunman is?' Jake asked.

'He's one of ours.' Kat didn't feel like now was the time to get into the detail of Edison's involvement in the case.

He nodded, satisfied with the answer. 'Colchester's on his way,' he informed her. There was a collection of television crews and cameras assembling along the line of the cordon that had been hastily erected around the scene. Jake added, 'He'll need to do his piece to camera.'

Kat nodded and walked away. Mo was arguing with the junior police officer who had been put in charge of the cordon's security. She walked over and confirmed that he should be admitted.

'Are you ok?' Mo looked at Kat's bloodstained t-shirt and dust-caked hair.

'I'm fine. Edison's over there. He saved the day.' They walked over to where he was waiting.

'Where's the gun?' Kat asked.

Edison held it up.

'How the hell are we going to explain away the shooting of a suspect by an unregistered weapon?'

'It's registered,' Edison said. 'Just not to me.'

'What do you mean?'

'I got Tanya to register it in your name when I started working as an agent.' Edison remembered the request he'd made to the head of counter-terrorism on his doorstep as they'd bartered over his single demand for being recruited as an MI5 agent.

Kat's jaw dropped. It took a moment for her to find a riposte. Her phone rang, and she ripped her incredulous gaze from Edison's to answer it. 'Hello, Tanya ... Everybody from our section is fine ... Yes, the police will be managing the fallout ... Ok, we'll see you back at Thames House.' She hung up. 'She wants us back on the Grid. I'll go and let ... uh, someone, I don't know who's taken charge now Nick's been invalided ...'

'I have,' Colchester's voice behind them interrupted her. The two intelligence officers and Edison turned to see the uniformed superintendent bearing down on them. 'That was a close-run thing. But we got there.' He smiled, an expression that was ill-fitting on his features. 'I know you,' he pointed at Kat, 'and you,' pointing at Mo, 'but you,' gesturing at Edison, 'are new to me.' He paused, 'Or are you?' He studied Edison more closely. 'You look familiar. A friend of Charlie Harrington-Smith's I think.'

'Yes, Scott Edison. We have met before.' Edison didn't offer the police officer his hand.

'Indeed. Anyway, must be getting on. The press is overdue a statement. I am sure we will all debrief in due course.' He swept away in the direction of the waiting journalists.

'Pompous twat,' Mo muttered. And they all laughed.

'Why don't you get back to Thames House. I need to check in on a few things.'

'Can you let me know if you get any news on Nick?' Mo

pleaded.

'Of course,' Kat promised, touching Mo's arm, sensitive to the young man's emotional state. He'd spent the last two weeks with the police officer. They were a similar age and had got to know one another well. Also, although the whole team were still reeling from the loss of Natalie, Kat feared, too, that it was the junior officer who would feel it most keenly. Jock and Colin were hardened campaigners and knew the sacrifices of the job too well. Mo was naïve, borne of inexperience. He was vulnerable right now, and Kat felt responsible for him. Edison and Kat watched as he made his way back to the car, his head bowed, avoiding the gaze of the dozens of television cameras trained on the carnage that lay in the shadow of the stadium.

An army of police officers was hurrying around with sheets and shrouding, in an attempt to cover up the distressing sight of bodies. Kat turned to Edison but was distracted by a kafuffle. Over his shoulder, she saw two police officers restraining a member of the public who was making a fuss at the cordon. Kat thought she recognised the figure who was gesticulating wildly in their direction. Edison followed Kat's gaze and immediately recognised the man who was imploring the policemen to allow him past the barrier.

'Tony,' Edison said.

'Tony?' Kat sounded like the information didn't stack up, as if the mousey analyst and Edison's reclusive flatmate couldn't possibly be on the scene of a major terrorist incident.

Kat and Edison hurried over to where Tony was still begging the policemen to allow him over the barrier. He turned to them as they approached. 'They wouldn't allow me to come see you,' Tony whined.

Kat ducked under the police tape and offered an apologetic look to the two police officers who both looked relieved as Edison put an arm around Tony's shoulders and led him away.

'Where are the kids?' he asked.

Tony waved vaguely up the hill where a knot of people stood. Many were straining to get a better look at the police operation. Others were cowering, clutching one another, tears streaming down their faces. A handful of uniformed policemen were doing their best to calm the distressed whilst shepherding the more curious members of the public back away from where their colleagues were securing the scene below. Close to one of the policemen sat a young boy and a teenage girl. The little boy, with a floppy haircut and pointy, rat-like features, was unmistakably Tony's son. His sister, a head taller, was pretty and blonde. Edison didn't know his flatmate's ex but assumed the girl must have inherited her looks from her mother. The two children were sitting quietly on the grass, bewildered at the pandemonium that was unfolding around them.

Edison steered Tony up the hill. He looked wild-eyed and was muttering to himself about the horror of it all. He berated himself for bringing his family into this storm. Guilt knotted in the pit of Edison's stomach.

'He's in shock,' Kat said to Edison under her breath. Edison nodded.

'I should take him home.'

'No, we need to debrief. That's the priority,' Kat protested. 'We'll have to bring them to Thames House.'

They reached the children. The boy squinted up at them, shading his eyes from the bright light. 'Can we go home now, Dad?' he asked.

'Well behaved kids you've got there,' one of the policemen commented.

'Thank you, officer,' Kat replied when Tony ignored him, he wasn't taking his eyes off the van and the shrouded bodies. 'Are we ok to take them home?'

'Please provide my colleague with names and a contact number, but yes, it's ok to go.' The policeman eyed Tony, 'Does he need medical assistance? Looks like shock.'

'We'll look after him,' Edison said.

The small party shuffled toward the exit, showing Kat's ID to a dozen different police officers before they were allowed to escape.

Chapter Twenty-Three

1846, Sunday 9th July, Thames House, Westminster, London
The imposing facade of Thames House appeared as the taxi Kat had requisitioned for their journey sped across Lambeth Bridge. It had been slow progress through the police road cordons as they departed Wimbledon, and Kat had to regularly show her identification to the nervous but well-meaning police officers that blocked their route. In the back of the cab, Tony's son, Jason, was sandwiched between his father and Kat on the back seat. Edison and Danni, Tony's daughter, were perched on the fold-down seats, travelling backwards. They didn't speak as they sped through the empty streets of London.

The atmosphere was familiar to Edison, who had worked through all the major terrorist attacks in the capital of the past fifteen years. He had been a junior officer at the time of the July seventh bombings and remembered, after the chaos of the bombing scenes, the eerie quiet of the streets only a few blocks away as Londoners retreated to the safety of their offices and homes to watch the events unfold on their televisions. The subdued atmosphere never lasted long. London would be buzzing again within hours. Edison liked to pretend that such was the confidence the general public had in the security services and the police forces. Actually, it was the unrelenting pace of city living and its residents' collective stoicism that drove them, unerring, back to work, onto the transport system and to their next gig or sporting event.

'*We have no intelligence to suggest that there will be any follow-up attacks,*' Colchester had told the waiting reporters as part of his statement.

'The threat level will remain at critical until we gather a full picture of today's events.' That soundbite was being played regularly on the radio that the cab driver was listening to.

As they approached Thames House, Edison's thoughts turned to where they were going to debrief this time. He thought it unlikely that the Gosforth Arms would be considered a suitable location. Was there a safe house somewhere in Pimlico, he wondered, digging about in his memory. He had a recollection of a dingy bedsit where he'd housed an asset for a period back in 2008.

The taxi pulled up at the front of the building. Mo and Colin hurried out. Colin settled the bill with the driver. Tony, still looking dazed, took Jason's hand and helped the nine-year-old out of the taxi. Standing on the pavement alone, Danni was pale and appeared much younger than her fourteen years. Her shoulders were hunched, and she played nervously with a strand of hair, positioning herself a few metres away from the others as they exited the taxi.

Kat nudged Mo and muttered, 'Could you take Tony and the kids in, please? Find someone to keep an eye on them. They're all in a bad way.'

He nodded and moved toward Danni, offering her a reassuring smile, 'You look like you could do with a cup of tea.' Danni shot a suspicious glance at him then looked at her father. 'I think your dad could do with one too,' Mo continued. 'Come on, Tony.' Tony and his family followed him, zombie-like, into the building.

Colin, Kat and Edison were left on the pavement. The taxi driver, having been handsomely tipped for his service, had raced off. Edison looked up at the entrance to Thames House. 'Come on then,' Kat said and started up the steps. Edison hesitated, and she looked back at him.

'Edison,' she said, 'do you really think that you can solve this whole thing, shoot a terrorist and still not be allowed on the Grid?

Tanya's sorted your clearance. Come on. I want to debrief as soon as possible so we can sort out tying all this up.' She marched up the steps and into the cavernous hallway.

Edison followed, his heart beating hard in his chest. This was a strange homecoming. He nodded at the familiar face in the security box. 'Hello Edison,' said the uniformed security guard, reaching down to open the access gates.

'Hello, Craig.' The greeting rolled off Edison's tongue as if there had been no break in his saying the same thing every day. 'How is your mother?'

'Oh, she's not getting any younger, and she'll be mighty unimpressed that there wasn't more tennis today.'

It was a macabre joke but one that reminded Edison of the camaraderie that working at MI5 engendered. No one outside those walls would have understood why that joke was necessary. Only those charged with protecting the nation on a day-to-day basis, often at great personal risk, understood the need to see the lighter side in events such as those that had happened that day.

'Your pass is upstairs,' Kat explained. She had been exchanging a flurry of messages with the team on the fifth floor as they'd travelled across London. As they walked through the building, Kat quizzed Colin. 'Any ID on our bombers yet?'

'Not yet,' Colin replied.

'Any sign of Yousuf?'

'None.'

'Christoph?'

Colin shrugged and shook his head.

They were ascending in the lift. Edison was subdued, drinking in his surroundings, half wondering at what point he would be evicted again from this inner sanctum of the intelligence world. The lift doors opened, and they were met by a wall of noise. The entire section had been assembled, and the floor was a hive of activity. Intelligence officers and analysts were investigating every possible angle on the day's events. Edison let the hubbub wash over him.

'Want a drink, Edison?' Colin offered.

'Cup—' Edison began, but Colin interrupted him with a grin.

'Of tea, of course. Why did I even ask?'

Edison smiled. While he waited, he checked his phone. There was a message from Charlie. Edison dialled his voicemail. *'Edison, I'm sure I saw you on the news. There's always some idiot with an iPhone filming these things rather than making themselves scarce like any sensible human being would. Everything ok? We're on the road but will be back in London around supper time. Call me.'*

Edison speed-dialled Charlie, and he picked up within a ring. 'Edison – what can you tell me? Are you ok? Is Kat ok?'

'We're both fine. Where are you?'

'Somewhere around Watford Gap. What about you?'

'If I told you that, I'd have to kill you,' Edison joked. They both laughed. Kat appeared and pointed toward Tanya's office. 'Listen, Charlie, I have to go.'

'Ok – call me later on, Eddie.'

'Will do.' He hung up and followed Kat into Tanya's office where Jock, leaning heavily on a crutch, and Mo were waiting with the head of section. Colin followed, thrusting a cup of tea – exactly as he liked it – into Edison's hand.

'Is Tony ok?' Edison asked of Mo.

'Very shaken up. I've left them with Jenny,' Mo said, referring to a matronly analyst who'd been with the Service for over thirty-five years.

'Shall we sit down?' said Tanya, and they all took seats around the conference table. 'First of all, well done. We've avoided any civilian loss of life.' A frisson of apprehension circled the room at her use of the word 'civilian'.

'Is there any news on Nick Walsh's condition?' Mo asked the question on everybody's mind.

'Not as yet. My last report stated that he's in a critical condition at St George's.' She paused to allow the team to absorb the news but didn't linger on it. 'Kat, what are our top operational priorities from here?'

'Finding Murat Yousuf. Identification of the three bombers and investigation into any connections or sleepers they might be associated with.'

'Do we have reason to believe there are more waiting in the wings?'

'No, all our intelligence points to these three working alone, but a conversation with Yousuf could corroborate this. We believe they, all three, were brought into the country via the Grimsby fishing racket. And there's no suggestion that any more have come through that way.'

'You mention Yousuf. He's been pulling the strings, is that right?' Tanya directed her question at Colin.

'Yes. Barinak Holdings – the property company linked to both addresses we found – the CEO, Murat Yousuf, alias of Kerim Dastan, is behind this.'

'And how does Yousuf connect with the woman we have in custody?'

'Evidence at her flat suggests they were lovers,' Kat said. 'Anna's flatmate, Christoph, had been manipulating the trading algorithm at Penwill's.'

'And Murat Yousuf was a cover name for Kerim Dastan, whose brother was found murdered in a packing crate last summer,' Colin continued.

'What's the link there?' Tanya asked. 'Do we have any idea what his motivations are?'

'We know, from the background on the investigation into Metin's death, that Kerim had some shady business activities to his name, but his profile doesn't bear the hallmarks of an Islamic fundamentalist.'

Kat shook her head and shrugged. 'Motive is still a mystery.'

There was silence in the office. Outside, dusk was closing in on the city, and the clock on the wall told them it was almost nine in the evening.

'Jock, Mo, Colin, that will be all,' Tanya dished out the instruction, prompting Jock to hobble after Mo and Colin as they left the room.

Tanya turned to Edison and Kat, 'I need you two focused on Yousuf.' Edison sat up a little straighter as he received the instruction. He couldn't quite believe he was back at the heart of the team. He stood, preparing to leave. 'But before you go,' Tanya went on. Something in her tone made Edison's spirits sink, 'We need to talk about what happened on Friday.'

Edison's legs buckled, and he felt the full weight of the day's fatigue as he sat back down. Kat perched on the edge of her seat, looking from Tanya to Edison with concern. Tanya's lips were set in a thin line. She looked stern. 'I have moved heaven and earth to get you back on the Grid, Scott Edison,' she began gravely. 'Today's heroics, your role in unmasking the Penwill's mole and the location of the attack have been enough to deflect the worst of the criticisms I've fielded in the past couple of days.'

Edison shifted in his seat.

'But I can't have you gallivanting across the country and dragging old beefs into investigations.' Edison opened his mouth to speak, but she held up her hand, 'You have to promise me you'll set aside your grudge against the former DG.'

Edison bowed his head. His mind was racing. What mattered more to him? Returning to MI5 as an intelligence officer or pursuing his vendetta against Hughes? He longed to see him face the punishment he deserved, but in that moment, sat in Thames House, with the dust of the day's atrocities still a patina on his skin, he knew what he had to do.

'I promise,' he said.

As they all stood up to leave, Tanya slid a security badge on a lanyard across the table toward him. 'Make sure you get a more recent photograph taken as soon as possible.'

The brittle plastic of the security pass felt warm in his hand. He snuck a look at it. A much younger version of himself looked back from the mugshot – his features chiselled and dark hair coiffed. It was a far cry from the jowly jawline and tousled salt-and-pepper mop he sported now. As Edison walked from the office, he felt dazed. Those around him made congratulatory and welcome-back noises. He realised, with a rushing sense of relief, his time in exile was over. It truly felt like he was home.

*

2136, Sunday 9th July, Thames House, Westminster, London

The exhausted team gathered around Kat's desk. Kat's T-shirt was still bloodstained, and her hair was matted with dust. Despite her dishevelled appearance, her eyes were bright and alert. 'Ok, Mo, Jock, time to go home. Get some rest.'

Neither of the exhausted officers objected. Kat offered Colin an apologetic look. 'Is Pete expecting you home?' she asked, referring to Colin's long-suffering partner.

'He knows better than to expect to see me, with headlines like today,' Colin replied, smiling. 'What shall I work on? The bomber IDs?'

'You read my mind. Is Helen still around?'

'Yes, I think I saw her lurking in the kitchen – hopefully, she's caffeine'd up for this,' Colin grinned.

'She only recently left Oxford, she'll be primed for an all-nighter.'

'This is no Keats essay crisis though.'

'Much more exciting,' Edison joined the conversation. He'd been perched on the desk, listening to Colin and Kat's banter.

'Very true,' Colin said.

'I need a change of clothes,' Kat said. 'What do you think on how to smoke out Yousuf?' she directed the question at Edison. 'I'll leave that with you to ponder whilst I go get changed.'

Edison looked dazed. The speed with which he had gone from expendable agent at the periphery of the investigation to being on the front line was unbalancing him.

Kat hurried away to her locker, smiling to herself. The Edison of old, Head-of-Section-Edison, had been so calm, inscrutable and well put together. His response to being invited back onto the Grid was endearing.

Whilst he waited for Kat to return, Edison drank in the familiar buzz. Colin watched him. 'It's good to have you back.'

'It's weird to be back.' Edison daren't say he was pleased yet. He couldn't yet admit that to himself. It would leave him too vulnerable, should he be relegated off the team once the reality of Kat and Tanya's adrenalin-fuelled decisions become clear. 'So, what do we think on tracking down Yousuf? One of the Barinak Holdings properties?'

'That's a great shout, Edison. There were three addresses that Natalie—' the name of their dead colleague caught in his throat and Colin swallowed hard. He took a deep breath before continuing, 'That Natalie found.' He gestured at the board.

'Twenty Danesdale Road,' Edison read.

Kat reappeared. Her hair brushed, dressed in jeans and a white T-shirt. The T-shirt fitted her in all the right places, Edison thought, appraising her figure in the simple outfit. He checked the thought as it crossed his mind. If this was a permanent return to the Service, Edison would need to deal with his emotional entanglement with the senior officer. 'Do you have an answer for me?' she said.

Edison pointed at the address.

Kat's face lit up, 'Of course.' She snatched a set of keys from her desk, 'Let's go.'

Edison ran after her as she hurtled from the building into the night.

*

2142, Sunday 9th July, Thames House, Westminster, London

Mo left Thames House, deep in thought. He crossed the road and looked out over the dark waters of the Thames, smoking a cigarette. The high tide brought the water up to only a few feet below the balustrade on which he was leaning. The lights of the expensive flats on the opposite side of the river danced over the water, reflecting in Mo's eyes as he considered the day's events. His mind raced to the image of Nick Walsh being stretchered away from the scene, bloody and barely breathing, clinging to life.

To his left, the great bell of Big Ben began to chime, telling all those within earshot that it was quarter to ten. Mo considered the time, and spotting the orange light of an approaching black cab, raised his hand. He stubbed out his cigarette as the taxi slowed, and the driver wound down his window. 'Where to, mate?' he asked.

'St George's Hospital.'

The driver nodded, and Mo opened the rear door, knowing that the taxi was an extravagance his finances could ill afford. The Service paid well in job satisfaction, but the material compensation was sadly lacking. The taxi pulled away and made quick work of the drive to Tooting. London was beginning to come alive again after the day's events, but still, the roads were emptier than usual, and only occasionally did Mo see an intrepid pedestrian on the pavements.

'Days like today, make you wonder, don't they,' the driver said, and Mo looked up, feigning interest. 'Whether it's worth it? You know, I have a place in Barcelona. Always said to the missus that we'd go there more when I retire, but I couldn't move there, you know, with the kids and the grandkids being here. But sometimes, I think maybe we'd be better off upping sticks completely. It would be safer there.' Mo nodded not wanting to dispute the driver's claim that somehow the Catalan capital would be a safer place to live. Mo had been seconded to MI6 for a short period to work on an investigation the previous year when a link had been discovered between a British group, formerly known to the security services for their sponsorship of the IRA, to terrorism in the region of Spain so heavily divided in its battle for independence. There had been some minor scuffles and suggestions of a plot to target a largely British ex-pat condo complex, but the investigation had been wound down. He wondered what the taxi driver would make of that.

They drove south through Stockwell, Clapham and Balham. The driver chatted incessantly, and Mo nodded, on autopilot, having long tuned out the sound. The taxi pulled into the car park at St Georges. Mo thanked the driver, tipping him as generously as his stretched finances would allow, and got out.

'Could you direct me to ICU, please?' Mo asked of a bored-looking administrator at the information desk inside the hospital's cavernous atrium.

'Is there a particular patient you're looking for?'

'Nick Walsh.'

'The policeman? Are you family?'

'A colleague,' Mo explained, hoping that would be sufficient to justify a visit at this late hour.

The woman behind the desk sat up a little straighter, believing Mo to be another police officer. 'Down the hall, to the end of the corridor and then take the lifts to the third floor. The nurses' station is on the right as you come out.'

'Thank you,' Mo said and set off, following the instructions she had given.

He emerged onto the third floor and found the nurses' station. He was met by three uniformed women. 'I'm looking for Nick Walsh,' he explained.

All three gave him a sympathetic look, and the oldest of them, reaching out and grasping Mo's hand, said, 'Mr Walsh passed away half an hour ago. I'm so sorry.'

Mo felt limp. He looked up and down the corridor as if looking for an escape. He saw a buggy parked outside one of the rooms, and his thoughts flew to Nick's wife and baby. He began to run toward it, ignoring the protestations from the nurses. He heard one of them begin their pursuit. He reached the buggy to find it empty. He looked up and his eyes were drawn through a window into a room where Nick was lying peacefully beneath a white sheet, his eyes closed, the wounds on his head and neck cleaned and sutured. Beside him sat a young woman, Shelley, Nick's wife, her face red and raw, tearstains streaking her cheeks. Her unseeing gaze was fixed on the face of her husband. The baby was asleep, laid carefully next to Nick's lifeless body.

Mo gasped, he felt like a weight was pressing on his chest, and his eyes filled with tears. He pummelled a fist against the window, anger flowing through him. The nurse who had followed him begged him to stop. At the sound, Shelley slowly turned her head to look in his direction. She cocked her head, looking confused by the presence of the stranger. Wishing he hadn't drawn attention to himself, he opened the door. He felt guilty for intruding on the young family's moment of grief.

'I'm sorry, I work with Nick,' Mo said simply.

'Were you there today?' Shelley whispered. Mo was taken aback by the question.

'Yes, I was,' Mo spoke quietly, conscious of the sleeping baby. He took a couple of cautious steps into the room. The nurse hovered at the door.

'He loved that job,' Shelley said, looking at her husband. 'It was everything to him.'

Mo didn't know what to say. At twenty-four he had not really experienced death. He recalled his grandfather dying when he was ten years old, but he couldn't remember much about that. The rest of his family had been blessed with longevity, his other three grandparents were still going strong, well into their eighties. He felt woefully ill-equipped to deal with the situation.

Shelley reached out a hand and laid it on her husband's. On instinct, Mo moved across the room and sat down on the armrest of the uncomfortable visitor's chair. Shelley withdrew her hand and leaned into Mo. He encircled the woman beside him in his arms, and she shuddered as a gargantuan sob escaped her body. Mo cradled Nick's widow in his arms as she cried. He looked up. The nurse had disappeared.

When the tears finally subsided and Shelley had sat motionless in Mo's embrace for a while, she spoke, her voice barely more than a whisper, 'Thank you for coming.'

'Do you have any family?' Mo asked, thinking practically for the first time since the nurses had broken the news of Nick's death to him.

'My parents are on their way up from Crawley. Nick's family

are in Hull. They won't be here until tomorrow.'

As if summoned, a couple in their late fifties appeared in the doorway and rushed toward their daughter. Mo stepped out of the way and watched as Shelley's father enveloped his daughter in a bear hug. Her mother carefully picked up the baby and cradled her granddaughter in her arms.

Mo tiptoed from the room and down the corridor. He forced a watery smile for the two nurses, still keeping guard at their station and hurried out of the hospital, grateful for the cool night air that met him. He paused, his legs giving way beneath him, and he staggered toward a low wall where he sat and allowed the grief and the horrors of the day to release from inside him. He cried. His shoulders shuddered and his head ached.

'Are you ok?' a woman's voice cut through his sobbing. He rubbed his eyes and recognised the older nurse from the ward, standing nearby, puffing away on an electronic cigarette.

Mo pushed his shoulders back and collected himself, 'I'll be ok.'

'Did you work with him?' she asked.

'Yes, in counter-terrorism.'

The nurse nodded. 'I don't know how you do it,' she went on, flicking the switch on her vape stick and turning to go back into the hospital. 'I'm so bloody glad that you do though.' She smiled at him and retreated.

Mo smiled. He took a deep breath, collecting himself. He called Kat but didn't get a reply. He left a voicemail, letting her know that Nick had passed away. He trudged off into the night. Unable to face the circuitous night bus route that would get him home to New Cross, he walked the eight miles and fell into bed three hours later.

Chapter Twenty-Four

2219, Sunday 9th July, 20 Danesdale Road, Hackney
'Tell me you've still got that pistol on you,' Kat said as they pulled up around the corner from their target property. Edison nodded. She looked relieved. She reached into the back seat of the car. 'Here, put this on.' She thrust a stab vest at Edison and grabbed a second for herself. Edison pulled the body armour over his bulky frame and breathed in to do the clasps up. It was an uncomfortable fit.

With a mounting feeling of expectation, the pair made their way along the dark residential street until they found number twenty. It was a modern, pale-brick, three-storey terraced house. On the ground floor, a battered garage door sat crookedly on its hinges to the left of the front door. Above, the house was in darkness. Kat walked to the front door and listened.

'Nothing,' she whispered as Edison joined her. She laid a gloved hand on the handle. It turned, but the door didn't move. 'Let's try the garage.'

To Edison's astonishment, the garage door slid open, screeching on its wonky runners as it did. Somewhere, a city fox responded with a shriek of its own. As the noise subsided, they both strained to pick up any sign that the cacophony had raised unwanted attention. Still the house lay silent.

Kat switched on a pencil torch and tiptoed to the back of the empty garage, sweeping the beam back and forth as she moved. A door creaked open onto a hallway and a flight of stairs. The two spies crept up to the first floor. They passed through a kitchen at the top. At the doorway to the next room, Kat drew to a halt, and

Edison heard her take a sharp breath. He peered over her shoulder into a sparsely furnished living room. A pale orange light from the streetlights seeped in. Through the gloom, he could just make out an armchair. In the armchair sat a figure, perfectly motionless but for a pair of glassy eyes that flicked occasionally toward where they were standing. He reached for his gun.

'Murat Yousuf,' Kat said, her words echoing in the empty room.

The figure declined his head.

'Or should I say, Kerim Dastan?'

The man in the chair parted his dry lips and rasped, 'You should say that. Although you have shown no respect for that name in the past.'

Kat ventured forward, and Edison, one hand on the butt of his gun, followed, not taking his eyes from Yousuf.

'You killed one of my officers,' Kat said as she advanced.

Painfully, Yousuf turned his head to one side and spat. 'And you killed my family.' His breath was short.

Kat's eyes were locked on Yousuf. 'Your brother was murdered by thugs. Drug lords. What does that have to do with us?'

'You may not have pulled the trigger,' the man in the chair gasped for breath, and his hands spasmed, 'but you killed my brother as surely as you killed my sister and niece. It has everything to do with you. You and your Home Secretary killed them. You had to suffer. You had to know what it is to deny people their freedom. The Right Honourable Timothy Johnson signed their death warrants when he forbade them entry to this country. He should have died.' Yousuf's voice rose, 'He should have been dead today. He killed my family.' He was wheezing.

'Did you kill the captain of the *Boston Jubilee*?'

The headlights of a passing car briefly illuminated the room and picked out Yousuf's white teeth, set in a jackal's smile. He coughed. 'The ever-amenable Captain Jack Fleming. Yes, I killed him. Although, like me, he had nothing left to live for anyway.' His fingers clutched at the arms of the chair, and a small pill bottle slipped from his fingers. Edison dived to retrieve it.

Examining the label, he spoke, 'Kat, call an ambulance.' Kat fumbled with her phone whilst Edison turned to the dying man.

'What about Anna?' Edison fixed his gaze on Yousuf, sat on his haunches, his eyes level with the man in the armchair.

Yousuf gave a rasping laugh. 'Anna. The beautiful Anna. So many useful connections. Like the computer programmer …' He trailed off, wheezing.

'Christoph?'

'Was that his name? He was a mercenary.' He lifted a trembling hand as if to dismiss the topic.

'And Hughes? What about Sir Donald Hughes?' He felt, rather than saw, Kat shoot him a dark look, but before she could say anything, her call connected to the ambulance service.

Yousuf looked at Edison, a vacant expression in his eyes. 'This name means nothing to me.'

'Are you sure? Are you sure you know nothing about Sir Donald Hughes?'

'Maybe, maybe,' the words were uttered between short, gasps for breath. 'Maybe he helped sell the drugs. There was someone … Anna … mentioned.' His head began to loll. 'Metin was the messenger.' He was delirious now. 'I had no choice.' His chest was barely rising as he tried to suck air into his lungs. 'They were my only family. And you British pigs killed them.'

Kat hung up the phone. 'ETA eight minutes.'

'It's too late.' Yousuf's body slumped, lifeless in the chair, 'He's dead.'

Chapter Twenty-Five

2256, Sunday, 9th July, Moniedubh Estate, nr. North Ballachulish, Lochaber

'*Today's events at the All England Club have sent shockwaves through London. Our security correspondent is at the scene in South West London, where earlier, three men were thwarted in their attempts to blow up Centre Court at Wimbledon.*' The newsreader handed over to her colleague, who stood in front of the police tape, behind which an army of forensic scientists was hard at work, combing over the scene.

Hughes had watched the footage over and over again. Every time the news cycle repeated itself, he found himself drawn back to the television screen. He stood in the middle of his study, aghast at what he was seeing unfold. There were snatches of film from iPhones that the television crews had secured. He swallowed hard as he watched each of the men go down. He watched Scott Edison emerge from the debris of the crash and wondered whether he should have paid more attention to his attempted warning.

The Home Secretary had been on the phone, wanting his old friend's view on the atrocities, but Hughes could only bluster his way through the conversation. His thoughts were elsewhere. With Anna. Having hung up with Johnson, he'd tried to call her again, but it was going straight to answerphone. It just wasn't possible that she could be mixed up in all of this, he thought. In a daze, he paced the floor, imagining reasons why Anna might not be answering the phone. It was ok, he told himself, the phone signal in London is likely to be jammed in the circumstances. She'll call to reassure me soon.

The news coverage had moved on. '*We understand some links have been made to a boutique investment bank.*' The anchor was talking via video link to a reporter who was in Canary Wharf. '*That's right, we understand that the terrorist attack today has been linked to a money laundering arrest at Penwill & Mallinson just last week. The suspect hasn't been named, but we believe a man in his twenties and a woman, believed to be the office manager at the bank, are helping the police with their enquiries.*' Hughes' heart sank.

His desperation was soon replaced by panic. What if the investigation led back to him? He needed to do something. There were missed calls on Anna's phone. He put in a hasty call to Waring at the Met with instructions.

Hughes rewound through the coverage to Colchester's statement. He had listened to it enough times to know it by heart and had the sound on mute. But this time, he was focused on the cluster of people just visible over Colchester's shoulder. One of them was a gesticulating, fraught Tony. Panic consumed him once more. How much had he divulged to the halfwit? He was vulnerable and a vulnerability. He might say something. Something had to be done.

Hughes took a deep breath and picked up the phone again. He called Bantam on a secure line. The fixer answered. 'Awright guv'ner,' he said in his Cockney drawl.

'Bantam, I need to you to sort something out for me,' and Hughes went on to explain his requirements.

'No bovver guv'ner, but that's a bit out of the ordinary,' Bantam said and quoted a huge sum for his services.

'I'll arrange the money. Just get it done.' Hughes hung up. He never thought he would have to call on Bantam for a professional hit. He felt oddly exhilarated.

Lady Elizabeth knocked on the door. 'I shall be going to bed, dear,' she said. 'Such terrible news from London. I am very glad you decided not to join the Home Secretary.'

'Indeed,' Hughes said. 'Thankfully, my former colleagues seemed to have everything just about in hand.'

'That poor policeman though. They were saying on the news that he has a six-month-old baby.'

'Yes, quite terrible. But it could have been a lot worse.'

'Yes, I suppose so,' Elizabeth said, turning to go. 'Good night, dear.'

Hughes turned back to the television. His earlier fear was slowly being displaced by rage. How had he let himself be drawn into this? He poured himself a drink and took a seat by the window, watching the last rays of light fade from the hillside. His escape from this place was on hold for now. There are other ways and means.

Angus trotted over to him and laid his head on his master's knee. Absentmindedly, Hughes scratched behind the dog's ears, and the dog whimpered his contentment.

'Time, that's all we need,' he told the dog. 'Time.'

Chapter Twenty-Six

0710, Monday 10th July, Thames House, Westminster, London

The weather had broken overnight, and a thunderous storm had hit London in the early hours of the morning. Rain still hung in the air as Edison made his way to Thames House.

At just gone midnight, he and Kat had left the scene of Yousuf's suicide.

'What was in that bottle?' Kat had asked him.

'Coniine,' Edison replied.

'Hemlock. Like Socrates,' Kat mused. 'Convicted and sentenced to death for moral corruption and impiety.'

'The irony.' They were silent until they reached the car. They threw their flak jackets onto the back seats. Kat checked her phone before getting into the car. Edison hovered, preparing for the short walk home. She listened to Mo's voicemail. Her response had been muted. With her phone pressed to her ear, her shoulders slumped as she listened to Mo telling her that Nick had died earlier that evening. Her exhaustion precluded a more emotional response to the news. When she hung up, she relayed the information to Edison.

'I'll drop you at home,' she suggested, sliding into the driver's seat.

Outside the flat, they'd wished one another good night with a perfunctory hug. They had gone their separate ways, reeling from the events of the day, both too tired to consider what Edison's return to MI5 meant for their relationship.

With the majestic façade of MI5's headquarters looming above him, Edison fingered his security pass in his pocket and felt his heartbeat quicken as he approached the security gates. For a moment, he wondered whether the pass would permit him access. Perhaps yesterday's triumphant return to the Grid had been a one-off thing. But no, he bid Craig good morning and waved the plastic badge at the scanner, the gates parted and let him through.

The fifth floor, the home of the counter-terrorism section, was subdued, although there were already dozens of people at their desks. As he exited the lift, there was an urgent knocking on the glass that separated Tanya's office from the rest of the floor. Edison looked over and saw Kat beckoning him to join them.

'Where's Mo?' Edison asked, concerned for the young officer who had spent so much time with Nick Walsh in the past two weeks.

'I told him to take the day off,' Kat said. She waved a plate of pastries under Edison's nose. 'Want one?' she asked.

Edison took a croissant and looked around hopefully for a teapot. 'On the side,' Tanya said, and Edison moved across the room to pour a cup.

'We haven't been here long. I've filled the team in on last night. Also, Anna Graham has been charged,' Kat explained to Edison as he returned to the conference table and pulled up a seat. 'Colin was just telling us that we have ID on the three bombers.'

He studied the photos on the board that had been wheeled in. They were grainy images taken from the sighting equipment used by the armed police unit.

Colin looked around at the team, his eyes were bright, and his skin glowed. He never looked like he'd sacrificed any sleep to this job, despite Edison's strong suspicion that it was unlikely Colin had been home the previous night. He pointed at the first photograph, 'This is Anan,' he moved his finger along, 'Saada and Bakar.'

'Mohammed Anan, Zeki Saada and Asif Bakar. Anan and

Bakar are Yemeni. Anan is Syrian. We're checking with the respective authorities for any further intelligence. But all three have links to an extremist group with training camps in Northern Syria.'

'Good, that's been bothering me,' Edison said. 'Yousuf had a very personal vendetta, his own score to settle. But to achieve what he did, he would need access to a much bigger infrastructure to identify potential recruits, source weapons, buy explosives and so on.'

'You're right, of course,' said Tanya, 'but we all know what a minefield that is. Do we have any leads?'

'We'll work with Six to follow up, but those trails go cold pretty quickly. They're renowned for going to ground at the first sign of trouble.'

'What about Christoph?' Edison asked.

'It was the Hungarians who eventually owned up to recognising his picture,' said Colin. 'Ernő Török is a Hungarian national. He studied computer science at the University of Budapest. He was arrested a couple of times in the early 2000s for malware attacks on state institutions before he disappeared, they think to Israel. The Swiss were interested in the picture as someone matching that description was wanted in connection to a money laundering fraud at one of their private banks. A similar story from the Belgians.'

'A hacker for hire,' Edison mused, thinking back to his conversations with RubiksKube. 'You never know, we might be able to track him down someday.'

'Ok,' Tanya said authoritatively, 'other than a few loose ends, this operation has been pretty much put to bed.' Tanya concluded the meeting, 'Very well done, once again. Edison, could I have a quick word?'

Colin grabbed another pastry, and the team made their way out.

'How is Tony?' Tanya asked once they had gone. 'You live with him, don't you?'

'Yes,' Edison replied, 'but I didn't see him this morning.'

Tanya looked perplexed. 'We received his resignation by email first thing this morning, which seems like a rather extravagant response. Wouldn't you agree?'

Edison didn't know what to say. 'He may come around,' he ventured.

'Desk jobbers don't really appreciate what it's like in the field,' Tanya said. 'I think I'll have to accept the resignation, but we'll need him in for a proper debrief. This isn't the kind of job you can just walk away from.'

'Tell me about it.' Tanya smiled at him. 'What exactly is my status, Tanya?'

'Let's say you're here on probation.'

Edison raised his eyebrows, 'Probation?'

'You're one of the best intelligence officers this service has ever seen, Edison. I need you in the inner sanctum. But it's not simple. This is still a bureaucratic government department and …' she trailed off.

'And Sir Donald Hughes has many friends.'

'Yes,' Tanya shifted uneasily, 'including the Home Secretary. Who had a lucky escape yesterday. He was clearly the high-profile target that Murat Yousuf was after.'

'And the collateral damage was there to satisfy the fundamentalists.'

'Rather puts paid to your theory that Hughes was somehow involved. He wouldn't have plotted to kill his friend.'

'He's a mercenary, Hughes. Sells his allegiance to the highest bidder.'

'As I told you yesterday, you need to be careful, Edison,' Tanya warned him, her brow furrowing. 'I've waged a few wars to get you back on the Grid. If you pursue Hughes, it *will* have disastrous consequences.' She looked sternly at Edison and added, 'For us all.'

Edison nodded his understanding. Tanya turned her attention to her computer screen, dismissing Edison who made his escape. As he crossed the floor, Kat pounced on him.

'What are you thinking, Edison?'

'Have you been skulking there all this time?'

Kat shrugged and asked him again, 'Come on, what are you thinking? This isn't wrapped up as far as you're concerned.'

He pulled Kat to one side, Tanya's warning about Hughes still ringing in his ears, he lowered his voice and said, 'There's still the connection between Anna and Hughes.'

Kat's eyes widened, 'Come on Edison. It's more than your job's worth to pursue that. Anyway, how can you be so sure there is a connection?'

'Absolutely sure. He was involved in all of this in some way. Maybe just skimming money off at the top. Coordinating the drugs racket perhaps. He's got form on that front. I'm sure he was involved.' Edison's voice rose as the accusations rolled off his tongue.

'Keep your voice down,' Kat said urgently. 'It's all conjecture. I don't think there's anything that can be done.'

He looked over Kat's shoulder at the buzzing Grid. His colleagues, his friends, working diligently to tie up HAPSBURG and work on the hundreds of new threats that landed in their inboxes every day. Edison sighed, remembering his promise to Tanya, 'I agree.' Kat seemed surprised by Edison's willingness to let go, 'We've got our man.'

'And woman,' Kat said. 'Yousuf couldn't have done it without Anna. She was cool as a cucumber in the interview. And even now, with Yousuf dead, she's not breathing a word.'

'Unflappable. Office managers and assistants tend to be. They know all the secrets and how to keep them.'

In their efforts to prevent any of their colleagues overhearing their conversation, Kat and Edison had found themselves speaking with their bodies just millimetres apart. The intimacy of the situation dawned on Edison, and he took a step back.

'So, you're back then,' Kat said.

'On probation, apparently,' Edison pulled a face and Kat laughed. Edison reached for her hand and Kat looked around, pulling it back from his grasp. She looked awkward, shuffling from one foot to another. 'What's up?' Edison asked.

'If you're back, maybe we should cool off a little.'

'Oh,' Edison stuttered, 'um, ok. If you think it's best.'

'I think it is,' Kat said resolutely. And with that, she marched off across the office. Edison watched her go, unsure what to make of it.

His phone vibrated in his pocket. He retrieved it and was surprised to see a French number displayed. 'Hello,' he answered.

'Oh, hello, Edison, it's Gauthier.'

'Oh, hello, Gauthier, it's good to hear from you. How are you?'

'I'm well. I just thought I would give you a call, given what day it is.'

Edison looked around wildly for a calendar. What day was it? Monday in mid-July. Surely, he hadn't forgotten? Surely, he couldn't have, even with everything that was going on. He peered over Colin's shoulder at the lower right corner of the screen, and sure enough, there it was – the date, the tenth of July. How could he have forgotten?

Edison sighed and felt a lump come to his throat. The kindness of his father-in-law's gesture overwhelmed him. The exhaustion that had accumulated welled up inside him, and he sat down. 'That's so kind of you to ring.' His voice cracked as he spoke, 'How are you and Jane holding up?'

'Oh, you know Jane – she's ploughing through the flower beds in the garden as I speak.'

'And you?'

'I miss her every day, today is not different, it just feels a bit more ... I don't know how to say it ...'

'Empty,' Edison offered. 'It just feels a bit more empty today.'

'Which is crazy, isn't it? A thing is either empty or not, it's not relative.'

'Don't get too philosophical with me, Gauthier.' Edison tried to make a joke, but neither man laughed.

'I'm glad to hear you're doing ok,' Gauthier said. 'I'll leave something from you when I visit her today.'

'Thank you.'

'Take care, Edison.'

'And you.' Edison hung up.

Colin looked at him quizzically, 'Everything ok?'

'I need to go.' Edison rushed out of the building, berating himself. How could he have forgotten? How could he have forgotten Ellie's birthday? She would have been thirty-four years old, and Edison would have served her a mimosa in bed as was their birthday tradition. Even in death, he continued to fail her. As he strode out of the building, his head down, he ran into a man coming in the other direction.

'Eddie,' Charlie cried, 'I was on my way to see you.' Edison looked up, and on seeing his friend, collapsed onto his haunches, his head in his hands. Charlie crouched next to him, 'Oh Eddie, it was always going to be a tough day, and then factor in everything else that's been going on.'

'Jesus Christ, Charlie, even *you* remembered.'

'Come on,' Charlie hauled his friend to his feet. 'You're exhausted. Is it any wonder you lost track of the dates? I think,' he went on as they emerged into the daylight, 'you should come stay with us for a bit. Let's go get some stuff from your place.'

Edison allowed himself to be manhandled into a taxi and Charlie gave the address in Bethnal Green to the driver.

*

1126, Monday, 10th July, Nelson Gardens, Bethnal Green, London
As the cab made its way to East London, Edison collected himself. His past tangled with present as memories of Ellie criss-crossed with thoughts of Hughes. He screwed up his eyes and tried to think clearly. Manipulating all the information and half-truths he had available to him, he tried to create a coherent hypothesis about Hughes' involvement in the complex picture. As they inched down the Whitechapel Road, he turned to his best friend and took a deep breath. 'Hear me out on this,' he began, 'I'm pretty sure Hughes was involved in HAPSBURG in some way. But he didn't know it.'

Charlie attempted to interject, but Edison raised his hand and went on, 'Just listen to what I've got to say, and then you can tell me I'm crazy or deluded or just so hung up on the past that I can't think straight.'

Charlie nodded his head, 'Ok, try me.'

Edison recounted the conversation in Hughes' study with near word-perfect recollection. 'I think that Anna was a pawn in all of this. She was seduced by Yousuf, who was after her connections at the bank and also with Hughes.'

'Why Hughes?'

'Because he'd already got an import line and distribution network for the drugs that Yousuf was bringing in. Anna seduced Hughes. I think he had designs on running away with her, you know, all financed by their ill-gotten gains. She may well have seduced other investors in the crypto fund too but that's by the by. What mattered was Hughes' connection to the drug-runners. He may not have been aware that she was involved with a bigger plot – everyone's protestations that he is a noble patriot being, depending on your definition, accurate. I *know* him. When I suggested links to terrorists, he was genuinely shocked. That wasn't bravado. But he's evidently still very active on the black markets. It makes me so angry that he wriggled out of all this the first time.'

The cloud that had been hanging over Charlie's features lifted, and Edison felt a wave of relief wash over him. His friend believed him. Charlie opened his mouth to respond just as they arrived at their destination, and whatever he was about to say was interrupted by the formalities of settling the taxi bill.

The two men were welcomed by a picture of urban domesticity – a woman pushing a buggy, two teenagers kicking a football against a wall and further down the road a transit van unloaded as new rental tenants moved into their flat. They crossed the road. Edison's attention was drawn to a figure dressed in black, with a hood pulled over his head, emerging from the bottom of the staircase that led to a dozen apartments, including the flat Edison shared with Tony. The man's gaze met Edison's, but he looked away almost instantly. In that moment, a bolt of recognition passed across Edison's mind. He had handed that man a mobile telephone in the pub in Clapham. He thought he recognised the loping gait of the same man at Billingsgate. Was it possible that this was the same man? On instinct, Edison reached out to grasp the hooded man's arm, but he skipped forward and ran. Edison started as if to make chase but thought better of it – he was in no position to apprehend the man on half-supposed coincidences and possible recognition. He shivered as he watched the figure retreating. A gold chain glinting on his left wrist.

'What was that about?' Charlie asked.

'I think I've seen that man one too many times in the last few weeks for it to be a coincidence.'

They both looked up the flat. A sixth sense, honed over many years, was tingling in both of them, and they rushed up the stairs, a smell of gas growing stronger as they reached the front door.

'Shit,' said Edison, as he fumbled with his keys, a sense of trepidation at what he would find on the other side filling him. Charlie was already dialling 999 when Edison opened the door and rushed into the kitchen. Tony's body lay on the floor by the oven. Edison pulled him away. He turned off the gas.

Edison dashed to open the window before turning his attention back to Tony's limp and lifeless body. He felt for a pulse. He already knew he wouldn't find one.

Charlie took a piece of kitchen towel and picked up an envelope that was propped on the sideboard. He extracted a piece of paper on which was typed a very short note.

'Fuck,' Edison cried, sitting back against the kitchen cabinets. 'Those poor kids.'

Charlie disappeared into Tony's room. Edison followed. On one of the computer screens, there was a document open. 'That's the note,' said Charlie.

Edison scanned the other screen. A few keystrokes and he pulled up a web-browser. Charlie whistled.

On the screen was the last message Tony had written, via a Dark Web messaging service, *Hughes, Tell me what's going on?*

Edison was floored. 'He's been watching me!'

'Who has? Tony?'

'Hughes has. Using Tony. And that bloke we just passed on the stairs. He's one of Hughes' fixers, I'll bet.'

'Edison,' Charlie said, the urgency in his voice couldn't be ignored, 'can you get rid of that?'

'Yes, but why? It's useful evidence.'

'Screenshot it, but we should make it disappear before it slides into official channels. Everything you've told me, everything makes sense. But it's not going to be easy to prove. And we certainly haven't got enough evidence at this stage to connect Hughes to the drugs let alone HAPSBURG. If you go in with what you have at the moment, they'll laugh at you and probably rescind your security clearance.' Edison tried to object, but he knew his friend spoke the truth. 'Your credibility is still rather fragile.' Edison nodded. 'Also, you know he's got friends everywhere.' Charlie's meaning was implicit.

'So, what do I do?'

'*We*,' Charlie stressed the collective noun, 'wait. We watch. We find out who that man was. We work out exactly what Hughes is up to. But we do this quietly. He cannot know. No one can know. We'll bring him down properly this time.'

'Ok,' Edison said as the sound of a siren signalled the arrival of the ambulance. He turned to the computer screen, and with a few keystrokes, the message was gone.

The two men gave one another a look and went out to meet the paramedics and police officer. The latter began gathering the required forensic evidence for suspected suicides. The formalities over, Edison called Tanya.

Charlie was starting to pull together Edison's belongings when his friend hauled himself up the stairs to join him. He let out a long, exhausted breath and collapsed on the bed. 'Thank you,' Edison said, looking up at his friend.

'For what?'

'For believing me.'

Charlie stuffed another pair of socks into the holdall and picked up the picture of Eloise on Edison's bedside table. He sat down next to his best friend of twenty-five years, holding the picture between them. 'It's not going to be easy, you know?' said Charlie, not lifting his gaze from the photograph.

'What?'

'Bringing down Hughes.'

The End

Did you enjoy reading Ethereum?

Would you help others discover Scott Edison, Sir Donald Hughes and the rest of the MI5 team?

Please support the author by:

- ✓ Leaving a review on Amazon or Goodreads
- ✓ Recommending the book to a friend
- ✓ Sharing the book on social media

Thank you.

Facebook: @NCManderAuthor
Twitter: @NCMander_Author
Instagram: @NCMander_Author

A nerve agent attack.
A mysterious disappearance of a Cold War spy.
A race across Europe.

Scott Edison returns in Matryoshka

But will Edison and his team track down their double agent before the Russians do? As Edison dashes across Europe to find one of MI6's most valuable assets, his life starts to unravel in his absence. Soon he must choose between the operation and those he loves.

Sign-up to N C Mander's mailing list for sneak previews and news on release dates www.ncmander.com.

Notes from the Author

What a rollercoaster it has been bringing Scott Edison, Charlie Harrington-Smith, Sir Donald Hughes and the rest of the cast of Ethereum to life.

I have to thank my husband, Dominic, for his endless love, patience and support. Not only has he dutifully read draft after draft, gasping, laughing and nodding in all the right places, he has endured my endless questions about the viability of my computer programming ideas around which so much of Ethereum is built. I have certainly ended up going with what is plausible rather than accurate when it comes to some of the more technical aspects of the book.

To Anna-Jean Hughes who helped me wrestle the early drafts into a coherent manuscript and to Miranda Summers-Pritchard – you are never overexplaining nor being too pedantic!

To my friends and family – it's here. No longer do you need to ask how the book is going. Rest assured I will regale you of the news of book two in due course.

About the Author

N C Mander writes espionage and mystery thrillers. 'Ethereum' is her debut novel. The book is the first in a series of espionage thrillers featuring MI5 intelligence officer Scott Edison.

Like any spy worth their salt, N C Mander uses an alias. When not working undercover as a thriller author, N C Mander is known as Natasha.

She lives in South London with her husband and draws inspiration daily from the buzzing city she calls home.

When she isn't poring over her laptop, Natasha enjoys long distance running, which she likens in discipline, to writing novels.

Printed in Great Britain
by Amazon